If Dantine pushed the curtain aside, she might see the movement. So instead he watched the two of them from above, through the white lace at the window.

He was experiencing sensations he hadn't felt in years. A kind of excitement, as though he were a schoolboy. A smile crossed his lips. Claudia had come, after all. Her photographs, her image on the television screen, none did her justice.

She was here. It was all that mattered; she had come this last part of the way freely, of her own, tacit choosing.

He opened the lid of the small, worn wooden box in his hand. The simple melody began to play. Slowly, one note at a time.

CATCH UP ON THE BEST IN CONTEMPORARY FICTION
FROM ZEBRA BOOKS!

LOVE AFFAIR   (2181, $4.50)
by Syrell Rogovin Leahy

A poignant, supremely romantic story of an innocent young woman with a tragic past on her own in New York, and the seasoned newspaper reporter who vows to protect her from the harsh truths of the big city with his experience — and his love.

ROOMMATES   (2156, $4.50)
by Katherine Stone

No one could have prepared Carrie for the monumental changes she would face when she met her new circle of friends at Stanford University. For once their lives intertwined and became woven into the tapestry of the times, they would never be the same.

MARITAL AFFAIRS   (2033, $4.50)
by Sharleen Cooper Cohen

Everything the golden couple Liza and Jason Greene touched was charmed — except their marriage. And when Jason's thirst for glory led him to infidelity, Liza struck back in the only way possible.

RICH IS BEST   (1924, $4.50)
by Julie Ellis

From Palm Springs to Paris, from Monte Carlo to New York City, wealthy and powerful Diane Carstairs plays a ruthless game, living a life on the edge between danger and decadence. But when caught in a battle for the unobtainable, she gambles with the only thing she owns that she cannot control — her heart.

THE FLOWER GARDEN   (1396, $3.95)
by Margaret Pemberton

Born and bred in the opulent world of political high society, Nancy Leigh flees from her politician husband to the exotic island of Madeira. Irresistibly drawn to the arms of Ramon Sanford, the son of her father's deadliest enemy, Nancy is forced to make a dangerous choice between her family's honor and her heart's most fervent desire!

Available wherever paperbacks are sold, or order direct from the Publisher. Send cover price plus 50¢ per copy for mailing and handling to Zebra Books, Dept. 2886, 475 Park Avenue South, New York, N.Y. 10016. Residents of New York, New Jersey and Pennsylvania must include sales tax. DO NOT SEND CASH.

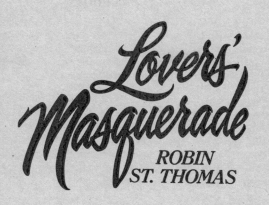

Lovers' Masquerade

ROBIN
ST. THOMAS

ZEBRA BOOKS
KENSINGTON PUBLISHING CORP.

ZEBRA BOOKS

are published by

Kensington Publishing Corp.
475 Park Avenue South
New York, NY 10016

First printing: February, 1990

Printed in the United States of America

For John Kelly
and for James, Gene . . . and Flo

Prologue

She stood before a gate that was fashioned of tiny flower buds nestled within a tangled mass of vines. At the slightest touch of her hand to the latch, the gate swung wide to admit her, and the buds blossomed into hundreds of blue and white morning glories.

Claudia walked up the path toward the magnificent house. Its door was open and waiting.

Everything inside glistened. Sparkled. All the furnishings were made of finest woods and covered in shining gold brocade.

On each wall hung heavy, ornately carved gilt frames. But they were empty.

Where are their pictures? she wondered.

She began to toss and turn, and hoped she would awaken.

The empty frames continued to appear. They traveled up the walls of a vast staircase.

At the top was a beautiful woman looking down upon her.

I've seen her before! Claudia thought. But where? The woman was dressed in a flowing gown of blue, and was carrying a small box in her hands.

She glided down the staircase and seemed, somehow, to hover in the air.

Then she opened the box.

Claudia felt a tap on her shoulder from behind. When she turned, a male child held out his arms.

And music began to play.

They danced. The song was a waltz. But it was playing too loudly, too quickly, and without harmony. A single note at a time clanged like a tower bell and crashed into the next; the melody, if indeed there was one, was indistinguishable.

The boy led her across the floor with assurance.

And now they were dancing inside a huge ballroom.

He spun her faster and faster as the atonal chiming grew more and more dissonant.

She wanted to press her palms against her ears to shut out the sound.

And all the while, the beautiful woman in the blue gown looked on.

"Claudia," came a voice from outside the dream. "Claudia!"

Her eyes opened.

Nick's eyes looked down at her.

She ran her fingers over the stubble on his cheek. "Is it morning already?" she asked.

"Not just yet," he answered, kissing her lips. "You were dreaming."

"Oh . . ." she answered, suddenly happy to be awake. "Yes . . . I was."

"The same dream?"

"Oh, Nick," she said. "The music was louder than ever, and . . ."

"And what?"

"I saw the woman's face clearly this time."

8

She sat up in bed and, cradling her knees in her arms, said, "It was my face, Nick. I'm the woman in the dream."

Chapter 1

"Your mother called," Bonnie was saying. "She'll be by around noon and says to leave room for a *fabulous* lunch. The underline is *her* emphasis—that's the way she said it."

Claudia smiled. "I bet it's because Eleanor is convinced that all the restaurants in the rest of the country are either McDonald's or Burger Kings. She thinks a book tour means the wilderness."

The secretary said, "Well, she also mentioned something about wonderful news."

Joshua Samuelson came out of his office then and stopped at Claudia's desk. "I just spoke with your publicist. Judy's shooting for the number six spot—at the very least—on the best-seller lists, so let me offer fair warning: If any of this success turns your head, I'll hire us another advice maven—maybe lure Zazz away from the *Sun Times*. Oh, yeah—and I *know* it'll cut into your royalties, but I do expect a signed copy, gratis . . ."

Claudia shook her head and laughed. "You've got it, Josh."

"On one condition," Bonnie put in. "You have to promise not to pass the book around. Not even to your wife. The rest of the world can fork over nineteen ninety-five plus tax to read it. Authors shouldn't be expected to hand out freebies."

"Watch it, Newcomb," said her employer. "You can be replaced."

"*That's* why I didn't suggest that you buy *your* own copy, Josh. But someone's got to look out for Claudia."

"Thank you both, but I can look out for myself. And I promise to remain kind, sweet, humble—and modest—even if we hit number one on the list." She waited a beat, then added, "And just think what that would do for the paper's circulation, Josh."

"Touché," he said. "Seriously, though, we've got just enough advance columns to last a month. So don't start thinking about retiring or writing a novel in Bermuda."

"Even if I decide to run off and join the circus, Josh, I'll send the column by express mail," said Claudia.

"Deal," said her editor. "And tell Nick if he wants some company to give me a ring. I'll teach him to play poker."

Josh knew Nick hated cards. "I'll remind him," said Claudia. "He'll be ecstatic."

She and Bonnie spent the rest of the morning sorting her mail. Personal correspondence went into one file, letters from readers into another. The reader file already contained stacks of letters, most of which had arrived over the weekend.

"There's another one from New Orleans," Bonnie observed, pulling a gray vellum envelope from among the rest.

At the mention of New Orleans, Claudia felt herself flush. The color subsided immediately, and she wondered if Bonnie had even seen it—or if, in fact, she had imagined it.

The gray vellum in question always bore a New Orleans postmark. The letter inside wasn't signed. Nor did it offer a return address. Still, it told enough about its sender to pique Claudia's curiosity. The stationery was top quality, the handwriting, in black fountain-pen ink, bespoke an artistic flourish, its author apparently someone who could afford the luxury of time.

The letters were never crank letters. Nor did they contain obscenities. Claudia had received her share of both; that, she'd learned five years ago, went with the territory. The letters from New Orleans were instead well thought out and intelligently articulated.

Some of the letters Claudia would have liked to answer personally. But because they bore no signature, she had no recourse other than to answer them in print. Her correspondence-in-print, then, had begun a year ago; she remembered because the letters had started to arrive only a week after Barton Gage's funeral.

Her adoptive father had suffered a fatal heart attack, right in the middle of the hospital board meeting. His passing was one of the reasons Claudia had written the book. One of her readers had experienced a similar loss at the time, and in seeking the words to comfort the reader, Claudia had uncovered answers to some of her own questions. They had led to *Dear Claudia,* a collection of heartfelt, probing letters. Not, however, letters from her readers; these were from the author to herself.

But the gray vellum from New Orleans were not from Claudia.

"I'll bet he's a secret admirer," Bonnie had remarked after Claudia had received the third or fourth mysterious missive.

"How can you tell my admirer is male?" Claudia had asked.

"Well, that's true. It could be some militant feminist inviting you to sample the joys of a lesbian relationship."

13

"I've gotten letters like that, but they're always signed — and generally include a phone number."

"So who is this Cyrano of yours?" Bonnie had said. Claudia had shaken her head.

But this morning, as she glanced at the postmark once more, she felt, very strongly, that she was about to find out.

She was more certain when she unfolded the letter and read: *Now is the hour. Until next week.*

New Orleans was the fourth stop on the publicity tour.

Eleanor Gage arrived ten minutes late, but Claudia was so immersed in last-minute details that she hadn't noticed the time. As Josh waved through the glass wall of his office, Eleanor smiled her frequently photographed smile.

It's true, Claudia mused, she does light up her surroundings. Eleanor wasn't only attractive; she possessed exquisite taste, an understated elegance that her adopted daughter had inherited.

Claudia laughed silently at her own choice of words. Emulated or absorbed were more appropriate; inherited didn't apply.

She watched as Eleanor, her gray-blond hair never too blond, her cashmere dress never too tight, strode toward her.

"Hi, Mom!" greeted Claudia, rising to embrace the woman.

"Hello, darling." They kissed each other on the cheek, and Eleanor apologized for being late. "There were some problems about next week's fashion show at the yacht club," she said. "I just couldn't get away."

"Careful, Mom," warned Claudia. "Never expect sympathy for the girl on the yacht."

They both laughed. "That has a familiar ring to it," said Eleanor.

Claudia nodded. "You told me years ago. An old editor friend of yours, remember?"

"Ah, yes. The memory really does begin to dull at a certain age."

"That's one thing about Ellie," said Josh, coming up behind her. "Never afraid to admit she's past fifty."

With a sly grin, Eleanor pointed a scolding finger and said, "Be careful, Josh. That ice you're walking on is very thin." But it was obvious that Eleanor Gage hadn't taken offense.

Strange, thought Claudia. In some ways we really are similar. She found it even stranger to be thinking about these similarities so often lately. People who didn't know Claudia was adopted usually commented on how much she had taken after Barton Gage.

"She's just like her father," the unaware observer would comment. And it was true about their personalities; Eleanor Gage was generous and warm, outgoing and affable, yet unflappable; Claudia and Barton Gage, on the other hand, had shared what Eleanor called a "flair for living," her own personal description of someone with a passionate, sanguine nature.

There were some who thought Claudia even resembled Barton. She remembered reading, years before, that children often took on many of the physical characteristics of their adoptive parents. Claudia seemed to have "taken after" Barton Gage. She was tall, dark-haired, with a healthy, glowing tan, and just slim enough. Her confident stride was a compromise between grace and athleticism. So like Barton.

Eleanor, by contrast, was pale; her complexion was milk-white porcelain. She was fashion-model svelte, but her height came up only to Claudia's shoulder. Eleanor's carriage—indeed, both her internal and outer demeanor—was inbred, a product of generations of Davenport wealth and power. Barton Gage had been a self-made man, and all the more proud for it.

Not unlike Nick, Claudia reflected.

Eleanor broke in on her thoughts after an exchange of noncommittal chitchat with Josh and Bonnie. "Darling, I've reserved a table at the Pump Room. And I don't know about you, but I'm famished!"

"The Pump Room!" said Bonnie, smiling. "Need anyone to walk three paces behind and carry your briefcase, Mrs. Gage?"

Eleanor laughed. "Well, after all, this lunch *is* a celebration of sorts."

Claudia tucked several envelopes into her purse, then zipped it shut. "Mom, that's lovely, but I thought dinner last Friday was in honor of the book—"

"And today is in honor of something else, darling. Let's get a taxi before we lose our table."

Claudia rose from her desk. "You're on." But she doubted the maître d' at the Pump Room would deny Eleanor Gage a table just for being fifteen minutes late. Barton had entertained clients too often at the posh restaurant.

It was a short ride from the *Examiner*'s offices near the Tribune Tower to the Ambassador East Hotel. Claudia tried twice to pry the news from Eleanor, but her mother had said, both times, "I've waited weeks for this, darling. And you know how I adore surprises. It can keep for a few more minutes."

The older woman alighted first from the taxi, and Claudia observed the doorman's appreciative appraisal of her mother's face and figure. But today there was something more. It had to be Eleanor's news; she always glowed when she had good news.

Even when they'd been greeted by everyone they knew and settled at their regular table, Eleanor persisted. "Not until we've ordered champagne," she said, perusing the wine list while Claudia studied her menu.

"Mom, white wine would be fine. And you know I'm not wild about bubbly."

"Well, today you'll have to humor me. White wine just isn't festive enough for the occasion."

Eleanor ordered a bottle of Dom Pérignon and then, when at last the cork had been popped and the filled glasses were before them, she lifted hers, clinked it with Claudia's, and with a mischievous smile, said, "To Dr. Seward."

Eleanor never referred to Nick as Dr. Seward; they were too fond of each other for that.

"Mom," said Claudia after taking a sip, "just what is all this—" She interrupted herself. "It's the . . . *appointment!* The job came through!"

Her mother didn't answer, but her nod and the pleased expression on her face confirmed it.

"Mom! That's terrific! But Nick called just before you arrived at the office. He didn't say a word—"

"Nick doesn't know, darling," said Eleanor. "The official announcement hasn't been made yet."

"Then how did you—" That's a silly question, thought Claudia. Dad was on the hospital board, and his lawyer still is. And Mom had promised to pull some strings.

She took another sip of champagne. "You know, you were right. Wine wouldn't be appropriate." She leaned forward and clinked her glass once more against Eleanor's. "Thanks, Mom. For everything."

"There's no need, darling. Nick's qualifications spoke for him as loudly as I might have. Otherwise, I couldn't have done a thing."

The waiter arrived and took their orders. When he had gone, Claudia said quietly, "Mom . . . would you do me a favor?"

Obviously teasing, Eleanor asked, "Another favor?"

"Yes. Would you . . . not . . . tell Nick that you or I had anything to do with the appointment?"

Eleanor nodded. "You're not going to tell him either, are you?"

"No. You know how he feels about that kind of thing. I want him to feel that the medical board chose him as chief of psychiatry strictly because of his work and his credentials."

"Well, darling, that's the truth, after all—"

"Yes, but it wasn't without a gentle . . . shove . . . from the Gages."

The waiter returned with their orders. Then Eleanor said, "I suppose that's refreshing, in a way."

"What is?" asked Claudia.

"Dr. Seward's high ideals and morals. I wish we had a Nick Seward in Washington."

Claudia understood her mother's meaning, but she wasn't in the mood for a serious discussion of politics, either on the local or federal level. "You're right, Mom," she said as their seafood salads arrived. "And just think. If Nick had been in Washington during the Reagan administration, people could have consulted the shrink, instead of the astrologer . . ."

Eleanor didn't say another word on the subject for the rest of their lunch.

As they came out of the restaurant onto Michigan Avenue, they heard Claudia's name being called.

Both women turned to see Judy Fargo, Claudia's publicist and tour coordinator.

"Well, ladies," said Judy. Her hair, which was blonder than Eleanor's, seemed shorter than when Claudia had seen it that morning. And her nails were newly manicured.

Claudia had needed a trim for a week but just hadn't

18

had time. And she'd filed her nails short to make polishing them unnecessary.

"How on earth do you find time for everything?" she asked Judy. "With your schedule, I mean?"

"Simple. I do three things at once. I had a sandwich and a manicure while I was under the dryer—and finished reading through our revised itinerary. Pack lightly—we're not spending much time in any one place."

"Oh, good," said Claudia. "I can repeat."

"Just bring enough along for the TV shows; viewers do a lot of channel hopping during the commercials, and you don't want it to look as if you're hopping from one studio to another all in the same day—"

"Even if I am . . . ?"

All three women laughed.

"Did you two just have lunch in there?" asked Judy, indicating the restaurant's entrance.

Claudia explained that they had—and the reason for it.

"Nick must be so thrilled!" exclaimed Judy.

"Nick doesn't know yet," said Claudia.

"You're celebrating—and he doesn't know?" said Judy. "How's that going to sit with him?"

Glancing furtively at Eleanor, Claudia answered, "You know Margo's line from *All About Eve* . . . ?"

Judy shrugged her shoulders. " 'Fasten your seatbelts . . . ?' "

Claudia nodded and finished the famous phrase: " 'It's going to be a bumpy night.' "

She accompanied Eleanor to Marshall Field's, where she allowed her mother to coax her into a teal blue silk dress.

"It matches your eyes and will photograph beautifully on color television," said Eleanor.

"I know, Mom, but I have enough clothes."

"We'll call it a going-away present." Eleanor and Claudia seldom disagreed; they got along as friends. But they didn't see eye-to-eye on extravagance. Claudia liked to spend her money on other things: "You can wear only one dress at a time, Mom," she'd often said. "I'd rather put money to better use."

Her mother's gentle rebuff had always been the same. "Claudia, wealth can be shared only to an extent. It's the old story about the British crown jewels. If they were divided equally among the entire population, they'd amount to less than sixpence apiece. And the Gages have always done their share—there's no need to feel guilty about our wealth."

It wasn't guilt. It was simply that Claudia preferred to buy and wear what suited her taste, not what fashion editors chose to dictate for this season or that. She liked the lines of certain designers, but she'd never once flown to Paris for the "collections" or fallen slave to the latest darlings of the industry. The cliché "I know what I like" didn't seem a hackneyed phrase to her.

As now, when they passed the lingerie section. "Mom, I tell you what. I'll accept the silk dress willingly if you don't say a word about that." She nodded toward a filmy, sexy ecru lace teddy, which she knew was not Eleanor's taste.

But it was Nick's taste.

The salesclerk handed Claudia her package and receipt. Claudia tucked the charge slip into her purse, alongside the dozen or more letters she'd brought from the office.

"I thought you were taking the afternoon off to relax before your trip, darling," said Eleanor.

"I did. Why?"

"Well, that stack of letters can't *all* be personal correspondence," said Eleanor. "Does Josh really expect you to work on the column while you're away?"

Claudia shook her head. "No. Call it habit. Actually, the only letter I meant to bring along was this one." She withdrew the gray vellum envelope with its New Orleans postmark.

Eleanor took out her reading glasses. "There's no return address. How can you answer it?"

"Through the column. That's the 'mystery writer' I've told you about."

"You didn't tell me the letters came from New Orleans," said Eleanor.

"I must have. Are you sure, Mom?"

With a seriousness that Claudia couldn't understand, Eleanor said, "I'm absolutely positive."

Eleanor had waited for her driver and the Mercedes, but traffic was congested and he was late, so Claudia took a taxi home from Water Tower Place. She was eager to finish packing, and also wanted time to prepare a special dinner for Nick—even though she'd have to pretend, until he told her the "news," that the candlelight and flowers and boeuf Wellington were solely in celebration of her book.

By six o'clock, the sun was setting over Lake Michigan and casting an Impressionist's palette through the wide expanse of living-room windows. It was too hot for Claudia to serve dinner on the terrace, but she did the next best thing: she moved the round table from its usual corner to a spot directly facing the unobstructed view of the water twenty-two floors below.

She'd picked up fresh flowers—iris, gladiola, and roses—and arranged them in a cut crystal vase that was low enough to be the table centerpiece without interfering with Nick or Claudia's ability to see each other.

She doublechecked the place setting to make certain

she'd forgotten nothing. Then, adding the larger crystal wineglasses—for a Clos Vougeot, to go with the meat—she repaired to the kitchen. Nick would know how special she wanted tonight to be; this Wellington would be homemade—from scratch.

By the time she heard Nick's key in the lock, the pastry crust encasing the filet and the pâté topping had turned a mouth-watering golden brown. Claudia's perfume would have to compete with the aroma emanating from the oven.

She had showered and slipped into the new lace teddy before wrapping herself in a silk dressing gown of almost the same shade of ecru. Her long hair was damp from the steam, so she swept it up into curls at the nape of her neck; the effect was soft and romantic.

"Anyone home?" Nick called from the living room.

Claudia was standing before the mirrored wall in their bedroom. Now she saw his reflection as he joined her. "Mmm," he murmured, taking her in his arms, "something smells deliciously inviting . . ."

"Dinner's just about ready," she answered, returning his kiss.

"I wasn't talking about dinner . . . just yet."

"Nick," she said, trying to wriggle out of his embrace, "I spent all afternoon in the kitchen—"

"Good. That means we can spend some time in here, now."

"Darling . . ."

"Mmm-hmm?" His lips were kissing her again, gentle little kisses on her mouth, her cheeks, her ears. His hands had moved from the back of her shoulders to her face, and now they began traveling slowly down the bodice of her dressing gown, tracing the outline of her body through the sensuous silk fabric.

22

The gown was closed only by a softly knotted belt, which Nick untied with one hand while the other moved back up toward Claudia's breasts.

"Nick . . ." she protested in a whisper, "I have to turn down the oven . . ."

"I'd say the heat is just right," he answered, sliding the dressing gown off her shoulders to reveal the lace teddy . . . "For me . . . ?" he teased, brushing his fingers across her nipples through the peekaboo lace.

"Well, I didn't buy it to wear for anyone else," she said, giving in to the sensation his hands provoked.

"It's lovely, darling. Thank you. And now . . . why don't you take it off?"

"I'd rather have you do it for me," she whispered.

"Your wish is my command," he answered, sliding the thin satin straps from her shoulders and starting to undrape the lace as someone would unwrap the most precious of gifts.

"But . . . dinner. . . ." she tried only once more.

"First we eat," said Nick, as the teddy dropped to the floor. "And later we dine. . . ."

As his hands parted the lips between her thighs, Claudia abandoned all thoughts of the boeuf Wellington that might be overcooking; of the lighted candles possibly dripping; of the red wine that still needed to breathe. She forgot about everything but an overwhelming fire rising inside her.

Nick dropped to his knees and pressed his face to the curly mound of pubic hair. Then his tongue began to explore the secret parts of the woman he loved all the more for his intimate knowledge of her.

Claudia moaned as Nick's tongue worked its magic on her velvety flesh. She began to feel the familiar, lightheaded dizziness as his hands grabbed the backs of her thighs and her own hands sought his face, wanting to kiss him yet not wanting him to stop his journey inside her.

"Nick!" she cried out softly. "Oh, Nick—yes—oh, yes! Ohhh!" She grabbed his shoulders as one orgasm exploded after another. Her hands now went to his dark, curly hair and pulled at it until he threw back his head and, looking up into her eyes, asked, "Shall we . . . ?"

Her wanton laugh during their lovemaking had always surprised her, but it excited Nick. He stood up and led Claudia to the bed while her hand caressed his erection through the gray wool of his pants.

"Take those off," she said pleadingly.

He shook his head. "It's your turn . . ."

She tore off his shirt and tie, his belt and slacks. He helped with the rest and joined her on the bed.

Her mouth moved down his chest, over his stomach, toward his penis, but Nick's hand restrained her. "Later. I can't wait—I want to be inside you—now!"

She lay back and he entered her so quickly, so deeply, that she gasped for breath.

"My God!" he cried. "You're so . . . ready! Jesus, I love you like this!"

With his steady, rhythmic thrusting, he brought her closer and closer to climax. Her fists pummeled the pillows on either side of her head; her legs were wrapped around him more tightly than a vise.

"Claudia!" Nick panted, pumping faster, "it's . . . now!"

"Yes!" She screamed with pleasure.

Then, together, they climaxed—joyously, ecstatically. Afterward, they remained locked in spent embrace.

Finally, he slid from her and fell back against the pillow.

When they had rested in each other's arms and quiet enveloped the room, Nick looked down into her eyes and whispered, "Well . . . we can't live on love alone. I don't know about you, but I'm starving."

"Christ!" she exclaimed, jumping up as the food smells reached her nostrils. "If dinner's a disaster, it's your fault—you started this!"

"Okay, then tonight you can start. But in the meantime . . . when do we eat?"

Giving him a sly grin, Claudia said, "I thought you had. . . ."

He'd brought champagne for the same reason Eleanor had ordered it at lunch. They began with that, although Nick hadn't told her his news yet, so Claudia assumed that it was to celebrate their last night together before the book tour.

He waited through the salad, then through the Wellington—"which did not overcook, no thanks to you," she teased—and the broccoli hollandaise.

When they'd finished the red wine and moved on to the strawberries in Marsala, Nick said at last, "I have an announcement to make."

Claudia was pouring the espresso. She sat down next to him and, in the soft glow of the candlelight, said, "Well . . . ? Don't keep me in suspense. What is it?"

His hand reached out and clasped hers. "I didn't want to . . . to upstage you . . . I mean, this is *your* night—"

"Darling, it's *our* night. So tell me . . ."

Nick's eyes were wide and bright. "I've been made chief of psychiatry—head of the entire department at the hospital!"

"That's wonderful! What a surprise!" Claudia leaned forward to kiss him. But for a split second she averted her eyes, and Nick felt the slightest withdrawal of her hand from his.

"I'd have told you sooner," he said, "but I didn't find out myself till four-thirty this afternoon, and it wasn't news I wanted to share over the phone. And then when I came in and . . . you looked so . . . well, so tempting—"

She was smiling. "Nick, darling, you don't have to explain. I'm thrilled about it—really I am."

Then why did he have this ridiculous notion that she was keeping something from him?

Occupational hazard, he chided himself. Always analyzing. Not advisable to take the job home at night, Dr. Seward.

Still . . .

"I tried calling you at the office this afternoon," he said. "Not to tell you the news, but just to let you know what time I'd be home."

"I took the afternoon off. Lunch with Mom."

"Where'd you go?"

"Oh, you know Eleanor. Only the poshest. We . . . went to the Pump Room."

There it was again. The smallest hesitation.

"That's not where you usually have lunch," he said.

"No . . . Mom wanted something special. You know, to celebrate the book. . . ."

She saw him looking at her curiously. "What is it, darling?"

He shrugged. "Nothing. But it's a good thing you don't have a clandestine lover hidden away somewhere."

The remark surprised her. "What a strange thing to say. Why would you even think that?"

"Because," he said, "you'd make a lousy liar, and I'd find out about it."

Claudia went into the kitchen on the excuse of making more coffee. But her mind wasn't on the espresso. She was wondering if Nick suspected Eleanor's hand in the appointment—and if not, how that revelation would "sit," as Judy Fargo had said, if Nick should find out.

Chapter 2

Nick watched as the chairman of the board took a sip of water and continued. ". . . So, it is with pride that we, the directors, announce the appointment of Dr. Nicholas Seward as Chief of Psychiatry at Lake Shore General."

Raymond Fenwick stepped away from the podium and joined in the hearty applause. The chatter of automatic camera shutters filled the room as Nick crossed the small platform in a strobe light burst of flashbulbs. Hand-shakes of friends, acquaintances, and strangers alike were offered for quick congratulations as he passed by.

He had reached the podium, but before he could speak, Fenwick grabbed his hand and whispered, "Richly deserved."

The words moved Nick. He had wanted this position. It felt good to have it.

"Thanks," he replied with a beaming grin. He adjusted the stem of the microphone upward to accommodate his height, and looked at the smiling faces before him.

"I accept this undertaking with awareness of its responsibility," he began, "and with the knowledge that I will do my utmost to fulfill the trust shown in me." When drafting his acceptance speech, Nick had kept it short, to

27

leave time for questions from the handful of newspaper reporters present.

They started almost immediately:

"How do you feel about being the youngest appointee in the hospital's history?"

"What changes do you plan to effect?"

And, from one of Claudia's *Examiner* cronies, the expected joke: "Will you be asking Miss Gage for advice?"

Nick chuckled good-naturedly, joining the group's laughter. "Only about the color of my tie," he answered.

The small crowd had filtered down to twenty or so, once the trade journalists and newspaper people were gone. Those who remained were colleagues and board members making polite chitchat with Nick between sips of their drinks. It was this part of "the job" he had previously found disconcerting. He'd been taken aback, months ago, at Claudia's observation during a similar function.

"You're good at this," she'd said.

He knew she'd meant it. He wished she was at his side now. Her presence always helped.

Nick glanced at his watch. One o'clock. Her flight was scheduled to depart at 2:15 P.M. He was glad they'd had last night, and his thoughts lingered on their past evening. He missed her already, but there'd been no possibility of her attending this afternoon's ceremony. She's probably still packing, he thought. A private smile curved his lips at the image of her frantically cramming last-minute choices into a suitcase before the limousine arrived.

Limousines. How quickly he'd become accustomed to a life that included such luxuries. He worked hard, but the outward symbols and pleasures of his precocious rise to success had taken some getting used to. Again, Claudia had been instructive; none of it had ever been new to her.

"You're looking happy," said Raymond Fenwick.

"I am. For a few days there, you had me sweating."

Fenwick smiled. "Given your credentials, there was never any doubt in my mind."

"And the . . . others?"

"Very few dissenters. I brought them around."

"I'm glad. But . . . who . . . ?"

"Not on your life, m'boy," Fenwick joked. "That'd be grounds for blackmail! But enjoy your victory. Soon, you may have enough work to make you wonder if it's worth it."

"Oh, it's worth it."

The older man put a hand on Nick's shoulder. "That's how I felt when I took over the firm. Now, retirement's looking mighty tempting."

"Raymond, I didn't know you were such a cynic," Nick said with humor.

As if in response, a male voice laughed too loudly from a corner near the bar. Both men turned to see John Downing's mirth dwindle into a coughing spasm. One of the people in Downing's group poured a glass of water and handed it to the portly doctor. As he accepted and drank, his eyes met Nick's, then darted back to another guest.

"Has he offered his congratulations yet?" Fenwick asked

"I don't think that's forthcoming. The competition isn't . . . friendly. At least to me, these days."

"Downing has never been what I'd term a sport," said Fenwick. "But it's understandable, I suppose. He's older. Saw the post becoming his by way of tenure, I'd imagine."

The gathering was thinning out as Fenwick's wife came over to remind him it was time to go. They left, and Nick decided he'd stayed long enough to follow suit.

Saying his goodbyes, however, would involve a confrontation with Downing. Nick had hoped that Downing would leave first, but that hadn't happened, and there was no telling how long he'd go on drinking.

Nick reasoned that contact between them was both inevitable and unavoidable. He stalled until the last two people near Downing had gone for their raincoats. An encounter would be less awkward without witnesses.

Nick approached Downing, whose eyes were boring into him, and held out his hand. It was not accepted.

"Well," his older colleague said in a low, toneless voice, "You've gotten this far. What's next, the White House?"

"John, the post is hardly one of political significance."

"Oh, come now, Doctor Seward! You know better than that. It's all politics. Who one is in bed with, as it were."

"Excuse me?"

"No, excuse *me*. Most . . . unfortunate . . . choice of words. But I hope at least you're treating your lady friend's mother to a celebration dinner."

"What are you talking about?"

Downing stared at him with a mock look of wonder. "My God . . . can it be that you honestly don't know?"

Nick tried to keep his mounting anger from affecting the sound of his voice. "Know what, John?"

"Why, the chairman of the board . . . your buddy, Lawyer Fenwick. His firm counts the Gage estate as one of its most important clients. They handle all of Eleanor's money." Downing took a final swig of his Scotch, then added, "Probably Claudia's money, too. Congratulations . . . on your connections, Seward."

Nick left the large conference room and managed what felt like a pasted-on smile for the last of the well-wishers. Once deeply outside in the hospital parking lot, he breathed deeply and pulled up the collar of his jacket against the first drops of a summer shower. At last he

30

allowed his face to form the grimace he hoped had remained hidden upstairs.

He tried telling himself it didn't matter. When that didn't work, there was nothing left to do but admit his anger with Downing.

No. With Claudia. Himself. The world, for permitting appointments on boards under false pretenses. Did that make sense? Think clearly, a private voice cautioned. Why be so upset? Physician, he mused, heal thyself!

That helped; he hadn't lost his sense of humor entirely. But it offered no solace from Downing's innuendo.

Nick pulled his vintage dark-green Jaguar out of the lot and into traffic, halting for the light at the corner. The windshield wipers beat back and forth at a steady monotonous rhythm that didn't improve his mood.

He questioned whether Downing would have made the remark in front of Claudia. He was relieved she hadn't been there, after all; he knew how she would have reacted.

Or do I? he wondered, gunning the motor. Downing hadn't lied—not about the Fenwick-Gage business relationship, at least. That was common knowledge. But had his further implication been true as well?

Sure, Downing was jealous, observed Nick. Maybe even drunk . . . But that would explain only why he'd voiced it.

Suddenly it seemed very important for Nick to know whether he'd gotten the appointment on the basis of merit or through "pull," from influence he didn't even know he had—connections, as Downing had put it.

Nick hoped Claudia hadn't been involved; if any favor-trading had occurred through Raymond Fenwick, Nick could live with it more easily, provided that Eleanor Gage had acted on her own—independently and without her daughter's knowledge.

But what if she hadn't?

The only way to find out was to reach the apartment before Claudia left and ask her face-to-face. Nick knew she'd tell him the truth . . . Which brought to mind another question: Did he want to hear it?

He found a parking spot across the street; it was faster than maneuvering through the cavernous garage within the bowels of the Edgewater Towers building. Still, in spite of his haste, he sat for a moment behind the wheel, more to calm himself than to rest. He looked up through the windshield. The rain was lifting to a soft mist, and he could see the outline of their apartment terrace twenty-two floors above. The beachfront directly east was almost deserted, and Lake Michigan was again glassy-smooth, the whitecaps of earlier in the day flattened and gone, as though the lake were grateful to be free of invading bathers and boaters who impeded its flow toward shore.

Across the lake lay Michigan, and north of that, Canada, where Nick and Claudia had taken a week following Barton Gage's death. Then they'd visited Quebec and Montreal, where Claudia's French and her familiarity with both cities had seen them through. Nick hadn't traveled extensively, except for psychiatric conventions in San Francisco and New York. Even medical school had been back home in the Midwest. No complaints. But it did seem, by contrast, that Claudia had traveled everywhere.

And now she'd be traveling again, without him. The thought didn't appeal to him. She always seemed to be in flight.

The flight! Nick jumped from the driver's seat, got out and locked the door, and dashed across the street just as the block-long black Cadillac limo halted before the canopy over Edgewater Towers' main entrance.

"You here to pick up Claudia Gage?" he asked the liveried chauffeur breathlessly.

"Yessir. Sorry I'm a little late."

"Stay put. I'll tell her you're here." Nick rushed past the doorman toward the bank of elevators at the rear of the oak-paneled lobby. He was moving so fast, he almost slipped on the slick white marble floor.

"C'mon, hurry!" he hissed, pressing the UP button with vehemence. There was even less time than he'd planned on.

He unlocked the door and glanced around the living room. The mauve silk draperies were drawn across the glass walls and door leading to the terrace; the translucent fabric diminished the glare of the sun emerging after a midday rain, and cast a soft pink glow onto the off-white carpeting.

Nick saw no evidence of last night's celebration. Despite his mood, he smiled, wondering what the maid must have thought this morning. When he'd left for the hospital at dawn, the dishes, stemware, even the candle stubs in their crystal holders, had remained on the table. Only leftovers had been put away. Now, the table had been moved back to its customary corner, fresh candles had replaced those used at dinner, and even the flowers had been changed. The room still looked warm and inviting, but not the same kind of inviting Nick remembered from last night.

He could hear quiet cursing, punctuated by struggling, grunting sounds, coming from the bedroom. Nick walked to the doorway and nodded to himself. He'd guessed right. Claudia was leaning all of her hundred and twenty pounds on top of a suitcase that refused to close.

"Bon voyage," he said.

She let out a yelp and spun around. "God! You scared me! I didn't hear you come in!"

"Sorry," he answered.

Her hair was hanging loosely, and the comb that

33

sometimes kept the left side swept back and off her face was missing; it fell forward and gave her a very mischievous look. Her gray silk-jersey dress clung to her breasts and hips, and Nick had to fight his stirrings of renewed excitement. There just wasn't time.

She smiled and came toward him. "How'd the ceremony go?" she asked by way of greeting.

He shrugged, and Claudia impulsively pulled his face down to hers. Their lips met, and Nick noticed that she smelled of almond-scented soap and the new perfume he'd given her.

"I'm proud of you," she whispered.

"I know," he answered quickly.

Too quickly. "Something wrong?" she asked.

"The car . . . limo . . . is downstairs." He moved past her to the suitcase. "Let's get this closed."

Claudia leaned on the lid while Nick snapped the locks shut. "Thanks. I spent twenty minutes working on it — and there's stuff I didn't pack!"

He didn't reply, but picked up the two matching taupe leather bags and carried them into the hall, dropping them beside the door.

"You know," she said, following him, "New York is only a few hours' flight."

Nick shook his head. "I'll be up to my eyes getting the hang of the new job . . . and you'll be having interviews from dawn to dusk."

"Nick . . ." she began, then stopped. There was something going on, something more than their pending separation.

His back was to her when he asked, "Raymond Fenwick is your mother's lawyer, isn't he?"

"For as long as I can remember. You know that."

Now he turned to face her. "Did Eleanor have anything to do with my new appointment?"

"What are you talking about?"

"You don't know . . . ?"

Claudia paused, then dropped down onto the deep-rose silk love seat in the hall. "What have you heard?"

It was apparent to both of them, as he spoke, that Nick was furious. Claudia had never feared him physically, and she didn't now. But they respected each other's temperaments, and she knew that he was choosing his words carefully and trying to control his anger.

When at last he'd finished speaking, she said, "Will you sit down?"

"You have a plane to catch."

"Nick, there are other planes, and the car will wait."

"I'll stand. Go ahead and talk."

"All right," she began. "Mother frequently entertains the Fenwicks, among her other friends. She did recently, as a matter of fact, and of course your name was mentioned at dinner. There's nothing sinister about it."

"My name should never have been 'mentioned at dinner,' Claudia."

"Nick, you live with her daughter. If anyone asks about me, you are—logically—included!"

"You're telling me Eleanor's money had no influence on the board?"

Claudia rose from the love seat. "My mother isn't a blackmailer, for God's sake! Nick, my father was on the board! And if Eleanor was able to swing things in your direction, why not?"

"Then she did!"

"To the extent that she pulled a few strings . . . yes! It's done all the time, Nick! It's how I got my first job on the *Examiner*—and what's wrong with it?"

Nick was staring at her. "I never knew that," he said.

"Well, now you do. But I worked hard for five years and that's how I finally got my column. Nobody could 'buy' it for me. It's a success, and *I* did *that*. It's something I've earned—just as you've earned this ap-

35

pointment."

"Claudia, I know things like this are done. I just don't like them being done in my behalf."

She went to him. "It would have been dishonest only if you weren't qualified and got the job anyway."

"Dammit, don't you see?" he said. "Under these circumstances, I could be a moron and still have landed the job!"

"But you're not a moron, are you? You think John Downing didn't try the same thing on his side of the fence? Nick, your deserving the job didn't ensure your getting it! What if Downing had been appointed—he is a moron! What would have happened to the department of psychiatry then?"

Nick was studying her. Gradually a smile began to form. "Downing . . . it would have been chaos, I admit."

"Yes," she replied, moving closer to him. "It was a simple case of making sure the right man got the post."

"No matter the means . . . ?"

"Oh, Nick . . . no. You're acting as if we went around slinging mud. Or killed somebody."

"Maybe I am." He bent to kiss her, then said quietly, "But in the future, please leave your family's connections out of my career?"

They didn't speak while the elevator took them to the lobby. The doorman and the limo chauffeur loaded her two bags into the trunk. The rain was beginning again in a slow, steady drizzle.

Claudia climbed into the rear seat and lowered the window.

"You're getting wet," she said, as he leaned in and kissed her.

"I don't care," he said.

"I'll call you when we get to the hotel."

"Good. I'll . . . miss you."

"Sure you can't fly down for the weekend?"

"I can't." Nick took a breath and exhaled. "I love you, you know."

His eyes held hers. Claudia stammered, then answered, "I . . . never meant to hurt you, Nick."

It wasn't what he wanted to hear.

"I know," he said.

Then the limo pulled away from the curb.

Chapter 3

Judy Fargo leaned back in her aisle seat and took the first sip of her second Manhattan.

"So who won?" she asked.

"It's always a draw." Claudia continued, staring out at the clouds. "He's stubborn," she added.

"And you're not?"

Judy was smiling when Claudia turned to her. "It's a family trait, I'm told. Barton was mule-headed, too."

"I'd hate to think what my daughter has inherited from me," Judy replied with a broader grin.

"Well, mine is learned. I'm not really sure what I've inherited."

"I am," Judy said, popping the maraschino cherry into her mouth. She turned toward Claudia again. "Was that uncouth?"

"Not from you . . . But I didn't mean the money. Lately I've been thinking about things that never bothered me before."

"Are you so different? From Eleanor and Barton, I mean?"

Claudia sipped at the Scotch and water she'd been nursing. "Not in ways that seem . . . important. But I do sometimes wonder . . . well . . . why I am the way I am."

"If you ask me—and you didn't—I'd say you got pretty lucky to draw the Gages."

"Oh, I know that. But I had no part in who adopted me . . . maybe that's why control over my own life now is so important."

"Back up a minute, hon," Judy said. "You mean committing fully to Nick would relinquish control?"

"Oh, I don't know what I mean . . ."

"Claudia . . . no one has a say in who they're born to *or* adopted by. If they did, my own spawn would have chosen the Gages over me in a minute."

"Are you two on the outs again?" asked Claudia.

Judy shrugged. "She's a good kid, I guess. But she seems more concerned about her stock portfolio than about her life. She's confused over priorities." Judy pulled a stray blond hair from her mascaraed lashes. "And she certainly didn't get that nature from my set of genes, believe me!"

"Is Annie still working for her father?"

"No, but he throws her as many accounts as he can. Incidentally, we're having dinner with the two of them tonight."

Although the invitation was sincere, Claudia knew it was being extended so she wouldn't be relegated to a lonely meal at the hotel—even if the hotel was the Plaza. She hadn't met Judy's legendary ex-husband or the prototypical yuppie daughter, but joining them tonight hardly seemed like fun. For Claudia or for Judy.

"No," Claudia answered. "Thanks. But you go without me. I'd only be in the way. Besides, I have to get to bed early if I'm going to be on time at the network at the crack of dawn tomorrow."

"We both have to be there," Judy reminded her.

"Yes, but you don't have to be on camera, looking great and oozing wit and wisdom."

"You have a point. But it'll come easier to you—the beauty part! You're a few years my junior."

Claudia grinned; Judy admitted to forty-two.

"I wonder," said Judy, "if he's still dying his hair."

"Frank?"

Judy nodded. "He thinks too much gray would hinder his way with women—or rather, with girls. At least Nick doesn't fool around, does he?"

"No. He doesn't."

"Have you?" Judy asked. "Would you?"

Claudia looked intently at her publicist and friend. "No, Judy. I haven't," she said.

"That's one answer to two questions."

"Did you . . . while you were married to Frank?"

"No. Not that it didn't cross my mind, after I found out about him. But he said it would never happen again. Of course, what he meant was that he wouldn't get caught again."

Claudia finished her drink, then said, "But he did—get caught again?"

"Yes," said Judy. "Anyway, you're not *married* to Nick . . . and you still haven't answered my second question."

"What if I don't know the answer?"

Judy took her hand. "Then you'd better find out. Nick wants to put a gold band on that ring finger of yours."

Claudia didn't need someone else to tell her that. "Judy," she said carefully, "can we switch to publicist-and-client now?"

"In other words, shut up and change the subject?" Judy asked with an apologetic smile.

"Something like that . . ."

Within minutes they were immersed in the revised version of the tour's itinerary. It amazed Claudia the way her publicity agent could change gears so easily—and the way she drew her client into her sphere of enthusiasm. Before long, Claudia was just as excited about the personal appearance schedule as the woman who had arranged it, and the worries she had left behind in Chicago dimmed in the light of the new turns in her career.

"Now, tomorrow," Judy said, gesturing with a perfectly manicured hand, *"Good Morning America*—that's ABC—is followed by a taping for CBS News—the five-fifty spot with what's-her-name, Jill Rappaport. Then a photo session for *Cosmo* to go with the excerpt, then lunch with your editor and publisher at '21', then the book signing at B. Dalton on Fifth Avenue—the store is right around the corner from the restaurant—and after that, you and Sue Simmons go *Live at Five* on NBC, and . . ."

The early part of the evening would include a cocktail reception at her publisher's, dinner—Judy wasn't sure where—and theater, "but only if you want to." *Donahue* was set for the next day. "And we may even have time for some shopping. Then we take the shuttle to Boston."

Claudia nodded wearily as the FASTEN SEAT BELT sign flashed on. Judy's mere recitation of the schedule had exhausted her, and they were still circling above New York.

"My office is trying to line up airtime in Seattle and Dallas," Judy went on, "but we may have to wedge them in. San Francisco and L.A. are no problem. And we may do one day in San Diego—I'm working on it . . . And oh, by the way, even with all the changes, New Orleans is still the fourth stop on the tour."

"Yes . . ." said Claudia.

Judy hadn't noticed her client's reaction. The publicist leaned back and smiled contentedly. "I believe in the old adage about leaving no stone unturned. And, darlin', if I have any say in the matter, you'll be into a third printing before the tour's half over. There won't be a soul who hasn't heard about *Dear Claudia*."

"All they have to do is buy it, Judy."

"They will. It's a good book."

"Which doesn't guarantee a thing."

"Look, if I had to sell ice cubes to the Eskimos, I could do it. But it's easier to push something I believe in . . . and I think your book is terrific."

Claudia squeezed Judy's wrist in thanks. "I just hope it helps people. That it offers good advice."

"You're not getting cold feet on me, are you?" asked Judy.

"No. I'm just aware that sometimes I need good advice, too."

Judy leaned in close to her. "Do me a favor? Don't say that on the air!"

"It's a deal." Claudia managed a nervous laugh.

"And don't worry. That's what I'm here for." Judy's voice took on a more serious, businesslike tone. "Another thing. When you get face-to-face with the book-buying public, there's more than a chance that some of your fans will want instant, on-the-spot solutions to their problems. Be polite . . . but brief. This isn't an oral column."

Before Claudia could speak, Judy continued. "And don't endorse any product, no matter how heartfelt. First, it could be in conflict with the sponsors of the local shows you're guesting on, and, second, you endorse nothing for free. If it's not for money, you only plug the book."

"It looks as if you've covered all the angles," said Claudia.

"Listen, I work on commission. The bigger your take, the bigger my percentage."

"Oh?" said Claudia, trying to suppress a grin.

"Something amuse you?"

"I was just thinking . . . perhaps Annie did get some of those genes from her mother."

42

"Beyond the good looks, you mean?" asked Judy.

The engine's roar as they landed obliterated Claudia's reply.

McClintock Publishing had arranged for a car and driver to pick them up at La Guardia Airport. Unfortunately, their arrival coincided with New York City's rush-hour traffic, so a trip that should have taken twenty-five minutes lasted an hour and a half. Some things are universal, Claudia reflected as they crawled over the bridge; whether Chicago, Paris, or Rome, evening traffic was evening traffic. And no matter which city she visited, the approach always made her eager to get there.

When she and Judy stepped out of the air-conditioned limousine and onto the pavement in front of the hotel, the July humidity enveloped them in a blanket of moist air. Claudia had long been fond of New York, although she tried to avoid the city during winter and summer. Still, flowers were in bloom everywhere, and their perfume, mingled with the smell of trees and grasses, carried on the damp breezes from Central Park across the way.

Overhead loomed the enormous stone-and-metal canopy of the Plaza's main entrance. The huge banners suspended over it hung limp and still in the muggy air. With relief, Claudia and Judy climbed the short flight of steps and pushed through the revolving doors into the lobby.

The atmosphere changed immediately to one of busy elegance and efficiency. The green-beige Oriental carpeting, Claudia noted, even with thousands of guests traipsing over it each day, showed no signs of wear. A three-foot-high spray of fresh flowers fanned out from the mammoth urn at the center of the rug. It was past the hour for high tea in the Palm Court, but strains of violin music still floated above the "white sounds" of low-pitched conversation.

As they headed toward the registration area, Judy took a quick detour. "I've got to take a peek," she said, sticking her head into the staid, wood-paneled Edwardian Room while Claudia waited outside.

Judy nodded as if confirming her own suspicions. "I confess it," she whispered. "I'm impressed."

They continued to the right, which brought them to the marbled lobby and the front desk.

The Gages had stayed at the Plaza many times, most often during Claudia's childhood and adolescence. Barton, in particular, had been fond of the hotel, despite its gradual transformation in recent years toward its present "streamlined" look. Gone was the expanse of lobby in which a six-year-old Claudia had sat and pretended to be Kay Thompson's Eloise while her parents dressed for dinner. Bejeweled guests no longer felt inclined to linger or stroll; in their place were conventioneers wearing badges and joking loudly. A smattering of "old money" opulence and style was still visible, but only to the discerning eye. Claudia noted sadly that they were outnumbered by the nouveaux riches and yuppies. Judy's daughter, she mused, would feel right at home — the way I used to feel, here.

As Claudia glanced around the bustling lobby, Charlie Chaplin came to mind. "The Tramp" had looked forward to his final visit to New York just to see the Plaza one last time. Claudia recalled now that Barton had told her the story during his own final visit to the hotel.

Had it been only a year ago?

With mixed feelings Claudia signed her name to the guest register. She didn't want the tour stop in New York to evoke bittersweet memories, but her resolve was rapidly dwindling. When McClintock Publishing had suggested the Plaza, she had readily agreed, primarily because Judy had been so eager. But, she reflected now, the Pierre or the Waldorf might have been a wiser choice.

They found messages waiting at the desk. There were three for Judy and one for Claudia, who saw that hers was from the *Examiner*'s office. She'd return the call later; suddenly her energy was depleted.

"You all right?" asked Judy. "You look a little pale."

Claudia nodded, gazing off into the distance. "I'm fine. Just tired."

A uniformed bellhop unlocked the door to Judy's room.

"We're practically next door," said Judy. "Get some rest and call me later."

"I will," answered Claudia, continuing down the hall.

The bellhop opened her door to reveal a spacious enough room; the yellow decor was overdone in one of her least favorite colors, but at least her request had been granted: the single window looked out onto Central Park. Even at the twilight hour, the view presented was a monochrome of dense, lush green. During her last visit it had offered a variety of yellow, rust, and red.

On the mirrored dresser, two large bouquets filled the room with their scent. The first card, accompanying the two dozen roses, read: "For *Dear Claudia,* best wishes from McClintock Publishing." The second, tied to a basket of tiger lilies, read: "I still want that free auto-graphed copy!" Signed "Josh," it was obviously from him, personally, and not from the entire *Examiner* staff.

"Will that be all, ma'am?"

Claudia had completely forgotten about the bellhop, who had placed her two suitcases on the luggage rack and was standing near the door waiting for his tip. They used to be less blatant about expecting it, she mused, opening her wallet and taking out a five. She tossed her purse onto the bed and handed the money to the bellhop, who thanked her and left.

She was alone. The muted traffic noises coming from the street below were still audible over the drone of the air conditioner, but they sounded blurred and far away.

Claudia glanced from the window to the bed, where her purse lay open. She noticed some paper peering out of a partially unzipped pocket flap. The corner of an envelope. Gray vellum. From New Orleans.

Now is the hour.

Claudia suddenly felt a chill.

Until next week.

She was startled by the telephone's ring.

"Hello?" she answered.

"Hi! You sound out of breath!"

"Nick! We just arrived—your timing is perfect!"

She heard him laugh. "I'm calling from my new office. Thought you should have the phone number."

Claudia grabbed a memo pad and pen from the night table. "I was supposed to call you," she said after jotting down the number.

"I couldn't wait. Besides, with the hour's difference, I won't get back to the apartment until at least seven-thirty or eight, your time."

"Well, now I can interrupt all kinds of important meetings and whisper in your ear whenever I want to," she teased. "How's it going?"

"A madhouse. This is the first break I've had since you left . . . Oh, your mother phoned . . . to congratulate me."

"What did you say to her? I mean, you didn't . . . ?"

"No," he answered with a chuckle, "I didn't. Even if I was sorely tempted to. I just thanked her." In a different tone of voice, he said, "I miss you."

"I miss you, too. I hate it when we fight."

"I wouldn't call it a fight exactly, would you?"

"Well, maybe not. Still . . ."

As they talked, Claudia felt some of her earlier tension beginning to ease. It was reassuring to know that things were all right between them.

"Good luck tomorrow," he was saying. "I'll tape the morning show so I can watch you when I get home from the hospital."

"Let me know how I look — and how I come across on the tube, okay?"

"You tired?"

"Yes. I'll have to call Eleanor, and Josh left a message. But then, I think a nap is in order."

"Dream of me," said Nick.

But she didn't dream of Nick. She awoke, hyperventilating and damp with perspiration.

The setting of her nightmare was by now as familiar to Claudia as this hotel; however, unlike the Plaza, her dream evoked fear, not nostalgia. And although the locale of its setting still eluded her, this time she had seen more clarity in its images and, in particular, its sounds. The blare of music had dulled to an off-key, almost recognizable — but not quite — melody. It was played slowly, one note at a time.

She had felt closer to understanding the dream than ever before, which fueled her frustration and anxiety. With comprehension just beyond her grasp, the images were that much more real — and, therefore, more frightening. Claudia was no longer certain that she *wanted* to know their meaning.

She swung her feet onto the carpeted floor and sat up on the edge of the bed. What had brought on the dream this time? — induced it, to use Nick's terminology. They'd discussed it when the dream had occurred before, joked about the luxury of having a psychiatrist "on call" at home. "My live-in shrink," she'd teased.

Claudia reviewed the past hour, her thoughts and actions. Arrival at the Plaza. Memories of her father. Nick's call. Then the conversation with Eleanor. All underscored her sense of loss at Barton's passing. Her dream had to be somehow related to her family or life at home. She was convinced that the strange, yet familiar tune, still echoing in the outer recesses of her conscious mind, linked the distant past and present.

What had come next? she asked herself. After Nick . . . Eleanor . . . then the call to Tina Berenson's office at McClintock . . . and another to Josh Samuelson. That had been all.

No. There'd been something more. She'd noticed the gray vellum envelope.

The phone rang again. Only once. Probably someone who had dialed the wrong room number, realized it, and hung up.

Christ! she thought, glancing at her watch. It's nearly seven! I forgot to call Judy!

Claudia rang the room and, while waiting to be connected, perused the room-service menu that she found in the night-table drawer.

"Hi," she said when Judy answered. "I just woke up."

"Good. Feeling rested?"

"Not completely. I had that dream again."

"Dammit!" said Judy. "You're probably more tired now."

"Well, sort of. I could really use the night off. It might be my last one this month."

"You sure I can't get you to change your mind?" asked Judy. "And don't start saying you'll be in the way. I can use moral support for this reunion, hon."

"Judy . . ."

"All right, all right, I'm trying to manipulate. Sue me. Want to meet me downstairs for a cocktail before I make my way unto the breach?"

48

"What I want to do is take a shower and get into my robe, order some wine and a sandwich from room service, curl up, and spend the rest of the evening watching TV."

"Then do it, hon," said Judy. "To be truthful, I envy you."

Claudia asked to have *The New York Times* sent up with her club sandwich and wine. She opened the paper to the book section and found her publisher's advertisement: "Come and meet Claudia Gage! Have her autograph your copy of *Dear Claudia!* Tomorrow afternoon only!" They'd run her photograph below the copy, and beneath that, the location of the booksellers and the time.

She'd turned on the radio after her shower. On the classical station, following a Mozart concerto, an announcer spoke words similar to those she'd just read in the *Times*.

She was beginning to feel uneasy. Stage fright? she wondered. There's going to be this kind of advance publicity at every stop on the tour. And it all starts rolling tomorrow . . .

Fine, Claudia decided. But for tonight, I'm going to relax.

She flicked off the radio and didn't even turn on the television set. Maybe later. Right now, she preferred the quiet, the air conditioner humming in the background, the traffic noises fading outside as night fell over the city.

She sipped her wine and relished the rarity of an evening with nothing to do. At home, the column required long hours, much of it away from the office and on frequent occasions intruding on her time with Nick. Letters from deeply troubled readers often meant consulting qualified professionals — Nick among them — before composing a reply.

This evening, then, was a welcome respite from the battery of psychiatrists, psychoanalysts, and therapists who formed her counseling network. And even though a conscientious Bonnie Newcomb had stuffed a stack of unanswered letters into her boss's briefcase, Claudia was going to treat herself to a mini-holiday until tomorrow.

Just for tonight, she promised, I'm not going to think about letters.

Any of them.

Chapter 4

Each of the television interviews shared one factor: speed. Claudia was whisked into a dressing room, made up under blazing hot lights, rushed to the station's "green room," and invited to wait.

Each host—or each host's assistant—carried a copy of *Dear Claudia*. She wasn't certain that any of them had read it.

Then a cup of coffee—*another* cup of coffee!—a quick powder retouch to counteract shine, and "Miss Gage, we're ready for you."

"Well," she commented to Judy as they entered "21," "at least I didn't trip over any cable or call the book by the wrong title."

"You were terrific," said Judy. "You even managed to keep your face three-quarters to the *right* camera."

"*That* was an accident," Claudia admitted.

"There's no such thing, hon. Oh, look! There's Tom Wolfe"—she waved to the tall blond man in the white suit and pink shirt—"and there's . . . my God, it's *Liz!*"

"Judy," whispered Claudia, "I can't believe it—you're

impressed! You work with famous people every day, but—"

"Why do you think I went into this business? Part of it was for the money, and part of it was because I never thought Frank was going to get out of debt. But the *real* reason," she confided in a hushed voice, "is because I get off on the glamour."

Claudia was about to answer, but at that moment Sean Connery passed by, and she admitted to herself that she, too, was "getting off" on the glamour.

Her editor, Tina Berenson, arrived on time. The tall, very slim strawberry-blond wore a black linen suit with a blue silk blouse only a shade lighter than the teal-blue silk dress Claudia was wearing—the dress Eleanor had insisted on buying for her.

"Well, it looks as if lunch will be a hen party," said Tina as the maître d' led them to their table. "Ken couldn't get away." Kenneth McClintock was the chief executive officer of McClintock Publishing, one of the last independent holdouts left after recent years' conglomerate takeovers.

"Good," said Judy. "If Ken were along, we'd have to play ladylike. Now we can dish instead!"

But they didn't "dish." They discussed the book. "Orders are very strong" from Tina; "We can make them even stronger" from Judy.

And throughout the huge chef's salad and wine, Claudia felt that part of her was there, and part of her was somewhere else, although she had no idea where that somewhere else might be.

She didn't miss any of the conversation; she even contributed to it every now and then. Maybe it was the whirlwind—and the fact that she was at its center. Even at her busiest, she'd never crammed a hairdo and makeup session, two television interviews, a photo shoot, and lunch into the first half of a day that had begun at five in the morning. And it was only halfway over.

"Well," Tina was saying to Judy, "there's the possibility, according to all reports, of *Dear Claudia*'s being published in French, Italian, German, and Spanish editions."

"I'd like that," said Claudia.

"She'd like that," echoed Judy. "An extra several million copies in print and 'she'd like that.' " But it was clear that Judy was teasing affectionately. She knew Claudia didn't sit at her desk and figure royalty percentages as a habit. She knew Claudia didn't have to.

". . . and at the reception," Tina was saying, "I may have a reporter or two, so be forewarned."

"You know," said Judy, "we may not have time for a real sit-down dinner tonight. I've got us tickets to *Phantom of the Opera,* so it depends on how late the reception goes."

Claudia nodded and finished her salad.

Judy had advised her to be ready for the onslaught, but when they arrived for the book signing at the B. Dalton, Claudia saw crowds assembling inside and for a moment thought that some famous Hollywood celebrity was holding court — or that several hundred copies of an international best-seller had suddenly gone on remainder . . .

That was until Judy said, "Claudia, they're waiting for you."

One by one they stepped up to the table. Most were shy or pleasantly friendly — "I read your column every week" and "I'm so eager to read your book." In the first thirty minutes, Claudia asked each person's name, and then wrote a personal dedication on the title page. As the hour wore on and the crowds grew more dense instead of thinning out, Claudia's left wrist began to tire. She wasn't

53

ambidextrous, so she couldn't sign autographs with her right hand. The dedications were dropped unless they were specifically requested, and "Best wishes from Claudia Gage" grew more and more illegible. As the second hour was drawing to a close, she was opting for her signature only, scrawled hastily beneath the title and barely resembling the boldface italics of her printed name above.

Judy stood off to one side. She observed people from all walks of life, all styles of dress, all ages; young children with their parents, others accompanying their grandparents, sophisticated New Yorkers, pastel-printed-and-polyestered tourists, — everyone wanted Claudia's book. And Judy's work behind the scenes had helped; they also wanted the author's autograph.

Judy was leaning against a stationery display. She closed her eyes for a split second just to rest them. When she opened them again, she noticed the man. But only for an instant. Then he was swallowed up by the crowd.

He had stayed in the background. He preferred it that way.

It was interesting — fascinating — to watch without being watched. He'd been studying Claudia and her smile. It was genuine and warm, and made each person buying her book feel special. He knew; he'd felt special when she signed his copy — a dedicated and autographed copy; he'd been there since the first half hour.

He'd learned where she was staying from the listing in *Celebrity Service*. But he wanted to observe her here. He often found the key to subjects' natures when they were unaware of posing; it was not unlike a child absorbed in play and made suddenly self-conscious by the appearance

54

of a camera. The last thing he wanted was for Claudia to become self-conscious over him.

He waited. Then he made his way through the still-packed throng until he reached the manager's desk.

At the end of the second hour, Claudia's hand was almost numb. Finally the crowds had thinned out, and Judy, intervening to placate the stragglers, insisted that Miss Gage was late for an interview.

It was true. Fortunately Judy knew shortcuts through building entrances and exits, so they made it from Fifty-second Street to the RCA Building and NBC with two whole minutes to spare.

They'd been in such a rush that the manager of B. Dalton didn't realize until after they were gone that she hadn't given Claudia the gray vellum envelope handed to her by the tall, dark-haired man in the ivory-colored suit. She hoped it wasn't important. Probably a fan letter. Some admirers were more bashful than others. She'd send it to Claudia's editor for forwarding.

Live at Five was fun, at least. Sue Simmons had read the book, and because one of NBC's breaking stories had no tape as yet, Claudia's interview ran almost six full minutes—twice as long as either of those at dawn. By now, Claudia's timing took into consideration the seconds ticking away until the commercial; her subconscious mind had edited out all hesitation, bearing out what she'd read years before: that only a first interview is truly spontaneous. Even the second and third have, by their order of appearance, been rehearsed. In fact, when she and Sue "wrapped up" the spot, Claudia was sorry it was over.

She was also sorry because that meant another crowd scene downtown.

McClintock Publishing occupied the top floors of a high-rise tower, and Tina Berenson's office afforded a panorama of the New York skyline which, as much as Claudia adored Chicago, she admitted was unique in the world.

An open bar had been set up, and waiters wove their way among the guests. Knowing that this might well be dinner before the theater, she indulged. With a month-long schedule like the day just past, calories were a trifle. She could throw caution to the proverbial wind.

She tried to memorize names, but too many of them were thrust upon her at once. "Judy, stay near," she whispered. "I don't want to slight anyone; strangers seem to know me—"

"Relax, Claudia. They know you because they've been working on various stages of your book for the past year. Just be yourself."

Despite the advice, being herself was the most elusive and difficult aspect of all.

Finally, Judy and Claudia thanked Tina Berenson and Kenneth McClintock, made a quick round of goodbyes, and headed for the elevator. The party was still going strong.

Judy had gotten them tenth row on the aisle. Claudia leaned back in her plush seat and slid her feet out of her shoes. The brooding sets and dark lighting helped her to relax and compensated for the overloud music blaring through the speakers. Sitting up straight so that no one seated nearby would notice, she closed her eyes and, while first-time audiences oohed and aahed over the Phantom, Claudia fell sound asleep.

He had fought the impulse to go to her hotel. But now,

as darkness descended over Manhattan, he made his way to the Plaza. He paused at the fountain, even took a detour for an espresso at a nearby café. There he unwrapped his package and leafed through the pages of Claudia's book. He felt not as if she were addressing a vast, impersonal audience, but as though she were writing to him. Just as her columns were written to him. It wasn't an illusion, a fantasy of his mind's creation. She would understand one day. But not before it was time. And there were other considerations.

Among them, the child.

No. The time and setting were wrong. But soon . . . very soon . . .

He closed *Dear Claudia* and paid the check. From within the inner jacket flap of the book he withdrew another sheet of gray vellum paper and an envelope. Then, after unscrewing the cap of his gold fountain pen, he began to write.

The clerk handed Claudia and Judy their keys and said good night. As the women left the desk, Claudia heard the clerk call out after her. "Miss Gage, I beg your pardon."

Turning, she said, "Yes?"

"I almost forgot," he said. "There's a letter for you."

"A letter? Are you sure?" Who would be sending her a letter at the hotel so early on the tour?

"It was delivered by hand," he said, giving her the envelope.

Looking down at the familiar color and texture of the paper, Claudia said, "A messenger delivered this?"

"Well, I don't think he was a messenger, Miss Gage," answered the clerk. "He was . . . I mean . . . the gentleman was very well dressed and didn't seem . . ."

She nodded. "Thank you." To Judy's inquiring expression, she said, "New Orleans."

"New Orleans . . .?" repeated her friend.

"He must be here. . . ."

Suddenly Judy grabbed Claudia's wrist. "He was *there*, too!"

"What do you mean . . . there?"

"B. Dalton!" Judy said excitedly. "I'll bet it was the same guy!"

"Judy, what are you talking about?"

"*I'm* not even sure myself. But there was a guy at the book-signing—really gorgeous—blue-black hair like in the movies, and the bluest eyes you can imagine. And this weird sensation, too—"

"What do you mean . . . weird?" asked Claudia, not frightened but not altogether calm.

"Well you know me with faces and names. I never forget one. And I know I've never seen this guy before in my life. But still . . . "

"Judy . . ."

"Okay, it's just that I have this very strange feeling that I have seen him somewhere before this afternoon. Even though I know I haven't."

"How can you be certain you haven't? Maybe you sat next to each other on a plane trip, or passed by at a party, or . . ." But even as she spoke, Claudia sensed that was unlikely. Judy remembered faces, even those she'd seen for only a second in a crowd.

"Listen," she said, "it's been an incredibly long day, and I can hardly keep my eyes open. Let's get some sleep."

"Aren't you even curious?" asked Judy as they waited for the elevator.

"Sure I am," she answered. "But whoever 'New Orleans' is, I have more important matters on my mind right now."

"Such as? Aside from Nick, that is?"

"Well, for one thing," said Claudia, "these quickie interviews aren't as hard as I'd expected, but tomorrow, on *Donahue,* how the hell do I hold an audience for an entire hour?"

"Hon, with all those commercials, it'll be like a dozen of those quickie spots you did today. And Phil reads books. It'll be a snap."

"You ought to go in my place."

Both of them laughed as the elevator door opened.

"Don't forget to peek under the bed," advised Judy as she reached her room.

"You could have a whole new career as an actress! You say that as if you're serious."

"Considering 'New Orleans'—or shall we call him "Gray Vellum?"—I'm not entirely joking."

They said good night and entered their separate rooms. Glancing at the bed, Claudia smiled.

But her smile faded as she opened the gray envelope and unfolded the note inside. The message in the familiar handwriting read:

The blue of your dress matches the color of your eyes. You must wear it always.

Claudia was looking up from the foot of the staircase, where the woman stood. At first it seemed as though a mirror reflecting her own image had been placed on the highest step. But then the image began to move. The long blue gown floated behind her, and, as always, in her hands was cradled a small wooden case. When the image was close enough to touch, Claudia saw her eyes—her own eyes, which matched the color of the woman's gown—staring back at her.

"I wear it always," she whispered to Claudia as she lifted the lid of the box.

Gentle bells rang out. Claudia was just able to hear part of a melody, when a screaming, wailing sound from far off shattered her sleep.

She counted four sirens before the fire engines had sped across Central Park South and faded away. Now only the white noise of the air conditioner remained to break the silence.

Claudia switched on the bedside lamp, then leaned against the headboard of the bed. She concentrated on slowing her breathing until the palpitations were gone. She'd escaped the fear once more — once more by awakening from her dream.

The clock read 11:45 P.M. She'd barely dozed. She felt a restlessness and knew that the harder she tried to fall back to sleep, the more sleep would elude her. She could take a pill, although she disliked such crutches. But a quick inventory of her purse's contents told her that she hadn't packed her pillbox. She couldn't call Judy so late; they both had to be up at dawn.

The note still lay beside the clock. Its words echoed her dream — or did the dream echo the note?

". . . wear it always." She was tempted to tear the sheet of gray vellum to shreds. Something, however, stopped her.

The room was too chilled. Claudia rose from the bed and adjusted the air conditioner's setting to low-cool. She lingered at the window and looked out over the busy street. It was still early, at least for New York.

Ten minutes later, hastily dressed in slacks, a T-shirt, and loafers, she came out of the hotel into the humid night.

Central Park South was crowded with traffic and pedestrians. People strolled slowly, seemingly unhampered by the smoky air, a mixture of dampness and car exhaust that created a thin layer of fog over the scene.

Claudia hoped a short walk along the thoroughfare would relax her enough to induce a good night's sleep.

She glanced at the vast black stillness across the street. She'd always loved Central Park, but she knew it had changed; rather, times had changed, and it was dangerous to enter the park at this hour. Better to walk along its perimeter, which was well lit and not deserted.

She turned east. The elegant, canopied entrances to the luxurious hotels made Fifth Avenue luminous in the diffused, misty light.

She crossed to the little square at Grand Army Plaza and stood before the statue of Sherman on horseback in his perpetual march downtown.

From over her shoulder Claudia heard a loud whinny. This wasn't another dream, so it couldn't be Sherman's mount. There was a line of hansom cabs behind her; she noticed one horse munching on a sugar cube from the palm of a man's hand. The scene was silhouetted against the lights of the fountain and made Claudia smile at the picture-postcard prettiness.

The man had turned just in time. Although he was certain she couldn't make out his features at this distance, he wasn't ready to risk discovery.

The horse finished the sugar. The man thanked the driver and glanced uptown. He saw her as she passed Sherman's statue and crossed to the park side of the street.

He'd told himself that one glimpse of her would be sufficient. For now. But surely there was no harm in looking. Watching. Just for a little while longer.

She was facing the tree-lined path leading to the zoo. It wasn't actually inside the park, she noted. After all, the walk was no more than twenty feet parallel to the noise and lights of Fifth Avenue. Safe enough.

61

Rows of benches curved in toward the zoo's entrance. Lovers sat, kissing passionately, oblivious of Claudia. But they made her think of Nick. She wished he were here with her.

Inadvertently her thoughts had taken her farther along the path and into the park than she'd realized. Now she stopped. She'd heard something. Not from the rush of nearby traffic.

She listened, and recognized what sounded like the cry of a wild animal.

The zoo! she realized. Talk about one's mind being somewhere else! She turned quickly, intent on leaving the park. The fog was thicker than before, and she couldn't see the lovers on the benches.

But she could see the shadow of a man. Heading toward her.

My God! she thought, as mental images raced by. What if *he's* been following me? He was at the book-signing— and at the hotel, when he left the note. What if he's been staying at the Plaza and waiting for me to do something just like this, just like going out alone at midnight?

She might run, but where? Claudia's eyes darted left and right. High fencing guarded the foliage. Behind her, the zoo was closed. Ahead, the shadowed figure was fast approaching.

She froze as he raised his arm. He was almost upon her.

Before a strangled cry could form in her throat, his hands fell heavily on her shoulders. The putrid, sour smell of alcohol sent her reeling backward.

"Hey, lady," he slurred, "where the hell am I, anyway?"

Claudia shoved him off. "Get away!" she yelled, moving past him and hurrying down the path as he stumbled and fell.

In the darkness she could see another man seated on a bench. His head was bowed, his face hidden from view.

Had she passed him before? No matter; he seemed to be asleep.

I will be soon, too, she thought. She was suddenly exhausted. I'll be fine as soon as I'm back at the hotel, dream or no dream.

The man had been overwhelmed by rage at the sight of the drunk's hands anywhere near her. He'd been tempted to help, but she'd handled it on her own, and he hadn't wanted to frighten her off. Still, he'd stayed close, first on the bench in the shadows, and now as she went past, so close that he could have touched her if he'd dared.

Now he followed behind, maintaining a discreet distance as she came out onto the street, crossed it, and headed for the Plaza. Only when she had climbed the steps and gone through the revolving doors did he feel reassured and calm. She was safe. And when it was time, she'd be even safer.

With him.

Chapter 5

Claudia didn't bring up the note or her late-night encounter, when she and Judy were whisked off to NBC at dawn. The two women were less than awake, and the limousine ride came close to lulling them completely back to sleep. Neither uttered more than a yawned "good morning." As a result, Judy had no idea that every time the limo slowed for a traffic light, Claudia expected to find a handsome stranger with blue-black hair and mesmerizing blue eyes peering at her through the smoked glass of the rear passenger window. Judy didn't know that her client had even checked out the chauffeur's coloring before stepping into the car. Blond hair and hazel eyes had reassured Claudia, which was why she'd been willing to climb inside.

During the short ride to Rockefeller Center she remained on constant lookout for the man answering Judy's description of "Gray Vellum," for anyone vaguely resembling the drunk in the park or, for that matter, anyone she might have seen before. No suspicious-looking faces appeared, however, and within minutes they were at the entrance to the RCA Building.

Claudia couldn't avoid scanning the other passengers in

the elevators, and later, the studio audience and camera crew. Paranoia was adding to her television nerves, but the feeling of being watched—stalked—just wouldn't go away.

She'd worn the teal blue silk once again, despite Judy's protestations that she should not wear the same dress more than once in the same city.

Claudia wasn't sure why she'd insisted. Because he might show up? That seemed an unlikely reason.

Or a very neurotic one, she mused.

She refused to allow such ruminations to invade her thoughts or ruin the interview, so she turned her concentration to the questions put to her by Phil, who had, per Judy's prediction, read her book. The show proceeded smoothly, and Claudia was sorry it was over so soon.

Before she knew it, she and Judy were aboard the Eastern shuttle, headed for Boston.

"Well," said Judy, "now we can talk. You were terrific, but I had the feeling you were acting. As if you were there and at the same time somewhere else, you know?"

"I tend to do that sometimes," said Claudia evasively.

"Hey, this is Judy Fargo, remember me? C'mon. Tell me. Did anything happen in the past twenty-four hours that I haven't heard about?"

"How could it?" asked Claudia. "Except for your dinner with Frank and Annie, we've been together since we got here—it's as if we're joined at the hip." She felt foolish enough for having gone out alone so late at night—especially since she'd unwittingly ventured into the park. To tell Judy about it would make her feel more ridiculous.

But Judy persisted. "You've been alone—or at least I've assumed as much—once we've said good night."

"Meaning?" asked Claudia.

"Meaning that I just wondered if you're holding out on me. Details of a clandestine meeting . . . secret telephone calls at the stroke of twelve . . . a knock at the door by Frank Langella or Louis Jourdan in formal dress, a flowing black cloak, and fangs?"

Claudia burst into laughter. It was a welcome release. She'd explain everything to Judy later. Just not yet.

They arrived at Logan Airport in the middle of a hailstorm. The plane was forced to circle for forty minutes before the pilot announced that yes, they would be able to land, after all. The relief in his voice was audible through the speaker system.

"We don't have to be sociable tonight, do we?" asked Claudia as they deplaned.

"Listen," suggested Judy, "I know a wonderful little restaurant on Newberry Street, and they do a shrimp in garlic sauce just the way we both love it."

Claudia's mouth was watering. That afternoon had included a canapes-and-wine reception consisting mostly of chicken and pork saté on skewers. Each of Claudia's mouthfuls had served as a cue for someone else's question. She'd finally given up on lunch altogether.

Unlike the separate rooms in New York, their Boston accommodation at the Copley Plaza was a suite consisting of living room, dressing room, kitchenette, huge bathroom, and two large bedrooms.

"It's so big," said Judy, "we could have a book-signing here—"

"Don't you dare!" interjected Claudia, flopping down on the bed and kicking off her kidskin pumps.

"Only teasing." Judy was standing at the windows. "God, will you come and look at this!"

66

"I'm too tired. You tell me. I got turned around when we got off the elevator. What view are we facing?"

"No, I mean the rain! It's like a sheet—you can't see anything through it!"

"Nuts," offered Claudia. "And I'm starving."

"Well, I suppose we could send out for pizza."

Judy had meant it as a joke, but an hour later, they had changed into jeans and T-shirts and were sitting on the carpeting of their luxurious suite with a "picnic" spread out before them on the floor. The magnum bottle in the mini-refrigerator contained an ordinary white table wine, but Claudia poured generously into two water tumblers taken from the bathroom counter; she handed one of the glasses to Judy with ceremony, as though it were lead crystal from Baccarat, the vintage, a Corton Charlemagne '68.

"Salut," said Claudia.

"Salut." Judy took a sip and then began to slice the pie.

"What's on our schedule for tomorrow?" asked Claudia as she gently tore into a third slice of the pizza *capricciosa*—a pie with everything on it.

Judy had a mouthful of cheese and was trying to disentangle a long string of mozzarella that refused to be pulled free of the half-eaten slice in her hand. After swallowing and washing it down with more wine, she answered, "Another couple of three-minute interviews—one of them is for a PBS show on books, speaking of classy—and a few signings."

Her voice trailed off as Claudia's eyes gazed at the windows which, even though they were only on the fifth floor, reverberated from the violent winds and rain hitting the glass with almost gale force. It was so strong that when Nick called before they went to bed, he had to yell into the phone just so Claudia could hear him.

"You sound as if you're talking through a bottle!" he shouted.

"It's the same at this end—the connection is terrible!"

"How's it going?"

"Fine! How 'bout you?"

"Great!" His reply was underscored by a loud thunderclap.

"I'm sorry I'm not there with you!" She loved the drama of watching the storms over Lake Michigan.

"I'm sorry, too! But I'm going hoarse from screaming!"

"Why don't we talk tomorrow night?" yelled Claudia at the top of her lungs. "I'll call you when we get to Atlanta!"

"That's if you can get out of Boston!"

"What . . . ?"

"Tomorrow! I love you—and I'm horny! But don't repeat *that* out loud, or every guy at the Copley will be pounding on your door!"

Claudia heard enough of his remark to laugh. Then they hung up, and she and Judy finished the rest of the pizza.

As the TV weather forecast had predicted, the storm ended by morning. But it had moved south, and when Claudia was still shaking hands at the second book-signing, Judy arrived with a newly revised itinerary.

"The bad news is that the airport in Atlanta is closed. The report said something about a hurricane watch. We're stuck here overnight. The good news is that I may be able to book you—pardon the pun—for a TV interview with—"

"Another interview?" said Claudia.

While Judy went to the telephone in her bedroom to

take advantage of their imposed stayover in Boston, Claudia called Nick in Chicago to tell him of their change in plans. He was at a meeting, so she left a message with his secretary. Then she changed into black linen slacks, a black crepe de chine shirt with handpainted flowers on it — and black lizard flat-heeled loafers. *If the TV camera is willing to shoot me from the knees up,* she mused, *I'll do as many interviews as Judy can cram into our schedule. May as well strike while the iron is hot. . . .*

She flopped on the bed and, reaching for her tote bag, went about unearthing a Band-Aid for the blister on her baby toe.

"Hey, no kidding!" Claudia heard Judy's voice cry into the phone all the way from the other bedroom. "That's great news — I'll tell her right away!"

Her face appeared in the doorway. *"New York Times,* hon!"

"What about it?" asked Claudia, who'd been leafing through the pages of *Vogue* while sprawled across her bed.

"The best-seller list! You're on it!" As Claudia's eyes widened, Judy amended, "Well, you will be as of this Sunday — and guess what position?"

Claudia shrugged her shoulders, but she sat up straight. The news was reviving her waning energy.

"Number six — the first week out! There's only one way to go from there!"

Claudia laughed. "I hope that's up!"

Judy came all the way into the room and Claudia rose to hug her. "You know, you've done a fabulous job, Judy. I owe this all to you — "

"My percentage is all you owe me. You're the one who wrote the book — "

"Okay, we'll form a mutual fan club. But right now,

69

let's go out and celebrate!"

"Fine with me. But first I have to make a few more calls—"

"I'm too excited just to sit here," said Claudia. "I'll try Nick again to tell him the news, and then why don't I meet you downstairs in the lobby?"

"Give me fifteen minutes?" asked Judy.

Claudia nodded and lifted the phone as Judy went back to her room.

Nick wasn't in his office, so Claudia added a second message to the first. Then she grabbed her black purse and linen jacket and headed toward the door.

Judy found her seated quietly in a corner of the lobby. The enthusiasm of a quarter hour before had dissipated, and a somber Claudia looked up at her friend with a puzzled, troubled expression.

"Hey, what's the matter? You and Nick have an argument long distance?"

Claudia shook her head. "He wasn't in. I left word."

"Well, then what—?" Judy's voice cut off as Claudia handed her an envelope. Not an ordinary envelope, but the color and kind of vellum they'd both seen before.

"Isn't that the note you received at the Plaza?"

"No," replied Claudia. "This is a new one. It was left for me today . . . here, in Boston."

"How do you know?" Judy took the folded gray sheet of vellum from the envelope and opened it. *Television cannot hope to capture your essence; only an inspired artist might dare.*

Judy looked up, glanced around the lobby, then returned her eyes to the stationery. "There have been good-size crowds at all the signings—and the TV show, too. Especially considering the weather. Did you notice anybody who—"

Claudia interrupted with a shake of her head. "No one. And believe me, I was keeping an eye out." She thought back over the day, to the autographing sessions in local stores. She'd signed more than a hundred copies of her book, and while answering questions amicably—and briefly, as coached by Judy—she'd been unable to avoid speculation whenever a man answering Judy's description stepped up to the desk. However, at least a dozen male fans were tall, dark, and good-looking, with blue-black hair and deep-set blue eyes.

"You didn't see him either . . . ?" asked Claudia.

"I would have pointed him out," said Judy.

"But who in his right mind would follow me from New York to Boston? Groupies go after rock stars, not for Joyce Brothers or Ann Landers, or—"

"You may have just hit it on target," interrupted Judy.

"What do you mean?"

"He may not be in his right mind. He could be some kind of obsessed lunatic—you saw *Fatal Attraction*. You and Nick even mentioned that there's a lot more to it than just sexual obsession—"

"Oh, come on!" said Claudia, taking Judy's arm and guiding her toward the lobby exit. "The next thing you'll tell me is that this guy perceives me as another Jodie Foster. Maybe we'd better call the White House and warn the President!" But for all her joking, she felt a growing uneasiness.

"Well, whoever he is and whatever he's up to," said Judy, "I'm not going to let you out of my sight till we reach Atlanta. And right now, we're late, so c'mon!" Her arm went up just as a taxi pulled up.

"Late for what?" asked Claudia.

"C'mon. I'll tell you in the cab."

Claudia had finished her makeup and was pinning a

circular brooch of diamonds and pearls to her Chanel-inspired summer knit jacket when the phone rang.

"Judy?" she said automatically into the phone.

But it was the desk clerk. "Miss Gage, a gentleman is on his way up to see you. He asked me not to ring you—he preferred it to be a surprise—but I felt it my duty, nonetheless, in case it might be an admirer who happens to know that you're staying with us, and—"

"Could you . . . describe him to me?" Claudia asked.

The clerk answered, "Well, let me see. He's tall, dark-haired, he's wearing a light suit—"

"Th-thank you," Claudia interrupted. "It'll be all right." Or it would be if she could escape from the room immediately.

"Then he's someone you know, Miss Gage?" asked the clerk, misinterpreting her reply.

"In a manner of speaking." She thanked him again and hung up, grabbed her purse and key, and hurried toward the suite's entrance. If she could make it to the lobby before he got upstairs, there'd be people around, and she'd be safe.

She peeked down the corridor in both directions, but saw no one. Quietly closing the door, she walked as fast as she could along the hall toward the elevator.

Just as she turned the corner and was beginning to breathe more normally, the door to the exit stairs opened.

But it wasn't a stranger.

"Nick!" she cried, her head beginning to spin. "What in God's name—?"

Nick dropped his briefcase and packages on the carpet runner and rushed to her. She flung her arms around him.

"Hey," he said, embracing her, "your heart's going a mile a minute. What's the matter?"

"I . . . d-didn't expect you to t-take the stairs. . . ." she stammered.

"You weren't supposed to expect me at all," he said. "There's a mob fighting for the elevators, and I couldn't wait. What happened, the desk clerk couldn't keep a secret?"

"S-something like th-that." Her arms were still wrapped tightly around him.

He took a step back and looked at her. "I thought you'd be happy to see me — but you look upset."

"N-no. I'm thrilled." She reached up and tenderly stroked his cheek. "It's just . . . I mean . . . what about your schedule?"

"Priorities. I missed you too much. I'd planned to surprise you in New Orleans this weekend, anyway, but things worked out. I was able to juggle a few appointments, and —"

"Christ!" she interrupted. "Judy will kill me!"

"Judy?"

"She's waiting for me in the bar. I'm doing some kind of panel discussion at the Harvard Club this evening."

Nick lifted the sleeve of his jacket to check his watch.

"Can't you get out of it?" he asked. "I had a more romantic evening in mind."

"Oh, Nick," said Claudia, frowning, "I promised Judy. It came up at the last minute."

"Then why don't you tell her that something else has come up at the last minute?" His innuendo made her smile.

"I can't, darling. Judy's doing a favor for a friend."

"Not exactly. You're the one who's doing the panel."

"Nick . . ."

"I'm being selfish, I know. I flew all the way from Chicago to spend an evening with you, and you have —"

"A previous commitment. If I'd known —"

"Priorities."

"What?" she said.

"Nothing. What time is this gig over with?"

"Not late, I'm sure. I won't stay late, anyway, even if they go on till dawn."

"If you'll let me have your key, I'll be waiting for you. I'll even chill the wine and serve the lobster."

That was when she saw the package alongside his briefcase.

"I'll be back as soon as I can, I promise."

He nodded. "Is the whole tour going to be like this?"

She heard the note of disappointment in his voice. "It's . . . only for a month," she said.

"Yeah . . . only for a month. . . ."

She leaned closer and kissed him. "The book's going to be on the best-seller list this Sunday," she whispered.

"Congratulations," he said, trying to keep his ego and a sudden childish reaction from coloring the word.

Nonetheless, she'd heard it.

Chapter 6

The first week of the tour was over. New York, Boston, and, finally, Atlanta too, were out of the way. *Dear Claudia* had moved upward on *The New York Times* best-seller list — according to Judy's sources, the book would be number four in the forthcoming Sunday edition. And, with few exceptions, Claudia had begun to enjoy the whirl.

One of the drawbacks was Nick. Their night together in Boston, already cut short by Judy and Claudia's appearance at the Harvard Club, had culminated with the recurrence of Claudia's dream. She didn't tell Nick, this time. It would have necessitated telling him the rest — that the dream's images were becoming clearer.

Nick had noticed her reticence at breakfast and later, when he and Claudia and Judy shared the limousine to Logan Airport. But he sensed that whatever it was, she was in the process of working it through. If Claudia needed his help, he could only hope she'd trust him enough to ask.

When Nick boarded his flight to O'Hare, Claudia couldn't avoid feeling split in two; it seemed as though half of her was returning to Chicago, with him, and the other half—the part en route to New Orleans—was just going through the motions.

Now, as they were being shown to their rooms at the elegant, French-inspired Royal Orleans Hotel, Claudia's mind was divided once more, this time between thoughts of Nick and speculation over the gray vellum note she'd expected—but not received—in Atlanta. There'd been no envelope awaiting her arrival here, either.

She recalled Judy's quip earlier at the front desk. "Remember the saying, hon: no news is good news. Of course, there's another saying, too . . ."

"What saying?" Claudia had asked absently.

"Well . . . New Orleans is 'where he's coming from.' Literally. You ought to be ready for anything."

That, observed Claudia, was far easier said than done.

They walked to the first autograph party and arrived a few minutes late, despite their having dressed in a rush. Upon leaving the hotel, the heat and humidity had made both women long to turn back to the air-conditioned cool indoors. Even by eleven A.M., the southern sun burned hot and bright and demanded a slow, deliberate pace.

Claudia had given the teal blue silk to the valet service for cleaning; its long sleeves and high collar would have meant agony in this weather. Still, she was troubled by the sensation of having considered wearing it. Am I so concerned, she wondered, about pleasing "Gray Vellum"?

The off-white washed silk with its halter top showed off her tanned shoulders to advantage. They glistened, however, with perspiration after she and Judy had taken only a few steps outside. Although an occasional, meager breeze blew in from the Mississippi a few short blocks away, the heat rising from the pavement and descending from the sky enveloped them.

Claudia glanced at Judy. Originally she'd thought her

friend's attire was too much; now, instead, she envied the wide-brimmed straw hat and the oversize sunglasses. They acted as a shield against the architecture, which contributed to the sultry atmosphere of the day. The sun, reflecting off the stucco buildings of pink, orange, and aquamarine, caused a blinding glare, and Claudia's gray-tinted aviator glasses did little to help.

The four blocks to the bookstore were the most she'd seen of the city since their arrival, yet she felt a certain familiarity; New Orleans in many way resembled parts of Europe, a blending and occasional clashing of France and Spain, a strange amalgam of style that was Old World, though she couldn't quite refer to it as quaint. Claudia found herself responding to a beauty that seemed to express a challenge, even a dare, to be loved.

Turning the corner at Canal Street was akin to an awakening slap across the face, an unwelcome shock that forced her back into the present with its gleaming glass-and-steel towers of the modern, urban world.

Lining both sides of the broad avenue, huge, nondescript hotels vied for space in the skyline. The only vestige of the old quarter was the St. Charles streetcar, an anachronism for which the traffic grudgingly made its way.

"Brace yourself," Judy muttered as they approached the bookstore. Outside, the throng had queued up for the signing session. One window was completely given over to copies of *Dear Claudia*. They surrounded a poster-size photograph display of the author.

As she and Judy entered the shop, Claudia's readers and fans greeted her with a warmth she found touching. Some reached out to grasp her hand, and they all addressed her by her first name, as they would a friend.

"It's as if they already know me," she whispered, amazed, to Judy.

"That's because you make them feel as if you know

them," her friend answered.

The thought warmed Claudia even more.

An hour into the book-signing, the line snaked from the entrance to the rear of the store, where Claudia sat behind a makeshift desk. Judy had already made one coffee run, and had carefully scrutinized each waiting face both on her way out and on the return trip.

She stood at Claudia's side now, sipping her now-tepid brew and looking out into the crowd.

"I still don't see him," she said.

"Are you sure you'd recognize him again?" Claudia asked, craning her neck to gain a better view of the faces farther back.

"Of course I would. In addition to my photographic memory for faces, his wasn't one you'd forget." Judy leaned in closer to Claudia's ear. "Besides, I told you, I've seen this face before . . . somewhere."

Another fifteen minutes passed. People continued to join the line. The noon hour brought office workers who were willing to sacrifice their lunchtime for a glimpse of *Dear Claudia*'s author and to have her name scrawled across the title page. This had happened in the previous three cities, but not in such vast numbers. Claudia marveled at the response to her words; that they could have such an impact became a heady experience.

The line might have moved more quickly if they hadn't all paused to chat. But chat they did, and Claudia wanted to remain polite. Some didn't seem to care about the book or her signature; they wanted, or needed, to talk. Claudia recognized in many a desperation to communicate—even to confess; she'd discussed this aspect of her work with Nick. Usually she found it was enough to listen, her own comments not essential.

Throughout, Judy's hand remained close at Claudia's

elbow, urging her to move on to the next person in line. And if that next person requested no more than an autograph, the one behind invariably brought a plea for help.

Judy was right, Claudia reflected; this mustn't turn into an oral extension of the advice column. But how could she be rude, when the letters addressed "Dear Claudia" now had faces? Bodies? Voices?"

"My son is a cocaine addict."

"My wife is alcoholic."

"I'm pregnant."

All in whispers. All spoken in the distinct New Orleans blend of southern drawl and Brooklyn.

If unable to offer an easy, brief solution, Claudia invited her fans to leave their addresses for a written response. The stack of these requests had already accumulated and filled the bottom third of a shopping bag. Added to it were letters, prewritten and folded tightly or sealed in envelopes to keep the words secret from any but Claudia's eyes.

Not since beginning to write the column had she been so conscious of her responsibility. Although she had been aware from the start that her advice could influence the lives of her readers, she had never before felt it so keenly.

And all the while, without distracting her attention away from the confidences and compliments offered, Claudia searched the crowd for "Gray Vellum," even if she was depending on Judy to spot him first; Judy was standing, so she could better see into the mob. And, after all, Judy was the one who had actually seen him — or at least had thought to.

A tall woman said thank you and moved past with her autographed copy.

Claudia took a quick sip of cold coffee and as she put down the cup, a small voice said, "Hello."

Claudia lowered her eyes to the left edge of the desk.

She saw a mass of shining blue-black curls. A pair of intense blue eyes stared up at her over a stack of unsigned copies of *Dear Claudia*.

Claudia exchanged a glance with Judy, while people waiting in line behind the child began to smile.

"Hello, there," replied Claudia. "Can I help you with something?"

"Yes, thank you," answered the handsome little boy. He came around to the side where they could see each other more clearly. "I've just purchased your book, and I would very much like to have it inscribed."

Claudia suppressed a grin at the formality of his speech. He was either small for his age or extremely precocious; he looked no more than seven years old.

He placed his copy of the book on the desk before her and straightened his tie. It was, Claudia noted, the exact shade of blue as his eyes, and was all the more vivid against the crisp white of his shirt. She took in the fine tailoring of his ivory linen jacket and the matching short pants.

"You look very nice," she said.

"Thank you," he answered. "They try."

Judy leaned over to address him. "Don't you think this book is a tad grown-up for you?"

"I doubt it. In any case, it's a gift for a friend. An adult friend." From his inside jacket pocket the boy withdrew an old-fashioned mother-of-pearl fountain pen and offered it to Claudia.

"Would you please autograph your book with this?" he asked.

"Certainly. Is there anything in particular you'd like me to write?"

"Yes, please. Simply say, 'For Sirena. I hope this will help.' And underneath, of course, your signature."

Claudia unscrewed the cap of the pen and began to write. The words flowed out in purple ink. "That's Sirena with an *i* followed by an *e*, please," he added.

"Does your friend read Miss Gage's column?" Judy asked, more from curiosity than from amazement.

"She has no choice, really." The lyrical cadence of the boy's accent underscored the courtliness of his manner.

Claudia handed him the autographed copy and returned his pen. "Is your friend here? I mean, is she in the store right now?"

"No," he said. "She doesn't even know I'm here. This is a surprise." He replaced the pen in his jacket pocket and tucked *Dear Claudia* under his arm. Then, with a small bow, he turned and walked past the waiting line until he disappeared into the taller crowd of adults. Claudia watched his departure, transfixed, noting that he'd had the same effect on others. People smiled, and more than one commented on "such an adorable little gentleman."

"What a gorgeous child," Claudia said.

When she heard no reply, she looked up at Judy. Although the boy was no longer within sight, Judy was still gazing after him, toward the store exit. "Yes . . ." she answered absently. "Beautiful eyes."

The note lay opened in Claudia's lap. She stared at the words, written in the same familiar hand across the gray vellum page.

"What are you going to do?" Judy asked.

"I don't know."

"What do you want to do?"

Claudia thought for a moment. She didn't like admitting it, even to herself. But the answer was clear.

"I want to go, Judy."

The two women looked at each other, both knowing that it was now more than simply a desire to satisfy a growing curiosity. The letters were, surely, a form of enticement, and Claudia's reply was evidence of their

81

partial success.

The note had been waiting for her at the message desk of the Royal Orleans when they returned to the hotel that afternoon. Claudia resisted the temptation to read it until she and Judy were upstairs in their suite. But the moment they closed the door, she sat down on the bed and tore open the envelope.

"No wonder he didn't show up at the bookstore. He was here, delivering this," she said after reading the note aloud.

"Claudia, this is . . . well, getting a little scary, don't you agree?"

She glanced up at Judy without answering. Claudia was feeling several sensations at once, but "scared" wasn't among them. Enervated, yes . . . perhaps a bit guilty, as if her thoughts or emotions were some form of betrayal of Nick.

She didn't reply to Judy's question; instead, she asked one of her own: "You think the boy is his, don't you?"

Judy came to sit beside her on the edge of the mattress. "Yes, I do. His eyes, Claudia. There's something about his eyes."

"Do you think he sent the boy?"

"I don't know. It doesn't make sense. I mean, why would he?"

Claudia shrugged. "There's only one way to find out."

"You're not going there."

"I have to, Judy."

"You don't have to do anything."

"All right, then. I want to. If just to find out what this is all about."

"Claudia, you're not going alone."

"Judy, don't start sounding paranoid again—"

"I'm not! What if this—this Sirena-with-an-*i*—is hiding in wait, wielding a knife, or something?"

"Oh, c'mon, you're getting carried away."

82

"It's getting carried away—in a hearse—that I'm worried about!"

"Judy . . ."

"I'm going with you, and I won't take no for an answer."

"No . . . !"

They settled on a compromise. Judy would give her an hour. Then she and Claudia would meet at the Napoleon House.

"The Napoleon is actually nearer to the hotel than where you're going," Judy said. "Maybe we should pick a bar that's closer to—"

"It's fine," said Claudia. "It's within easy walking distance." She checked her watch. "Speaking of which, it's time to go."

Judy leaned over and kissed Claudia on the cheek. "Take care of my author, will you? She's more to me than just a client."

Claudia smiled gently. "I promise. See you later."

In the elevator, she read the note once again.

Dear Claudia,
Please come to tea at three o'clock today.
The number is 1130 Royal Street.
Now is the hour.

Chapter 7

Six short blocks had seemed like twelve. The onset of midafternoon had not cooled the streets, and Claudia's own anticipation added to the glow of perspiration dotting her skin. A cloudless sky permitted sunlight to cast sharply defined shadows across the stucco buildings that looked as though they were hot to the touch. Each window, every door, was shuttered, most of them closed against the still-scorching glare.

Everywhere there was music. A wind had come up, carrying melodies over from Bourbon Street a block away, where they mingled with those from the lace ironwork balconies above. These lined the entire block on both sides. Some were stately and black, but a few had been painted in garish colors and strung with Christmas lights. Chinese lanterns danced to the tunes of wood-and-metal wind chimes being played by the hot breeze. The frenzied clanging joined the sounds of horns and drums . . . so many that one single refrain was indistinguishable from the rest; the noise created was not unlike an off-key orchestra playing for a bygone Mardi Gras. The changing winds only muted or amplified the cacophony, while offering little relief from the surrounding heat.

Judy had lent Claudia the wide-brimmed straw hat, and this time she'd remembered to wear sunglasses. She passed few other pedestrians along the way. It appeared that most had taken refuge in the bars on the next street, and Claudia momentarily envied them their cool drinks and comfort.

But she had reached the 1100 block of Royal Street; she was almost there.

Then, she saw it.

She didn't need to check the address; she knew this was the house. Exactly as she had envisioned it. And somehow out of place. The street — the entire French Quarter — was characterized by a pervasive seediness that both attracted and repelled. Claudia had read about the city's turbulent history, but its ravages and excesses were here to be seen; they were etched into the rusting facades that layers of paint could no longer hide.

Yet this particular house stood preserved as in its prime, still boasting a gleaming white elegance amid the run-down neighborhood scarred as much by a century of carnival as by battles fought long ago.

It was the tallest structure within view, and was set in from the pavement. A small yard of newly cut grass was bordered by a four-foot-high cast-iron lacework fence, whose design repeated in the scalloped arches and posts of the second-floor balcony where iron flowers opened in perpetual bloom. The shutters of the house, also black, were fastened over the windows, which made the white facade of the outer walls glisten more brightly.

Claudia walked to the center of the fence. A word had been inscribed into the gleaming metal of a high gate: Dantine.

"Gray Vellum" now possessed a name.

She lifted the latch and pushed. The gate swung open on noiseless hinges and closed behind her with a quiet click as Claudia strode up the front path. The shutters on the door were not drawn shut.

She paused before the stone steps. It was still possible to turn back.

She didn't.

At the door, Claudia let the polished brass knocker fall twice. And waited.

From inside came the light footfalls of someone approaching. But the door did not swing open. Claudia, instead of knocking again, spoke her name.

"It's Claudia Gage," she said. "I'm . . . expected."

A lock snapped. A bird flew from its perch of iron morning glory, and the door began to move.

Claudia found herself looking down into the face of the little boy from the bookstore.

He was still wearing the ivory linen suit with short pants.

"Welcome," he said with a happy smile. "You're most punctual. I'm Philippe, by the way."

They shook hands and he half bowed. Claudia smiled, amused once more by the boy's decorum, which far exceeded his years or the occasion. She was not unaware of her response to him, which was more that of an old friend than of an adult to a child.

The boy beckoned her inside and closed the door. The foyer seemed unnecessarily dark. Then Claudia remembered and removed her sunglasses.

The child straightened his tie in an already familiar gesture. "Please come with me," he said, leading her down a narrow hallway.

Handsome brass wall sconces supported gleaming crystal bowls whose light made the floors of dark, polished wood shine from beneath straw carpet-mats lying scattered throughout. Heavy oak doors closed off rooms to the left, opposite the winding staircase to the right.

As she followed her "guide," Claudia caught a glimpse of the kitchen before the boy opened another door at the far end of the hall and said, "This way, please."

They passed under a trellis of live morning glory and stepped out into an enclosed courtyard with a circular garden at its center. The air was sweet with the scent of jasmine and azalea rising from the flagstone beneath their feet.

"Drinks are over here," the child gestured. "You must be thirsty."

"You've read my mind," Claudia answered, going eagerly to the table in the corner of the yard.

She had expected ice water; at most, Perrier, lemonade, or iced tea. But an impromptu bar had been set up under a magnolia tree. A few yellow blossom-petals had fallen over the silver ice bucket; the glass tabletop reflected the gleam of crystal goblets. In matching decanters were scotch, vodka, and the requisite bourbon. Beside them sat a wooden bowl of fresh mint with its own crusher.

"I haven't learned yet how to prepare a proper drink," Philippe said with apology. He stood on the opposite side of the courtyard beneath a large tree that was dripping in Spanish moss.

"I can manage, thank you," said Claudia. "May I pour you something?"

"I think perhaps a lemonade. Without sugar, please."

Claudia first took a drink of cool water. It had seldom tasted so refreshing. As she drank, she noticed a small building tucked farther back in a corner beyond the magnolia tree. The structure was made of stone rather than stucco, and was too small to be a shed. Its high, slanted roof was a skylight of frosted glass. Two small windows at eye level were covered from within by drapery, leading Claudia to doubt that this could be a hothouse.

She set herself to preparing the drinks. The sounds of ice dropping into glasses emphasized the courtyard's quiet and solitude, while only a short distance away, the street noise was formidable. Claudia mentioned this when she handed the boy his lemonade and took the first sip of her vodka and tonic.

"It's a trick of the wind, so I'm told," he explained. "Although it must have something to do with the way the walls of the yard were constructed."

"I see," said Claudia.

They seated themselves on white wrought-iron garden chairs beside a matching round table. For a while neither of them spoke, and Claudia began to wonder if she had been invited to the Dantine residence to pass the early evening with the child. Had he been left here all alone and unattended? And if not, where was . . . his father?

A low-hanging string of moss tickled her brow, and she pushed it aside.

"Do you know the legend?" asked Philippe.

"What legend is that?"

"About the moss." He raised a small hand and set the black strands of the moss to swaying. "They say that an Indian maiden died. Her lover cut off her hair and hung it over the branches of the tree under which he'd buried her. After that, there was moss."

"I see," said Claudia. "I've never heard the legend before. . . ."

If he pushed the curtain aside, she might see the movement. So instead he watched the two of them from above, through the white lace at the window.

He was experiencing sensations he hadn't felt in years. A kind of excitement, as though he were a schoolboy. A smile crossed his lips. She had come, after all. Her photographs, her image on the television screen, none did her justice.

She was here. It was all that mattered; she had come this last part of the way freely, of her own, tacit choosing.

He opened the lid of the small, worn wooden box in his

hand. The simple melody began to play. Slowly, one note at a time.

Claudia had asked Philippe about his schooling. He'd explained about his tutoring at home. "But he's vacationing in Europe for the summer, and—"

"Pardon me," she interrupted.

He stopped speaking and listened with her. But all she heard was the rustling of the moss. More magnolia petals fell in the warm breeze.

"I'm sorry," she said at last. "I thought I heard . . . something." Claudia knew she'd heard it. Music. Too distant to recognize the melody, but music, nonetheless.

"It's all right," said Philippe with a smile. "Sounds often drift over from Bourbon Street . . . especially when there's a wind."

Hopping down from his chair, he said, "I'd like another lemonade, I think. Would you care for a second drink?"

She handed him her glass. "You might add some ice and tonic to this, thank you."

Again the boy executed his courtly half-bow and went to the bar tray.

Claudia glanced at her watch. A quarter hour had elapsed and still she didn't know whether any other member of the Dantine family was due to join them. The child, though precocious, couldn't possibly be the mysterious admirer with whom she had been corresponding.

She rose from the chair and was midway between the table and the bar when she stopped short and drew a startled breath.

Claudia didn't know how long the woman had been standing beneath the trellis over the shadowed doorway, but it was clear that she was staring—and continued to do so even after Claudia's eyes and hers had met.

A mass of shining, tight black curls fell over her high

temples and cascaded down and across her shoulders. Her deep, rich tan accentuated the pale green of her eyes—cat's eyes, Claudia thought. Eyes that bored into their guest relentlessly, alternately curious and . . . angry? The woman wore no makeup, except for a slash of red over her full lips that opened into a slight pout. She wore a white peasant blouse and a red ruffled skirt of Indian cotton. Claudia's first thought was of Bizet's *Carmen*. And yet this woman didn't strike her as a Gypsy. Almost, but not quite . . .

Claudia wanted to say something—anything that would end what appeared to be a contest between them.

But the woman spoke first.

"Philippe! Come here, please."

The boy turned. A joyous smile spread across his face.

"Sirena!" he cried, running to her and wrapping his arms over her hips while her long ivory fingernails fondled the black curls of his hair.

"Sirena," he said, remembering his manners, "I should like to present Miss Claudia Gage."

"Ah, yes . . . I have your book," Sirena said in a thick drawl.

"It was . . . Philippe's idea," said Claudia.

The woman just nodded, but the boy, running to the bar, called out, "Sirena! Let me fix you something to drink! Then you must join us for a visit!"

Sirena crossed the length of the courtyard and, stopping at the table, took a sip of Philippe's lemonade. "It's too early for spirits," she said, looking at Claudia. "For me, at least. Besides, it's time for your nap."

While Philippe protested—for the first time behaving like the child he was—Sirena picked up Claudia's glass from the table and began freshening their guest's drink.

"No, thank you—I hadn't planned on a second one," said Claudia. "I really can't stay long, and—"

But Sirena placed the refilled glass in Claudia's hand.

"Your . . . home . . . is quite handsome," Claudia ventured, hoping to strike up any kind of small talk.

"Yes, the master of the house does keep it nicely."

"Mr. Dantine . . . ?"

Sirena nodded imperiously. "Armand. He should be down shortly."

A bird had landed on the ice bucket. They both watched it fly off to the glass roof of the building beyond the magnolia tree.

"That isn't a shed, is it?" Claudia asked politely.

"No. In the past, it was used as slave quarters. Armand had it converted to a studio. He stores his canvases there, too."

"Canvases. He paints?"

Sirena nodded again. "His pride and joy is hangin' in the parlor. You ought to have a look at it. I'm sure you'll find it . . . interestin'. In fact"—she took Philippe by the hand—"it's too hot out here. Come inside." The woman and child began walking toward the house.

Claudia put down her drink and followed them back down the hallway through which she and Philippe had entered the courtyard. At the foot of the staircase, Sirena stopped.

"Jus' through that door." She gestured in the direction. "He won't be long now."

"Good," said Claudia. "I mean . . . well, I must be going soon, and—"

"You're not staying to supper?" asked Philippe. "I was hoping, just this once . . . " His voice trailed off, crest-fallen.

"I can't. Perhaps another time?" She offered her hand. "You've been an excellent host, Philippe. Thank you."

He giggled and shook her hand with a firm grasp, after which he bowed and started up the stairs.

"And perhaps we'll meet again," Claudia said to Sirena. The phrase seemed to amuse the woman. She smiled

and answered, "I have no doubt of that, Miss Gage."
Then she followed Philippe up the staircase.

Claudia watched them until they were out of sight. So,
she thought, that was Sirena-with-an-*i* . . . She couldn't
help wondering who the woman might be — or what
position she occupied in the Dantine household. She'd
been aloof, yet not completely rude. It was more in what
hadn't been said.

But she was beautiful. And the boy had bought
Claudia's book for her. There was clearly a mutual
affection between them. She wasn't his tutor — Philippe
had explained as much — but she didn't strike Claudia as a
governess or nanny. Housekeeper? It was apparent that
she wasn't mistress of the house — unless she was Armand
Dantine's mistress . . .

I wonder what I'm doing here, Claudia mused. And
why I was invited . . .

She turned toward the door across the hall. To the left
was the entranceway . . . and exit. She debated whether to
stay or to leave, then checked her watch.

She could stay a few minutes more if she chose to. . . .

So she made her decision and opened the door to the
parlor.

The sun was blocked by heavy draperies that were
drawn over the tall windows reaching at least fourteen feet
to the ceiling. Around the top of the wall, fluted cornices
caught the eye's attention and pulled it to ornately designed medallions set into the ceiling. A magnificent
crystal chandelier — Waterford, Claudia guessed at once —
was suspended over the center of the room.

Bright, flowered slipcovers over the furnishings seemed
ordinary and out of place. But, Claudia said to herself,
it's only as protection against the summer sun.

She was momentarily taken aback by her observation.

It wasn't something she had read or heard. Or even deduced. She knew it as fact, just as she knew that beneath the slipcover she would find fabric of gold brocade.

If she looked.

With relief she discovered she was wrong. The design under the cover was silk moiré, and the color was pearl gray.

She was still wearing Judy's wide-brimmed hat. Now she removed it and placed it on a small table. Then she continued her tour of the room.

The decor struck her as strange, eclectic, a combination of American nouveau and nineteenth-century Italian, in keeping with the Italianate design of the house itself. Somehow the styles blended, and created a warm, if formal, atmosphere. As in the hallway, straw carpet-mats had been strewn across the floor, again as concession to the New Orleans summer heat.

An imposing marble fireplace occupied the far wall. And above it, as Sirena had said, hung the painting.

She'd called it his pride and joy. Claudia could see why, although its impact on her emotions was less easily understood.

Tears began to fill her eyes as she stood gazing up at the large canvas framed in an ornately carved, gilt-wood frame, the kind found on museum masterpieces.

The woman in the portrait smiled down at her, and the kindly, loving expression in her eyes moved Claudia deeply.

The model was beautiful, but it was more than that. Her pose was a standing, full-length portrait turned three-quarters toward the viewer. Her dark hair had been painted with rich, warm highlights. The long waves framed her delicate, fine features and fell from a center part to her bare, marblelike shoulders. Her deep-blue eyes looked directly out from the confines of the two-dimensional canvas and appeared to follow the observer. Her skin was flawless, her bone structure that which any professional model would admire. Jeweled adornments were unnecessary; nothing distracted one's eyes from her compelling beauty.

She seemed no more than thirty, captured by the artist's brush at the peak of her loveliness. Her figure was slim, yet womanly, beneath a strapless gown of shining satin. Her left hand displayed a single ornament, a gold wedding ring; her right held a small wooden box.

Claudia wiped the tear from her eye. For some reason, the wedding band had touched her, just as the wooden box had stirred something painfully sweet. The woman was peculiarly familiar to her.

Then she realized the reason for her feeling of déjà vu. The satin gown was blue. Teal blue. And the face was enough like her own to send shivers through her.

"She is beautiful, no?" said a male voice behind her.

Claudia turned with a start.

Philippe's face, matured into manhood, stared back at her. A lock of thick black hair fell rakishly over one brow. A thin line of silver hair at each temple softened the chiseled angularity of his cheekbones. The same blue of the child's eyes was darkened by his years, but was no less intense. A deep cleft chin accentuated the strength of his jaw. He was tall, with an athletic body clothed in well-cut, casual attire. His white silk shirt was opened at the neck, and his long legs were encased in close-fitting black linen slacks.

Claudia found her voice and answered, "Yes . . . she is. Who . . . is she?"

"My late wife." He looked up at the painting once more, then took a step toward her and held out his hand. "Thank you for coming. I am Armand Dantine."

His voice was a low, well-modulated baritone that held the slightest musical lilt of an accent. Claudia accepted his hand; her own felt moist, and the warmth of his palm against her skin caused a sudden rush of blood to her head. She hoped she wasn't blushing — or if she was, that Armand Dantine couldn't see it.

"Thank you for inviting me. I'm Claudia Gage. But . . . of course you know that."

What's the matter with me? she asked herself. I'm practically stammering. The dizziness had passed, but she was having difficulty in controlling her shaking knees. Her hand was still in his and he pressed it gently. They were very close. She could smell the faint aroma of his cologne.

At last she removed her hand, in the pretense of keeping her shoulder bag from slipping off her shoulder. She looked quickly up to the portrait to avert his gaze.

"What was her name?" she asked.

"Noelle," he replied.

Claudia could feel his eyes still upon her.

"Sirena told me you're an artist."

"I'm a painter," he corrected.

"Uh . . . yes . . . Well, it's very good. Wonderful, in fact."

"You know something of painting?" he asked.

"A little, yes. I've collected a few things here and there. I've been told that I have a discerning eye."

"Good. You must. I am a very good painter."

Claudia turned, surprised at his words. He'd spoken them as a matter of fact, not as a boast.

She glanced back at the portrait. "Philippe's mother?" she asked.

He nodded, then stepped back, gesturing her to the love seat. He seemed to have sensed her wish to create physical distance between them.

She declined the offer and remained standing.

"May I offer you something?" he asked. "A drink?"

"No, thank you." She smiled. "Philippe was extremely

cordial."

"He's a precocious child."

"How old is he?"

"Eight. He is small for his age."

Eight, thought Claudia. How long ago since the woman in the painting . . . Noelle . . . had died? The presence of the portrait as the focal point in the room made it obvious that her memory was revered—or perhaps still mourned.

"May I ask why it was Philippe who answered the door?"

"Yes. I wanted to watch you for a while."

Again, his directness caught her up short. "You were watching us—in the courtyard?"

"No. Only you."

She didn't ask why. Instead, she said slowly, "That wasn't the first time, was it?"

"No. I've been following you. But you know that."

Claudia took the gray envelope from her purse and held it up. "And this?"

He shrugged. "To pique your interest, I admit it."

She put the note down on the table beside Judy's hat. "This is all a mite melodramatic, don't you agree?"

"Perhaps," he said. "But you're here, aren't you?"

Yes, she thought. I am. "Touché. And now I must leave."

It didn't seem to faze him. "I will see you again."

"By following me?"

"If I must. But please don't worry. I have no intention of making a nuisance of myself. However, I do think we must spend more time together."

"Do you? Why?" His nerve had made Claudia smile.

"Because you are curious. And so am I. As I have been, from the beginning."

"And just when was that?"

"The day I saw your photograph printed with your

column in the newspaper."

"You read advice columns?"

"I read many things. But Sirena has been your faithful admirer." He hesitated for a moment, then added, "She was, at any rate."

Claudia nodded. "Until today?"

"Yes."

She glanced at her watch. "I . . . I do have to leave, now. I have a reception this evening."

"As you wish," he said.

She picked up the hat and he escorted her down the main hall, his hand lightly touching her elbow as they went. At the door, they stopped and looked at each other. Without speaking, he took her hand and brought it to his lips.

"Again, thank you for coming," he said. When she withdrew her hand, he raised his and gently brushed a stray tendril of hair from her cheek. "Your hair is so soft. . . ."

Claudia turned the knob and the door opened.

The sun was not as bright as it had been an hour before, but still the glare made her put on her sunglasses as she walked to the edge of the stone steps.

Suddenly, she turned. He was standing in the doorway, still watching her.

"Armand," she said. He made no reply, but his eyebrows rose attentively. "The Royal Orleans ballroom. Eight o'clock. Just tell the maitre d' that I've invited you."

Claudia spun around quickly as soon as she'd blurted out the words. She rushed down the steps and through the front gate.

She did not look back.

Chapter 8

Judy was flirting good-naturedly but distractedly with the bartender when Claudia entered the bar. The relief that spread across the publicist's face was apparent, and Claudia realized only then how worried Judy must have been.

"Well, Frank, here she is at last," she said. To Claudia, "Same name as my former, I know. But that's where the similarity ends. This is one helluva guy."

"She's an excellent judge of character," agreed the bartender without a trace of a southern accent.

"He's from New York," Judy explained. "Frank, meet Dear Claudia, herself, live, and—thank God—in person."

It was clear that the drink in front of Judy wasn't her first.

Frank said, "Nice to meet you . . . in person. What are you drinking?"

Claudia ordered a glass of white wine and took a seat beside Judy.

"Well," said her publicist, "don't keep me waiting. What happened?"

Claudia told her. Relating the events of the past hour so matter-of-factly seemed to alleviate some of the mystery, although the image of the portrait remained strong in her mind, as did the scent and the strange little melody . . .

All of it, she admitted to herself. Armand, the boy, and . . . that woman. There was a look, an expression, in Sirena's eyes . . . Not one of menace, but disturbing, nonetheless. Claudia wondered if the threesome would appear as they had, transported to another setting. Surely if they'd met at, say, a Holiday Inn, or taken tea at McDonald's, the atmosphere would have been less intense.

But the boy had come alone to the bookstore, and still . . .

". . . So it wasn't anything weird after all?" Judy was saying under her breath.

"Uh . . . no. Nothing like that."

"Well, then . . . ?"

"Well, then what?" asked Claudia.

Judy exhaled loudly. Just as loudly she said, "Frank, I don't know about my buddy here, but I could use another one." Turning to Claudia, she said, "What's he like?"

"I told you. You described him perfectly the first time you saw him."

"No, I don't mean what's he like physically. I mean . . . well, are you attracted to him?"

"He's a very attractive man," answered Claudia.

"I know," said Judy. "That's why I'm asking. Claudia, have I had too much to drink—or haven't you had enough? One of us has me very confused."

"Probably both. I'll have another glass of wine to catch up."

Frank didn't hear her, but he saw her place her empty glass on the bar and brought her a refill immediately.

"Okay," whispered Judy when he'd gone to take another order, "what's the bottom line?"

"There isn't any," said Claudia. "I'm involved with Nick."

"Oh, Christ!" exclaimed Judy. "I forgot. He called—"

"When?"

"A minute or two after you left the room."

"Did you tell him where I was going?" asked Claudia.

"Uh . . . actually, I didn't. For some reason I thought you might not want me to say anything."

"No? Why wouldn't I?" asked Claudia. But it was a rhetorical question, and they both seemed to understand it, because Judy offered no reply.

They walked slowly back to the hotel. Frank and Judy had made a date to meet later. For a while the women didn't speak, but just strolled leisurely along, smelling the heavy sweetness of the magnolia, feeling the weight of the damp night air.

At length, Judy said, as though half in thought, "So she's wearing teal blue, too . . ."

"Hmm?" said Claudia.

"The woman in the portrait. His wife."

"Oh . . . yes."

"And you don't find it weird?"

"Find what weird?"

"That he likes you in teal blue—and that you're a double for his late spouse."

"There's a general resemblance, Judy. I'd hardly call her my twin—"

"Listen," said Judy, "all jokes aside, this Armand hasn't named the house Manderley, has he? And Sirena-with-an-*i* doesn't go by the last name of Danvers, does she?"

Claudia laughed. "No, Judy, and this governess, or tutor—or whatever she is—doesn't look anything like Judith Anderson." Then, to herself, she said aloud, "God, everyone's always telling me *I'm* melodramatic!"

"Okay," said Judy as they reached the hotel. "I won't say another word about him."

"Good. Because I've invited him to tonight's reception."

"You've whaaat?"

"You promised."

"That was before you dropped the bomb! What're you trying to do—play with fire?"

A raucous group of tourists interrupted Claudia's answer, but the question was very much on her mind as they entered the hotel.

Dusk was settling over the skylit studio, casting pink and violet hues over the dark corners of the room under cover of subdued light.

Armand Dantine stood before the easel, tracing the contours of the painted figure on the canvas with his fingertips. He heard the door open and turned.

Sirena was silhouetted in shadow. Her green eyes assumed an almost phosphorescent glow in the falling night. Her rich black curls and burnished copper skin took on depth and mystery at the twilight hour, a sensuousness he felt was lacking when the bright sun burned overhead.

"She seems almost willin'," said the woman in a low, husky voice that mocked while it provoked him.

Abruptly, Armand threw the white drapery cloth over the canvas. "It's none of your affair," he said.

"No, I suppose not." She smiled, a teasing, upward curve of her full lips, but didn't move from the doorway.

"I've told you not to visit my studio."

"But then I wouldn't see what—or who—you choose to paint."

"You'll see when it's time, not before."

She laughed in the throaty, knowing laugh that excited yet repulsed him.

"Come on," he said, taking her by the wrist.

"Where are we goin'?" she asked coyly, as though this

were both a nightly ritual of dialogue and action—and at the same time as if it were completely new and foreign to them.

"Upstairs," he said, continuing the scene and leading her away from the studio. "And then I am going out."

"Where?"

"To a reception at the Royal."

"Her reception?" she demanded.

"I once told you I would never lie to you. Yes. To her reception. She has invited me."

"But you'll go because you want to, not because she invited you."

"Yes."

"There are times, Armand, when I despise you," she said.

"Yes," he answered. "And that makes it all the better, doesn't it?"

His hand was gripping her wrist now, and she winced slightly at the pressure of his touch. But she said nothing. Neither of them spoke as they entered the main house and went upstairs, past the room where the child Philippe lay napping, past the room through whose window he'd first seen Claudia in the courtyard with his son, and finally into his room, where he beckoned her to enter, after which he closed and locked the door.

She stepped out of her sandals and stood just inside the door. He drew her to him and pulled the fabric down from her shoulders until the elastic border of her blouse barely concealed the tips of her ample breasts.

"You'll make love to me, but she is the one you want!" said Sirena.

"Yes," he said.

His hands had begun to knead her breasts. "You like this, don't you?" he asked.

"You're a bastard, Armand."

"Yes," he said.

Her nipples hardened, and the place between her legs was growing hot. His hand went beneath the hem of her skirt and up to the source of her heat. His other hand pulled her head back by the thick, black curly hair, and his tongue moved slowly across her neck and down her chest, stopping long enough at each nipple to take them, one at a time, into his mouth.

"Armand!" she cried, closing her strong thighs tightly as his hand parted her lower lips and thrust his fingers inside her.

"And you like that," he said, taunting her as she had taunted him before.

"Bastard!"

He pulled the skirt to her ankles and ripped the blouse back up over her head.

She wore no underclothes beneath them.

Perspiration made her body glisten in the semidarkness of his room. He scooped her up into his arms and carried her to the bed.

She lay still, slightly coiled like a panther poised to spring upon its prey.

He tore off his clothes and stood at the foot of the four-poster bed. He regarded the woman at its center with a different look than that with which he had earlier contemplated the reclining nude on his canvas; his expression was more than one of lust. Desire was fused with contempt. Whether for Sirena or for himself, he didn't know.

Sirena lay there waiting. Or perhaps she lay in wait.

She was well aware of her hold over Armand. And of the threat presented to them both in the unknowing person of Claudia Gage.

"You want her," Sirena teased. "But you cannot have her. You can have only me!"

That moved him to action. Armand came to her and slapped her face. She kicked him, and he straddled her, trapping her beneath his muscular thighs. She reached out to scratch him, but he held her wrists in a viselike grip.

"You're no better than a bitch in heat," he said, hating her, and hating himself for wanting, needing her.

"And what can you do about it?" she said, flashing her teeth as she struggled and pretended to try escaping her captor.

"I will take you," he said, his penis growing stiff and erect. "I will make you want me all the more—"

He paused to position himself for entry and then, with a plunge so deep inside her that it made her gasp for breath, he spat the words: "And then, when you have had your pleasure and I have taken mine—I shall go to Claudia Gage's reception!"

It was as though his words released some kind of wild fury deep within her. She climaxed, hating him for having such control over her, hating herself for permitting it. He came seconds later, in a frenzied burst of passion mixed with loathing. If they shared in lust, they shared in disgust even more. For themselves and for each other. It was a disgust borne of their need.

Claudia was wearing palest pink. Yards of pink silk crepe de chine, cut on the bias and flowing from a backless, sleeveless halter. Delicate golden butterflies were embroidered on the low-cut V bodice. The gown was utter simplicity, to show off her swanlike neck and bronze tan. Her only adornment was a pair of diamond studs piercing her ears.

Judy had teased her about blue. "After this afternoon, I'd have expected you to wear teal."

"I would have," Claudia countered, "but I haven't anything appropriate for evening in that color."

"Well, then, let's hope he'll recognize you in the midst of so many people."

They both laughed. Claudia and Judy were standing at the entrance to the ballroom. It had been decorated, for reasons Claudia couldn't discern, to look like a turn-of-the-century festival.

"More like an early 1900's brothel, if you ask me," she commented.

"Is that the voice of experience?" Judy asked with a wink.

Claudia didn't answer. She'd been scanning the room as the last-minute touches were being added: wicker baskets filled with pink roses; carved-ice centerpieces with more pink roses frozen inside.

"What're you thinking?" asked Judy.

Claudia's reply surprised her. "It's neither sexy nor profound. Just that this whole show reminds me of a christening Mom and I went to a couple of months ago."

"Pretty ritzy, hmm?"

Claudia shook her head and smiled. "Schmaltzy is more like it. I couldn't help wondering what the parents will do for an encore."

"You mean when the kid gets married?"

"I guess."

"Well, hon, this bash is a christening in a way—the book is, after all, your baby. Look at it like that."

"I have been," said Claudia. "And it just smacks of what Nick was talking about before we left Chicago."

"I didn't think I understood then. Now I'm sure I don't."

"Well," said Claudia, trying to settle it in her own mind, "I keep wondering what all the glitz—not the book-signings, where I'm actually meeting readers, but this"—she indicated, with a wave of her arm, the entire room and its gaudy decor—"what all this has to do with my book. D'you know what I mean?"

Judy shrugged; she was accustomed to such remarks from Claudia. "Look, you could have sent your mom out to buy a zillion copies of the book, just because she can afford it. That would have put you in the number-one spot on the best-seller list in a minute. You could have ordered another zillion copies to give or throw away. You didn't. You wrote the book and you're letting it speak for itself. Sure, your publisher is doing the advertising hype. But the public is responding by plunking down its money. In short, you're not buying your success — you're earning it! Now do you know what I mean?"

Claudia nodded, although she and Judy both knew it was a nod just to avoid polemics; the ballroom was beginning to fill up.

"Don't get philosophical on me tonight," advised Judy as she adjusted her "professional" smile and moved toward the entrance. "Just play the game. You can run off to a desert island and become a hermit . . . after the ball . . ."

The band played too loudly, and the guests drank too much champagne. But the crème de la crème of New Orleans society turned out to meet Miss Claudia Gage. She was introduced to southern Aristocracy and southern Business; southern Charm — and, in a few cases, southerners who hadn't been advised that the Civil War had ended more than a few years ago. Claudia was widely traveled, and only in Paris, when her boarding-school French met with disdain, had she encountered snobs. She was surprised to find that in her own country she could feel so much a foreigner.

The southern belles were the worst, with their pasted-on smiles and fluttery eyelashes. Even those from "connected" families looked as if they were rehearsing a scene from *Gone with the Wind*. But only after an hour did Claudia begin to understand that it wasn't because she was a Northerner — with a capital *N*.

Sally Tremont — "Jus' call me Sugah, 'cause everybody 'round heah calls me that" — explained after a none too subtle head-to-toe appraisal of the guest of honor, "Why, Miss Gage, you put us all to shame with yo' tan." The way she pronounced the word, it came out with two syllables instead of one. But Claudia got the message: she wasn't white enough. She felt another color — red — beginning to rise at "Sugah"'s implication.

However, Claudia's embarrassment was upstaged by the late arrival — and entrance — of Armand Dantine.

Sally "Sugah" Tremont eyed him, and then commented to her hostess and to the air in general, "Why, jus' look what the breeze blew in. I wonduh what brought him all the way ovah heah."

"He's an invited guest," replied Claudia coolly.

"Really!" Sally flashed a dazzling, insincere smile. "Well, I must say when he washes off all that paint and gets prettied up fo' a pahty, he shuah cleans up nice." She began moving in his direction.

Claudia heard someone else behind her mutter, "Isn't that Armand Dantine?"

And the reply: "Yes. I didn't think he went anywhere in public these days. I'd heard he'd become something of a recluse."

"Eccentric, but he is somethin' to look at, isn't he?" said another.

"An' that's the truth . . ."

He hadn't moved from the entrance to the ballroom, even though he was aware of the stares. He was looking for Claudia.

And when his eyes found hers, she was crossing the room to him. How beautiful she is! he thought, transfixed and unaware that his feet were moving him toward her.

107

Sally Tremont is a fatuous ass, thought Claudia. But she's right about one thing: Armand does "clean up nice." The white dinner jacket set off his tan—which, Claudia noted, "Sugah" didn't seem to mind in him—and if the lapels were a bit broader than those of men's latest fashions, so what? Brooks Brothers was for "establishment" dressing, anyway. Stockbrokers. Bankers. Yuppies. And Armand Dantine certainly was none of these.

Neither is Nick, warned a silent voice as Armand reached her and lifted Claudia's hand to kiss it.

"I'm glad you could join us this evening," said Claudia, aware that they were the center of the room's attention.

"As I am," he replied. "May I have the pleasure of this dance?"

The band was playing a medley of old standards, all of them dreamy, all of them romantic. Claudia's mind was on its guard as Armand's right arm held her gently but firmly, and his strong yet slim artist's hand clasped her fingers in his.

They weren't simply dancing; they were gliding, as though the polished wood floors were made of smoothest glass.

"You're very graceful," he said.

"I'm just following a good lead," she answered.

Judy stood off to one side with Frank, who had arrived shortly before.

"What's he doing here?" asked the bartender.

"Who?" she asked, knowing exactly whom he meant.

"Dantine. Your friend doesn't strike me as kinky."

"Claudia?" Judy laughed. "She's the last person on earth I'd call"—She interrupted herself—"Wait a sec! Why'd you say that?"

Frank shrugged self-consciously. "Look, Judy, they're only rumors—"

"Don't do that—I hate when people do that! What rumors?"

"Well, it's just that he lives with his kid and that mulatto woman who comes across like some voodoo priestess."

"Oh, c'mon, just because she looks like a Gypsy—"

"Nobody knows who she is or where she comes from," Frank cut in, "but she lives at that house with Dantine and the kid, and—"

"And Claudia also said the little boy—Philippe—is very fond of her. He even bought a copy of the book and had it inscribed. To Sirena." She smiled, remembering the way he'd said it: "Sirena with an *i* and an *e*."

"Yeah, well, my last name is Saggio. In Italian that means wise. And the name Sirena means . . . siren."

Judy laughed off the remark. "At least it doesn't translate to my favorite after-dinner liqueur," she said.

"What's that?" asked Frank.

"Strega," she said. "I may not be Italian, but I know the word means witch."

"You got it," he answered, draining his glass of champagne. "Just be sure to keep a watchful eye on your friend."

There were other rumors, too. Rumors Judy wanted to tell Claudia before the evening ended. But she wondered if there'd be a chance. Claudia had mingled earlier, but since Armand Dantine's arrival, she had seldom left the dance floor—or her partner's arms.

Frank had mentioned Dantine's money, of which there seemed a bottomless supply. The painter was considered to be a gifted artist. However, his reputation stemmed from teachers or other artists with whom he had worked

109

or studied as a younger man. Years had passed since he'd been seen in public. And his paintings were never shown.

Judy had speculated to Frank that perhaps Armand Dantine was one of those rare artists who—truly, not only in lip service—painted solely for himself.

She could tell from Frank's expression that she hadn't convinced him. How could she? Judy hadn't convinced herself.

The party continued on, with Sally "Sugah" Tremont holding court and the rest of the glittering guests wining and dining in air-conditioned splendor.

Judy spotted Armand and Claudia as they danced farther away from the band and moved, in each other's arms, closer to the ballroom exit.

Frank had refilled their champagne glasses and now returned to Judy's side.

Following the direction of her eyes, he shook his head. "You can't crawl inside her head. She's old enough to know what she's doing."

Judy clinked her glass against his. "I hope you're right," she said. "But just the same, let's drink to that . . ."

Chapter 9

Claudia studied Armand as he talked. He seemed to be enjoying, or pretending for her sake to enjoy, his narrative of the famous street. The blinking lights of white and colored neon flashed across his handsome face, which still, despite his smile, wore its slightly melancholy attitude.

They strolled through Bourbon Street where, he told her, some bars never closed. Barefoot, shirtless men, drag queens, and women in bikini tops blended among visitors in ties and jackets, polyester leisure suits mingling with, as in the case of Claudia and Armand, the silk of formal gowns and dinner jackets. All seemed welcome; no one was out of place.

Outside the Maison Bourbon a long line of people were laughing, joking, waiting for admittance. Few appeared to be listening to the hot jazz blaring from within. On the right, a black man in tuxedo barked his invitation to "Big Daddy's amateur Cajun-style female wrestling!"

They passed the Old Absinthe House and the Old Absinthe House Bar, two different establishments and ownerships, he explained. "And the first evidence of what is popularly called gentrification," Armand said, pointing

111

to a Mrs. Field's Cookies shop.

"It's an anachronism," said Claudia. "So out of place."

She was glad to be here, though, away from the polite, forced gaiety of the hotel ballroom which, in contrast to the careless festivity in the streets, seemed even more false than it had an hour before.

"But you love it, don't you?" she asked, reading the expression on his face.

"Yes," he answered. "And I hate it, too."

She would have asked him to explain, but he had taken her arm and was drawing her to a bar with a street-service window. He ordered, after which they continued their stroll while sipping brandy from plastic cups.

They had exchanged little in the way of conversation except for small talk and tour-guide information. Nonetheless, Claudia was aware of a tacit understanding between them. Perhaps because of his letters and her replies via the column, it was as though they already knew each other and had no need of preliminaries. And although Claudia had many questions she wanted to ask, their answers didn't seem important.

Claudia was intrigued by a mannequin standing out in the street. Obviously it had been placed there to catch the eyes of potential patrons and lure them into the shop. But its pasty white face was painted with black brows frozen in surprise, and a single blue teardrop was outlined on its cheek, giving it a ghostly expression of mock sadness. It wore a plain white T-shirt, a threadbare brown fedora, and no shoes.

Claudia looked up at Armand. "It's so hideous," she said. "Why would anyone — ?"

"Wait," he said. "Watch."

She did so. Perhaps thirty seconds passed. Nothing happened. Then, suddenly, the dummy moved.

Claudia gave a short cry, then laughed in embarrassment. With the stiffened, jerky gestures of a wind-up toy, the mime stood on one leg, tipped his hat, and bowed. He stared directly at Claudia, cocked his head, and stretched out his arm toward the entrance to the shop.

Her eyes followed his direction. On a wooden sign above the door was a word painted in black and red.

"Voodoo," she read aloud.

"Come," Armand said, leading her away.

"Oh, let's go in."

"No."

"Just for a minute," she said. "Come on, it looks like fun."

"There's a museum around the corner that you can visit on your own, if you're so interested." He stared at her when she didn't follow him. "Claudia . . . I insist."

A smile broke out across her face. "You insist? Armand, it's just a little tourist trap. What are you afraid of . . . zombies?"

But his hands went to her shoulders and he pulled her to him. "What do know of these things?"

"Armand, let me go." She faced him directly. "You're hurting me."

He released her immediately, seemingly shocked by his own behavior.

Claudia pushed an errant lock of hair from his brow. "What is it?" she asked.

"Nothing," he answered, recovering his composure. "You're right. It's only a tourist trap." He took her hand and now began leading her toward the shop.

She drew back and stopped, distrustful now of the mercurial change in his attitude. "Well, come on then,"

He stood beside the mime, who held out his palm for an offering. Armand dropped a coin in the fedora, and the mime winked at Claudia.

Armand called her name and, extending an open hand, beckoned her. "Come! Satisfy your curiosity!"

She didn't like his tone. It was a dare.

She tossed her empty plastic cup into a trash receptacle outside the shop and, without looking at Armand, entered the "tourist trap."

A moment later Armand followed her inside. High-pitched chimes rang out, and Claudia heard the mime laughing as the door closed behind them.

The small store was dimly lit by a bare bulb in a ceiling socket and some twenty candles of different lengths and colors. Paint that at one time had been a shade of mauve now peeled over the walls in curls and cracks. Two glass showcases were positioned at right angles, and beyond them a beaded curtain blocked off what was presumably the entrance to a back room.

Armand remained near the door; Claudia knew he was watching her and was displeased at her for having come inside. She glanced around the place, taking in as much as she could as quickly as possible. But there was so much to see.

At first she'd thought the shop was empty. That was before she saw the figure sitting in a high-back chair off in a corner of the room. Claudia started to say something in the form of a greeting, then shrank back with a gasp.

The figure was a human skeleton, dressed in a man's suit—complete with hat and sunglasses. Claudia shivered at the grisly joke, and abruptly turned her attention to the vetrines.

An array of baubles and trinkets was spread over dusty black velvet. Several of them caught the twinkling light of the candles, but most of the objects were strange and disturbing charms and statuettes—or idols—with malformed limbs and mutated heads. A woodcarving depicted grotesque Siamese twins grasping the handle of a watering can. A coiled python displayed a ridiculous smile. Amulets and pendants of teeth and feathers hung from leather straps. From the top of the counter Claudia picked up the small clay image of a little man burdened

114

with an enormous, erect penis.

"Dat is Legbra," she heard a voice say.

A black man of perhaps fifty—the proprietor, Claudia assumed—stood in front of the velour curtain. The tight black curls of his hair showed strands of white. He was dressed entirely in a yellow cotton shirt and pants and wore a red bandanna around his neck.

Claudia returned the statuette to the counter. "He has the same . . . problem . . . as Priapus," she said.

The shopkeeper laughed, showing rows of white teeth. "Aha! De lady knows mythology! But dat little fellow is African, not Greek."

"Claudia," said Armand from the doorway, "we should be going."

The proprietor looked up in surprise and cried, "Alo, alo, Mistah Dantine, sir! We do not see you too much these days!"

Armand left his post beside the door to join Claudia. "No, Uncle Leo. I prefer my house to your shop."

The black man leaned toward Claudia and said in a stage whisper, "Time was when Mistah Dantine found many things in my shop to his liking. He once bought my most prized possession."

Claudia looked from Uncle Leo to Armand, whose face was flushed with anger. "You're quite through?" he asked. Claudia wasn't certain whether the question was for her or for the shopkeeper.

"A moment longah," said Uncle Leo, resting a hand on Claudia's wrist. He directed her eyes to the opposite side of the showcase, where a Bible lay open. A tiny crucifix marked the place: Psalms 18 through 21.

"Voodoo is a mystery, miss," he said. "Like dis book. People come heah for good magic."

Claudia removed her hand and took Armand's arm. "I'm sorry," she said. "I don't believe in magic."

"But you should, miss," said Uncle Leo. He came from

behind the showcase to stand beside the skeleton in the chair. "Magic is de mothah of science."

Claudia hadn't noticed the wooden cup in the skeleton's lap. Uncle Leo picked it up and held it out to them. "Dis is Papa. He is de doctah. You put money in his cup. Make a wish. De doctah fix it up. Papa make it real."

Armand withdrew a coin from his pocket and threw it into the cup. "Shall I tell you my wish, Uncle Leo?"

The black man snickered and returned the wooden cup to Papa in the chair. The chimes rang as Armand opened the shop's door.

"Everyone has wishes, Mistah Dantine!" Uncle Leo called after them. "You tell dat Sirena girl come see Papa!"

"I'm sorry," said Claudia once they were out in the street again. "I didn't think you knew each other."

Armand shrugged. "It doesn't matter . . . but it's malicious nonsense."

"It didn't seem like more than spooky theatrics," she said.

"They're thieves. They steal things . . . personal things to make their dolls and charms."

Claudia held out her hands in an open gesture and said, "Look. Nothing missing." Taking his arm, she added, "Except your sense of humor."

At last he smiled. "I suppose it is amusing after all. But he and I have known each other a long time."

"And . . . Sirena?" Claudia asked cautiously.

"Uncle Leo is . . . fond of her. She stopped going to see him when she came to me."

"Why?"

"I do not wish to have Philippe's head filled with that mumbo jumbo."

They walked for a while in silence. The music grew dim

116

as they moved farther away from the bright lights and the crowds. They turned down a darkened street; ahead of them was the corner of Dumaine and Royal.

As they continued along Claudia realized that a few blocks to the right was her hotel; to the left, Armand's house. Her hand was in his, and the quiet between them was stronger and louder than the raucous voices they'd left on Bourbon Street. The area immediately surrounding them was deserted, and all the doors and windows were shuttered, barring the light of the full yellow moon.

"Armand," she began, "you said before that you love the city as much as you hate it?"

He nodded. "The way you feel about Chicago."

"You're right," she answered, smiling. "But how did you know?"

"You've said as much in your column—even in a reply to one of my letters."

"Why did you begin writing to me?"

"Out of need," he said. "And when you wrote back in print, I confess, the prospect of a public correspondence appealed to me. The world watching our progression. We were no longer secret."

Claudia looked up at him. "Secret?"

"My thoughts . . . my feelings . . . were expressed at last, you see."

"Doesn't painting serve that purpose?"

"I do not show my work."

"Except for the portrait in the parlor."

"Yes," he said, turning to her. "Except for Noelle." He paused, then added casually, "Barton Gage painted too, didn't he?"

Claudia stopped short. The moon over his shoulder made him a silhouette before her. "Armand, I never wrote that in a column."

She heard hesitation in his voice when he answered, "But you know about art. I assumed . . ."

"Perhaps, but you couldn't have assumed my father's name. Or that he dabbled in watercolor as a hobby."

There was an awkward silence, heightened because he wasn't facing her.

"Let me look at your face when we're talking," she said, moving around him. She could see apprehension in his eyes when he turned with her and was lit by the moon. "You've been investigating me—is that it?"

"I want only to know you." He stepped closer. "And for you to know me." Armand put his hands on her bare shoulders. "I see your fear, and that is wrong. I do not wish to cause you harm. Only to protect you from it."

"What harm?" she asked in a hushed voice. Who is this man? she wondered.

"The hurt . . . the damage . . . that the world can do. Even those who say they love can cause pain."

"But that's part of living, Armand. You . . . we . . . can't hide ourselves away from it."

"Yes. We can. I can teach you so much."

"How to fear, you mean."

"That, too. As in Uncle Leo's shop. The next time, you will listen."

"If there is a next time."

"Never say that!" Armand's voice rose and his fingers increased their pressure. "There must always be a next time."

Claudia looked down at his hand on her shoulder. "Is this my first lesson in fear?"

He released her. "Forgive me. You are different. I . . . tend to forget that."

"Armand," she said, "this isn't just an ordinary pass. What do you want from me?"

He smiled. "You are different. I want you to accept me into your life. Forever."

"Forever? Armand, I'm leaving Tuesday."

He was telling the truth, she knew that. But it was only

his truth. Claudia sensed that his real wish was to absorb her into his life.

"You would grow to love New Orleans," he said.

"My life is in Chicago."

"You find the Vieux Carré unacceptable?" he whispered softly. His lips brushed her own. She felt his breath on her cheek as his hands came up to her neck, tenderly this time. He clasped her face within his palms and began tracing kisses along her ear and across her throat. "Come with me tonight," he murmured.

"I can't . . ." she answered, barely able to breathe.

"I will beg you if you like." He tilted her face upward and kissed her closed eyelids.

"Armand, I don't want . . ."

"But you do. I know you do." He was looking down at her, his lips so close to hers that they were nearly touching. "The house. We're almost there. Just a turn to the left."

Claudia broke away and half stumbled to the pillar support of an adjacent balcony. She shook her head to clear her thoughts. Her own words had restored her self-control. *My life is in Chicago. With Nick.*

"No, Armand." She pulled herself erect against the column and faced him directly. "I don't really think one accepts the Vieux Carré . . . one succumbs to it. And I can't do that."

"Or . . . you won't. Yet," he said.

"Take me back to the hotel, now, please," she said.

They passed late departing stragglers from the ballroom as they swung through the revolving doors of the hotel. The last of the glittering crowd took no notice of the guest of honor who had left her own party so early.

Claudia and Armand had said little more to each other

for the rest of the walk along Royal Street. Now he said, "I'll see you to your door."

"I have to check the message desk," she told him. She headed across the lobby and expected him to follow. Instead, he remained where he was standing. Claudia turned and came back to him. "What is it?" she asked.

"I feel that I should apologize in some way . . . although I am not certain for what."

She smiled. "Funny. That's just what I was going to say."

"Then you will let me make it up to you?"

"Armand, I . . ."

"A simple brunch. Excellent food"—he, too, was smiling now—"in the company of my son . . . and in the safety of daylight. At noon."

"I can't," she answered, aware that he'd chosen the word safety with care. "Judy's trying to arrange an appointment—rather, an interview—"

"Come afterward."

"Armand, I . . . I can't very well run off and leave my publicist at—"

"Bring her."

His offer surprised her. "Look, I . . ."

"I insist."

Clearly it was important to him, and something made her want to know more, and why. "Well, I . . . in that case, I mean, if you're sure. . . ."

"Positive. Any opportunity to be with you, even if we are not to be alone."

She weighed the situation. The prospect of Judy's presence clinched it.

"All right then. Noon it is."

He seemed pleased, and his smile was less enigmatic as he escorted her to the message desk.

"Here we are, Miss Gage," said the clerk, handing her a note.

She opened it. *Surprise!* it read. *Arriving Sunday* A.M.*!*

120

Nick.

"You're blushing," Armand said. "It must be from Dr. Seward."

Claudia didn't reply. She disliked that he knew about Nick as well. What else did he know about her personal life that hadn't been printed in her column?

"I'll say good night here," she said, putting the message inside her purse.

"Please, allow me to see you to your room."

It was easier to say yes than to argue—and would probably require less time. They walked to the bank of elevators, and all the while Claudia's thoughts were of Nick. Suddenly she could hardly wait to see him. She needed to see him. And needed to talk.

The elevator arrived. They were alone in the car. Claudia pushed the number 4 and said, as the door closed, "Armand, I'll have to cancel brunch, after all . . ."

"But . . ."

"Please don't ask me to explain. It's impossible to come. You'll just have—"

"Bring him, too," interrupted Armand.

"What . . . ?"

"I said for you to bring him."

The doors opened and moments later they reached her room. Claudia unearthed the key from her purse. He took it from her and unlocked the door.

"You're smiling," he said, returning the key to her. "Why?"

"I just wish Judy—or somebody—could have seen what you just did. Men haven't done that for women since before the fifties, Armand."

"Old-fashioned, perhaps. But I can be polite."

"Yes, you can."

She thought he was going to kiss her, but he didn't, and she was grateful; she wasn't sure what her reaction might have been if he had tried.

"You'll come with your friend Judy and . . . Nick, is it?"

"Nick," she repeated with a nod, trying to remember whether she had told him Dr. Seward's first name—or if he had known that, too.

"We will have an . . . enlightening afternoon," he said. "I promise."

Chapter 10

Claudia was surprised only by the absence of her dream that night. In fact, she didn't dream at all. Probably due to the heat and flat-out exhaustion, she thought.

Exhaustion, or denial. Claudia mused that Nick would have diagnosed the latter, and she wouldn't have been able to argue; her senses were being bombarded by too much information in this strange city.

By the time Nick arrived from Chicago looking as hot and sticky as Claudia felt, they had less than an hour in which to shower and dress for brunch Chez Dantine.

"We don't have to go." This time it was Claudia who offered the choice.

"No," said Nick, unknotting his tie, "I'd like to. Breakfast on the flight was lousy, and I'd love to see inside one of those old houses in the French Quarter—maybe find a few buried skeletons on the premises. Or shrunken heads . . ." He laughed at the expression, partly because he liked the pun, but mostly to disguise his underlying motive for visiting 1130 Royal Street: on his way up to the room he'd bumped into Judy in the lobby, and she had told him about the enigmatic trio of the artist Armand Dantine, the precocious child Philippe, and the woman, Sirena-with-an-*i*, whatever she was to each of them.

Judy had triggered Nick's professional curiosity.

And Eleanor Gage's conversation at dinner the night before had kindled his interest even more.

"I'm glad you're joining Claudia in New Orleans," she'd said over cherries Jubilee at the Pump Room.

"Well, it's been a hell of a week," he'd said, "between getting used to the new post, my regular schedule of patients, and squeezing in that overnight trip to Boston—something I shouldn't have done."

"I wasn't referring to your spending the weekend with Claudia, Nick, although I know she'll be more than delighted to see you."

"Then I'm afraid I don't understand—"

"It's New Orleans," she'd said.

"The city? What about it?"

Eleanor's face had colored slightly and she'd said no more on the subject. Rather, she'd seemed to purposely elude it, as though she had begun to tell him something and for some reason had reconsidered.

A sixth sense—or shrink's sense—told Nick that Claudia was at the center of whatever Eleanor had decided not to share.

He and Claudia showered together, but on this occasion it was more for the sake of punctuality than as a prelude to lovemaking. Somehow the atmosphere of the French Quarter—even in air-conditioned comfort—precluded hurrying of any kind.

Claudia noticed that Nick was taking more than extra care with his appearance for brunch at Armand Dantine's. She wondered what, if anything, Judy had told him. Or what he'd guessed.

What is there to guess? she mused silently. Aloud she said, "I like you in that jacket," and nuzzled her head against the ivory-colored raw silk.

"Thanks," he answered, his arms going around her. "I like you in that, too." Claudia was wearing a bare-back eyelet cotton sundress in a sherbet shade of shrimp pink. Her accessories were white linen and straw.

"Of course, I like you even better in what you weren't wearing in the shower," he said, drawing her lips to his.

She laughed and ruffled his still-damp hair.

"Do I have to wear a tie?" he asked.

Claudia shrugged. "Armand said it's casual, but . . . well, he seems a rather formal kind of person, so . . ."

"Okay. But if his shirt is open—"

"I'll have room in my purse for your tie . . . That reminds me." She opened her suitcase and took out a monogrammed lace handkerchief, which she tucked into a pocket of her straw shoulder bag.

"C'mon," she said, picking up the room key, "let's get Judy and start walking."

"You mean we're not going to take a streetcar named Desire?"

"That streetcar," she answered, smiling, "is a bus. Besides, we're already on Royal Street. It's a very short walk."

"Oh, yes. I'd forgotten that you've been there before. To tea, wasn't it?"

"Yes." She heard, but ignored, the upward inflection in his voice. Then, repeating his line about the streetcar, she added, "By the way, that was a horrible pun."

"Blame it on the heat," he said, closing the door behind them.

Judy was her usual, cheerful self, despite the weather. She chatted about the sights Frank was planning to show her later. "I'm passing up a jazz brunch at the Commander's Palace with my new boyfriend, just to see what 'Gray Vellum's' inner sanctum looks like," she said.

Nick laughed at Judy's name for Dantine, but Claudia's thoughts seemed to have drifted elsewhere.

"Want to come with us tonight?" asked Judy.

"Where to?" said Nick.

"Arnaud's, for dinner. Then we're going to Forty-one-forty-one. Frank says it's *the* place for dancing. We can make it a foursome."

"Sounds good to me," said Nick. "How about it, Claude?" he asked, using his pet name for her.

"How about what?" she asked, distractedly.

"Dinner. Dancing. Or are you already somewhere else?"

"Oh . . . I'm sorry," she answered. "It's the heat. Makes my mind wander."

"And brings out the awful puns in me," said Nick. "What a great all-purpose excuse. I never thought of using it before."

Claudia, ignoring his innuendo, said to Judy, "Dinner and dancing sound lovely. And we'll probably be famished. Sirena is gorgeous, but she doesn't strike me as the domestic type. God knows what we'll have to eat this afternoon." She paused, then said, "Maybe Sirena's cooking is why we're the first guests Armand has had to the house in years."

"Are we?" asked Nick. "How'd you know that?"

Claudia indicated the front gate and said, "He told me. And . . . we're here."

This time it wasn't the boy Philippe who answered the bell. The woman about whom they had been speaking pulled back the heavy door and said, "Come in. You're expected."

126

Judy and Nick looked at each other. Claudia kept her eyes straight ahead as Sirena led them toward the parlor—the room with the portrait.

"I'll take your things," she said, reaching out for Judy's hat and Claudia's tote bag. "It's too hot to be waitin' out in the courtyard. And he'll be right down. Just wanted to wash off some paint."

Nick observed the woman from several points of view; with his objective, professional eye, which so far told him nothing, and from a strictly physical appreciation. In the translucent cotton caftan, with no makeup but lipstick, and no jewelry other than hoop earrings, Sirena presented a sensual, provocative "mistress" of the house. She'd sized up Nick—or tried to; he'd felt it the moment they entered the foyer. But whether the slightly closed eyelids were because she'd had a late night or to evoke a response, he couldn't say yet. She'd given Claudia a once-over, too. At the same time, she'd paid no attention to Judy.

This brunch could be interesting, he decided, whether we eat or not.

"She is gorgeous," whispered Judy the moment Sirena had left the three of them alone in the parlor. Then she noticed the portrait.

"Je-sus Chr-ist! No wonder you were having the creepy-crawlies! You could have modeled for it! It's amaz—"

She stopped as the door opened and Armand Dantine entered the room.

He was wearing fitted black slacks and a rust-colored silk shirt that was open at the neck. Nick shot a glance at Claudia, as if to say, "See, no tie," and her smile told him she'd understood.

"I am sorry to keep you all waiting." He extended his hand as he came forward. To Nick, he said, "You must be Dr. Seward."

Nick nodded and, shaking hands, said, "Nice to meet you, Mr. Dantine."

"Please. My name is Armand." Before Nick could return the courtesy, their host turned to Judy and said, "Miss Fargo. We met last night at the reception." He lifted her hand and kissed it.

But it wasn't quite the way he kissed Claudia's hand. Judy could see the look in his eyes, just as Claudia could feel it. Nick, though trying to remain objective, found it difficult. It's a natural response, he thought, however possessive or immature it may be, and I doubt very much that Dantine and I are going to become the best of friends. You don't become friends with a guy whose eyes are bluer than Richard Burton's and whose hair makes Superman's look dull. Not when that guy is after the woman you love.

So what's his reason for inviting all three of us together? he wondered. To meet the competition, see what he's up against? Judy was obviously included as an accessory, like a pair of gloves or a hat. But what's his motivation for inviting me? Is it just because I showed up for the weekend and he couldn't think of a good excuse for asking Claudia not to bring me along?

Nick and Judy made the obligatory remarks about the house in general and, in particular, the painting. Armand offered the same history that he had previously given Claudia.

"Your wife was very beautiful," said Nick.

"Yes. We are both very fortunate men, Dr. Seward, in being surrounded by beauty."

128

Nick nodded politely. He sensed that he was being given a cue to say, "Oh, call me Nick." But in this case, he preferred the formality of Dr. Seward. It would enable him to ignore his host's offer of first-name familiarity; distance could be maintained by addressing him as Mr. Dantine.

"As I was saying, Dr. Seward, we are both fortunate men. I assume, considering your profession, that you have been curious about my fascination with Miss Gage—of which I also assume she has told you?"

Nick recognized this, too, as an opening, and he smiled noncommittally. You want to play a game of chess, mister, he thought, that's fine with me. But don't try little games to find out what Claudia has or hasn't told me. That's high-school psych class, and we're all too old for it.

Armand continued. "It began, of course, when I first noticed the striking resemblance between my late wife and your . . . friend."

This time Nick's smile broadened. Dantine's pause had been almost transparent—but not quite. Which meant it had been deliberate.

Nick decided not to answer. Judy diplomatically put in, "Well, they say everybody has a double."

Armand seemed not to have heard. His eyes moved toward the door, as though he could see beyond it to the other side. At precisely that moment it opened, and Philippe, dressed like a miniature prince, came in.

He made a beeline for Claudia as soon as he saw her and bowed. She felt the urge to hug him, but he was too much the little gentleman for that. Instead, she kissed him on both cheeks as his face went bright pink and he said, "I'm so pleased to see you." Then, turning to the others, he bowed once more.

To Judy, whose hand he kissed in imitation of his father, he said, "We met when Claudia signed Sirena's

129

book. Have you met Sirena yet?"

Judy smiled at the boy. "Yes, when we first arrived. But now she seems to have disappeared."

"Oh, she's just supervising in the kitchen. We've ordered specialties for today's guests." To his father, he said, "You don't mind that I've told them, do you?"

Armand smiled at his son. A genuine smile, Nick noted.

"Not at all." To his guests, he said, "It is so seldom that we entertain. Sirena can manage for just the three of us, but for today, I could not entrust her or burden her with such responsibility."

"You mean just the three of you take care of this entire place?" asked Nick. He'd purposely included the boy, but it seemed impossible that Dantine and the woman Sirena were the only adults on the premises.

Armand answered, "I have workers who come in for various repairs and upkeep. Maintenance. Gardeners, landscape people, and such. And cleaning help, as well. But as to your question, Dr. Seward"—again, Nick noted the way Dantine's eyelids seemed to reflect the intent behind his words—"the three of us are the only ones who actually live in the house."

Armand turned sharply then to his son and said, "Philippe, we are both forgetting our manners. You have not yet introduced yourself to Dr. Seward."

Nick and the child shook hands. "I am pleased to meet you, Doctor," said Philippe, almost bowing.

To the boy, Nick said, "My pleasure, Philippe. And I hope you'll call me Nick." He marveled at the child's Little Lord Fauntleroy behavior and wondered what effect a Cubs or White Sox uniform might have on him. Maybe it'd turn him into a real kid. He also wondered what might happen if anyone tried.

Sirena came in then to invite them to the dining room, and Nick temporarily abandoned further speculation.

The dining room's centerpiece was not on the table but hung overhead. It was a magnificent crystal chandelier, whose glistening prisms, despite the fact that the lights were turned off, dazzled in the rays of sun that filtered in through the closed shutter slats.

The chandelier reflected in the polished rectangular mahogany table, and again Nick wondered whether the task of keeping the crystal fixture sparkling and the table gleaming fell to Sirena or to someone else.

He noticed that the table was set for five, not six. To Philippe he said, "Aren't you going to sit with us?"

The boy nodded. "Yes, of course."

The master of the house, seating himself at the head of the table, answered Nick's question. "Sirena has made other plans. She won't be joining us."

Armand invited Claudia to sit on his left, Judy at his right, and Nick found himself seated beside the boy Philippe.

Well, thought Nick, you're the one who decided to come down for the weekend. May as well make the best of it.

Claudia was surprised, as were Nick and Judy, that despite Sirena's "other plans," she first served the meal to Armand's guests. It was more than clear that she had been asked—or told—to do so; her eyes remained half-lidded as she placed each platter or bowl on the table.

The stemware was Waterford and matched the decanters, although these were not filled with wine or a variety of spirits. Armand, after placing his damask napkin across his lap, announced, "I apologize for bringing you all directly to the table without first offering

131

you an aperitif, but since it's early and the sun is so hot, I thought we might eat and drink at the same time."

"I think it's a great idea," said Judy. "That way we'll all stay lucid."

"In that case, may I pour something for you?" asked Armand, reaching for one of the decanters.

"Thanks," she said. "I'd love a glass of wine."

Sirena, who had just placed a crystal bowl of mint leaves on the table, turned to her and said, "We are serving only mint juleps."

Claudia thought back to the courtyard and the tray of assorted whiskies, but made no mention of it. If mint juleps went better with whatever they'd be eating, then bourbon was fine with her.

"I hope the three of you like crawfish," said Armand. "I did not think to inquire before."

For this meal, he explained, he had ordered the preparation of his favorite foods.

On finest Wedgwood china, accompanied by antique Gorham sterling flatware, they were served a spicy seafood gumbo, followed by a featherlight crawfish soufflé. Home-baked cornbread sticks and hot biscuits were heaped into a silver-filigree basket, with a variety of jams and preserves in individual, faceted crystal jars.

Coconut pralines were served for dessert, with strong, rich French coffee. The meal was utter perfection.

The single flaw was in the service. While they ate, Armand conducted the conversation as a travel guide might advise visitors. "You must see this" or "You must visit that." However, with each new course—brought in by Sirena—his tone became dictatorial, although Sirena didn't seem to notice.

But Claudia noticed it, and wondered, as she had before, just what Sirena's position was in the Dantine house.

Judy regarded the woman and thought back to

Frank's comments. "Rumors," he'd said. And even Armand had admitted that the three of them were the only inhabitants of the house.

Nick observed the color of Sirena's skin and the way in which she moved, the manner with which she spoke to Armand Dantine. It wasn't Nick's imagination; there was a certain, undiscernible look that occasionally passed between Sirena Mars and Armand Dantine.

Master and servant? he speculated. Or were they master . . . and slave?

After the meal, Armand escorted Claudia and Judy on a tour of the downstairs quarters of the house. Nick declined in favor of talking with Philippe and getting to know him better. At the table, he'd seen the boy's eyes light up at the mention of baseball; it had made Nick wonder if the "little gentleman" was ever allowed to be the eight-year-old he was. Moreover, Nick knew that children often possessed a deeper awareness of what was going on around them than adults generally gave them credit for.

"Claudia tells me you don't go to school," said Nick as they settled into wicker chairs in a shutter-cooled corner of what Philippe called the sunroom.

"No," he said. "I have a tutor."

"I envy you. I used to hate getting up in the morning for school. Especially in winter. Of course, that's because Chicago is so cold at that time of year."

"It's nothing to envy, really," said Philippe. "In fact, sometimes it's lonely. I'm glad my father has invited guests to the house today. Especially you. And . . . Miss Gage."

"Well, I'm glad, too," said Nick. "It would have been nice if one of your friends could have been here, too."

"Oh, Sirena is my friend," said the boy immediately.

133

"I bought Miss Gage's book for her."

"Yes . . . I know. But . . . I meant friends of your own age."

Philippe looked up with his wide, blue, innocent eyes and said, "I don't know anyone of my age, Dr. Seward . . . I mean, Nick."

That explains much about his manner, thought Nick. Poor kid's around adults all the time—and those two adults in particular would make any child of eight come across like a genius—or a midget.

"So . . . you like baseball," Nick ventured.

"Well, from what I've seen on television. I've never actually attended a game. We don't have baseball in New Orleans. Just football."

"And you don't like football?"

"It doesn't seem to require the strategy that baseball does. I'd like to try playing it someday. Pitching looks like fun."

At least the word fun is part of his vocabulary, thought Nick. "I tell you what. If you can talk your dad into bringing you up to Chicago sometime, we can all go to a game together. And maybe you can throw me a few pitches. I used to be a pretty decent batter in Little League."

"That would be very nice," answered Philippe. "To attend a game, I mean. Especially with you and Miss Gage. I doubt very much, though, whether my father would allow me to play."

Considering the past several hours, Nick wasn't surprised by the child's remark. Somehow, he couldn't shake the feeling that the Dantine household—and its inhabitants—for all the preserved beauty and order, was suffering from time warp. There was something too cosmetic about it all, something akin to a stage setting that dazzled the beholder and made the audience believe in the story unfolding onstage, while behind the scenes a vastly different life existed. Here, too, inside this house, there was more to the threesome than that which merely met the eye. Nick felt as though he were witnessing a magic show. And the basis of magic, he knew, was illusion.

"Where are you going?" asked Armand when the guests had gone.

"Out," said Sirena, moving toward the door.

"Where?" he repeated, holding on to her wrist.

"You'll know when it's time," she answered. "But not now. Not yet."

Armand tightened his grip.

"Let go of me," she said, "or I swear I'll ruin all your plans."

He released her hand and she hurried from the house.

If Nick had suffered misgivings at the Dantine house, they only increased after he and Claudia and Judy returned to the Royal Orleans.

They hadn't spoken much on the walk back to the hotel; it was hot, they were tired, and each was lost in thought over the afternoon just past.

Once they were in the elevator, Judy took off her straw hat and said, "Damn it all, anyway!"

"What is it?" asked Claudia.

"Oh, it's just the little porcelain rose I pinned to the grosgrain ribbon. See?" She held up her hat to show Claudia and Nick that it was gone.

"I gave my hat to Sirena when we arrived, and either she dropped it and the pin fell off, or . . ."

"Or what?" asked Claudia.

"Oh, never mind. I get bitchy when I meet someone so gorgeous who doesn't do a thing to become that

135

way."

"What do you mean?" asked Nick, suddenly interested in Judy's hat.

"Oh, I was going to say maybe she stole it, and that's not fair at all. It didn't have a safety catch, and I guess it must have been loose."

"You can call and ask Sirena if she's seen it," suggested Claudia.

"You're right. I'll do that when we get upstairs."

Nick and Claudia agreed to meet Judy in the lobby at seven, when Frank was due to arrive. Meanwhile, Claudia wanted to flop down on the bed and take a nap.

The air conditioner had chilled the room to freezing, and as Nick went to adjust the thermostat to warmer, Claudia sneezed; too-cold temperatures had always made her sneeze.

She reached into her tote bag for her purse-size packet of Kleenex, but found that she'd used it up.

She sneezed again and laughed. "Well, I suppose I can use a handkerchief. That's what they were originally intended for, anyway."

She opened the side pocket compartment of her bag, where earlier she'd put the white lace square.

"That's strange," she said to Nick. "It's not here."

"What's not here?"

"My handkerchief. I distinctly remember taking it — for brow mopping, because it's so hot out."

"I saw you put it in your purse before we left," said Nick.

For a moment they looked at each another. Then Nick said, half joking, "Maybe Armand stole it to put under his pillow at night."

"Oh, stop it," she said. "This is very odd. Things

136

don't just disappear into thin air."

"Well, maybe the kid took it. He is precocious, and he seems to have a crush on you . . . must run in the family . . ."

She shot him a look of "Oh, c'mon!" But she didn't answer.

Finally, he said, "Claude, you're not starting to think along Judy's lines, are you?"

She shrugged her shoulders. When she replied, it was slowly, and half to herself. "I don't know, Nick. But when I went to tea at the house, I was wearing Judy's hat. Sirena may have mistakenly thought it was mine."

"Well, what difference would it make whose hat it was if what she wanted was the pin?"

"Yes," agreed Claudia, "but then, what about my handkerchief?"

Chapter 11

The tomb was little more than a small brick house with a roof sloping down from the central point. The sun penetrated through the half-dead branches of a tree and illuminated the name Marie Laveau. Sirena fell to her knees.

To her right, a cement pedestal that was only a few inches off the ground supported an urn in which a flame perhaps once had burned. But not for at least the past hundred years, Sirena reasoned. With trembling hands she placed her canvas tote beside her on the parched grass and studied the facade of the mausoleum. It was in sorry condition, especially in comparison with the clean white cement or granite of the other gravesites surrounding it. Now she knew why they were called oven vaults. From the way they looked.

She had tied her long black hair carelessly in a red bandanna to keep her neck cool. Stray strands had escaped and now stuck to her damp skin. She removed the bandanna and used it to wipe her brow. But she knew her excessive perspiration was due to more than the heat.

She was uncomfortable here. Not from fear—she respected the dead. Strange, she thought, the way some folks find charm in a place like this. Well, maybe their ancestors aren't restin' here—ancestors, according to rumor, who included the woman whose remains were inside the tomb in front of which Sirena knelt.

She had never visited the graveyard before. She had successfully avoided having to until now. Her people had come to assume she was afraid. How could Sirena have explained that it was her attempt to resist temptation, and not fear, that kept her away?

Since early childhood, she had heard the legend of Marie Laveau, the voodoo queen. Sirena had been raised with the notion that she herself possessed similar powers, powers that thus far had not manifested themselves. Whether they existed at all or merely lay dormant and untried had always gnawed at her curiosity. Uncle Leo had told her on numerous occasions that she, too, had the "special gift," but Sirena had fought the urge to call forth that gift and exercise it.

She had decided to encourage her people to believe she was a "modern" woman, and hoped her practiced look of disdain was enough to convince them that she thought their ways backward and ignorant.

Yet all the while she had wondered . . . what if it's true? What if I am special in that way?

These temptations she had confessed to her priest.

"It's wrong," he'd said, "to turn your back on your family and friends. Somehow you must find your way without submitting to pagan ritual." He had termed such ritual as Godless.

But is it Godless? Sirena asked herself as she retied her hair with the bandanna, then removed a small garden spade from her bag. Isn't it true that God exists in all the *vodoun,* in every spirit? She had prayed to

God, at first for Armand; matters had only become worse. Then she asked for strength within herself—and found herself weakening further. Philippe was all she had left; she must not lose him.

But Armand, she thought. One day he'll be wantin' me to give Philippe over to him and that woman.

Sirena almost laughed at the irony; she had been the one to bring Armand's attention to Claudia's newspaper column; she had pointed out the striking resemblance to Noelle. Two white women, neither of whom she knew, encroaching on her life as Armand became more and more preoccupied with the existence of past within the present.

I'm bein' pushed out of the world inside that house, she thought, the fury rising inside her.

She feared only the power of her increasing hatred. She grew lightheaded at the excitement that such power could generate in her . . . and in Armand. Something uncontrollable. Something that must be quelled . . . or ended. And God alone had not been enough.

Now she would ask for help from the spirits, despite the priest's counsel. But hadn't Uncle Leo spoken of the invisible line between religion and magic? And wasn't it time for her to cross that line?

Others had. The evidence was all around her. The mausoleum's grounds were strewn with objects that unknowing eyes would term as debris: wooden crosses, rosary beads hanging from a jagged brick, the tiny skull of a small bird, and a variety of trinkets scattered about.

Sirena looked around her. There were a few tourists at a tomb some hundred yards away. Their backs were facing her, and no one else was close enough to watch.

With a forceful blow, she stabbed at the dry earth with the point of the spade and began digging the hole.

140

When she had reached a depth of six inches or so, she put down the spade and reached again into her tote. Withdrawing the knotted lace handkerchief from the bag, she laid it on the ground beside the little grave she had dug, then untied the two ends to reveal a pin. It was made of porcelain and fashioned into a delicate rose.

There had been no time to look at it carefully when she'd taken it from the hat. Now she admired the exquisite detail work. Sirena loved pretty things, and the pin was most definitely that. Once, long ago, Armand had bought such things for her.

It seemed a shame to bury the pin; she would have preferred to keep it. Perhaps not to wear it—Armand's eyes rarely escaped even minutiae; he was likely to remember where he'd seen it—adorning the ribboned border of their guest's straw hat.

Sirena had been tempted to tear it from the grosgrain band the first time the Gage woman visited the house. Opportunity had denied her the chance. But earlier this afternoon, when the *other* woman, the one named Judy, had come to brunch wearing the same hat—and had placed it in Sirena's own hands—well, it had just proven too easy.

She remembered then her true motive for the theft: the blond woman, Judy, had obviously borrowed the hat which, along with the pin, belonged to Claudia Gage. *That* made the porcelain rose important as well as pretty. The lace handkerchief was only an afterthought, an extra little stab of malice.

Sirena picked up the fragile flower and studied it more closely. Then she resolutely lowered her hand and placed the tiny rose at the bottom of the hole.

Soon it was buried beneath the dirt. She emptied the last spadeful of earth into the handkerchief that was spread out on the ground. She tied the ends together, placed the lacy sack inside her tote, and threw the spade in beside it.

She remained on her knees for another few minutes and thought through the possible consequences of her actions. She considered herself a good woman. Perhaps not so good as before Armand Dantine had entered her life . . . but certainly she wasn't a bad sort. She wished no harm to anyone. She wanted only for her problems to vanish. So she closed her eyes and carried out the final part of her mission.

She murmured the words she had learned as a child, and invoked Marie Laveau to intercede in her behalf, to drive away Claudia Gage.

When she had finished, Sirena brushed off her skirt and left the graveyard, her tote bag clutched tightly in her fists.

The light was fading. It didn't matter. The work hadn't gone well this afternoon. Too many distractions hindered his concentration.

Brunch had been awkward at best. The "good doctor" Seward could prove an eventual problem; the extent of Nick's love was apparent in the way he looked at Claudia. Armand had found it almost impossible to bear. Fortunately, Seward would depart the following night.

And Claudia would leave on Tuesday. So little time.

Visions of Claudia danced before his eyes — eyes that should have been focused on her painted likeness.

Perhaps it was best to take a cue from the waning sun and stop for the day. But it was difficult to do.

Many times he had stood at the easel, day after day, barely eating or sleeping, in a frenzy to capture a picture on canvas before the image in his mind had become a blur. He had once finished a painting in just three days. A fine painting.

Such was not the case with the current portrait-in-progress. He was painting her slowly, elongating the process, savoring and making it last. Although this afternoon's work had been less than rewarding, the study was nonetheless beginning to assume the form and texture of the living woman. And something more. His own love for her was making itself known through the pigment, through his brushstrokes. In the blue of the eyes, the play of light on the smooth white throat, the dark hair that draped across a shoulder blade and traveled downward to rest on the swell of gently rounded breasts. His imagination would have to do the rest for now. Until the time when his own hand would rest upon the flesh and hold her against him.

Armand surrendered himself to the fantasy. They would be here, together again, joined in perfect union. He foresaw days and days of their endless lovemaking. And at the very center of the dream was the pastoral vision of a family. Three, not two. Armand, with Claudia as his wife and the mother of his son, Philippe.

Scores of unframed canvases lay about the studio. Most were good. But none was as inspired as the one before him now. This would be his finest achievement, his masterpiece. If only he could look upon the woman as she appeared here, revealed to him alone.

He had felt this satisfaction in his painting only once before, with the completed portrait of Noelle. But the rendering was not displayed in the house to boast of his talent; it was to have her with them always, watching over them. Neither her image nor memory would ever be dimmed by time. Philippe would look at her face and remember the stories Armand had told him. In that way, her beauty, her grace, would live forever.

And this new painting, the portrait of Claudia, would be that and more. He had begun it months ago, yet only in the days since their first meeting had it taken on life. With her portrait Armand was being freed, given full rein to convey the passion he had wished to express in everything he painted — but could not.

The phone rang. Once. Twice. Three times.

"Damn!" he cursed aloud, putting down his brush. "Where is Sirena?"

Then he remembered that she had gone out. Either she hadn't returned, or was playing one of her games by not picking up the phone. Lately she'd found all kinds of excuses to disturb him.

But his work was finished for the day. He left the studio and answered the hall extension on the fifth ring.

"Mr. Dantine?" a familiar voice asked.

"Yes, this is Armand speaking, Miss Fargo."

"Oh . . . uh . . . well, hello," Judy stammered self-consciously. "I hope I'm not interrupting anything . . ."

"I would have told you if you were, Miss Fargo. What may I do for you?"

"Well, it's just that I seem to have misplaced something . . ."

Philippe sat on the floor of the parlor with his legs crossed before him, elbows on his knees and head in his hands. He'd heard the telephone ring but ignored it. He'd never been encouraged to use the instrument. However, by the fourth ring, a nervous fluttering had begun in his stomach. Armand would expect Sirena to answer it, and this interruption of his father's work could cause another screaming battle between them, followed by that familiar silence in the house.

He was relieved when the ringing stopped, although he couldn't tell whether it had been answered, or if the caller had hung up. For Sirena's sake, he hoped it was the latter.

He readjusted his legs, and his attention returned to the portrait of Noelle.

He had always wished he'd known his mother. Her name meant Christmas; she must have been wonderful. Even though he felt a deep affection for Sirena, Philippe had been taught that a special place in his heart must always be reserved for the woman in the picture. But only part of him could remain faithful; the Noelle in the portrait was made of canvas and paint.

He reflected on the day at the bookstore, the day when Noelle had seemingly stepped through the gilt-carved frame and come to life. The wonder of it had overwhelmed Philippe; he'd tried hard to behave in a grown-up manner, not to gawk at Claudia Gage, but still it all had appeared miraculous to him.

Philippe heard the key turn in the front-door lock, but he remained motionless in his position. Sirena was home at last.

The parlor door opened and closed. Her footsteps came closer, and he felt her lips on his cheeks as an arm enfolded him.

"My little man," she said in her low voice, putting her tote bag on the floor. "No greetin' for me? Didn't you even miss me?"

She was kneeling beside him. She smelled like the hot summer day. He turned and kissed her on the cheek. "Yes, I did."

"Why aren't you outside playin' in the courtyard?" she asked. "It's a lovely evenin'."

"He's still working. It was easier to stay quiet in here."

A flash of anger passed through Sirena; she hated that the child should be forced indoors by his father's tyranny. Philippe needs friends of his own age, she thought. He should be allowed to attend school, be sent off to summer camp like other kids, and not be cooped up inside this suffocatin' old house.

"Listen," she said, "maybe after supper, you and me, we can play a game. Scrabble or somethin'."

Philippe hugged her tightly. "You hate Scrabble, Sirena."

"I'm just no good at it, is all."

He laughed, but his gaze had returned to the portrait.

That one again, thought Sirena. My prayers need more time. She fought back the resentment and tenderly brushed the hair from his forehead. "What're you thinkin' about that's so serious, little man?"

Philippe shrugged without answering. This wasn't the first time Sirena had found him like this, seated on the floor and staring up at Noelle's picture.

In a lighter voice, she said, "Well, you can see her a lot better with a light on. It's gettin' dark in here."

She turned on the Tiffany wisteria lamp and hoped it would bring a change to the mood in both the room and the boy.

He didn't move. Finally, he said, "It's not Noelle. I mean, it is, but . . ." He looked up helplessly at Sirena. "How can they be so much alike?"

She knelt beside him again and took his small hands in her own. "I can't explain it to you, little man."

Not yet, at least, she thought.

"She's awfully nice, don't you think so?" Philippe asked with expectation.

"Miss Gage? Oh, she's . . . all right, I guess. Anyway, I suppose it's good that you like her."

"Why?"

Sirena paused. "Philippe," she began cautiously, "if . . . if things were suddenly to change around here, could you be happy with Miss Gage?"

He stared into her eyes. The expression on his face was a troubled one, but Sirena detected a spark of comprehension. He must know there was more to the question than her words could convey. The deep blue eyes that she loved filled with tears. He gave a sad, shy nod, then lowered his curly head and studied his clasped hands.

"Not if I had to choose," he said with difficulty. He spoke so softly that Sirena could barely hear him. "I love *you,* Sirena."

She drew him to her and squeezed him fiercely. Her own tears dampened his dark ringlets of hair. "And you know I love you, darlin'. But things are happenin' . . . things we can't always control."

Philippe's arms went around her neck, and Sirena realized that she'd do anything to keep him from harm. Even, she realized in that moment, if it meant giving him up.

But not without a fight.

She forced herself to release him and they faced each other. "Now look at us," she said, smiling. "We're both an awful mess!"

Philippe laughed as he brought a hand to her cheek and wiped away the tears. "You're too pretty to cry, Sirena."

"And you, little man, are already too handsome and charmin' for your own good."

She reached into her bag for a tissue, and saw the little handkerchief filled with earth. "Listen," she said quietly, "will you do me a favor?"

"Anything."

She lowered her voice still further to a conspiratorial

147

whisper. "This belongs to Miss Gage. I mean to return it to her. Will you keep it for me until I ask for it again?"

Philippe took the tiny sack from her and replied, also in a whisper, "You don't want . . . him . . . to find out?"

"No. I was gonna hide it in here, under the sofa . . ."

"I'll hide it under my bed," he offered.

He didn't ask why a handful of dirt wrapped in Claudia's handkerchief should be kept a secret. Again, Sirena was overcome by love at his complete and total trust.

They both started at the loud slam of a door followed by the sound of footsteps coming down the hall and drawing closer.

Philippe stood up and stuffed the handkerchief into the pocket of his short pants, after which he gave Sirena a quick, happy wink before turning to face the door.

It opened, and Armand entered.

"So, there you are," he said.

He was wearing his old paint-spattered cotton smock over his shirt and pants. "When did you get back?" he asked Sirena.

She rose to her feet, picking up the tote bag and holding it in her right hand. "Just now. What are you scowlin' about this time?"

"The telephone disturbed me."

"It didn't kill you to answer, did it?" She tousled Philippe's hair and crossed the room until she was standing before Armand. "Let me pass. I'll start supper."

But Armand didn't move aside. "Where did you go?" he asked.

"To visit . . . a relative." Her answer brought a smile to her lips.

He grabbed her arms, but she shook herself free and stared him down.

Philippe watched as the scene began to play. Armand was accusing her of having stolen something; he even pulled her tote bag from her and went through it.

"What are you doin' ?" Sirena demanded.

"Looking for a missing pin."

Philippe didn't understand, but at the mention of a lady's handkerchief, he suddenly realized what he had tucked away for Sirena. He glanced down and noticed an edge of the tell tale lace. He quickly shoved both of his hands deep into his pockets and pushed the handkerchief far out of sight.

Sirena was still facing Armand. Over her shoulder she called Philippe's name. "Go outside and play for a while. And make all the noise you want. Your father's through with work for today."

Philippe came closer to them and stopped next to Sirena. "Are we still going to play Scrabble?"

"Yes, darlin'. Later."

"Then I'll go up to my room and get the game," he said, looking directly at Sirena. "It's under my bed."

"You do that, little man," she answered. "Then go into the courtyard and get some fresh air."

Armand opened the door. As soon as it closed behind Philippe, their voices rose, as they did so frequently these days.

Once inside his room, Philippe removed the handkerchief-sack from his pocket. Then he crouched down on his hands and knees, and placed it as far beneath the bed as he could reach.

Moments later he came back downstairs with the Scrabble game tucked under his arm. He put it on a chair in the kitchen before going to the courtyard door. There, he stopped to listen.

The house was quiet again.

Philippe went outside and seated himself at the garden

149

table, where he would remain until he heard the sounds of Sirena preparing supper in the kitchen. Then he would know it was all right to go back inside.

The sun had fallen low, and deep shadows filled the corners of the courtyard. Philippe sat gazing at the Spanish moss, which was stirring in the evening breeze. From the gentle way in which the moss moved and swayed, it was easy for him to believe the story of the Indian maiden.

But it wasn't her hair that he saw. It was Sirena's. Philippe didn't understand why it made him want to cry.

Chapter 12

Nick was still mentally replaying his phone conversation with Judy Fargo when the light on his intercom began to blink and the buzzer sounded.

"Yes, Margaret?"

"I'm sorry to interrupt, Dr. Seward. I know you said to hold all calls, but I thought it might be important."

"Who is it?" he asked.

"Mrs. Gage. On line three."

Christ, thought Nick. I promised to call Eleanor as soon as I got back. "Thanks, Margaret, you were right—and I'll take it."

He leaned forward and noticed that his belt felt a bit tight around his midsection. He hoped that Claudia's mother wasn't going to suggest another meal at the Pump Room. After nonstop—albeit fabulous—food in New Orleans, he was thinking about skipping a dinner or two.

"Hi, Eleanor, sorry I didn't call when I got in. It's been hectic. And . . . to tell the truth, I just plain forgot."

"That's all right, Nick," she said. "I thought perhaps

you'd decided to stay an extra day."

"With this schedule?" He laughed. "I hope none of my private patients is heading for a crisis. I mean, the timing would be way off."

Eleanor laughed, too. "Speaking of which, tell me, did you and Claudia have any time together at all?"

"Not as much as I'd have liked," he answered. "But I knew in advance I wouldn't be able to monopolize her." He smiled to himself at his own choice of words. "One does come across some very interesting personalities on a book tour, though," he said.

"Interesting," repeated Eleanor. "That's a word I use when I can't quite find another one that's more appropriate."

"Well, so do I, I guess. But 'interesting' is the word I meant just now. Pathologically speaking."

"Why? What . . . who . . . were the 'interesting personalities' you met?"

Eleanor had hesitated, but Nick couldn't tell whether it was deliberate or because she didn't want him to know she was prying.

Hey, Dr. Seward, he cautioned himself. She only paused while she was forming a question. Even you've done that.

But still. . . .

"Well . . .?"

"Oh, yes. Sorry. I'm groggy. Not enough sleep." He yawned to support his excuse. "Let's see. Claudia had a couple of appointments, interviews, you know. And Judy Fargo and Frank—"

"Frank?" interrupted Eleanor. "Her ex-husband?"

"New boyfriend. Tends bar in the French Quarter. Very down-to-earth guy. I think he really likes Judy. And the glamour doesn't seem to impress him. Anyway, the four of us had dinner at Arnaud's, then went to a club to hear some jazz. And . . . oh, yes," he added as though it were an afterthought, although Sunday afternoon remained uppermost in his mind, "we were invited to brunch in the French Quarter. That was very interesting."

"Interesting in what you call your pathological sense?" asked Eleanor.

"That, too, but . . . well, I admit — unprofessionally — that I wasn't exactly nuts about our host."

"Why not?"

"Well, I don't go crazy over any guy who tries to horn in on my territory." Then he remembered he was talking to his "territorys'" mother and said, "What I mean is—"

She laughed. "Nick, I know exactly what you mean. You don't want someone making overtures to Claudia. And I can't say I blame you. But I wouldn't be worried."

"No, you're right. And I won't worry — as soon as she leaves New Orleans." He looked at his watch. "That should be in another hour or two, which is fine with me. Both the city and this Dantine guy are too seductive-looking for my taste."

"Did you say . . . Dantine?" asked Eleanor.

This time, Nick knew he'd heard hesitation in her voice. And not simply a pause during a question.

"Yes," he answered. "Armand Dantine. Don't tell me you know him?"

"No, I can't say that I do."

But her breath was shallow and unconnected to her voice. Nick didn't need to see her to know that.

"Eleanor . . .?"

"Yes, Nick?" Now she sounded almost anxious. "I beg your pardon. The name Dantine reminded me of someone else . . . someone Barton used to know in

New Orleans."

"Is that all?" he asked.

"Why, yes. For a moment I thought it was the same name. But I was mistaken."

No she wasn't, Nick reflected after they'd hung up. Otherwise, she wouldn't have insisted that he accept her invitation to dinner.

And not at the Pump Room. At her duplex on Lake Shore Drive. "Where we can be alone and talk," she'd said.

His professional training and experience had taught him to put his own problems, concerns, life on hold during his fifty-minute sessions with patients. Objectivity, he reminded himself, was the key to his effectiveness. And there were days, such as today, when objectivity was easier achieved than maintained.

During his breaks—the last ten minutes of each hour—Nick leaned back in his chair and tried to analyze the reason why Eleanor had reacted nervously—why, in fact, she had reacted at all—simply at his mention of the Dantine name. She had clearly, audibly, flinched, and Nick couldn't figure it out.

But each series of ten minutes between patients passed quickly, then Margaret buzzed him on the intercom to announce the next arrival.

Mr. Peters was overcoming his acrophobia, and that gave Nick a good feeling; they'd worked for months and now the young stockbroker could peer out a window at the top of the Sears Tower with no more than mild anxiety.

Mrs. Lefferts was experiencing fewer and fewer panic attacks lately. "I walked here on my own today, Dr. Seward. No one had to cross the street with me. And

154

my progress is thanks to you—and those pills you gave me."

"No," he assured her, "the pills—and I—only help you to help yourself. It's okay to give yourself the credit." In truth, Nick was gratified by Mrs. Lefferts's growing confidence.

But Wendell Jackson was still experiencing severe bouts of depression, and at one point during his hour, the troubled painter spoke again of suicide. Nick had worked hard with the handsome, tortured young artist. "But we're not God," he said aloud, repeating the words of Dr. Emerson, head of the therapy group Wendell was attending. No, Nick reflected, we're not God. We're not magicians, either. And despite myriad breakthroughs in the field, we're still pioneers exploring areas of the psyche that continue to hide more than they reveal. Some people, like Wendell, need—or unconsciously want—to hold on to their problems more than they need or want to solve them.

Thoughts of Wendell's profession, as well as memory of the repressed hostility revealed in his canvases, returned Nick's mind to the French Quarter and another, very different artist named Armand Dantine. Then Margaret buzzed, and it was time for his final patient of the day.

Eleanor was wearing black silk hostess pants and a cream-colored silk poet's shirt. Just the right amount of jewelry. Good stuff. A woman of exquisite taste, taste she had instilled in Claudia.

She greeted him at the door. "Nick, dear! I just got home myself. I'm heading the committee for the up-coming costume ball at the Art Institute, and you wouldn't believe the work involved! Anyway, I had no time to arrange dinner instructions with Imelda, so I've ordered something up from the little place around the corner. I hope you won't mind."

She took his arm and led him into the drawing room.

"I'm trying to take off a pound or two as it is," he said, following her and taking a seat on the greenish-gray velvet sofa.

"Well, that makes two of us," she said, crossing to the bar. "At my age, it's harder to take weight off, so I'd rather keep it off in the first place."

"Eleanor," he said, "you look terrific. And I think you know it."

"Oh, dear, is my vanity that apparent?" she asked with a laugh.

"Only to a man in my field. And I don't mind—that or a take-out dinner. What're we having, Chinese?"

"Too much sodium, dear." She took the chilled bottle of Chardonnay from the ice bucket and said, "But a few glasses of wine with dinner thins the blood and"—she grinned mischievously—"relaxes inhibitions." She considered her own remark. "Goodness, please don't misinterpret that!" She busied herself with pouring the wine into two faceted crystal wineglasses. They reminded him of Armand Dantine's stemware.

"I thought we'd rough it this evening," Eleanor was saying. She placed the bottle on a lacquered tray alongside the two filled glasses and brought it to the brass-framed glass coffee table.

"Well, cheers," she said, handing one glass to Nick and clinking her own lightly against it.

They had each taken a sip when the doorbell rang.

"That'll be dinner. I won't be a minute." And she left the room.

Nick glanced around at the splendor displayed throughout. Understated elegance, he thought. Where

Claudia grew up. No wonder she's so accustomed to this. Luxury no longer made him feel uncomfortable—especially when, as here, it wasn't ostentatious—but he'd had to acquire the ease; Claudia had been born with it.

Well, maybe not. Sometimes it was difficult to remember, given Claudia and Eleanor's closeness, that Claudia was adopted.

Eleanor—or her maid, Imelda—had arranged a bouquet of fresh flowers in a delicately woven basket on the coffee table. Beside it was a heavy crystal ashtray, although Eleanor didn't smoke and disliked when others did. But Barton Gage had puffed on the occasional cigar, so Eleanor had probably left the ashtray there as a reminder of his presence.

Still holding his wineglass, Nick got up from the sofa and walked across the room to one of the gilt-framed mirrors hanging over the matching Louis XVI—or were they Louis XIV?—console tables. He'd been in this room many times, but he'd never checked himself in either of the mirrors.

Now he took a long look. He wasn't displeased with the image staring back. He just wished Claudia were here, too, standing beside him.

Well, he thought, at least she's left New Orleans. There were smoked almonds in another crystal dish on the coffee table, and Nick helped himself to a handful. Diet or not, he was hungry. He washed the nuts down with a long swallow of wine just as Eleanor reentered the room, followed by a uniformed waiter pushing a room-service-style cart.

"We'll just have to move two chairs," she said. Nick helped, and within minutes—in the moments required to carry over two of the tapestry-covered chairs—the cart had been transformed into a sumptuous feast-laden

157

table.

"I'll have to remember this when Claude gets home," Nick said, lifting, one by one, the heavy metal plate-warmers for a peek.

"Lobster and pheasant? And the soup"—he sniffed—"Mmm! Smells wonderful! What is it anyway?"

"Leeks. They do it up very nicely, don't they? Wait until you see the lovely pearl onions and new potatoes. So tender. And I ordered *porcini* mushrooms because Claudia's told me how you adore them. I think you'll like dessert too. Come, sit down while I see Harman to the door."

Nick bristled for a split second. At first he thought she'd said Armand.

After the waiter had gone, they both abandoned their diets. Eleanor even invited Nick to loosen his belt. "I plan to roll up my sleeves and dig in, as one says, so please, don't stand on ceremony."

He complied, and Eleanor unbuttoned the pearl-buttoned cuffs of her blouse and rolled them to her elbows. "There," she said. "Much better. I really grow weary of those charity luncheons where everyone is expected to eat like a bird."

Nick nodded. He'd been to a few.

They ate without much conversation, punctuating dinner occasionally with a comment about the spices or garnishes used in preparation of the meal. Nick was beginning to wonder if Eleanor would ever get around to her underlying reason for inviting him—especially after she'd had such a busy day.

At last his patience was rewarded. They'd finished their portions of mocha Bavarian mousse and had gone from espresso to brandy—poured from a stunning Wa-

158

terford decanter, which was a far cry from "roughing it," Nick noted—when Eleanor said, "I'd like to hear all about New Orleans."

"Why?" he asked, looking directly across the table at her.

"Why? Well, my daughter has a book on the best-seller list, she's on a publicity tour, and New Orleans is a fascinating city. Why wouldn't I want to hear about it?"

"No . . ." said Nick slowly. "I mean . . ."

They were interrupted by the sound of a timer. "What's that?" asked Nick. He knew the kitchen was too far away, even if Imelda had prepared something to add to the dinner they'd just finished.

"Oh, I'm glad I set the clock, or it might have slipped my mind," answered Eleanor. "The interview that Claudia taped for WGBH in Boston—you remember, that ten-minute chat with the book critic?—well, it was preempted on channel eleven here by some news bulletin or other, and it's been rescheduled for tonight. In five minutes, to be precise. Why don't we take our brandies into the den?"

The interview had been edited, and lasted less than five minutes. When it was over and the emcee went on to the next author, Eleanor turned off the set and refilled Nick's glass. "So, tell me about this Dantine person. Sounds mysterious."

"Well, I don't know about mysterious, but his eyes look as if they can see right through the person he's addressing or listening to. Very intense."

"He's not a psychiatrist, too, is he?" Eleanor asked with a slight smile.

"No. He paints. And judging from the one canvas I

saw, he's damned good at it."

"Does he show in galleries up here?"

"He doesn't show anywhere, according to Claudia. His choice."

"Well, I suppose he doesn't need to—" Eleanor cut herself off and Nick noticed immediately that her face was flushed bright pink. It wasn't from the brandy; she was still nursing her first.

"No, he doesn't need to. But how did you know?"

Eleanor swallowed nervously, then said, "You told me earlier, didn't you?"

Nick took a sip of his drink, his eyes on her. "Did I?"

"Yes. Unless it was Claudia. Over the phone. Yes, perhaps I'm mistaken and she mentioned it. Something about the grandeur of his house, I think."

Eleanor had made a slip, and they both knew it. She excused herself on the pretext of changing into more comfortable shoes, and Nick was alone in the den.

He leaned back on the mocha leather sofa and held his brandy snifter up to catch the light's reflection. While the amber liquid swirled and warmed to the touch of his hand against the bottom of the glass, he gazed through the clear upper half of the crystal to the desk on the opposite oak-paneled wall.

Stacks of correspondence lay atop folders. A small portable electronic typewriter sat to the right of the telephone. Alongside the phone were an engagement calendar, a lacquered pencil holder, and two photographs, framed in silver. One was of Claudia, the other of Barton Gage.

Nick took another sip of his brandy and stood. Eleanor returned just then, and he sensed her following him with her eyes as he crossed to the desk and picked up the photograph of Barton.

160

"I hope Imelda cleaned the den before she left for the day," said Eleanor. "I'd hate to think you've found smudges or fingerprints on the frame."

Nick smiled. Eleanor wasn't generally bothered by such things, but that was because she seldom had cause to be. Her apartment was always immaculate.

"Something funny?" she asked.

He nodded. "I was just thinking that habits aren't hereditary. For a moment, I forgot." He looked again at the picture of Barton. "It's easy to forget. Claude reminds me so much of your husband."

"Well," said Eleanor, "I've read that adopted children often grow to favor their adoptive parents. Although I must admit that I don't see a resemblance."

"It's not their features that make me say that. It's more of a certain . . ." He couldn't find the word.

But Eleanor supplied one. "Essence, perhaps?"

He shrugged. "It'll do, I guess."

"I'd agree with you there, Nick. But it's only natural that Claudia took after Barton in a number of ways. She adored him so."

He could hear the emotion in her voice. Eleanor had adored Barton, too. It's unfair, he thought, to open wounds that are still undergoing the healing process. Better to change the subject.

"You asked me about New Orleans," he said, placing the photograph back on the desk and returning to the sofa. "And we were talking of resemblances. That reminds me of the 'interesting' brunch I told you about."

"At the Dantine residence, you said?"

"Yes. And that painting I mentioned. It's a portrait of his wife, Noelle. Amazing how much she looks like Claudia."

Eleanor's face suddenly went ghostly white. She re-

161

covered both her color and composure a moment later and said, "Noelle . . . it's a pretty name."

"But it seems to have upset you," said Nick.

"Not at all. I'm afraid your mention of it coincided with one of my hot flashes. Usually they occur when I'm alone. In company, it's terribly embarrassing."

"Eleanor, I'm also an M.D. There's nothing to be embarrassed about." But he knew—they both knew—that she was in her late fifties—and postmenopausal.

"Noelle . . ." he said, consciously watching for a repeat of Eleanor's reaction.

There was none, but Nick sensed the effort in her calm when she said, "Odd where names come from, isn't it? Unless, of course, they're family names handed down through generations."

She'd unwittingly handed Nick an idea. "Who is Claudia named for?" he asked casually. "Someone on the Davenport side, or one of the Gages?"

"Neither," answered Eleanor. "Claudia was already eighteen months old when she came to us. Her . . . birth mother . . . named her."

Nick and Claudia had once discussed Eleanor's remorse at never having been able to bear a child of her own. Perhaps that accounted now for her obvious reluctance to talk about Claudia's natural mother.

Nonetheless, Nick had to pursue the issue. Eleanor was hiding something, and both his personal and professional curiosity demanded a follow-up.

"Was Claudia born here? In Chicago?" he asked, as though it were a random question brought about by their conversation of names.

"Yes. Why?"

"Just wondering. She and I haven't ever discussed it. Did you and Barton adopt her through a local agency?"

"Of course, Nick. Where else . . .?"

162

"No, I mean . . . well, I'm trying to find a discreet way of asking if you went through regular channels."

"By 'regular,' I take it you mean legal?"

He nodded. "All right, yes . . . I mean legal."

"Nick, I know Barton had powerful connections, but they were in the business world, not the underworld. Not the world of black-market babies, or whatever they're called."

"I didn't mean to imply—"

"Actually, you did. But I don't mind. You're in love with Claudia. It's only natural that you'd want to know everything you can about her. And her . . . background. Especially if the two of you plan to marry and have children of your own. You'd want to be as sure as you can that her birth parents were healthy and, as they say, of sound mind and body."

"How can we ever be sure of that?" he asked. He knew it was one of the reasons why Claudia consistently shied away from talk of marriage and family; it had come up before.

"You can be reasonably certain," said Eleanor. "The information was made available to Barton and me at the time of Claudia's adoption. And of course, Claudia herself is healthy and strong. I really wouldn't worry about it if I were you."

Nick shrugged offhandedly, as though to dismiss the subject.

Eleanor had finished her brandy. Now she stifled a polite yawn. "I'm sorry, Nick. It isn't your company. It's just that I've had a more active day than I'd realized. And," she added with a short laugh, "I'm older than I realized. It's past my bedtime."

Nick nodded and took the hint. "I've had a long day, too," he said, rising from the sofa. "I'll say good night."

163

She walked him to the elevator and kissed him fondly on the cheek. "When you speak with Claudia, be sure to give her my love."

"I will," he promised as the doors closed between them.

On the way to his car, he ruminated over the evening's conversation. It was clear, though he didn't know the reason, that he'd been invited to dinner so Eleanor could pump him. Instead, he'd wound up pumping her.

The next morning as soon as he arrived at the hospital, Nick placed a call to the Cook County Hall of Records. It required his pulling a few strings, dropping the right names, then waiting interminably on hold, but finally the switchboard operator said, "One moment, please, Dr. Seward. I'm going to transfer you to the supervisor in charge of birth records."

The supervisor will probably figure that this shrink needs a shrink, thought Nick.

"It'll take some time with only a first name to go on, Dr. Seward," said the woman. "Why don't you give me your number and I'll get back to you?"

Nick waited hours. Two meetings and four patients later, the supervisor called back.

After he'd hung up, Nick sat back in his chair and closed his eyes to help him concentrate. The information—or lack of it—perplexed him.

Eleanor had told him that Claudia was born in the city. Chicago was part of Cook County.

"The records show that only eight baby girls given the first name of Claudia were born in Cook County on June sixth, 1960," the supervisor had told him. "Each of them was legitimate. Fathers' and mothers' names are listed for each infant."

"Only eight? You're sure?" Nick had asked. "Chicago's a very big city, and Claudia isn't what you'd call an unusual name."

"Dr. Seward, the information is in the computer. In addition, certain names become popular for a time, then fall from vogue. Are you sure you have the right birth date? With adopted children, sometimes the exact date is difficult — or impossible — to track down. Perhaps June sixth is the incorrect date of birth for the Claudia in question."

"Yes . . . sure. Maybe that's it. Thanks for your help."

He sat mulling over the possibility of a mistake. No. A mistake was too easy an answer. There had to be more. Eleanor had lied to him. He had no proof, and he couldn't just pick up the phone and ask her.

But one way or another, he had to find out why.

Chapter 13

Claudia still felt cowardly about not having said good-bye to Armand, but too many questions remained—questions about what Judy called the enigmatic genius, to be sure, but those which Claudia found more unsettling were the questions Armand Dantine had provoked in her about the future. And about the past.

He had begun to write to her for a reason, and whatever that might be, the "Gray Vellum" Claudia and Judy had previously joked about was, in the flesh, intense and not the least bit funny. He knew too much about her. And, although she hadn't mentioned it directly to his face, these were disturbing facts: he had taken the trouble to investigate her past; had learned of her itinerary and followed her; he had even used his son as messenger to lure her to his house.

Why did I go? she wondered. Why was I drawn there? Because of the boy? But Claudia knew herself too well to accept that as truth.

Just as she knew herself too well to believe that the

farewell promise made to Philippe was for the boy alone.

The child had come to the hotel in secret; neither his father nor the woman Sirena must know, he'd told her.

"Sirena might not understand," he said. "And I love her very much."

"She loves you, too," Claudia replied. "That's easy to see in her eyes."

"Yes," he said shyly. "And she loves my father. But he is sometimes unkind to her. It's a strange thing to say, Miss Gage—"

"Claudia," she interrupted.

Philippe blushed and lowered his eyes. The double-thick black lashes swept his cheeks, and Claudia wanted to embrace the child and tell him that the worries and concerns of the adult world need not be his as well. Not yet. Still she felt that the "little man," as she'd heard Sirena call him, was exactly that: no longer a child, but a miniature version of himself ten years ahead of time; for now, protected by his own innocence and only instinctively, intuitively aware of matters that his intellect could not interpret.

"Well, as I was saying . . . Claudia," he continued, "my father can be a difficult person to understand. I suppose it comes from his artistic nature." He looked away; he seemed incapable of lying to Claudia.

When she said nothing, he went on. "Anyway, Sirena is more . . . well, she's a very devoted kind of person."

"She's lucky to have someone as loyal as you for her friend," said Claudia.

"Oh, she's more than that. Sirena's like my mother." This admission seemed to bother him. "What I mean is, even though I don't remember my mother . . . except for her portrait."

"I understand what you mean," said Claudia. "My mother died when I was very small. I don't remember her at all."

"Then who took care of you?" asked Philippe.

Claudia smiled and took his hand. They were seated on the flowered sofa in the living room of Judy's and her suite.

"A wonderful lady named Eleanor Gage. That's why I know how you feel about Sirena. Except that I've always called my adoptive mother Mom, not Eleanor."

He shrugged apologetically. "I'd feel . . . well, not altogether right about calling Sirena that." He thought for a moment. "Besides, my father wouldn't allow it."

No, reasoned Claudia. Not in view of his obsession over the woman in the painting.

And with me, added a silent voice. My resemblance to Noelle Dantine has created a fixation for her husband. That's why I haven't called to say good-bye.

That . . . and something more. . . .

Philippe cut in on her ruminations with the same thought. "Does my father know you're leaving?" Not an accusation, but still . . .

"No, I've been so busy. All those appointments and" — perhaps the boy would carry Claudia's hint home with him — "my boyfriend, Dr. Seward, was here for only two days, so we wanted to spend as much time together as we could — "

"But he has left already, hasn't he?" interjected Philippe.

What else hadn't escaped the "little man"? she wondered.

"Yes, he flew back to Chicago. And I'd best get

packed, or I'll miss my plane."

"But you'll come back, won't you?" He asked it politely, but Claudia saw the pleading in his huge, round eyes.

"Well, someday, I'd like to," she began.

"No, no! I mean soon! As soon as your tour is over! Please, Miss Ga—I mean Claudia—you'll come back, say you will!"

"Philippe," she said slowly, repeating the very words she had spoken to his father a few short nights before on a walk through the Vieux Carré, "my life is in Chicago." Then she added Armand's own phrase. "With Dr. Seward."

In a sudden show of affection—and need—the child turned and threw his arms around Claudia. "Oh, please, promise me you'll come back! Just for a while. Everything has been so much nicer—he's been so much happier since you came to visit!" He realized that he was behaving like a very young child and unlocked his hands from the back of Claudia's neck. He lowered his eyes once more, sheepishly studying his bare knees, and added, "I've been happier, too. At first I thought it was because you look so very much like my mother."

"And you don't think I do anymore?"

"Oh, no, now more than ever!" he cried, frantic that she might misunderstand him. "But I . . . I'm not as confused by it as I was before. I like you very much, Claudia. I'd like for us to be friends. And"—the bashfulness was returning—"friends invite other friends to visit them. Especially when they bring happiness into someone's house the way you do."

If she'd speculated for a moment that his father might have put him up to this, his last remark negated that possibility. More than his words, it was the trusting honesty in the boy's eyes. An openness that she found irresistible. It was clear to Claudia that Philippe was captivated by her.

As she was by him. Partly for his loneliness; partly for the shared loss of their mothers so early in life. But most of all, there was something about the child, something that made Claudia feel as though she knew him. As if she'd known him always.

That was why, while accompanying Philippe down the hall to the elevator, Claudia had agreed to return to New Orleans.

"As soon as your tour is over?" he'd asked, stepping into the cage.

"The very minute," she had answered.

"Say you promise! Then I know you'll come back!"

"I promise."

Then the doors had closed and he was gone.

It is because of the boy, she thought now as her eyelids slowly lowered despite the brightness of the sky outside the porthole window.

It's because of the boy, Claudia repeated silently. One must never break a promise to a child.

Perhaps she'd convinced Judy, who lay napping alongside her.

Now, she thought, all I have to do is convince myself . . .

Somewhere between New Orleans and Mobile, Claudia heard the familiar tune and dreamed her famil-

170

iar dream. It didn't frighten her, but this time the images were interspersed with fragments of the recent past and peopled by faces both known and unknown to her.

While she dozed, the boy Philippe sat holding a small wooden box. When he lifted the lid, it played the little song. Armand entered, and both the boy and the music disappeared. The woman in the painting, Noelle Dantine, stepped out of her picture frame and down from the mantel. Sirena, dressed as a Gypsy and wearing the porcelain rose — Judy's rose — changed places, and costumes, with Noelle.

Now Noelle wore a peasant dress and sandals; Sirena wore the teal-blue gown. And Sirena held the little wooden box. But when she lifted the lid, there was only silence.

Claudia, in her semisleep state, smiled to herself. All that was missing from the dream on this occasion was the presence of Nick. Or Sigmund Freud.

Neither appeared, however, and gradually Claudia opened her eyes and checked her watch. All that psychodrama, she mused, in only fifteen minutes!

She laughed softly under her breath, just as Judy sighed and came awake.

"Ohh, that felt good!" she exclaimed, bringing her seat to an erect position. "I don't know why they call it a cat nap, or forty winks, but I feel completely rested. How 'bout you?"

Claudia nodded. "Me, too. Except for my dream."

"You mean . . . *the* dream? The weird stuff?"

"Yes. But it seems to be getting . . . closer."

"What's getting closer? The why and wherefore, or is the weirdness getting weirder — if there's such a word as weirder?"

171

"Well . . . do you remember that old song called, 'Where or When?' "

"Some lyrics about déjà vu and having been there before. It's an old standard. What's that got to do with your dream? Is that the melody you've been hearing in the background?"

"No," answered Claudia. "I don't know the name or where I've heard it before, but I'm sure it isn't 'Where or When,' because I *am* certain of that song's tune."

"You could hum it for me," said Judy. "You've never tried that. Unless it's something archaic, like opera—"

"No, it's a simple melody set in a waltz tempo." She began to hum, leaning closer to Judy so they wouldn't attract an audience from the rest of the first-class passengers.

"*La*-da-di-*da,*" she hummed, remembering. "La-*da*-da-*da*-di-da."

"Jesus H. Christ!" exclaimed Judy. "Why didn't you ever do that before now?"

"Do what?"

"Sing it for me?"

"Well, because until now the melody wasn't coming through clearly enough—once I woke up, I mean." Then Claudia noticed the excited look on Judy's face.

"What is it? Do you recognize the song?" she asked.

Judy nodded. "I sure do," she said, "and it's giving me the creeps."

"Why? What's the name of it anyway?"

Judy's voice dropped to a whisper. "It's called 'Now Is the Hour.' Ring any bells?"

"You mean . . . ?"

Judy nodded. "That was the message on the note from 'Gray Vellum,' wasn't it?"

Involuntarily, Claudia shuddered. The note that Ar-

172

mand Dantine had sent—or delivered—to the Royal Orleans, the one with the invitation that had summoned her to the house at 1130 Royal Street, had ended with the name of the song.

"It could be coincidence," said Claudia.

"You're as certain as I am that there's no such creature as coincidence on this planet," said Judy. She glanced up in search of the flight attendant. "Now I could use a cup of coffee, even if it is that watery stuff they serve up here."

Claudia laughed, trying to shake off a sudden apprehension brought on by Judy's identification of the melody in her dream.

When they'd both been served coffee—tepid, in addition to being weak—Judy said, "Well, even if it leaves a lot of unanswered questions, at least the whole matter is over and done with."

"What is?"

"New Orleans. 'Gray Vellum.' 'Now Is the Hour.' Unless he's wacky—or sick—and decides to follow you to Mobile and God-knows-where-else."

"Judy . . ."

"Hmm?"

"I'm going back to New Orleans."

"You're . . . what?"

"Oh, not till week after next. Once the tour is over."

"You're kidding. Tell me you're kidding."

"I'm serious."

"I think I'd better call your shrink in Chicago. Why on earth would you go back to New Orleans—and don't tell me to listen to jazz, because we've got that at home. It must be for the Cajun food." To herself, but aloud, Judy said, "Yes, that's it. Claudia Gage will return to New Orleans for a bowl of shrimp gumbo. It

173

has nothing to do with a gorgeous, lunatic painter who lives on Royal Street . . ."

"Judy . . . I promised his son."

"You promised his son," parroted Judy. "So for the kid's sake, you're willing to open Pandora's box."

"Children live in a state of trust and expectancy— unless someone betrays that trust."

"You're starting to sound like a shrink, Claudia. All kids think they're the center of the universe. So does Sirena-with-an-i's 'little man,' no matter how grown-up he seems. So it's time for him to wake up and realize that the world doesn't revolve around him. Maybe his father should learn the same lesson."

"That's not it, Judy."

"Claudia, you once said to me that kids—and I mean younger ones than Philippe—live in an almost psychotic state. Well, I don't have to be a shrink—or living with one—to know that an adult with the same infantile tendencies can be as hazardous to your health as smoking. And, while I hate to say it, I get the feeling it's a case of like father, like son."

"Judy, I promised Philippe. It can be for just a day, but I'm not going to break my word."

Judy was studying Claudia's face. "You're really stuck on this kid, aren't you? I mean, I've seen you around other children, and you're terrific with them, but with this one it's almost maternal."

Claudia couldn't deny it. She was surprised only that her feelings about the child were so easy to read. She wished that her unresolved feelings concerning his father were as simple to interpret.

And not so easy to read . . .

* * *

174

Judy had asked no subsequent questions about Armand for the remainder of the flight, but Claudia sensed that her publicist was refraining from doing so because of their friendship; Judy clearly didn't believe for a moment that Claudia's promise to Philippe was the single reason for her planning to return to New Orleans at the end of the tour.

By the time they checked into their suite at the hotel in Mobile, they were tired once more; their naps aboard the plane seemed to have been nonexistent. Judy flopped down on one of the king-size beds, and Claudia dropped onto the other. They were both beginning to doze.

And the telephone rang.

"It'll be Nick in Chicago," said Judy, not opening her eyes or reaching over for the phone.

"No, it'll be Frank calling you from the bar," said Claudia. She was also too exhausted to move.

"Wanna flip for it?" asked Judy, still not budging.

"That means one of us has to get up for the coin," answered Claudia.

"C'mon, that's five rings. One of them will think we're in bed with the bellhops."

That made Claudia laugh, and the laughter brought her fully awake. "All right," she said, reaching over for the phone.

Armand's voice erased the playfulness in hers.

"You didn't tell me you were leaving. I had to learn it from the hotel when I called."

Obviously Philippe hadn't told his father that he'd gone to see Claudia.

"I felt that was wiser," she said.

Judy heard the tone in her friend's voice and sat up on the bed.

175

"Claudia," he said sternly, "I've tried to assure you that I have no desire to harm you. You must believe me when I say this. If I were to do anything against your wishes, to offend you in any way, it would be no different than if I were to offend myself. But"—now his voice became softer, coaxing—"I must see you again. You must come back."

"Now is the hour . . . ?" she said, her throat parched and tight.

"Or when your tour is finished," he said, making not the slightest reference to the song's title or to the fact that he'd used it in one of his notes to her.

She had wondered how to visit Philippe without his father's knowing that the boy had come to see her. She'd considered registering at the hotel and trying to phone him at the house, all the while feeling ridiculously like a woman arranging a tryst with her clandestine lover.

"I may be stopping in New Orleans on my way home," she said as casually as he'd just spoken. "For a day or two only. Perhaps you and Philippe and I could meet for lunch."

She'd expected him to balk at the suggestion that he bring his son, but Armand Dantine never seemed to suffer a lack of surprise.

"Philippe will be ecstatic when I tell him," said Armand. "My son adores you, you know."

"I don't think that's particularly healthy for your son," she said pointedly.

"Why not let his father be the judge of all such matters?" he answered.

Then, before she could reply, he added, "I must go for now. When shall we expect you?"

"I'm not sure yet. My itinerary is subject to . . .

change."

"I hope you will not allow that. My son would be heartbroken."

Claudia was tempted to ask if Sirena would join them for lunch, but thought better of it. Perhaps if she treated Armand—and whatever relationship he shared with the mulatto woman and his son—in an impersonal, casual manner, he would "receive" the message.

The only problem was that Claudia wasn't sure what message she wanted to send.

Chapter 14

Claudia and Judy found San Francisco mercifully cool after the debilitating heat wave they'd left behind in the South and the East.

Two messages, both from Frank in New Orleans, were waiting for them when the women checked into the hotel. "Ah," sighed Judy. "My bartender beau of Bourbon Street." She placed a call to him as soon as they were ensconced in the elegantly appointed presidential suite.

While Judy dialed the long-distance operator, Claudia unpacked . . . again. She was glad the tour was almost at an end. The perpetual packing and unpacking had grown wearisome; despite the enjoyment of travel, this trip had made her realize that living out of a suitcase was not the life for Claudia Gage. She longed to spend some time in one place. Home.

She bent over to arrange her lingerie in the dresser and envisioned Philippe's sweet face staring up at her. He was standing in the drawing room just beneath the painting of Noelle.

The image disturbed her. Home. That meant Chicago. Nick, and Eleanor. Not Philippe . . . not Armand.

After the phone call to Frank, the silence in the room was broken by the sound of Claudia's shower running at full force. Judy checked the cabinets in the dining alcove and, finding no bar, placed a drink order with room service. Then she kicked off her pumps and flopped on the sofa to relax.

The knock at the door wasn't the arrival of drinks, however. A bellhop stood holding a ceramic vase overflowing with magnolia blossoms.

"Just put them on the coffee table," said Judy, going to her purse for a tip. These welcoming bouquets from the radio and TV stations are enough to put me into bankruptcy, she mused, taking out a five-dollar bill. It never seemed to fail. When she had a wallet full of singles, no flowers arrived. But a five spot meant another delivery from the florist. She'd already tipped five for the roses. They were "compliments from the hotel"; how could she ask for change?

What about these sickeningly sweet-smelling magnolias? she wondered, turning up her nose at their perfume. Who had sent them?

A small card protruded slightly from its envelope, and Judy's customary curiosity prompted her, as soon as the bellhop was gone, to read it and find out who had cost her this five.

Come home to us was all it said. Instead of a signature, the card bore an initial: the letter *A*.

* * *

Claudia emerged from the bedroom wearing a purple-and-black polka-dot silk shirtwaist dress. She carried a matching purple silk jacket with black jet beads sewn along the gently padded shoulders.

"You look fabulous," Judy observed. "I ordered up drinks." She gestured toward the tray, which the waiter had placed beside the magnolias.

"Thanks. I'm thirsty." Claudia took her glass, and in doing so, her nostrils filled with the strong scent of the flowers. She experienced the same sensation as she had upon smelling them in New Orleans: a mixture of sadness and nostalgia, and a sudden, brief twinge of . . . of what? She couldn't identify the feeling with so much as a word.

Claudia immediately noticed the card. With a quick glance toward Judy, she picked it up and read it.

Judy speculated on the reaction; however, her friend's expression was indiscernible. Claudia dropped the card back onto the table and, taking a sip of her drink, said, "I'm going out for a while. To the bay." She took another long swallow of her drink, then set her glass on the tray and headed toward the door.

"Claudia . . . ?"

Claudia's hand was on the knob. She looked back at Judy, who was curled up on the enormous, cushiony sofa.

"Yes?"

Her friend paused, then said slowly, "I wish I'd never scheduled New Orleans as one of the stops on the tour. I wanted you to know that."

"I don't think that would have mattered, Judy. Something tells me I'd have ended up going there eventually, anyway." She dropped the room key into her purse. "I'll see you later."

The door closed and Judy was alone. She glanced at the bouquet and was taken by a sudden urge to heave the vase across the room. These goddamn magnolias! she thought. I ought to throw them out!

She was saved from temptation by the telephone. Judy rose from the sofa and went to the small table next to the dining alcove.

"Hello?" she said into the receiver.

"Claudia, darling, is that you? It's a terrible connection."

"Eleanor? I can hardly hear you—this is Judy! How are you?"

"I'm fine, dear. What about you?"

"Okay, thanks!" Judy almost yelled. "You just missed Claudia—she's gone out. She'll be gone for"—Judy checked her watch—"about an hour. I'll have her call you when she gets back!"

As the interference on the line subsided, Eleanor said, "Actually, that won't be necessary, dear. I really wanted to talk with you."

Upon Claudia's return to the hotel that evening, Judy related part of Eleanor's telephone conversation. "She asked me about New Orleans—mainly about . . . him. She didn't have to say his name."

Eleanor's reference to Armand struck Claudia as strange. But even stranger was that Eleanor had told Judy of her late husband's aversion to the city. Barton had regaled Claudia with stories and anecdotes about his travels. But never once had he mentioned New Orleans—or that he had ever visited there.

Claudia's dream had begun appearing nightly. The elusive melody that accompanied each recurrence, now that the title was identified, took on new importance. Only Armand Dantine might be able to explain the meaning behind the words.

The final leg of the book tour was serving merely to postpone Claudia's decision, although she already knew what that decision would be, what it had to be. Some matters, she reasoned, offered no choice.

Two more days passed. The last book-signing had occupied the previous afternoon; the final interview, that night. Claudia and Judy had awakened at dawn to finish packing. Then they'd said good-bye, and Judy was on her way.

To Chicago. Where I should probably be headed, too, Claudia mused.

But she had chosen instead to stroll the steep hills of the city, and now she was back at her favorite spot on the bay.

Claudia checked her wristwatch. It was almost one. She hadn't realized it, but she'd been walking for hours. No wonder she was exhausted.

Still, she wasn't ready to return to the hotel. That meant telephoning Nick, who would expect her to arrive with Judy. How much longer could she put off the call?

She looked down at her watch again. My God, she thought, it's nearly three o'clock in Chicago. Judy's already there.

And Claudia's own flight to New Orleans was scheduled to depart in two hours. There were no more excuses, no new ways to stall. It was time either to go—or not to go. And how could she not?

Judy absently overtipped the driver and was out of the limo before he could come around to open the rear passenger door for her.

She looked up at the building that housed her apartment in Old Town. Judy liked the 1880s style of most of the dwellings on her street, although whenever returning from a trip, she was sorry not to have opted for a glass high-rise on the lake—with a doorman to help with her luggage.

Marty, the super, came out of the basement apartment just as she was trying to juggle three suitcases with only two arms.

"Can I give you a hand, Miss Fargo?" he called.

"More than one, Marty—thanks!" He took two of the bags while Judy readjusted her grip on the small beauty case that was perilously close to falling.

She was on the top step of the entrance when she remembered. "Marty! There's a fold-over in the trunk—can you manage that for me, too?"

"Sure!" He ran to the limo, and Judy pushed open the door to the foyer.

Her mailbox in the vestibule was crammed full of junk mail. At least it's nothing written on gray vellum, she mused. That made her think of Claudia, and New Orleans. The book tour might be over, but until her friend was home, it wouldn't be ended.

As she entered the elevator and pressed the top button, the phrase "business as usual" ran through her mind. This trip had been anything but.

The small cubicle opened into her foyer and Judy turned the key in the lock. She'd seldom been this happy—or if not happy, then relieved—to be home.

She peeled off her creased red silk jacket, kicked off her matching red sandals, and flopped down on the sofa. She wiggled her toes, whose nails matched those of her fingers, and sighed.

Then she looked at her watch. Claudia should be boarding her flight about now. There was no way to call her, yet Judy was seized by a sudden need to make contact.

Well, she thought, trying to quell her own misgivings, Claudia has said—on more thán one occasion—that she's a "big girl."

Sure. But the big girl would be alone . . . there.

She considered calling Claudia's editor at McClintock Publishing, on the pretext of reporting on the tour, checking up on sales . . .

No. Too transparent.

What about phoning Josh at the *Examiner?* Just to see how the column was doing with Claudia out of town? She dismissed that, too. Josh would say, in his inimitable style, that the column was in lousy shape—and why wasn't Claudia back and asking him herself?

Then I'd have to explain. And what the hell would I say?

She waited till Marty had brought up the rest of her luggage. Then she stretched out on the sofa in her office off the living room and closed her eyes. New Orleans, Armand Dantine, and Claudia had given her a headache, not unlike some kind of emotional hangover.

That brought Frank center stage in her mind. She couldn't call him at the bar; he'd be too busy to talk.

Later, at his apartment. She could ask him to look in on Claudia.

Claudia again! Judy's conversation with Eleanor still bothered her. Something about it had put her off.

On an impulse, she got up and rummaged through her purse for her personal phone book. She scanned the two pages of *S*'s until she found Seward. Then she touch-toned Nick's number at the hospital.

"Just a moment, please," said the switchboard operator. Judy was put on hold, and instantly the Muzak of cascading voices and a hundred strings filled her ear with its lulling melody. A shiver passed through her when she recognized the refrain. It was anything but lulling; it was "Now Is the Hour."

The music was cut off abruptly by Nick's voice.

"Judy! Where are you?"

"In Chicago. At my apartment."

"Is Claudia there with you? Put her on."

Immediately, Judy regretted having made the call. Of course he'd ask for Claudia—they'd been expected on the same plane.

"Uh . . . she's not here, Nick . . . Hasn't she called you?"

"Not since yesterday afternoon. Did she go directly to our place?"

"Uh, she's . . . still in San Francisco." The clock on the desk confirmed it. Claudia's flight might have boarded by now, but it wasn't scheduled to leave for at least another quarter hour.

"A last-minute interview, huh?" Nick said with a laugh. "Well, I guess if it helps sell the book, I can wait a little longer. Maybe I'll call her at the hotel. Listen, Claudia didn't say much about it yesterday. How

185

did everything go?"

"I'm not too sure. From the book's standpoint, it was perfect . . ."

"And otherwise?"

Judy paused. Then she answered, "Nick, that's why I'm calling. Something's bothering me."

"Let me guess," he said. "Armand Dantine?"

"Well, that's part of it," Judy admitted. "Specifically, it's Claudia's mother, though, who's been on my mind."

"You and me both. How so with you?"

Judy related the crux of her long-distance conversation with Eleanor, adding at the end, "And Nick, she was glad that I'd answered the phone. I got the feeling . . . well, that she was pumping me. For information."

"About Dantine?"

"Exactly, but there was more to it than that, somehow. I mean, If this guy is just a stranger — or a fan — then why should Eleanor be so worried?"

"I don't know, Judy," said Nick. "I got the same feeling from her." He told Judy about his dinner with Eleanor Gage.

"And was she curious about this Noelle person with you, too?"

"Yes. What do you think is going on, Judy? You've spent more time down there with this gang than I have."

"Nick . . . I don't know. Claudia's been having that dream — the same one every night. And that song she hears in it? The words in the title are the same words Dantine wrote in a note he sent her."

He was listening quietly.

"And, Nick," Judy went on, "there's one more thing. While I was talking to Eleanor, she made a slip."

"What kind of slip?"

"Well, she referred to Noelle Dantine as . . . Genevieve."

"Genevieve? Who the hell is *that?*"

"Damned if I know, Nick. Eleanor tried to pass it off by saying she'd gotten the French names mixed up. But I don't think it was that at all."

Nick nodded to himself. Finally he asked, "What did Claudia make of all this?"

"I . . . I didn't tell her everything Eleanor said. She's already confused, Nick."

"No wonder. Look, Judy, I appreciate your concern, and I'm glad you called me about it. When Claudia gets home tonight—"

"Nick," Judy said cautiously, "she won't be getting home tonight . . ."

Chapter 15

What the hell is happening? Nick asked himself. He was pacing in front of the bank of elevators. His watch and the overhead clock both read 3:30 P.M. His workday was almost over, still, it would be easier not to bump into any of the other members of the hospital staff. He hadn't missed the expression on Margaret's face when he'd told his secretary he was leaving for the day. Nick hoped this whole business with Armand Dantine would be cleared up before his colleagues began to notice how much time he was taking away from his work.

At last the elevator arrived. He was relieved to find it empty. No need to invent excuses or polite chitchat. He pushed the button marked Garage and leaned back against the chrome paneling.

His talk with Judy had been edifying, if annoying. That annoyance had been compounded by Claudia's call only moments after Judy's.

"I'm at the airport," she'd said. "My flight leaves in a

few minutes."

Nick had decided to make no mention of his conversation with Judy. "So that should get you to the apartment well before eight."

"I doubt it. I have to make a stopover."

"Oh? Where?"

"New Orleans." She'd said it with trepidation.

And Nick had heard it in her voice.

"Claudia, the flight from San Francisco doesn't make a stopover in New Orleans."

There'd been silence at her end of the line. For a moment he'd thought they'd been cut off. Then, speaking in a soft, deflated tone, she'd said, "I know. Nick . . . I've got to go back."

"Why, Claudia?"

"Because I . . . I promised Philippe—the little boy. You remember him, don't you?"

"Yes. I remember."

"It's just for a day or two. I . . . I can't explain, Nick. Believe me. I wish I could."

He didn't want to say it, but it came out nonetheless. "His father . . . Dantine . . . holds no interest for you at all?"

"Oh, Nick . . . my darling! There's—how can I say it?—something of me is there, Nick. I . . . I have to go back."

"Claudia, I'm being as patient as I can. But how do you expect me to react to this?"

"As my friend."

"I'm more than your friend."

She paused. "Then as a doctor. I think maybe you can help me that way, too."

"You're saying you need a shrink—not a lover?"

189

"I need you as both, and—" Her voice was interrupted by the amplified voice of a woman in the background. "Nick," said Claudia more loudly, "they're announcing my flight."

"Claudia, wait! Don't do this! Come back!"

"Nick, I can't! Please—this is so difficult!" She sounded as if she was fighting tears. "I'll be at the Royal Orleans again. Good-bye, darling!"

"Claudia—!"

"I've got to go!"

And she hung up.

The elevator doors opened onto the garage level. Nick dug into his jacket pocket and found the keys. The Jaguar was parked directly ahead of him.

A blast of heat from inside the car hit him as he climbed behind the wheel. Nick slid out of his jacket and tossed it onto the backseat. Then he started the ignition and waited for the air-conditioning to cool him off. In more ways than one, he mused.

He turned on the portable CD player. A little Mozart might help.

It did. After several minutes he was cooler. Calmer. He pulled the car out of the garage and headed north toward Lake Shore Drive, where he hoped to find some answers.

Eleanor Gage sat alone in her formal salon. She had spent little time in this room since her husband's death. The exquisite surroundings had previously given her pleasure; now, instead, the grandeur seemed too vast. In the months following Barton's passing she had come to feel that her own being was of an insufficient size to adequately fill the space.

It wasn't as though she was overpowered by the money that had provided the furnishings; she had always been accustomed to wealth and position. Perhaps, then, it was the absence of Barton's personality which, now missing, reminded Eleanor that she was left to carry on. To control alone what they had controlled together.

However, the only control she cared to exercise was the kind that could help those close to her.

But was there anything she could do—some way in which she might influence the outcome of an impossible situation? Boundaries had been crossed, overstepped.

Eleanor, seated in a reclining position on the gray satin chaise, suddenly realized that she had begun twirling the large diamond on her left hand. It was a habit Barton had often found amusing.

Thankfully he's been spared the indignity of this . . . this outrage, she thought, closing her eyes and letting the tension ebb away. She tried to put herself in Barton's mind. He would have known how to handle the matter. He'd known once before. Together they had seen it through to the end.

Wait, she told herself, sitting upright as the spark of an idea took hold. That's exactly what Barton would do now—put an end to it.

Because, of course, this must be stopped.

Eleanor rose from the chaise, her energies newly revived. The contracts were old. Revised, once, and marked Confidential. They would be kept under lock and key, which meant one of three places: in the bank vault downtown, or in Fenwick's safe at the firm.

Or in Barton's wall safe.

Eleanor slid her stocking feet into the satin mules on the floor and made her way down the hall to Barton's office.

Yes. She was certain. The papers would be here.

She opened the door and, even this late in the day, Eleanor had to shield her eyes from the glare of bright sunlight streaming through the sheer window draperies. The colors of the Persian carpeting were vivid jewel tones against the sheen of the polished parquet floors. Eleanor made a mental note to thank Imelda for keeping the office so neat and clean; she herself hadn't been inside the room for the past several months.

Many years before, Eleanor had transformed the large alcove off the master bedroom into her own office. With louvers serving as doors that permitted privacy while at the same time allowing sound to travel through to her, she had been able to arrange her charity work and social calendar and still keep an ear on the then-small Claudia.

Months ago, she'd briefly considered moving the filing cabinet and desk to her late husband's office. But now, standing on the threshold of Barton's library/ study, Eleanor understood why she preferred her bou- doir/office. This room, furnished in dark, heavy woods, solid brass lamps, and black leather upholstery, bore the unmistakable stamp of Barton Gage. It had been his domain, and so it would stay.

And Eleanor sorely missed him.

She shook her head, as if the physical action would dislodge any distracting sentiment or emotion from her task. She closed the door with a movement of her left shoulder, and crossed the room.

On the wall beside a large, beveled antique mirror was a small painting of a little girl. It hung inconspicuously in its plain wooden frame, and Eleanor remembered with a smile the steep price at which her husband had acquired the portrait and the quiet pride with which he then displayed it.

"It's not because it's a Renoir," he'd confided in an effort to explain the purchase of so small an item at so high a cost. "It's because the child looks so much like our Claudia."

He hadn't needed to justify the acquisition to his wife; the painting had remained their favorite. Still, he had kept it in his office; Barton had always disliked ostentation, and using Claudia as an excuse for displaying a Renoir would have struck him as precisely that.

On the opposite, facing wall, larger but still of modest proportion, was the Van Gogh. That brought a broader smile to Eleanor's lips. Barton's wealth had accumulated over the years, yet not to the extent that a genuine Van Gogh was affordable. Which was why he'd bought this excellent copy from a renowned art forger on Ibiza. The larcenous aspect, Eleanor recalled, had intrigued them both.

And now, as she stood before "Sunflowers," her hand reached out and tripped the latch behind the bottom right corner of the frame.

The fake Van Gogh swung aside on noiseless hinges to expose the wall safe.

Eleanor hadn't anticipated so many memories to come rushing at her, but they flooded her now—thoughts of those weeks on Ibiza following the heart-breaking news that she was sterile, and just preceding the joyous time when their adopted daughter came to them . . .

Even recalling the combination to the safe caused an aching nostalgia. Barton had devised it so they could both easily remember the numbers: *C,* the third letter, for *Claudia; I,* the ninth letter, for *Is; O,* the fifteenth letter, for *Our;* and fifteen again, for *Own.* Left three, right nine, left fifteen, and right fifteen.

Claudia Is Our Own.

The combination clicked and the safe opened. One by one, slowly but with her pulse quickening, Eleanor leafed through the yellowing documents. Finally she found the large manila envelope marked Fournier. The logo in the upper left-hand corner was another reminder of the time that had passed.

So many years ago, she reflected. Appleton, Finney, Fenwick, and Noyes. All gone, except for Raymond Fenwick, who now headed the firm.

Eleanor closed the safe and swung the Van Gogh back into its place. She took the envelope over to the inlaid rosewood desk and sat down to study the contract and papers pertaining to the . . . situation.

Barton had once remarked that the way to reach an adversary was through his wallet. Eleanor hoped to find the means to end the matter of New Orleans inside the envelope. For good.

As her manicured hands pulled back the butterfly clip on the flap, the lobby intercom buzzer sounded.

"Damn!" she said under her breath. It was Imelda's day off and she hadn't told the doorman to tell all callers she was out. She hadn't expected that to be necessary.

Still holding the envelope, she went to the intercom in the entrance foyer.

"Yes, Warren?" she asked into the speaker.

"Dr. Seward to see you, Mrs. Gage."

"Dr. Seward? Here? Now?"

"Yes, Mrs. Gage."

Well, she thought, the doctor must be psychic, too. "All right, Warren. Please tell him to come up."

She slammed the receiver back on its hook and quickly retraced her steps down the hall, heading back toward Barton's office.

The telephone rang.

Talk about timing, she said to herself. She went to the nearest extension on a three-legged table just off the dining room.

"Yes, hello!" she answered, hoping it would be a wrong number.

Nick pushed the doorbell for the second time. From inside he heard, "Just a moment — I'm coming!"

After a minute or so, the door opened. Eleanor stood there, elegant as always in an aqua-colored silk jacquard blouse and matching hostess pants. But Nick could see that her eyes looked tired. Also that she was holding a large manila envelope in one hand, her reading glasses in the other.

"I'm sorry, Nick. I've been working on . . . some legal matters. Then the telephone rang, and—"

"That's okay. May I come in?"

"Well, I'm in the middle of . . . something. But if it's important . . ."

The habitually unflappable Eleanor Gage, Nick

noted, was flustered.

"It won't take more than a minute," he said.

With the back of her hand, Eleanor brushed a stray wisp of blond hair behind her ear. "Come in, then." She stepped aside to let him pass.

After she closed the door, Nick waited for her to lead him down the hall into the drawing room. But it soon became obvious that no such invitation would be extended today. He'd purposely not called—he'd wanted to surprise her—but as a result, Eleanor remained in the expansive foyer; she was making it clear that Nick's move was next.

"Eleanor," he began, "I don't want you to think I'm prying, but . . . well, the fact is, I feel I have a right to know what's going on."

"Going on?" she repeated. "What do you mean?"

"Claudia's gone back to New Orleans."

He watched for her reaction, which was evident without any close scrutiny. He saw her color drain away, and then she averted her eyes, trying to cover the moment by arranging her reading glasses across her head as though it were a ribbon or a hairband.

"She can't," he heard her say in a half-whisper. "She mustn't."

"She already has."

Nick related what Judy Fargo had told him, while omitting Judy's voiced suspicions about Eleanor. ". . . And we—Judy and I—thought you might be able to shed some light on all of this."

"I might? How?"

"Well, for one, you could tell me who Geneviève is."

Eleanor stretched an arm to lean against the door, and as she did so, the manila envelope slid from her hand and fell to the floor. Simultaneously, she and Nick knelt to retrieve it.

Nick reached it first, and Eleanor snatched it from him with an uncharacteristic yank.

"Excuse me," she offered. "I'm somewhat upset by all these questions."

"Apparently. Eleanor, who is this Geneviève?"

"I . . . I don't know. I mean, I suppose Judy mentioned the name to you. But it just came to mind. I had intended to say Noelle, and . . ."

"All right, then, who is—or was—Noelle?"

"Why, Nick, you told me that . . ."

"Eleanor, please!"

He could see that her hands were trembling, as was her lower lip when she answered, "Nick, I can't begin to explain any of this. I'm not even certain about all of it myself. But it must be stopped. And it will be. I'm going to see to that personally."

"How can you? Eleanor, I love Claudia. Tell me."

"I've already said I can't. But if you'll trust me . . . give me some time I think there may be a way . . . legally . . . through all of this."

"Your family connections again?"

She snapped her head in his direction. Glaring at him, she asked, "I beg your pardon?"

"You needn't beg. You've got it . . . and my apologies. I just don't want any more help coming my way via your social clout, if you'll forgive my bluntness."

Nick thought she understood him.

She had. That was immediately confirmed by her reply. "You didn't say no to the appointment at the hospital, did you, Nick?"

He opened the door and, turning back to her, said,

"I've had this conversation once before. Good evening, Eleanor."

She's told me more than she thinks, Nick reflected on his way to the car.

The envelope she'd dropped—and that he'd picked up—had offered information, too. The name of the firm was different now. Raymond Fenwick was the only surviving member of the original partnership. But all of the lawyers had been living when Eleanor's manila envelope was printed. And big-time law firms didn't use old stationery. When the firm name changed, so did the paper their legal work was printed on.

But what of the name he'd seen written in longhand across the front of the envelope?

I'll ask Ray Fenwick about that, too, he decided.

Claudia was too exhausted. She wanted only to sleep. But sleep would mean the dream again.

And the melody.

She lay down on the bed in her room at the Royal Orleans. It wasn't late, but she didn't want to call or speak with anyone tonight. Tomorrow was soon enough. She'd feel stronger, then.

In the meantime, maybe a light dinner and some wine would do. She picked up the phone and dialed room service.

At the same moment in Chicago, Nick was calling his secretary at her home.

198

"Margaret," he said when she answered, "something urgent has come up. I'll have to cancel all my appointments for tomorrow. I won't be in the office."

He didn't tell her where he would be. But he'd already made the arrangements with his travel agent. The earliest flight to New Orleans was in the morning. And Nick had booked a seat.

Chapter 16

Claudia hesitated before the door at 1130 Royal Street. The heady perfume of magnolia blossoms had followed her, intoxicated her, all the way from the hotel. This wasn't the first time she had entertained second thoughts about her decision to return. Before, however, they had been confined to her mind.

Now she was here. How could she turn back?

As if in reply to her unvoiced question, an old woman called through the gate, "You gotta ring the bell more'n once, miss, in case they be out in the courtyard." The woman waited, urging Claudia. "Go on, they be home. I seen the boy not more'n two hours ago."

At mention of Philippe, Claudia's index finger inadvertently pressed the black button. She heard several chimes ring inside.

Claudia turned her head toward the gate, but the old woman was gone.

She heard a creaking of hinges, and the massive door

opened.

Sirena stood facing Claudia. Each seemed surprised to see the other.

The dark woman spoke first, her words almost in a tone of challenge. "Mr. Dantine is paintin' in his studio. Always does at this time o' day. He doesn't like to be disturbed."

"I wouldn't dream of interrupting his work." Then, pointedly, Claudia said, "I've come to see his son."

"Oh?"

"Yes. I promised I'd stop by on my way back to Chicago."

"Hmm . . ." Sirena seemed puzzled as well as displeased at Claudia's return.

Perhaps she doesn't believe I'm here to see the boy, she reasoned. *But it's too hot for games. Let's try it again.* "Is Philippe at home?" she asked aloud.

Sirena nodded, still staring at Claudia as though she were seeing an apparition.

Perspiration was making even the spaghetti straps of Claudia's white cotton piqué sundress feel heavy on her shoulders. The sun was beating down and giving her a headache.

"Would you mind if I come in?" she finally asked outright. "I'm not accustomed to such heat, even with the intense summers we have in Chicago."

Sirena didn't reply at first. She stepped aside and allowed Philippe's guest to enter. The cool, dark hall made Claudia sigh with relief.

"Sun gets awful hot this time o' year," Sirena said at last. "Can make a body sick, especially glarin' down on your head all day. You need to be wearin' that hat o' yours."

201

"My hat?" asked Claudia, trying to understand. She seldom wore hats.

Then she remembered. "Oh, you mean the one I wore on my first visit here. You have a remarkable memory—I'd forgotten all about it."

"Your friend borrowed the hat when y'all came to brunch," said Sirena matter-of-factly, leading Claudia down the hall toward the parlor.

"You're almost right, except that my friend didn't borrow it."

Sirena stopped cold. "What d'you mean she didn't borrow it?"

Claudia heard the woman's question, but she was trying to answer one of her own: Why take an accusing tone at the mention of a borrowed hat?

"I was askin' you—"

"And I was telling you," Claudia interrupted, "that Miss Fargo didn't borrow my hat. I borrowed it from her." She was tempted to repeat the phrase; the expression on Sirena's face made her look as though she were lost in a trance.

But Sirena had heard Claudia. And now, as the words sank in, so, too, did their significance.

No wonder the Gage woman has come back! The porcelain rose pin belongs to someone else! It isn't that the magic holds no power—I made a mistake!

A bad mistake, she mused. I asked that the owner of the pin be removed from my life—from our lives. And I got exactly that—not what I wanted, but what I asked for! Judy Fargo—the pin's owner—is gone.

But what about the handkerchief? Does that belong to the Fargo woman, too? Is that why Claudia Gage is here now? She claims it's to see the boy, but just supposin' . . .

Just supposin' that's not true. A surge of anger began rising inside her as a silent voice suggested, What if the Gage woman has come for the boy's father?

Claudia was pacing slowly as she waited in the parlor. Sirena had promised to send Philippe downstairs as soon as he was "all cleaned up for company." She'd brought a tray of drinks and behaved civilly enough after her initial greeting at the door. Still, there was something about the woman's manner, a kind of looking-through, rather than looking-at, that disturbed Claudia and made her feel unwelcome.

And there's more, she thought. Something about this house. She glanced up at the portrait of Noelle Dantine; it was difficult to be in this room and not be drawn to the painting. Or to the woman; she wasn't sure which.

Examining the room's surroundings now with a better-acquainted eye, she was surprised that Armand Dantine was not in the habit of entertaining. The house appeared to have been built for parties, with its high ceilings and polished floors. There's probably even a ballroom on the premises, she thought, looking up and in that moment meeting Noelle's eyes.

"Perhaps things were different when you were alive," Claudia said aloud to the portrait. The woman on canvas had been painted in a gown clearly designed for dancing.

I wonder what's in that little wooden box in her

hand, Claudia mused, suddenly aware that she'd been unconsciously searching the room for just such an object while pacing back and forth.

But no little wooden box was to be found, and so Claudia poured herself a glass of iced tea, added a sprig of mint, and sat down to await Philippe.

Sirena paused to listen outside the bathroom door. The water was running in the shower, but the stream was steady, uninterrupted; that meant Armand hadn't stepped into the tub yet.

Several minutes passed, and for a moment she feared that he might open the door and catch her with her ear against it. Still, she didn't move, and at last she heard the metal rings of the curtain sliding across the shower rod. Then the water's direction changed audibly and Sirena knew that it was safe to continue on what she perceived as her mission.

She tiptoed into the master bedroom — not because Armand was likely to hear her, but because the boy, Philippe, was playing in his room and she wasn't ready to inform him of his guest's arrival. Quickly Sirena went to Armand's tan linen trousers. He'd emptied the pockets. Her eyes darted to the dresser. Yes. He'd deposited everything there.

She glanced over her shoulder at the sound of a floorboard creaking, then realized it had come from her own footsteps; fear was distorting her senses. No time to waste. Just do it and be done with it!

Almost silently Sirena removed the longest key from the gold ring on the dresser. Then she hurried out of the bedroom and down the stairs. From there she made her way past the parlor—she smiled at having remembered to close the doors; Claudia wouldn't hear or see a thing—and out back toward the little shack that had housed slaves more than a century before.

She had reached such a state that she almost fumbled the key in the lock. But it turned and she heard the click that told her the door was open. Accessible.

Then she retraced her steps, scurried down the hall and up the stairs once more, and, breathless from her task, returned the key to its chain just as the shower stopped.

Her heartbeat almost stopped with it. What would she say if he caught her? What would he do?

Taking off her sandals, Sirena backed away from the dresser. Her eyes never left the bathroom door as, barefoot, she slipped silently from the room.

Claudia glanced at her watch. Ten minutes had passed. How long could it take for a child to "get all cleaned up for company?"

Her question was answered then as the parlor doors opened and Philippe cried, "Claudia! You're here! Oh, I'm so glad!"

She held her arms out to him and he raced into her embrace. His little heart was thrumming.

"I was so afraid you wouldn't come back!" he said excitedly.

"I promised that I would," she replied, caressing the sides of his face.

"Yes," he said, "but sometimes promises get broken, or can't be kept." His eyes moved inadvertently to the portrait over the mantel, and Claudia wondered if

Noelle had once promised never to go away. How old was Philippe when she died? Claudia couldn't remember whether Armand or the boy had told her.

"Well," she said, "I've kept mine, and I've brought you presents." She broke their embrace and reached over to her tote bag, which was leaning against one of the sofa cushions. Her fingers felt around the bottom of the purse until they found two small packages, each wrapped in gift paper. She produced them one at a time.

"This is just for fun," she said, handing Philippe the first box.

"What's inside?" he asked, suddenly behaving like the young child he was.

"Just a souvenir from one of the cities I visited. Go ahead, open it."

He tore off the wrapping with relish. "It's beautiful," he said, his eyes widening with curiosity. "But what is it?" He tipped it upside down, but nothing moved.

"Well, you can use it as a paperweight, but it's actually a model of the Space Needle in Seattle."

For a moment he looked dejected. "I don't know what that means," he said.

"Never mind. I brought you booklets that I collected on the tour." She withdrew several pamphlets from her purse. "Here's one from San Francisco, and one from St. Louis, and . . . here we are, Seattle. All you need to know."

He started flipping through the first few pages, then remembered. Sheepishly, he said in a soft voice, "You mentioned, well . . . you said presents. Is there more than one?"

She laughed, and his face turned crimson. "I'm

206

sorry!" he apologized. "I didn't mean—"

"Philippe," she said quietly, realizing how terribly sensitive he was, "you were perfectly right. I said presents, and"—she reached into her tote bag again—"here's the other one." She handed him the flat, square box.

"What's inside?"

"Open it and see," she answered. "It's for special occasions, when you're all dressed up."

He had some difficulty in untying the knotted ribbon, but Claudia refrained from offering help; he seemed determined to do it on his own.

"Ohh!" he exclaimed, lifting one of the six white silk handkerchiefs from the box. "It's monogrammed with the letter *P!*"

"That's so no one else but you can wear it in your pocket. Do you like it?"

"Oh, yes!" He placed the box carefully beside him and flung his arms around Claudia once more. "I love all of them! And—"

He stopped.

"What's the matter?" she asked.

"I just remembered—I have something for you, too!"

Before she could answer, he had bolted from the room.

Sirena entered the parlor while Claudia's back was facing the doors. She felt the rush of air from the hall and turned. "Oh!" she said with a start. "I thought it was Philippe."

"He should have been downstairs by now. I told him—" She stopped, realizing that Armand might join them before she could set her trap. "I'm headin' for the post office to mail a letter," she explained, fanning herself with an oversize manila envelope. "But I wanted to deliver a message from Mr. Dantine." She waited for her nerves to settle, then added, "He said for you to meet him in his studio out back. He'll be comin' there directly."

The middle finger of Sirena's right hand twitched very slightly, almost imperceptibly, but she was certain that Claudia hadn't noticed. And even if she had, there'd be no way for Miss Gage to know it occurred only when Sirena was telling a lie.

"Well, thank you, then," said Claudia, rising from the sofa. "I'll go there right away." She was telling a lie of her own; she would wait for Sirena to leave the room, stay until Philippe returned, and then, together, they would go to Armand's studio.

The boy reentered the parlor moments after Sirena had left. Claudia wondered if they'd seen each other; somehow she sensed that the three inhabitants of the Dantine household were in the habit of keeping secrets.

He was holding something in his hand. From the sofa it appeared to be a sachet, although Claudia could smell no scent. Well, she thought, relieved, at least it isn't anything to do with magnolias.

But when the boy came closer and placed it in her lap, she gave a little cry. "It's . . . my handkerchief!"

Philippe misinterpreted her reaction as delighted surprise. "I've been keeping it for you the whole time you were away!" he said, smiling because he thought she was pleased.

She understood his innocence, but not the rest. "Thank you, but Philippe, can you tell me what's wrapped up inside?" The lace was soiled, as if by dirt.

"Well, I hope you won't be angry with me," he answered. "I was awfully careful; still, some of it spilled out when I was putting it under my bed." He glanced over his shoulder at the door. "I'm sure he doesn't know about it, though."

She was trying to sift through his words to find their meaning without interrogating or frightening the child.

"Was there some reason why you didn't want your father to find out?" she asked.

His large eyes looked up at her and in all earnestness he replied, "Sirena said . . . I mean . . ."

Claudia could detect his reluctance to betray the woman. She didn't think it stemmed from fear of his father. It seemed instead a reluctance born of loyalty to Sirena. Claudia was touched to discover the trait in one so young.

Before she could inquire further, he said, "It's all right, isn't it, Claudia? I can wash it out for you—I'll be glad to—and we can throw the dirt in the courtyard this very minute, can't we? Please, before my father—"

Claudia took his hand and interjected, "We can dispose of it now, on our way to his studio."

"But what if he sees us?" the boy asked.

"Well, we'll just have to make sure that he doesn't," she answered, dropping the dirt-filled lace sack into the depths of her tote bag.

Together they left the room and, Philippe's hand holding tightly onto Claudia's, they went down the hall, past the kitchen, and out back to the path leading toward the studio.

Claudia was just turning the doorknob when Sirena stopped them.

"Little man!" she called. "It's time for your afternoon nap!"

There was the sharp edge of a command in her voice.

Claudia whirled around. "You're back in no time flat. The post office must be very close by." She made no attempt to hide her sarcasm. Claudia knew that she and Philippe were the subjects of the woman's scrutiny, and she didn't like it.

"The letter fit in the mailbox down the block," drawled Sirena. "It's just by the corner." Then, to Philippe, in a less authoritative tone: "Come on now. Don't make me coax you, little man."

Something made Claudia want to ask Sirena about the handkerchief at the bottom of her purse. But something stronger told her not to.

"Have a nice nap," she said to him. "And when you get up, you'll be all refreshed, and we can spend more time together. Maybe your father will let me take you out for dinner."

"Oh, yes! I'd like that!" Turning to Sirena and taking her hand, he asked, "Do you think he'll say yes?" Then the boy must have remembered his manners, because he added, "Or maybe we can all have dinner together."

"Well, little man," answered the woman, "we'll just have to see . . ." To Claudia she said, "Mr. Dantine will be down shortly. You can go on inside." Then she tightened her grasp on Philippe's hand and led him back into the house.

None of them—not Claudia, Philippe, or Sirena—had any inclination that they, too, were being watched. Observed from the opened upstairs window of the room that had belonged to Noelle Dantine. Only when she turned the doorknob to enter Armand's studio did Claudia hear—and for barely seconds—the faint, tinkling melody that she had hummed for Judy on the plane. The melody from her dream.

But now she knew its name. As she pushed open the studio door, she realized that Judy had been right in saying New Orleans was better over and done with. And Claudia had insisted upon coming back. The music played once more. *Now is the hour,* she thought, as what she saw on the easel registered on her brain.

Her heart was pounding in her ears, and her entire body was shaking. Claudia dizzily shook her head to convince herself that she was wide-awake. Then her mind began to sort out the information.

On the easel was a life-size canvas. The subject was a nude.

And the nude was Claudia.

That can't be!

Her brain rejected the illogic of it. But there it was, as large as—larger than—life! Who had posed for it? Sirena? But the model bore no resemblance whatever to the mulatto.

No. It was Claudia. Her face. Her figure.

But how . . . ?

The portrait of Armand's first wife flashed through her mind, but Claudia dismissed the implausibility. Noelle Dantine was dead.

Does that mean he's painted my face in only the time since we've met? she wondered. From memory? And the rest of me from . . . imagination?

Claudia didn't know why she found that possibility both disturbing and, at the same time, titillating. Nor why the duality of her own feelings should unnerve her so.

She hadn't closed the door behind her. Now she felt Armand's hands on her shoulders at the same moment the musky scent of his cologne reached her nostrils.

"I ought to ask how you managed to enter my studio," he whispered softly, "but I think I know the answer. And now that you are here, I have a more important question." He turned Claudia around slowly until she was facing him.

"Do you like it?" His eyes were searching hers.

She swallowed and tried to find her voice.

"I hope you do," he said, caressing her cheek with the tips of his fingers. "It's my best work. The finest thing I've ever done."

Chapter 17

"Come in, Eleanor," said the lawyer, holding his office door open for her.

Eleanor Gage rose from the leather sofa in the waiting area and walked past the receptionist's desk toward Raymond Fenwick. She offered a token smile and a nod of her head to his secretary and allowed Fenwick to take her arm. The mahogany-paneled, antique-furnished office, lined on three walls with leather-bound legal volumes, bespoke confidence and order, both of which she welcomed.

Fenwick could see immediately that Eleanor was tired and not in her customary good humor. Still, he observed, she looked good. They had been friends for many years, and it was clear that time was treating Eleanor Gage kindly.

He closed the door as she took one of the wing-back, studded leather chairs before his desk. She crossed her slender legs, and as she did, she leaned down to flick a speck of soot from her white spectator pumps.

Straightening up, Eleanor caught a glimpse of herself in the oval mirror on the lefthand wall. Then she turned away from the reflection and brought her attention back to the manila envelope she'd placed on Fenwick's desk.

"Gloria sends her love," he said, taking a seat in his swivel chair. "She thinks it's high time we had you over for dinner again. It's been too long since either of us has seen you. Socially, that is."

"Yes," Eleanor agreed, "it has. Tell Gloria I'll call her. Perhaps this afternoon. We'll try to arrange something for next week."

With the amenities over, they both settled back in their respective chairs. "All right now, Eleanor," Fenwick said. She could hear immediately that his voice had switched from friend to attorney. "What's on your mind?"

He knew, of course, what her reply would be. After Nick Seward's visit to his office yesterday, Eleanor's call for an appointment could hardly have surprised her lawyer.

"New Orleans," she said quietly.

Through the years that had passed, they had always referred to the matter simply as "New Orleans."

As Eleanor guardedly related the more pertinent events of the last several weeks, Raymond Fenwick compared her information with what Nick Seward had told him the day before. Even with Eleanor's side of the story, however, certain facts were missing, and less than illuminating. Still, Fenwick listened without interruption until she had finished and pushed the envelope toward him.

214

"I went over my copy this morning," he said finally, drawing a similar envelope from his desk drawer. "I'm well acquainted with the details of the contracts."

"Yes. I daresay the terms are not easily forgotten, Raymond. I was hoping you might find the loophole you . . . we . . . need."

"What exactly is it you'd like us to do, Eleanor?" he asked.

"Stop the money. Void the account."

"It's his money," said Fenwick.

"It isn't!" The words came almost as an outburst. She quickly composed herself and continued. "We gave him the money and now I want it back. It's as simple as that."

Fenwick slowly shook his head. "It's not simple at all, Eleanor. In the first place, the . . . endowment . . . came from Barton, not from you. Secondly, you can't possibly expect to recoup the vast sums already paid out over the years—"

"I just don't want him to have any more funds, Raymond! Barton may have set up the trust, but after all, it's my money, too, and I don't want Dantine—"

"It's not your money," Fenwick said gently. "Eleanor, after Noelle died, the guardianship was passed to her sister. Now—"

"Ray, I know all that," she put in.

"Bear with me," he said patiently. "Geneviève Fournier, legally and without contest, passed the inheritance to Armand Dantine at the proper time, and—"

"She had no choice in the matter."

"No, she didn't," said Fenwick. "Nor do you. Eleanor, whether it was in Barton's name or in Geneviève's, the money was always, legally, Armand's. It still

215

is — and will continue to be as long as he lives."

"Now just a second, Ray." Eleanor was twisting the diamond on her finger. "This isn't an inheritance. This is a trust. The money is entered into his account annually — there was never any lump-sum endowment. And all I'm asking is for the future payments to be halted."

Fenwick sighed and removed his glasses. Rubbing his eyes, he said, "Let me put this another way. The trust was set up by Barton. As his wish."

"Ray, I'm his widow! If I must, I'll sue to have it stopped."

"You'd probably lose, Eleanor."

"Really? How?"

"To begin with, you'd have to seek other legal counsel." Fenwick was speaking calmly and without inflection in an attempt to avoid an argument. "I would be forced to represent Dantine against you, Eleanor."

"But, Ray . . . why?"

"Because I am the executor of Barton Gage's estate. I am legally, as well as ethically, bound to see that his will is carried out. To the letter. Your contesting the validity of that will represents a conflict of interest. Barton's wishes are quite clear. In addition, the trust has been in existence for nearly thirty years — hence, there's considerable precedent." He leaned closer to her from across the desk. "Eleanor, even a second-rate lawyer would have no problem winning such a case against you."

"And you are anything but second-rate, Raymond," she said with a wry smile.

"Yes," he agreed.

She sank back in her chair and stared at the two

216

manila envelopes between them.

"Would you care for some coffee, Eleanor?" he asked in a more friendly voice.

She nodded. "Yes, Ray. I think so."

Fenwick buzzed his receptionist on the intercom. When he looked up again, he saw tears in Eleanor's eyes.

"Ellie, don't," he consoled, taking a box of tissues from his desk and handing it to her. But she had already taken a handkerchief from her purse and was dabbing at her eyes.

"Look," he ventured after a moment's awkward pause, "you can't possibly need this money, so why . . . ?"

"He's after Claudia," she answered.

"After her? You mean . . . ?"

"Yes, Ray, that's exactly what I mean. Notes. Letters. Flowers. God knows what else."

"And . . . Claudia?"

"She's gone to him. She's there now."

That was information Nick Seward had not offered to the lawyer yesterday.

"This is serious," said Fenwick.

Eleanor was fighting new tears. "Dear God — Ray, what am I going to do? What can I do?"

Fenwick had risen from his chair. Now he came out from behind his desk and stood beside Eleanor.

"It seems," he said finally, "there's only one way for this to end."

"How, Ray?"

He paused to weigh his words; they wouldn't sit easily, he was certain.

"Perhaps," he answered, looking directly into

217

Eleanor's eyes, "it's time that Claudia was told."

She seemed stunned by his suggestion. "Tell her? Ray, how can I do that . . . without destroying her father's memory?"

Nick walked through the lobby of the Royal Orleans. One of the guests was carrying a copy of *Dear Claudia*. The cover was hidden against the woman's chest, so Nick could see only Claudia's smiling face in the photograph on the back cover. Ordinarily it would have warmed him, made him smile back.

It didn't, now.

He registered and then checked the front desk for messages. There were none. Good, he thought.

"Is Miss Gage in her room?" he asked the clerk.

"Just a moment, Dr. Seward, and I'll see." He pressed three keys on the computer, waited, then picked up the house-phone receiver and rang. After half a minute or so he hung up.

"Miss Gage checked in last night, sir. However, she doesn't seem to be in her room right now. There are several restaurants in the hotel. She might be dining in one of them. If it's urgent, you might have her paged."

"No, thanks. That won't be necessary."

"Would you like to leave a message?"

Nick shook his head. "I'll try her room later."

A bellhop took his overnight bag and led him to the elevator.

Was it only weeks ago, he mused, that he and Claudia had taken this same elevator upstairs together?

Nick tipped the bellhop and politely dismissed him before the young man could begin the routine of opening draperies, turning on lights, and explaining the intricacies of hotel cable TV or other services. He wanted to be alone to consider his next move.

Once the door was closed, he sat down on the edge of the king-size bed to think. In his mind's eye, he'd envisioned his arrival as a reunion with Claudia. Being an intelligent and reasonable woman, she would then see the wisdom in leaving New Orleans—the sooner the better—and that would be that.

It was, he knew, a convenient and appealing fantasy.

Pride, as much as privacy, had kept Nick from telling Raymond Fenwick of Claudia's return to Dantine. At least Nick's apparent urgency had moved the lawyer to furnish him with some information, even if only bare-bones answers without any details.

Nick had surmised that Geneviève's last name was Fournier, and that much Fenwick had confirmed.

"She's dead," the lawyer added.

"And there was some kind of . . . business deal drawn up by your firm between the Fournier woman and the Gages?"

"Eventually . . . yes," replied Fenwick, nodding.

"But you won't tell me what."

"No, I won't, Nick. I can't."

"Was Armand Dantine involved?"

"I'm afraid I can't tell you that, either."

Nick paused then to rephrase his next question. "All right . . . can you tell me what Geneviève Fournier was to Noelle Dantine?"

"They were sisters," said Fenwick.

"And Noelle's dead, too. Dantine said so."

"She was the original party—what you'd call the principal—in the . . . transaction."

"And now the 'principal' is Armand Dantine," said Nick.

"That's right."

"This . . . transaction. Did it involve a great deal of money?"

When the lawyer nodded yes again, Nick asked, "Over what, Ray? Can't you say any more about it without betraying a confidence?"

Fenwick rose from his chair and moved toward the window. "Nick," he began, "I've never been convinced that this whole . . . matter . . . was handled in the best way. But it was Barton and Eleanor's choice, and as their attorney—"

"Their choice? So it really is tied up with the family, isn't it?"

Fenwick didn't reply but gazed out over the towers spiraling high into the overcast skies. On a clear afternoon his office afforded a view of the river all the way to the Merchandise Mart. This hadn't been one of those days. The humidity had all but shrouded the Windy City in gray, and Raymond Fenwick was feeling just as fogged in and grounded.

Nick turned away in frustration. "Ray," he said at last, "if everything is such a big secret, why tell me even this much?"

He was surprised by Fenwick's answer. "Nick . . . I want to help. I'd really like to see you figure this out on your own—and free all the parties involved."

"Dammit, Ray! All I'm asking is what the hell kind of hold Armand Dantine has over Claudia!"

"Let's just say he isn't Svengali, Nick. He just remembers more. His memory goes farther back."

"To what, for God's sake? Judy Fargo said the guy

knows things about Claudia's personal life that couldn't have been researched anywhere!"

Fenwick was staring at him, and in that instant Nick realized that he had answered his own questions.

Now, as he sat on the bed in his room at the Royal Orleans, he examined the facts once more. The mystery dealt with Claudia's childhood; there could be no other possibility. Armand Dantine knew something—or, as Fenwick had said, Dantine remembered. But what? What hold could he possess over Claudia that she herself didn't permit? Her recent dissatisfaction with the ignorance of her birth parents provided enough to make her fair game in whatever charade Dantine was playing.

Charade, Nick repeated in his mind. C'mon, Doc, he chided himself, call it what it is. Charade is what it's not.

"Seduction," he heard his voice say aloud. That's why you're so worried.

But if she doesn't see that yet, if she's responding only to her curiosity, doesn't she have a right to know whatever it is that Eleanor wants kept quiet? What if it has to do with Claudia's birth? She'd claimed to be returning to New Orleans on a promise to the boy. It had briefly occurred to Nick that Claudia might even be Philippe's mother. Stranger things had happened—he came upon them daily in his work. After all, they'd met when Claudia was twenty-six, almost twenty-seven. Hardly a kid. He had yet to meet a woman that age—with Claudia's looks and brains—who didn't have some kind of past.

That would explain why the painting in Dantine's

parlor was a double for Claudia; it might be a painting of Claudia.

But it would explain nothing else. They'd been living together for three years. Claudia hadn't lied about not having met Dantine before; Nick would have seen through that, and it wasn't his shrink's ego talking. And why would Dantine invite them to his house—and proceed to invent a dead wife named Noelle?

But Noelle wasn't an invention. Raymond Fenwick had attested to that.

No, Nick reasoned. It goes deeper. Farther back. Ray might even have been hinting with those words. He does want me to figure it out—so I'll be the one suffering sleepless nights.

Fenwick had disclosed that the law firm's name—the one printed on Eleanor's envelope—had remained the same until the death of Noyes. So the Fournier document, or contract, had been drawn up before the year 1962. Claudia would have been two years old and already adopted by Eleanor and Barton.

All right, thought Nick, trying to rub away the tension headache that had begun to form.

Well, it's a pretty good guess that she's at Dantine's house now. With him.

No, he amended. With the boy. That's what she said, and I'm going to believe her unless something happens to prove otherwise.

So what can I do? Go there and cause a scene? That's ridiculous. Whatever Claude's doing, it's her business. Yeah, no matter what that does to us . . .

He couldn't just sit on the edge of the bed and wait. Besides, there was no telling how long he'd have to wait.

Nick stood up, and the sudden movement made him lightheaded. Okay, he decided. I have to do something.

There were only two options. Frank Saggio at the Napoleon, and he'd already told Judy—and Nick via Judy—as much as he knew about Armand Dantine.

And, Nick recalled, there's the voodoo shop Claude pointed out the day we went to Dantine's brunch. The owner—Uncle Someone-or-other—had spoken of the servant woman, Sirena-with-an-*i*. Today Judy's phrase didn't make him smile.

But Claudia had mentioned that Dantine disliked the old black man in the shop.

In that case, Uncle ... Leo! Yes, that was it! Perhaps Uncle Leo held answers.

It was worth a try.

As Nick crossed the lobby and made his way toward the street exit, a sudden thought brought him to a halt.

The woman in the painting—Noelle—was Armand Dantine's wife. According to Raymond Fenwick, after Noelle died, her sister Geneviève took over the trust, or endowment.

But if such arrangement followed Noelle's death—and that had to be prior to 1962 because Noyes was still a living partner in the law firm ...

Christ! thought Nick. That would mean Armand himself couldn't have been more than seven or eight years old at the time!

So how could he have been married to Noelle?

The realization brought a myriad of questions. But somehow Nick knew that their answers—the real answers—lay just within his grasp.

223

Chapter 18

Sirena wanted to run, but in the afternoon heat her sandaled feet refused to move at a pace faster than a brisk walk. Even then, she arrived at Uncle Leo's shop breathless and with beads of perspiration dripping down the sides of her face to her neck.

In the blazing sunlight, the shop presented less than the forbidding enticements that both frightened and intrigued tourists by night; the charms and artifacts arranged in the window display appeared grotesque, not unlike the images inside an amusement park's fun house or wax museum.

Uncle Leo was seated on a stool behind the glass countertop, a newspaper spread out before him. The chimes over the door rang against one another as Sirena entered the shop, and the proprietor looked up from his reading.

"Well, what be bringin' you heah in dis heat, girl?" he said with a half-smiling, half-curious grin.

"I'm goin' to need somethin' stronger than what you

224

MORE PASSION AND ADVENTURE AWAIT... YOUR TRIP TO A BIG ADVENTUROUS WORLD BEGINS WHEN YOU ACCEPT YOUR FIRST
4 NOVELS ABSOLUTELY *FREE*
(AN $18.00 VALUE)

Accept your Free gift and start to experience more of the passion and adventure you like in a historical romance novel. Each Zebra novel is filled with proud men, spirited women and tempestuous love that you'll remember long after you turn the last page.

Zebra Historical Romances are the finest novels of their kind. They are written by authors who really know how to weave tales of romance and adventure in the historical settings you love. You'll feel like you've actually gone back in time with the thrilling stories that each Zebra novel offers.

GET YOUR FREE GIFT WITH THE START OF YOUR HOME SUBSCRIPTION

Our readers tell us that these books sell out very fast in book stores and often they miss the newest titles. So Zebra has made arrangements for you to receive the four newest novels published each month.

You'll be guaranteed that you'll never miss a title, and home delivery is so convenient. And to show you just how easy it is to get Zebra Historical Romances, we'll send you your first 4 books absolutely FREE! Our gift to you just for trying our home subscription service.

BIG SAVINGS AND FREE HOME DELIVERY

Each month, you'll receive the four newest titles as soon as they are published. You'll probably receive them even before the bookstores do. What's more, you may preview these exciting novels free for 10 days. If you like them as much as we think you will, just pay the low preferred subscriber's price of just $3.75 each. *You'll save $3.00 each month off the publisher's price.* AND, your savings are even greater because there are never any shipping, handling or other hidden charges—FREE Home Delivery. Of course you can return any shipment within 10 days for full credit, no questions asked. There is no minimum number of books you must buy.

4 FREE BOOKS

TO GET YOUR 4 FREE BOOKS WORTH $18.00 — MAIL IN THE FREE BOOK CERTIFICATE T O D A Y

Fill in the Free Book Certificate below, and we'll send your FREE BOOKS to you as soon as we receive it.

If the certificate is missing below, write to: Zebra Home Subscription Service, Inc., P.O. Box 5214, 120 Brighton Road, Clifton, New Jersey 07015-5214.

FREE BOOK CERTIFICATE

4 FREE BOOKS

ZEBRA HOME SUBSCRIPTION SERVICE, INC.

YES! Please start my subscription to Zebra Historical Romances and send me my first 4 books absolutely FREE. I understand that each month I may preview four new Zebra Historical Romances free for 10 days. If I'm not satisfied with them, I may return the four books within 10 days and owe nothing. Otherwise, I will pay the low preferred subscriber's price of just $3.75 each; a total of $15.00, *a savings off the publisher's price of $3.00.* I may return any shipment and I may cancel this subscription at any time. There is no obligation to buy any shipment and there are no shipping, handling or other hidden charges. Regardless of what I decide, the four free books are mine to keep.

NAME

ADDRESS _____ APT _____

CITY _____ STATE ____ ZIP ____

( )
TELEPHONE

SIGNATURE _____ (if under 18, parent or guardian must sign)

Terms, offer and prices subject to change without notice. Subscription subject to acceptance by Zebra Books. Zebra Books reserves the right to reject any order or cancel any subscription.   029002

GET
FOUR
FREE
BOOKS
(AN $18.00 VALUE)

gave me before," answered Sirena.

"What I gave you befo'," he repeated. "What was it, anyway?"

His laid-back attitude, in view of her predicament, angered her.

"You mean you don't remember?" she snapped. "What you told me 'bout the woman's pin and all?"

Uncle Leo scratched his head thoughtfully. "Oh, you be talkin' 'bout—"

"The magic! That's what I'm talkin' about! It didn't work!"

"All right, girl, you jus' tell Uncle Leo how it didn't work. Too hot a day to get all worked up ovah somethin' dat din't work in de first place . . ."

"You told me to steal somethin' of hers. And I did! Or at least I thought I did. A flower pin. I did everythin' you said."

"And it din't get rid o' de woman?"

"It did—but it was the wrong woman!" Sirena mopped her forehead with the hem of her skirt and mumbled under her breath, "I took the other woman's pin by mistake."

"Well, girl," said Uncle Leo with a wider smile, "why d' you come in heah accusin' me o' not givin' you strong enough magic? Ain't mah fault you got it mixed up, is it?"

Sirena looked away from him and her gaze took in Papa, his hatted, suited bones sitting motionless in the high-back chair, his teeth set for eternity in a mocking leer.

"Okay," she answered, half to Leo, half to the skeletal intruder across the room, "it's my fault. So what am I gonna do now? She's come back again."

"You mean she's come fo' . . . Mistah Dantine?"

She shrugged. "She says it's because she promised the boy. But I don't believe her for a minute. Neither would you if you'd seen them together. She's here for him, all right."

Leo nodded. "I seen dem togethah. An' I do believe you."

His words surprised her. "What d'you mean, you've seen them together? Where?"

"Heah, in mah shop," he said. "As I recollect, it be de night befo' you come to ask mah help.

"You didn't tell me that!"

"I knew you was all worked up already. No point to stirrin' up mo', I figger."

"Well, you 'figger' wrong! And now you've got to give me stronger magic—you owe it to me!"

"Girl," said Leo calmly, "I stopped owin' you de minute you left an' went to live at his place. Don't you be fo'gettin' dat."

Before she could argue, he held up his hand to show that he hadn't finished speaking. "Dat's jus' t' keep de record straight, Sirena-girl. Now"—he came out from behind the counter—"let's see what we can do to fix yo' situation, all right?"

He beckoned her behind a beaded curtain separating the selling part of the shop from his rear living quarters. Sirena stood just inside, next to the mini-refrigerator, until Uncle Leo motioned for her to take a seat on the flowered daybed in the corner. He went instead to an old wooden chair and pulled it closer to the square card table at the center of the room. Sirena was hidden in the shadows cast by the dim light of the parchment-shaded bulb hanging directly overhead.

226

"Now . . . run it all past me once mo'," said Leo. "You went to de cemetery—"

Sirena nodded. "And I buried the flower pin. Just the way you told me to."

"And you used all de words—"

"I did everythin' you said to! I even did more, just to be sure. I took the Gage woman's lace handkerchief—"

"You know fo' certain it ain't de othah woman's?"

New perspiration broke out on her face as Sirena considered that possibility. But then she remembered and said, "I do know. I took it from the Gage woman's purse. And it has the letter *C* embroidered on it. I made no mistake with that."

"Well, what'd you do? Bury dat, too?"

"No . . . it's back at the house." She felt cowardly at having asked Philippe to keep it for her. "Why?"

Uncle Leo sat thinking with his elbow balanced on the table's edge and his chin resting on his fist.

"All right, girl, dis is what you gotta do." He leaned in closer, although they were alone in the shop.

"You go on back to de house, get out dat piece o' lace handkerchief, and you make it into a little doll."

"Then what? Go and stick some pins into it?" she asked scornfully.

Uncle Leo shook his head. "Don't make fun, girl, not o' magic. You just set it out so's you can see it, so it's a constant remindah t' you o' what it is you want. An' you make a wish. You keep on makin' dat same wish."

"For how long?"

"Till it be workin' and de Gage woman go away."

Sirena had expected more. Some kind of magic whose potency would ensure success. "But will it

227

work?" she asked. "Is it enough?"

"Well . . . dat depend on more dan you, girl."

"Like what? What do you mean?"

Uncle Leo scratched the back of his head this time. "You ain't gonna like dis, Sirena, but it's also gonna depend on her. On yo' Miss Gage—an' on what *she* be wantin'."

Sirena rose abruptly. "That's no answer to give me! It can't depend on her! It's got to be left to *me!*"

Uncle Leo shook his head. "Girl, you gotta understand, de magic works only if she believes in it as much as you do."

"But how can I know that? What if she doesn't believe at all—then what good is your magic?" asked Sirena from the doorway.

Uncle Leo remained unperturbed. With another shrug, he replied, "Dat's a chance you gotta take, girl. Meantime, why don't you go on home and see about dat kerchief-doll?"

Sirena's response was formed not by words but in the rustling of the beaded curtains as she brushed past and out of the shop.

Uncle Leo came back out into the front of the shop and repositioned himself on the stool behind the counter. Business at this hour and in this heat would allow him to finish his newspaper without interruption. As he turned the page, he glanced up at the figure in the high-back chair and laughed. "Don't you go makin' fun o' me, Papa," he said to the skeleton's jeer, "she gotta believe in *somethin'*. We all gotta. Else we's likely to be goin' mad . . ."

* * *

At the same time that Claudia wanted to shift her shoulders from under Armand's touch, she found herself incapable of movement; she sensed instinctively that he would do nothing to hurt her, nothing that she didn't want him to do. It was her own duality of feelings that rooted her now and inhibited her speech.

She swallowed again. They were quick, parched swallows to cover the words that wouldn't come.

"I can read your thoughts," he said at last, breaking the silence.

Still Claudia made no reply; what would she have said? She knew that he was right.

They were both still facing the nude figure on the easel.

"You haven't answered my question," he said.

From somewhere, her voice finally appeared and she heard it reply, "What question . . . ?"

Slowly he turned Claudia toward him. Looking directly at her, without pretense or affectation, Armand said, "I asked whether you like my painting."

She tried to avert her eyes from his, but again was rendered immobile by her own ambiguous emotions.

"Armand, I . . ."

"A simple answer will do," he said. "Just tell me. Yes . . . or no."

Concentrate on the canvas, she commanded herself. On the technique, the brushstrokes — not on the subject.

"I . . . the . . . you're a very fine painter," she managed.

"Claudia, are you afraid of me?" he asked.

She could answer that. "No, Armand. I'm not. I hope I have no reason to be."

"You were not meant to see this portrait. You were

229

not meant to form the wrong impression of me."

"Armand, just what impression did you expect it to create? Or were you planning on my never seeing it?"

His fingers were featherlight against her skin as he replied, "The Bible tells us that for everything there is a season. I am not a religious man, but I find wisdom in those words. For years I have found comfort in them. And patience. I have waited so long, Claudia."

"For . . . what?"

"For . . . you." He took the tip of his index finger and tilted her chin upward. Then he lowered his mouth to hers and kissed her. Softly. Her eyes closed and her lips parted to his tongue, while his hands moved down the back of her sundress, stopping at the zipper just beneath her shoulder blades. They could hear each other's shallow breathing as the heat inside the studio heightened the intensity of his kisses.

"Your lips taste as I knew they would," he whispered. "And your skin . . . your hair . . ." His fingers gently slid the zipper down her back, and the bodice of Claudia's dress began to fall away. Now she felt his hands moving to her breasts, cupping them, his thumbs rubbing her nipples. A sudden moan of pleasure escaped from her throat.

Very slowly she opened her eyes — and immediately they came to rest on the nude painting at the easel. The canvas was like a splash of ice water on Claudia's face. She broke free of Armand's embrace and quickly readjusted her dress.

He stepped back, still watching her. After a moment he said, "I understand; 'she' makes you uncomfortable."

She wanted to tell him it was more than the painting — far more — but her thoughts, her feelings, were

230

jumbled, and she had difficulty in forming the simplest phrase.

"We will return to the house," he said. "I want to show you something."

"I think it might be better," she said, "if I were to say good-bye to Philippe . . . and go."

"Better?" he asked. "Or merely . . . safer?"

Again she knew that he could interpret her words and the motivations behind them as clearly as she could herself.

"Claudia," he said, taking her arm and leading her to the door of the studio, "at first I thought Sirena had ruined everything." At her quizzical response, he explained, "Oh, yes. You needn't tell me. Sirena arranged this. You see, I keep the door locked at all times."

"But—"

"Sirena's the one who opened the door. She's the one who told you to meet me inside. She wanted you to find the painting. She hoped it would drive you from here. From Philippe . . ." He paused, then said, "And . . . from me."

"Armand—"

"No. Let me finish. I had planned to wait until later. I wanted first for you to come to know me, to trust me, to understand, without misgivings, that your place is here. But now is—"

". . . *the hour?*" she interrupted, this time staring back at him in challenge.

"So . . . you remember the song."

"No. But my friend Judy does." Then she asked, "Is there some reason why you think the melody should mean something to me?"

"You didn't recognize it?"

231

"How could I, Armand, when I'd never heard it before?"

"That isn't so, Claudia. You know it isn't."

She felt suddenly vulnerable; it was one matter for him to be able to read her thoughts before she voiced them but quite another when he claimed to know her mind more intimately than she did.

"Come with me," he said. "You'll see and hear . . . and then you'll know." He pulled the studio door shut — and locked it — before beckoning her along the path and back inside the house.

"Where is Philippe?" she asked. The hallway was deathly still.

"He naps each afternoon at this time."

"And Sirena? Where is she?"

He shrugged. "Sirena is free to go out whenever she wishes. She is not my prisoner. Most likely she preferred to be away when you went inside my studio — that way she would be blameless for your departure."

"But —"

"But she was mistaken about you, wasn't she? Certain ties are too strong to be so easily broken. Sirena was foolish. She ought to have known that."

"Armand, you've got to understand —"

"Shh. Wait for me in the parlor. I shall join you there in a moment." He'd said it gently, yet she'd sensed an urgency in his request.

Has he placed me under some kind of spell? Claudia asked herself jokingly as she entered the room. And why, she wondered as she looked up at the painting of Noelle Dantine, do I have the feeling that those eyes — this afternoon, at least — are laughing at me? At all of us? Nick's right; the mind really can play many kinds

232

of tricks and games.

The thought of Nick prompted a guilty flashback to the scene in Armand's studio—and Claudia in Armand's arms. Just what is he doing? she silently asked herself.

Then she amended the question.

Just what is it I'm doing . . . ?

Armand stood outside the parlor doors and listened. No sounds issued from within. That meant she hadn't found it.

And he wanted her to find it.

He'd wait a few moments longer and then enter the room. If he had to, he'd show her the little wooden box. Still, he preferred that she find it on her own. That was why he'd placed it on the mantel, just below the painting. He'd originally hoped to show it to her upstairs, in Noelle's room, but that might be misinterpreted, and would serve only to drive her away, back to her psychiatrist-lover in Chicago.

So he had taken the box and planted it in the parlor before joining her in the studio. He'd guessed that Sirena would go out after returning the key to his ring on the dresser. With only slight alterations, his plans were proceeding on schedule.

Claudia glanced at the gold tank watch on its lizard strap around her wrist. Only five minutes had passed, but she was beginning to feel increasingly uneasy, as though she and Noelle Dantine had been purposely left alone together; the one to wait, the other to watch.

There were no magazines to leaf through in this

parlor, no albums to peruse. Only the painting.

And the little wooden box! Standing in the doorway, she hadn't seen it in the shadow of the clock. But now, seated on the slip-covered sofa and looking up at the mantel, she could see the corners jutting out from just beneath the gilt frame of the portrait. There was no doubt; it was the identical box Noelle was holding in the painting.

Claudia rose from the sofa and tiptoed—she didn't know why, but the house was so still—to the clock. She lifted the wooden box and for the first time saw that the lid was polished to a sheen without having been varnished. The box's lid in the canvas had been simply artist's license, a highlight for the sake of effect. But no, it was, in its three-dimensional shape, identical to the wooden box above it, framed by the subject's hands.

Claudia smiled as another of Judy's remarks came to mind: Pandora's box, she'd said. A small, nervous laugh escaped her lips, and then she lifted the beveled lid.

Her breath caught as she saw the glass-enclosed metal roll inside and the music began to play.

A lilting song in three-quarter waltz tempo.

"Now Is the Hour," she said aloud, holding the open box as she stepped back and sank onto the sofa.

It was Armand's cue, and he threw open the parlor doors.

"Now do you remember?" he asked, coming to join her on the sofa.

Instinctively she flinched and snapped the lid of the box shut. The tune stopped immediately.

"Claudia . . ."

234

"Armand, I don't know what game it is you're trying to play, but I'm not staying to find out, and—"

"Wait! Claudia, you misunderstand my motives! I thought the music would explain—"

"What are you talking about?"

"You recognize the music box—you can't tell me that you don't!"

"I told you, Judy knew the name of the song—"

"Not the song—the music box! It was *hers!*"

The feverish excitement in his voice made Claudia turn again to the woman in the portrait. The answer is there, she thought; it has to be there. I'm just not seeing it.

But the tinkling melody had stirred something inside her, a feeling similar to the one with which she awoke each time she had the dream.

"Who are you?" she demanded of the painting.

Noelle's eyes seemed to be smiling at her. Not mockingly, but . . .

Claudia's own eyes fell to the hands clasping the music box on canvas.

"This is for you," said Armand's voice from behind. She turned to see him holding something out to her.

It was a ring. A simple gold band, but its rosy hue and antique patina spoke of bygone years; in more recent times, the precious metal reflected far more yellow than pink, and widths of wedding bands, dictated by fashion, were slimmer now than they had been in the past.

Wedding bands.

Another glimmer, and her heartbeat fluttered.

Armand didn't speak. She sensed that he was waiting for her.

235

To what? she wondered. To say something? Do something?

To remember! Claudia's head began to reel, although she was still seated on the sofa.

He wants me to remember and . . . I *do!* Her throat closed, but not before she'd voiced the recollection.

"It's . . . her ring . . . !" she blurted out, neither rising nor taking the band from his outstretched hand.

"Yes! Then . . . you know!" The pupils of his eyes were dancing wildly.

Claudia found her head beginning to spin as her mind was catapulted into the eye of some bizarre hurricane of thoughts, images, sensations, whirling, converging upon her all at once.

Yet strangely—and she was conscious of the strangeness—Claudia was growing calm. It was as though, somehow, this cyclonic force, this bombardment of senses, had brought with it answers—those she had sought as well as those she hadn't thought to ask. Perhaps it was discovery of a center within the chaos. Her own center.

She didn't know what to call it, but she recognized and welcomed the new awareness, or enlightenment. Whatever its name, she recognized one fact: this was not denial.

A curtain had been withdrawn and, like Pandora's box, it could never, ever be closed again.

Slowly, Claudia repeated an act she had performed for no apparent reason on her first visit to this house. She pulled back a corner of the slipcover from the sofa on which she was seated.

This time she expected to find the pearl-gray silk moiré.

She did.

Now she looked up at Armand and said, "It was once gold brocade." She no longer phrased it as a question. There was no need to.

He nodded, never taking his eyes from her.

She turned her attention to the painting. "And the ring . . . is her wedding ring."

He nodded once again, and she could see his breath was rising.

Now she stood. Her legs felt shaky, but not for the same reason as before. In the studio she had almost succumbed to his touch. The memory of her own response made her queasy.

Keep your emotions out of this! she commanded herself. If you don't, you'll fall apart and even Nick won't be able to help you pick up the pieces!

Grabbing her purse and putting it under her arm, she walked to the fireplace and stopped directly in front of the painting.

She drew a deep breath, so deep it almost dizzied her, and said tonelessly, as matter-of-factly as her senses would allow, "I was born in this house, wasn't I?"

Armand didn't need to reply; his eyes told her the answer.

"And Noelle was not your wife."

"No."

It all seemed so logical, now.

"Noelle was . . . *our mother!*"

But voicing the phrase took Claudia by surprise. Suddenly the air in the parlor was stifling, suffocating, as it had been in her dream. Suddenly the woman in the portrait held new—and shocking—significance. So too did the dawning realization that Armand Dantine

237

knew—he had known all along! And despite his knowledge he had been willing to—trying to—

And she had almost—

Her brain refused to compute the data.

"Whyyyyy . . . ?" Her cry was born of torment and of anguish—the outrage—the madness—of this man, this house, of everything within it.

Claudia didn't wait for Armand's reply. She flung open the parlor doors and, overcome by her own fury, headed toward the front entrance hall, tears all but blinding her flight.

He ran after her. "Claudia! Wait! You don't understand! You belong here with me—with Philippe and me!"

She covered her ears to shut out the desperation in his voice. She reached the door and yanked it open. The hot afternoon sun poured in and flooded the hall with light.

And life.

She rushed forward, eager to embrace both.

She stopped just long enough to thrust her hand deep into her straw purse. She dug frantically along the bottom until she found the dirt-filled lace handkerchief.

Then, with all the force her buried rage had unleashed, Claudia hurled the lacy sack into the hall and, stumbling on the stone walk underfoot, rushed down the path, through the gate, and out onto Royal Street.

She looked back only once, not to the door where Armand Dantine still stood, but higher, toward a bedroom on the second floor where a little boy stood watching.

She thought her heart would break as her eyes caught sight of the blue-black curls on the small face framed

238

by the curtained window, a face that would grow even smaller as Claudia ran farther away.

At the corner, she glanced back one last time. She could no longer make out Philippe's features, but she was certain he was waving to her. She raised her hand in brief response, then turned and continued along Royal Street until number 1130 was far behind her.

Chapter 19

Sirena couldn't return to the house. Not yet. Not while she was still so confused.

She had decided against a drink, although she knew it would have calmed her; however, alcohol would also have dulled her senses, and she had to keep them sharp.

The Clover Grill on Bourbon Street was the next best choice to a bar, and so she sat now, sipping an iced tea at the Formica counter. The old diner's usual clientele of night people were for the most part absent at this hour of the afternoon. A few customers sat sleepily at tables behind her, either beginning their day or ending their night with breakfast. Sirena observed one frantic teenage girl of sixteen or thereabouts, who altered the scene by bursting through the door and rushing to the pay phone on the wall. She deposited her change and dialed, then listened, after which she hung up and ran back out into the baking street. This was repeated at fifteen-minute intervals, the last two of which Sirena

had witnessed with empathy; the girl's increasing outward hysteria matched her own inner anxiety.

Sirena sat down and ordered an iced tea. As she
sipped, she wondered what she was going to do. The
condensation on the outside of the glass dripped onto
the table, so she dabbed it dry with a napkin. That
reminded her about Philippe's promise to put the Gage
woman's handkerchief underneath his bed.

Well, then, she reasoned, I guess that'll be my first
stop . . .

It hadn't been difficult to find the place, once Nick
had recalled how small and unobtrusive the entrance
was. No mime stood outside when he climbed the steps,
no streetlights or neon illuminated the door, which in
the glare of daylight was a blazing orange.

The bell over the threshold rang as he entered the
little shop.

Uncle Leo was at work behind the glass showcase.
His back faced the door, and without turning around,
he said, "You go 'head an' browse. Ah be with you real
soon."

Despite the glare outside, the shop was still dark and
strangely cool, even without the help of air-conditioning. A wire fan oscillated back and forth on a small
table; its soft whirring was the only audible sound in
the place. Nick took in the bizarre atmosphere and
recognized many of the items and objects Claudia had
described to him — in particular, the business-suited skeleton seated in the chair.

The proprietor was dressed in white cotton pants. A
loose-fitting white chemise of a translucent, gauzy fab-

ric allowed his black skin to shine through the filmy material.

In his left hand he held a pint can of white enamel paint. With his right he decorated the wall with a brush.

He had painted a large, irregular circle. Inside it, strange symbols resembling Egyptian hieroglyphics had been more carefully executed. At the four points of the compass, the words *Life, Obe, God,* and *Juju* had been written.

"Dere! All done!" the old man exclaimed, turning now to face his customer. He smiled and placed the paintbrush inside the can, which he put on the showcase. The white paint dripped down the side and onto the glass.

"What . . . is that?" Nick asked.

"Dat, suh," answered the owner, "is magic. Inside de circle is de center of de Forces. Very powerful." As he leaned in, the breeze from the fan set his lightweight garments to billowing. "It should be on de floor . . . but I don' want no unsuspectin' tourist to step inside de circle and git jinxed."

Nick suppressed a grin. "That's considerate of you. And besides, it's more noticeable up there on the wall. Better for business, I'd imagine."

The black face studied him for a moment. "Also, yes. But business is good."

"Is the magic?"

"It's like anythin' else in dis life, mistah. It is what you make of it."

Nick came forward and offered his hand. "I'm Nick Seward. And you must be—"

"Uncle Leo, suh. I am to everyone, jus' ol' Uncle

242

Leo." He took Nick's hand and shook it firmly. "But you don't be wantin' magic, I 'magine, Mistah Seward, suh."

Nick didn't correct the title. "No, Uncle Leo. I'm looking for answers."

The old man shrugged his shoulders. "I maybe have some o' dem fo' you. Everythin' in mah shop is fo' sale, suh."

Nick nodded, this time unable to hide his amusement. He reached into his pocket, took out his wallet, and withdrew a ten-dollar bill. Uncle Leo eyed the money, then picked it up before the breeze from the fan blew it off the counter.

"Mus' be a very tiny question you got, Mistah Seward, suh."

"Well, I'll see what that much buys . . . okay?"

"Anythin', suh, to keep yo' faith alive. I sell dat, also." He picked up the can of paint and set it down on the floor. With a rag he wiped the white drops from the showcase glass, then leaned on it with his elbows. "So, mistah, now you ask me yo' ten-dollah question."

"I want to know about a woman named Sirena."

Uncle Leo rubbed the beard stubble on his cheeks. "Sirena . . . now dat be a most populah name, suh. Many gals wit dat name 'round heah—"

"She works for Armand Dantine."

"Ah! So . . . you be meanin' Sirena Mars!"

"Then you *do* know her."

The old man narrowed his eyes, but they twinkled mischievously. "Dis . . . could be expensive fo' you, Mistah Seward, suh."

Nick, looking directly at Uncle Leo, said, "I'm sure it'll be a bargain, whatever the cost. Who is she?"

"Why, she is mah very own li'l chile." The smile grew broader.

"What . . .?"

"Oh, yessuh. Mistah Dantine . . . he move her from mah shop to his house long time ago. He . . . buy mah faith in him—faith dat he take good care o' mah darlin' daughtah."

"I see what you meant," Nick commented.

"Suh?"

"About everything in the shop being for sale."

Uncle Leo obviously didn't like the remark. "Sirena . . . she do pretty well wit de . . . arrangement, believe you me."

"No doubt. Do you see her often?"

"I seen huh right where you be standin', not twenty minutes ago."

"Did she mention anything about a Miss Gage? Claudia Gage?" asked Nick.

Uncle Leo paused, then said, "You mean dat Deah Claudia lady? Oh, yessuh. She too be in heah once. Befo' ah reco'nize who she be."

"What exactly did Sirena say about the lady?"

"Oh, she jus' be jealous, mah Sirena, dat's all. She don' like fo' Mistah Dantine to be seein' so much o' dis Miss Claudia."

Nick leaned his palms on the glass and came face-to-face with Uncle Leo. "Did your Sirena by any chance tell you about a missing piece of jewelry . . . a pin in the shape of a flower?"

The old man glanced from Nick's eyes to the ten-dollar bill in his hand. He fingered it thoughtfully without answering.

Nick reached once more into his wallet and added

244

another ten to the first. Uncle Leo took it, smiled, and said, "Dere be a lace handkerchief, too, right?"

"Right," replied Nick.

"Well . . . you got to understan', Mistah Seward, suh. Sirena, she ain't no thief. She jus' believe in . . . crazy things, sometimes."

"Such as?"

"Look aroun' you, suh," the old man whispered. "Sirena's momma . . . she be descended from Marie Laveau—de voodoo queen!"

"Wait a minute," Nick said. "Are you telling me those things were stolen for—"

"Taken, suh, not stolen. To pray ovah. To send yo' Miss Claudia away."

"And you believe this stuff?"

"No, suh. Ah believe in makin' a buck. Ah got a business to run an' ah run it good." He gestured, taking in the entire shop. "Dis all fine tourist-trade bullshit dat ah learn from Sirena's momma. It keep de customers satisfied . . . an' it satisfy me, too."

"But Sirena believes in all this?" Nick asked. "In voodoo?"

Uncle Leo grinned. "Sirena be mah customer, too, suh. Mah daughtah's momma an' huh people, dey fill de chile's head wit many . . . legends. Sirena always be afraid o' de power her momma say she inherit. But now, mah Sirena, she be in a real tough spot. So she be tryin' anythin' to keep huh place in dat house."

"Would she harm Miss Gage—just to keep Dantine?" asked Nick.

"No, no suh! Dantine—he don't mattah no mo' to Sirena. She lose him already. It be de boy she fightin' fo'. She jus' wanna make yo' Miss Claudia go 'way, is

245

all. If she evah be doin' real harm to anyone, it be to Mistah Dantine."

"Uncle Leo, can you tell me how long ago Dantine's wife died?"

The old man looked genuinely puzzled. "Far as ah know, Armand Dantine ain't nevah been married."

"The names of Noelle or Geneviève mean nothing to you?" said Nick.

"Jus' dat dey be French names. I got a cousin name o' Geneviève. She live ovah in—"

"Wait a minute," interrupted Nick. "Slow down. I have another question—and another ten-spot."

Uncle Leo's eyes darted to Nick's wallet. "Shoot."

Nick placed a new bill on the glass counter. Then he said, "If Dantine has always been a bachelor, then . . . who is Philippe Dantine's mother?"

The old man's face assumed a wizened slyness as he pocketed the third ten-dollar bill and said, "Ah, Mistah Seward, suh, you seems t' be a smart fella. Now jus' who you think be de boy's momma . . .?"

Armand snapped shut the lock on his suitcase and glanced around the room. The closet door was still open, revealing a row of twenty or more suits in various shades and weaves. But there was no time—or need—to pack them. The two he'd chosen would have to suffice. He closed the mahogany dresser drawers; again, the shirts he'd taken were those he'd seen first. Dozens more remained, but he mustn't tarry; he could always buy more in Chicago.

He lifted the suitcase from the bed and carried it out into the hall, where Philippe stood leaning against the

246

banister. The boy was staring at his father, but **Armand** said nothing as he moved past and opened the door to the child's room.

By the time Philippe had followed him, Armand was throwing the boy's clothing haphazardly from the closet into another, smaller suitcase. Sweat glistened on his forehead. At length, he pushed a damp forelock from his eyes and, gesturing to the still-open suitcase, said, "If there's anything in particular you want to take with you, put it in here. Now."

Obediently the child went to his desk and picked up the Seattle space-needle paperweight. He took that and the sightseeing pamphlets Claudia had given him, and laid them carefully inside the folds of his packed clothing.

"Is that all you want to take?" asked Armand.

Philippe nodded. Then in a soft, tentative voice, he asked, "Are we going away for a long time?"

"I don't know, Philippe," replied his father. He knelt and placed his hands on the boy's shoulders. "You like Miss Gage, don't you?"

"Yes . . ."

"Well, then . . . perhaps we'll be seeing her where we're going."

The child hesitated but finally asked, "Is Sirena coming with us?"

Armand rose to his full height and looked down at his son. "No. She isn't coming."

Philippe's lower lip began to quiver in spite of himself, and tears rimmed his large, round eyes.

Armand tousled the boy's hair and added, "Maybe she'll join us later." The lie was necessary, considering Philippe's affection for the woman.

"When? How soon?"

"It depends. I'll let you know."

"May I leave her a note? She'd want me to say good-bye, and—"

"Philippe, there's no time for that. We have to catch a plane."

"I know, but—"

From downstairs they heard the ringing of the front doorbell.

Armand stiffened. It couldn't be the taxi. Not this soon; he'd called only minutes ago.

He looked at the child. Philippe had fallen silent at the sound. Now he stared at the floor and waited for his father's decision.

"Go and answer it," Armand said at last. "I've almost finished here. Send away whoever it is, then come back upstairs."

"But what if—" Philippe stopped. Armand was busy opening and slamming other drawers, and although the boy had seen his father in similar nervous states before, never had there been this accompanying, underlying apprehension that seemed to govern every movement, every word. It was the kind of negative energy that had a way of spreading to those in its sphere, and now Philippe himself was growing frightened. If only Sirena would come home in time.

A spark of hope flared inside him as he headed downstairs to answer the door. Perhaps it was Sirena! Then his steps slowed; she wouldn't ring the bell—she'd use her key.

Unless she'd forgotten it!

His pace quickened once more as he reached the bottom stair and ran down the long hallway.

He stopped short when he saw Claudia's soiled white lace handkerchief lying against the baseboard.

Most of the dirt had fallen out of the improvised sack. He picked it up and felt a twinge of fear.

The doorbell rang again. Philippe stuffed the handkerchief into his jacket pocket, and with his shoe tried to kick the telltale dirt under the straw mat. Then he straightened up and went to open the massive front door.

"Hello, Philippe," said the man he'd met before. "Remember me? I'm Nick Seward—I came here with your friend Claudia."

Philippe nodded politely but remained silent and made no move to admit Nick into the house.

"Is she here, Philippe? Miss Gage, I mean?"

"No," came the barely audible reply. "She left."

So she'd been and gone. "How long ago was that, do you know?" he asked.

The child shrugged. "I was taking my nap."

From above, Nick heard Armand Dantine's voice calling the boy.

"I have to go, Nick," he said, visibly nervous. He began to close the door.

Nick's hand went out to stop him. "Just one thing—"

"Please, I—"

"Tell your father I'm here. I have to speak with him. It's important."

"He won't like it," said Philippe.

"Please . . .?"

Reluctantly, the boy held the door open. "I'll go and get him. I . . . guess you can wait in there," he offered, gesturing toward the parlor.

Nick's eyes went immediately to the single spot in the room that held his interest—as well as the rest of the story.

Noelle Fournier Dantine looked down at him from her framed pedestal above the mantel. The striking, beautiful face, so like Claudia's, remained serene and regal as though presiding over her domain. She almost seemed pleased.

If only she knew, thought Nick. He wondered about her fate, and he was filled with conflicting feelings of both contempt and pity. Could she possibly have known the eventual consequences of her actions? However her history had ended, Noelle must have paid a high price for giving up the child.

Nick's gaze followed down the length of the portrait until it fell upon the clock below the frame. And on the object beside the clock. He hadn't really noticed it before.

He crossed to the mantel and picked up the small wooden box. It was the same box as the one reposing on canvas, in Noelle Dantine's delicate hands.

Before he lifted the box's lid Nick knew the name of the melody he would hear. Strange, he thought, that such a pretty little song should come to symbolize such pain. Now, as the simple, familiar tune played out, his mind went over all of the "actors" and their roles in the conspiracy: Barton and Eleanor Gage, Raymond Fenwick, Noelle and Geneviève. And Armand. They were all responsible.

The longer he waited, the angrier he became. And yet when he glanced at the clock once more, less than two minutes had passed. Nick let the lid of the box fall

250

shut, cutting off the music in the middle of its lilting song. He slammed the box back onto the mantel, opened the parlor door, and shouted, "Dantine!" He strode out into the hall and went to the foot of the staircase. "Dantine!" he called again. "I want to talk to you!"

The shouting from inside the house grew louder. The only difference to Philippe was that on this occasion, one of those voices did not belong to Sirena.

Where could she be? he wondered. He'd considered replacing the handkerchief under his bed, where she would expect to find it. But the thought of returning upstairs terrified him; he would have to pass his father, who was already enraged at Nick Seward's intrusion.

So Philippe remained outside in the courtyard, where he leaned against the tree and tried to decide what to do with Claudia's handkerchief. Had she accidentally dropped it? No, most likely she had thrown it away and didn't want it anymore. She had left and wasn't coming back.

What about Sirena? Would she return? How would she find him? Tears filled his eyes again. And then, resolutely, he made up his mind to keep the handkerchief for her. It was his reassurance. She would have to find him, no matter where he and his father were going.

Philippe untied the knot and, holding the lace by one corner, let the soil fall into the earth covering the roots of the tree. He shook out the handkerchief and put it back inside his jacket pocket as he looked up at the tallest branches.

The shouting inside the house continued, but Philippe was paying no attention to the words. He was watching the lazy sway of the Spanish moss that hung from above and encircled him within a curtain made of an Indian maiden's hair.

"I know everything!" Nick yelled. Armand had descended only halfway down the staircase and remained there during their heated exchange. Nick was aware of the superior position in which Dantine had physically placed himself; he was forcing Nick to look up at him.

"You couldn't possibly fathom all of it!" Armand cried back.

"I've learned enough to know what kind of manipulative . . . perverted games—"

"Dr. Seward! I haven't time to trade stupid insults with you! I told you Claudia is not here and I have no idea whatever as to her whereabouts!"

"If anything has happened to her, Dantine, I swear to you I will—"

"You'll what? Short of murder, Seward, there's nothing you can do! You're behaving irrationally, coming here with ridiculous accusations—I daresay you are in need of a psychiatrist!"

Nick was on one of the lower stairs and ready to take them two at a time when, seemingly from nowhere, a pistol suddenly appeared in Armand's hand. Nick halted halfway up; he was separated from his adversary by only half a dozen steps.

"I'm quite good with firearms, Seward. I don't miss, especially at close range. Now get out!"

Nick wondered if Armand would actually shoot him.

His instincts told him that yes, this man was capable of killing. And far more.

Thoroughly convinced—and not about to conduct a test—Nick retreated slowly down the stairs. He didn't turn his back until he reached the front door, which he slammed with what remained of his unexpressed rage.

Once outside on Royal Street, he took several deep breaths to calm himself. He was still furious, not only with the obsessive master of the house, but with his own lack of control over his emotions. Damn! he thought. If I hadn't lost it, I might have learned something!

But he had learned one thing. Claudia had left Dantine's and Nick was certain that the son of a bitch Dantine really didn't know where she'd gone.

But what had happened at the house? How much had he told her? How much had she guessed? There was no telling what psychological effect the truth—the entire truth—might have on her, especially if Dantine had first tried to . . .

Nick canceled the thought and entered the bar at the corner, where he found a pay phone and called the Royal Orleans.

"I'm sorry," said the hotel switchboard operator after ringing the room, "Miss Gage isn't here."

Christ! he thought. Don't tell me I've come all the way to New Orleans, and she's flown back to Chicago! "She hasn't checked out, has she?" He was conscious of having to work at keeping the frustration out of his voice.

He was asked to hold, and then: "No, sir. Would you

care to leave a message?"

"I'll call later. Thanks." He hung up and tried logic. Where else in this city could she be? She doesn't know anyone here.

Wait! Frank. Judy Fargo's Frank.

Nick's pace quickened into almost a jog as he headed down Royal Street for the Napoleon. It was a long shot, but worth the price of a drink.

Their suitcases were at the hallway door. There was nothing to do but wait for the taxi to arrive.

Armand went into the parlor, where he took the little music box and gently placed it inside his shoulder tote.

Then he looked up at the portrait over the mantel.

From outside, the taxi's horn sounded.

He moved toward the door and glanced back at the painting one last time.

"Adieu, Mother," he whispered.

Chapter 20

It would have been impossible to run with the hot sun beating down on her even if Claudia had been wearing lower-heeled sandals. But with three inches of stacked leather sinking into tar and catching in broken sidewalk cracks, she found herself stopping and starting, her legs behaving in much the same way as her breathing mechanism.

When she reached the corner she didn't look back. Nor did she consciously head in any particular direction. She had half expected her feet to guide her back to the Royal Orleans; after all, where else could they take her in a city she barely knew?

And yet when Claudia glanced up for the familiar landmark, the hotel wasn't there ahead of her. She laughed in spite of herself, in spite of all that had happened.

"The power of the unconscious mind . . . ," she said aloud to the air.

Her flight had led her to the one safe haven in this

entire town and to the only person there in whom she could confide.

She pushed open the door to the Napoleon and hoped against hope that it wasn't Frank's day off.

It wasn't. He stood behind the bar, talking and joking with one of the customers.

Claudia took several pieces of Kleenex from her purse and mopped the perspiration from her forehead and from the back of her neck. Even without pantyhose or stockings, her legs and thighs were damp, her silk slip sticking to her.

She wasn't concerned about whether she looked presentable; it was miserably hot, and more important, she was in need of help. Frank's help, if he was willing.

His eyes lit up upon seeing her. "Hey, it's Dear Claudia, live and in person!" Several people turned at the sound of Frank's resonant baritone.

But when she came closer at the far end of the bar, he joined her and, in a lowered voice, said, "Hey, babe, are you all right?"

She spoke in short, hesitant spurts: "I don't . . . know. I think so . . . now."

"Okay, let's pretend it's happy hour already," said Frank. He reached for a bottle and poured, then handed the glass to Claudia. She didn't bother to ask what it was. She drank.

The burning liquid—was it bourbon?—felt like fire in her parched throat, but it had an immediate numbing effect.

"Ohh!" she exclaimed at the alcohol's kick.

"Gets to you fast in this weather, doesn't it?" he asked. "After the second one you'll relax and tell me what happened."

"Hey, Frankie!" yelled a customer at the other end of the bar.

"Stay here," he said to Claudia. "Duty calls, but I'll be right back."

She nodded. She was too strung out to go anywhere. The reality of her encounter with Armand Dantine had been a shock, and now, seated at a bar in a city not her own, the shock began to wear off. It was fast being replaced by anger.

She wondered, thinking about the numerous discussions she'd had with Nick about the complexities of the human psyche, if denial was her reason for not having seen the truth before. Was it possible that she hadn't wanted to know the truth?

And what would have followed if such denial had continued? She and Armand might have unwittingly—

No. Not unwittingly, because he knew. He'd always known.

And as for me, well . . . I guess that says something about survival, doesn't it?

She was deep in rumination when Frank returned to her end of the bar.

"All right, now . . . Ah, wait! Your glass is empty, and that'll never do!" He made a great ceremony of retrieving the bottle of Jack Daniel's and refilled her glass with flourish.

Claudia managed a wan smile in appreciation of his attempt to cheer her up.

"Ah, Dear Claudia has rejoined us at last," he said, watching her but not letting her know that he was watching her. As soon as she could unwind enough to tell him what had occurred, he'd call Judy in Chicago; after all, she and Claudia were close, and he hardly

257

knew the author. Besides, it was an excellent excuse for calling Judy without coming on too strong.

Which made him ask Claudia, "Listen. Are you upset because some guy started hitting on you?"

"N-no. I'm not . . . upset."

"Oh, yes you are," he said. "C'mon, take a good swig. Then tell Frank what's up. You know what they say."

"Do I?" she asked after taking a sip.

"Sure. That bartenders and hairdressers carry the secrets of the world. Now if I tried to style your hair, you'd call the cops, I promise. Besides, it's known fact that hairdressers keep secrets like a sieve holds water. But bartenders . . . well, we're a breed apart. It's in our blood." He dropped his voice to a whisper. "C'mon. Give old Frank a try." When she didn't speak, he added, "Claudia, trust me. First of all, I'm a good listener. Second, your buddy Judy has me hooked—but don't tell her just yet. I'm only telling you so you won't think I have an ulterior motive. Now . . . trust Frank. What happened?"

She told him. All of it. More than he'd expected. And he was right; he was a good listener. As objective, she noted, as Nick.

And far less emotionally involved, in this particular case.

Claudia had lost track of time, but when she had finished with her story—as well as her third drink—the bar had filled with people. Frank checked his watch, then said, "Tell you what. I'll have Chris take over for me. Wait here while I get him and then we'll go."

"Go where?" Claudia asked, feeling better, though emotionally spent.

258

"To my place." He saw the sudden change in her expression. "Honey, if you go back to the hotel, Dantine might be there. And even if he knows better than to try anything stupid in public, still, you don't need to see him again so soon, do you?" He didn't wait for her to answer. "We'll go to my apartment—it's two blocks from here—and you'll take your shoes off, put your feet up, and if you want to, we'll call Nick in Chicago."

When she hesitated, he said, "Or we'll call Judy."

Again she didn't reply.

"Or we won't call anyone. But if I stay here, I've got to work, and just now, I'm more tempted to go to this son of a bitch's house and beat the living daylights outta him."

He didn't know why that remark should make her laugh when all other attempts had failed, but he'd stopped trying to analyze women's behavior long before now. Nick Seward's the pro, he reasoned. Let him go figure them out.

Sirena quickened her pace as she reached the corner and saw the taxi driver loading two suitcases into the trunk; she recognized the larger one as Armand's; the smaller belonged to Philippe. Her thong sandals, more than the intensity of the afternoon heat, kept her from breaking into a run. At first she didn't see the head of blue-black curls beside his father in the backseat; only when the cabbie slammed the trunk and climbed into the driver's seat did she realize exactly what was happening.

And the enormity of what had already happened.

Or had it? she wondered. Maybe they're leaving

259

because the Gage woman hadn't allowed anything to happen.

The taxi sped by so fast, it almost became a blur. Sirena stood staring after the car as the boy's face appeared and a small hand began waving frantically through the rear windshield. His mouth was open as he called to her, but no sound was audible thought the taxi's close windows. Sirena's last image of Philippe was recorded in her mind as though it were the ending of a silent movie.

But it isn't the ending! came her inner cry. It can't be!

And it won't be!

Hurriedly she made her way through the gate and up the stone path to the front door. She scrambled through her pockets until she found her housekeys.

She heard the top lock click. But the second one beneath it wouldn't budge. Damn! she thought. Can it be stuck?

She put her ear to the door and tried again.

That was when she understood. Armand had taken Philippe. And then he'd locked her out with the second key; he knew she had no duplicate.

In his haste, however, Armand had forgotten the courtyard entrance. Sirena separated that key from the others and crept around to the back of the house.

Within less than two minutes she was upstairs in Philippe's room. She crouched on her hands and knees and peered under his bed for the dirt-filled lace handkerchief that Uncle Leo had promised would work magic.

Nothing!

She turned on the night-table lamp beside the boy's

bed and looked again. Then she checked the four corners of the floor. After that she tried the dresser drawers and the closet.

Exhausted, she sank back against the door and tried to stop herself from shaking.

She began to reconstruct the scene as it must have occurred. Armand had confronted Claudia with the truth. Either that, or the Gage woman had figured it out. Whichever, she must have been shocked enough to run away. And Armand was obviously determined to follow her.

But why take the child, unless . . .?

Sirena's throat was choking her as she raced down the stairs and into the kitchen. She pulled the telephone directory out from the shelf beneath the wooden countertop and tore through the pages until her index finger reached AIRLINES.

But which one are they takin'? she wondered. There's gotta be more'n one airline flyin' to Chicago. An' supposin' they've gone somewhere else?

Then she reconsidered. The Gage woman is gone, and she lives in Chicago. Armand and Philippe are gone as well; the rest doesn't take much figurin'.

Sirena reached for the scratchpad beside the phone and noticed the pencil's impression on the paper. Seven numbers. She held the pad up to the light, but that didn't help. Then, remembering from a late-night TV mystery, she grabbed the soft lead pencil and colored in the numbers until the seven digits grew as clear as if Armand had purposely left her a sign.

And maybe, she reasoned, that's exactly what he did, even if he doesn't know it. Maybe there's part o' him that wants me to find out where he's goin' so that I

261

can follow him.

She picked up the telephone receiver and dialed.

When the reservation clerk answered, Sirena could barely control her voice. "When's the next plane leavin' for Chicago?" she asked.

"Well, ma'am, there's one in thirty-five minutes, but that's all booked."

"When's the next?"

"Just a moment, please." A pause, the sound of clicking keys on a computer, and then, "There's one seat left on the six o'clock flight —"

"I'll take it."

"Fine, ma'am. May I have your name, please?"

"Mars. Sirena Mars."

"Yes, Miss Mars. And will that be a one-way ticket, or round-trip?"

"Well," answered Sirena as she stared at her trembling fingers, "that all depends . . ."

It was a simple but cozy two-room apartment whose windows overlooked a small courtyard out back. Claudia had opted for Frank's living-room sofa; somehow the bedroom, despite his reassurance, seemed inappropriate. She didn't like the feelings of distrust that Armand Dantine had engendered within her; she hoped they would pass as quickly as a bad dream.

She dozed to the accompanying hum of the small air conditioner in the corner window. And although fragments of her recurrent nightmare appeared, they held no further mystery, and therefore could exact no fear.

Frank had asked if music would disturb her and she'd said no. Now, through the closed bedroom door,

Claudia in her half-sleep, half-awake state heard a familiar melody.

From her light nap she fell into a heavy sleep. It was a peaceful sleep, so deep that if Claudia dreamed at all, she had no awareness of it.

She was awakened by a loud rapping at the door, and it made her bolt upright in momentary panic.

"Frank!" she called softly. The music in the bedroom had stopped. Claudia rose as the knock came once more.

Her eyes came to rest on a yellow Post-it beside the telephone.

"Back in an hour," it read. "Didn't want to disturb your nap."

She looked around for a rear exit door to the apartment, but there was none. What if Armand had somehow managed to find her?

But then she heard, "Frank! Hey, are you there? It's Nick Seward—Claudia Gage's shrink!"

She burst into relieved laughter at his turn of phrase and flung open the door without even stopping to consider that he was here, in New Orleans, instead of where he was supposed to be, at his hospital office in Chicago.

"Nick!"

"Claude!" he cried, both of them wrapping their arms around each other as though they'd been apart for years.

Then she regained her senses. "Nick! What are you doing here? How—?"

"It's too long to explain. And too hot. I went to the Napoleon and the bartender said Frank had gone out with a 'real looker.' He trusted me enough to give me

263

the address, but"—this he said with a weak attempt at a joke—"he advised me to knock loudly in case you and Frank were . . . 'gettin' it on' was the way I think he put it."

She laughed again. "He . . . Frank . . . went out. But how—"

"I went to Dantine's, and you weren't there. Then I called the hotel, and you weren't there, either, so I—"

"You went to his house?"

"I sure as hell did—and it's too hot to talk about that, too, right now."

Nick entered Frank's living room and closed the door to shut out the stale, humid air in the corridor.

"I was there earlier," said Claudia.

"I know. You were the subject of our conversation."

"Nick . . . he's sick! I mean obsessive-sick—"

"I know that, too, Claude. He tried a little cat-and-mouse game on me, but I didn't fall for it."

"D-did he t-tell you he's . . . I mean . . . that he and I . . ." Her voice faltered; she still found it impossible to believe.

"He didn't tell me anything except that you'd been and gone." Nick reached for her hand and led her to the sofa. "Claude, he didn't have to tell me much. I've been doing some checking." Gently he stroked her arms while looking into her eyes. "I know who Noelle Dantine really was."

Claudia nodded and gazed across the room at the window, beyond which she could see a weeping willow swaying in the hot breezes of oncoming dusk.

"She wasn't Armand's wife, Claude."

"No," she answered. "Noelle was Armand's mother." After a hesitation, she added, "And mine, Nick. Armand Dantine is my . . . brother." Her eyes began to fill with tears, but not from the words she had spoken. They were tears for what might have been, if they had lived in the same house and been raised as brother and sister; if Noelle had lived.

"He's only your half-brother, Claude," Nick said softly, cautiously watching for her reaction.

"But if Noelle . . . I mean . . . I don't think I understand . . ."

Better tell her everything, advised the professional voice in Nick's mind. Tell her the whole story—what you've learned, and what's still to be uncovered. Then just be here with her, for her.

"Barton Gage was more than your adoptive father, Claude. He was . . . your natural father."

She looked up in wonder, yet at the same time with comprehension, as though her instinctive suspicions were at last being confirmed.

"But if Noelle . . . was our mother, then . . . ?"

"Barton wasn't Armand's father. Guy Dantine died long before you were born. Barton met Noelle when he was in New Orleans on business, and . . . she was very beautiful—like you, in fact—and . . ."

"And he had an affair with her and got her pregnant?" Claudia's voice rose at the implication. "You're telling me that while Eleanor was waiting at home in Chicago, Barton—"

"Yes, Claude."

"But, Nick . . . ! Why didn't he ever tell me?" She was feeling new anger, stronger than before, and it had nothing whatever to do with Armand Dantine and his obsession with her—or with their mother. "Nick—you're saying that Barton knew about Noelle's child—and knew about me! That he went home and told Eleanor and she forgave him . . . and they kept it a secret from me?" The rage in her was building to a crescendo. "How could they do it, Nick? How could *she* do it? Every time Eleanor looked at me, she was seeing her husband's mistress's child!"

"She loved Barton very deeply. So much that she was willing to forgive his . . . indiscretion . . . and raise his child as her own. And she loved you—still does. She'd do anything to protect you. We had something of an altercation over that just last night, in fact."

"What kind of altercation? Does Eleanor know—I mean about all this with Armand? My God, what have you been telling her?"

"It's the other way around, Claude. It's what she's been telling me. Or rather what she hasn't told me. That's what started me wondering in the first place."

"But . . . the whole charade about my adoption! How did they do that? And why? Didn't Noelle . . . want me?" Suddenly she felt a terrible vulnerability; she recognized it as irrational, yet she couldn't fight the feeling of having been rejected—or worse, negated—by her natural mother.

"Claude, I don't have all the details, but I plan to get them from Eleanor as soon as we get home. I don't know if Noelle had much choice in the matter. Barton set up some kind of trust fund—that's where Dantine gets his money—and I'm certain it's tied up with your adoption."

"Ray Fenwick would know," said Claudia.

"Maybe, but he won't share that information with me."

"Well, then, perhaps he'll share it with me," she said

tonelessly. "After all, if I'm Barton Gage's daughter"—
her voice caught at the word—"it sounds to me as if
this trust fund was intended to buy something. Noelle's
silence." She considered her statement for a moment.
"Or perhaps Noelle's child."

"Or both," Nick put in gently. His arms went around
Claudia. "Whatever the motive, you've got to remember
that Barton adored you, Claude. He did what he
thought was best under the circumstances."

"I suppose," she whispered between tears.

"And there's more." He turned her face toward him
and, looking into her eyes, said, "Eleanor loves you
very much. You'll see that if you can imagine yourself
in her place when Barton told her."

Claudia's anger was falling away. "My God, it's
amazing that she didn't hate me. Or at least resent me.
A woman who couldn't have children of her own,
taking in her husband's child by another woman."

"I've always admired Eleanor," said Nick, "but I
never realized before now just how . . . well, how fine a
person she is. There have been times when she's infuri-
ated me—the business about the hospital promotion,
for one. But I see how easily she might have played the
martyr, to manipulate and control Barton—"

"How . . . ?"

"By forgiving him, Claude, and using that as a
weapon. She's never done that. Your mother is the
woman who nurtured you, who raised you and taught
you and helped you to grow into the woman you are—
and into the woman I love. Eleanor's your mother,
Claude, not some idealized woman in a painting who
carried you for nine months. Prostitutes give birth and
abandon their babies, but that doesn't make them

267

mothers! You're Eleanor Gage's daughter, far more than you ever were Noelle Dantine's."

Through the tears streaming down Claudia's face, she asked, "Nick, I'm so confused . . . tell me what to do?"

"It isn't up to me, Claude," he said softly. "But I do have one suggestion that may help." His hand caressed her cheek tenderly. "We can start by going home," he whispered.

"Yes," she said, still sobbing intermittently but beginning to feel better. "Let's go home."

Nick's overnight bag and Claudia's luggage were sitting on the floor just inside the door of her suite. She freshened her makeup while he phoned the airline for reservations.

"When's the next flight to Chicago?" he asked. "We have two first-class tickets with open returns, and we'd like to book seats for—"

"I can get you on the eight o'clock direct to O'Hare," said the clerk, interrupting.

"Nothing earlier?" asked Nick, glancing at his watch.

"I'm sorry, sir," came the reply. "We have a six o'clock, but we've just sold the last seat."

Chapter 21

Claudia was surprised by her latent resentment toward Eleanor; it hadn't surfaced until the plane touched down in Chicago. Her hectic schedule upon returning to work proved a convenient excuse, but its proper name was avoidance, and eventually the issue would need to be addressed.

Claudia was home, and Dear Claudia was a celebrity just back from a successful book-promotion tour. That meant parties and lunches and dinners in her honor. The *Daily Examiner*'s circulation had increased as a result of the book's sales, and those sales had increased due to the newpaper's circulation. *Dear Claudia* was climbing still higher on the best-seller lists, and by the time its author and Nick had been back in Chicago for three days, the book was heading for that week's number-one nonfiction slot.

But Eleanor Gage knew this so-called whirlwind of activity was not the reason why her telephone calls with Claudia had been brief and audibly distant. She wondered what exactly had transpired in New Orleans and just how much her adopted daughter had found out.

She had considered dropping by Claudia's office at the *Examiner,* but she didn't want to push the matter. Besides, wasn't Eleanor herself using the preparations for the upcoming charity costume ball at the museum in much the same way? While she was eager to learn as much as she could, she felt it would be wiser to wait for Claudia to come to her, as she had done since earliest childhood whenever she was upset.

Yes, Eleanor thought now, but in the past she's always come to me in complete trust. Can she still? Will she? Perhaps we should have told her long ago; it seemed right not to, but . . .

Rather than continue fidgeting with the diamond wedding ring on her finger, Eleanor removed it and placed it beside the framed photograph of Barton on the desk where she'd been seated for an hour, answering a myriad of calls from various committee members.

She gazed at the image of Barton and shook her head sadly. "We may have done the wrong thing, after all," she said to him. "I can't expect her to fully understand. I'm not certain I ever did."

She removed her reading glasses and leaned back in the chair. Then she tilted her head and closed her eyes, remembering the day the baby Claudia had been brought to her.

And to the conversation with Barton, in this very room, that had preceded the child's arrival.

Perhaps she had made it too easy, in her customary need to keep the machinery of their life together running smoothly.

But what else could I have done? she asked silently,

as she had asked herself so often in those early years. How could I turn him away—I loved him!

Her heart ached for him as it had on that night almost thirty years ago when Barton confessed his indiscretion. "It just . . . happened," he said. "In New Orleans. I have no excuses."

And because of his honesty—and because she loved him—Eleanor Gage had forgiven him. How, then, could she have refused when he told her about Claudia—his own, flesh-and-blood daughter?

He had dearly wanted a child, and his wife's inability to conceive had been the single flaw in their marriage. Eleanor had willed herself to see it from Barton's side; that made it easier to accept the infant into her home, into her heart. And she had never regretted the decision; she loved the child from first sight of the large, curious eyes and the infectious giggle, the way Claudia's tiny hands had grasped Eleanor's fingers and held tightly as if fearing to let go.

And now as she recalled the past, Eleanor acknowledged her guilt. Never before had she considered the child's real mother, so happy was she to have a daughter of her own. But what of Noelle Dantine? Yes, she had died within the year of Claudia's "adoption"—the adoption through channels which, as Nick had suspected, were somewhat unorthodox.

But who, she wondered, could have known the outcome? Barton might have waited; yes, and Noelle might have lived. Who could say? The past couldn't be changed. Many comforting old clichés came to mind. But still, Eleanor remained uneasy, all too aware that in withholding Claudia's history from her, she and Barton had lied to the child—and later to the woman—who,

271

instead of driving them apart, had brought them even closer together.

"We've owed her the truth for a long time, Barton," Eleanor said, opening her eyes and looking again at her late husband's picture. "It would be easier if you were here, but . . ." She reached over, picked up the sparkling diamond, and rose. "But you're gone. And so . . . it's up to me."

"Well," Judy Fargo was saying, "that certainly explains why I was so sure I'd seen Armand Dantine before I actually met him!" Then, after another mouthful of Stroganoff, she changed the subject. "Look, hon, you can't go on avoiding Eleanor like this. You're both intelligent women—too intelligent for one of you to be playing games without the other one knowing it."

Claudia nodded and leaned back against the banquette. They were lunching at the Blackhawk Restaurant on Wabash Avenue, where she and Eleanor had spent so many Saturdays of her childhood. It was one of the reasons she had suggested eating there today; she needed the physical reminder, just now, of the closeness between mother and daughter the way it had been.

"It was always here or at Old Heidelberg, every Saturday without fail. Then shopping at Marshall Field's, Clippo the Clown—there was actually a marionette show for kids every week!"

She laughed. "If I misbehaved, I spent an hour in the children's playroom on the fourth floor. I always came out of there a mess, and Mom never said a word about it. In fact, she usually felt guilty for having stuck me in there, so she compensated by taking me to tea upstairs in the Walnut Room before meeting Dad for dinner."

Her voice broke at the memory. "So much of that is gone, Judy. Old Heidelberg and the chicken croquettes . . . the playroom . . . Clippo . . . and Barton."

Judy stole an anchovy from Claudia's Caesar salad. "You know, you're probably expecting me to say something like how unfair all this is, but I'll tell you a secret. I wish my real mother and I were as close as you and Eleanor are. And God knows my little wonder and I will never have that, either. So you want to hear my opinion—which I'll tell you whether you want it or not?"

She didn't wait for Claudia to reply. "I think you should enjoy your salad—the dressing's perfect—and then you ought to call your mom and invite her to dinner. Maybe you should bring her here, instead of me. It'll mean something to her, almost like saying things haven't changed—"

Claudia shrugged. "But they *have* changed, Judy."

"Okay, I'll grant you that. Still, what's changed is really a matter of information. Not her love for you—or yours for her."

"I'm so confused, though. I feel . . ." She shook her head as the words failed her.

"You feel betrayed. Please, don't compare what Eleanor didn't tell you with what Frank—past-tense Frank—didn't tell me. There's a big difference."

In spite of her mood, Claudia laughed at Judy's recently invented distinction between her ex-husband and her current boyfriend.

"Incidentally, I'm really grateful to present-tense Frank," she said. "He helped me out when I didn't know what to do next."

"Yeah, I like him, too. And, speaking of what to do next, Claudia you're evading the issue again."

"I am? What makes you think that?"

"Well, the fact that you're picking at your salad rather than eating it—and you're not getting up to make your phone call."

"My phone call . . . ?" asked Claudia distractedly as a departing luncheon guest passed by with a copy of *Dear Claudia* under one arm. He glanced at the author, then at his book, paused as though deciding whether to intrude on her privacy just to obtain an autograph, and finally headed toward their table.

Claudia was grateful for the interruption. She wasn't ready to confront Eleanor, and suspected that if the subject hadn't been changed, Judy might have been the one to make the call.

After separate telephone conversations with Claudia, Eleanor, and Nick, Raymond Fenwick reached the conclusion that the simplest way was the best: a meeting in his office for an open discussion, all parties present, no misunderstandings possible. The outcome that would follow was up to them.

In view of some of the more complicated cases he'd argued in his career, Fenwick might have considered the matter as insignificant. But it was of paramount import to the three principals involved; Fenwick had been the Gages' attorney for years, and a family friend before that. He felt compelled to do whatever he could to help calm the waters.

From the already varying versions and reactions,

274

however, he knew emotions would be running high—so he'd neglected to mention that they would all be present at the meeting.

Now, as he waited for his secretary to buzz him on the intercom, Fenwick laughed at his own wording on the engagement calendar: Round table—Gages. He recalled Nick's warning about the subtle psychological implications of the case. Well, he reasoned, I'm not King Arthur; all I can do is make the legal disclosures, and let the good doctor Seward handle the fallout.

Armand Dantine sat at the small writing desk in the suite of the Drake Hotel. Philippe had fallen asleep on one of the king-size beds almost moments after their arrival. His father was tired, too, but he would stay awake long enough to finish his letter.

He had reworded it several times, scribbling notes on the hotel paper before selecting the phrases he wanted to use and writing these, with his usual flourish, on the gray vellum stationery he'd brought for just such a purpose. It had to be perfect; she had to understand exactly what he wanted. Then she would see it his way.

He'd realized too late that rushing her would serve only to drive her from him. But nothing was done that could not be undone. His love was too powerful to admit defeat.

Sirena wasn't certain at first where to go. She had looked up the name of Claudia Gage in the Chicago telephone directory at O'Hare Airport, but had found nothing. Then she tried Information.

"I'm sorry, ma'am," said the voice of 411, "but at the subscriber's request, that number is unlisted."

"So how am I supposed to reach her?" asked Sirena.

"I'm sorry, ma'am," repeated the unembodied sing-song, "but at the—"

Sirena hung up. She had the same problem when she tried the name of Dr. Seward, although here an office number was available.

She'd been mulling over the prospect of phoning the Gage woman's boyfriend when another, better, idea appeared.

When Claudia and Judy had finished lunch and returned to the offices of the *Daily Examiner,* they found Bonnie waiting to enter the elevator as they stepped out.

"Are you the welcoming committee," teased Judy, "or have we kept you from lunch?"

Claudia checked her wristwatch, but they'd been gone almost exactly the length of time she'd told her secretary they would be.

"I'm eating lunch in today. But I'm running down to make a deposit at the bank. I've left your messages on the middle stack of papers on your desk, Claudia . . . and—oh, yes. You've got a visitor. A *weird* visitor."

"Weird? In what way do you mean?"

"Well, there's a woman waiting to see you. Gorgeous, but she looks like a runaway from a Fellini movie. Pitch-black hair, no makeup, kind of Gypsyish clothes, and the greenest eyes—"

"Sirena!" Claudia exclaimed almost before the implausibility registered.

"Sirena-with-an-*i*," said Judy. "Can you believe it?"

"She didn't give me her name," said Bonnie, clearly not understanding Judy.

"She didn't have to," said Claudia, walking toward her office and wondering why her legs felt weighted to the floor.

But Fellini's Gypsy was gone.

"Where—?" Claudia and Judy started at once.

Bonnie, from curiosity, had followed them back to the office. Now she seemed genuinely bewildered. "I said you'd be back at three. She asked me if there was a ladies' room, but she was still sitting here when I left for the elevator."

Josh stuck his head in at that moment. "Well, you gals give me the distinct impression that you've lost something," he said.

"No," answered Judy. "Someone." She described Sirena, and the editor gave out a low wolf whistle. "You're talking about Jennifer Jones's twin sister—what a looker!"

"That's the one," said Judy. "Did you see where she went?"

"Nope. I wouldn't mind to, though," said Josh. He paused, trying to remember. Then: "On second thought, I did see her heading for the water cooler a couple of minutes ago. Why?" He stepped out of Claudia's office cubicle, glanced down the hall, and said, "Now I get it. She's gone. Funny, I never realized how close the EXIT stairs are to the water cooler. Who is she, anyway—one of your fans?"

"Hardly that," answered Claudia, taking her seat at

277

the cluttered desk.

"I wonder what she wanted," said Judy.

"So do I," Claudia replied slowly. "And I also wonder why she's in Chicago . . ."

Claudia was the last to arrive. Eleanor and Nick had already exchanged surprised reactions at finding each other there, while Fenwick had made the perfunctory offers of "coffee—or something stronger." His two guests had declined, and the lawyer sensed that if the atmosphere remained this strained, he was going to be the one to need a shot of something stronger.

Nick had put two and two together, as he assumed Eleanor had done. Fenwick had a manila envelope on his uncluttered desk. Next to the envelope was an ivory file folder, and beside that was a contract; Nick could tell by the blue cover and the legal-size length of the papers. Since Barton's will had been read long before now, the contract had to confirm Nick's suspicions.

For Eleanor's part, she'd been mildly put off upon seeing Nick. It was nothing against him; rather, she was displeased at Fenwick's subterfuge. But then, when Ray had begun his familiar routine—the small talk and drink offers—she knew they were waiting for a third person. Only an idiot wouldn't have guessed who that third person was.

However, Claudia's reaction threw everyone off balance. She saw Nick first, and while the vision of him sitting there in one of Ray Fenwick's leather wing-backed chairs was a surprise, she wasn't unnerved by it.

Then she turned and saw Eleanor. "Mom!" So many opposing emotions converged upon her at once that she

278

didn't know whether to run into Eleanor's arms and embrace the woman who had loved her these many years, or whether to step away, to put physical distance between herself and the same woman who had, while loving Claudia, nonetheless kept such a secret from her.

The indecision about her own feelings immobilized Claudia; she suddenly envisioned herself at the age of four or five, bewildered by some new experience. The words came out now as they had then: "Mom, what should I do . . . ?"

But it was the first time Claudia had ever heard Eleanor reply, "I . . . don't know. I suppose . . . you might sit down . . . darling." Eleanor's voice was tentative, and her low-pitched pronunciation of "darling" lacked her customary self-confidence.

Claudia sank into the matching leather chair that Fenwick had set between Nick and Eleanor, although they had chosen their respective positions upon entering the lawyer's office; Fenwick hadn't indicated the seating arrangement with so much as a nod, and only now did he realize that Claudia was again—as she had been almost thirty years before—being placed in the middle.

Nick had heard the hesitation—and the reason for it—in Claudia's voice, as well as her choice of words. But he knew he mustn't interfere. He would have to sit and observe, much as he did with his patients. Sure, but that's easier, he thought. I'm not romantically involved with any of my patients.

The lawyer had closed the door to his office after instructing his secretary to take all calls. Now he took the seat behind his desk and, focusing his attention on the papers assembled before him, rather than on any one of the three people seated on the opposite side of the mahogany gulf that separated them, looked down at his folded hands.

"Well, you'll all have to forgive my . . . deviousness . . . in bringing you here this afternoon." He paused. "My reason wasn't meant to trick any of you. It was, in point of fact, to clear the air." It seemed to be a cue, because both Fenwick and Eleanor cleared their throats. Nick was sorry he'd refused a drink. Claudia's face masked whatever she was thinking.

"Eleanor," continued the lawyer, "you and I have discussed this matter, and"—he turned from her—"although it concerns you only peripherally, Nick, I wanted you present because you were instrumental in bringing the truth to light. Hence, you have some rights, here, too." Now he turned his full attention to Claudia and, feeling more like a stand-in father for Barton Gage than the prominent lawyer he'd been for thirty-five years, he said, "Most of all, I've called this meeting for Claudia's sake." He smiled gently at her. "And I admit, my dear, that it's long overdue."

He opened the envelope and withdrew the yellowed papers. "I won't bore you with all the legalese contained in these documents, Claudia, although, of course, you're free to read them later. However, from what I understand . . . you already know most of what's written in these pages."

He waited for her to say something, but she didn't speak, so Fenwick went on. In one way, he was relieved. He'd hoped to just state the facts as though reading a list, and then ready himself for questions and answers. He'd be the lawyer first, the witness second.

280

He wondered how he'd fare in cross-examination, and was privately grateful that he hadn't chosen to specialize in criminal law.

Still, he thought, it always helps to personalize. And so he continued with:

"Claudia . . . you know by now that Barton Gage was your natural father. And that your natural mother"—those two words did catch in his throat for a moment because of Eleanor's presence—"your natural mother was Noelle Dantine. Her maiden name was Fournier, before she married Guy Dantine.

"Armand Dantine was born to Noelle and Guy in 1953, seven years before your birth. Two years later, in 1955, Guy was killed in a fall from his horse. Noelle never remarried, but . . . in 1959, she and Barton met"—here again, Fenwick found difficulty in maintaining his professional distance but forced himself onward—"and a year later, you were born."

He paused to fill the glass on his desk with ice water from an adjacent pitcher. He used the moment to glance at Eleanor, then at Claudia, as though offering to share the water but in truth trying to read his clients. They were impassive and stony-faced. Fenwick looked at Nick, whose expression all but said "You started this, buddy, and you can finish it."

So, after a few sips of water, Fenwick continued. "Noelle Dantine suffered from a weak heart. She had apparently been warned against having a second child after her physical ordeal in bearing her son seven years before. However"—this directly to Claudia—"you were born to her, and Noelle's sister, Geneviève Fournier, moved into the house to help care for you."

Turning to Eleanor, Fenwick said, "Ellie, I know this

281

isn't among the legal papers, but I feel I must say it, for Claudia's sake as well as yours." Then, to Claudia, he said, "Barton never planned to leave Eleanor. Just as he never planned to give you up. I hope you'll remember both of these factors, my dear, and not judge your father too harshly. He was only trying to make the best of a . . . mistake."

And still, Claudia said nothing.

"Barton offered to adopt you, with Eleanor's full knowledge, of course. Noelle agreed. Barton set up a trust fund for her and for her son so they would never want for anything—"

For the first time since Fenwick had begun to speak, Claudia leaned forward and said, "In other words, my father . . . bought me. From my mother, who was willing to . . . sell me?"

The incredulity, and the weight of the words—made weightier for the lack of accusation in Claudia's voice—confounded even Fenwick. He could only nod, although in an attempt to soften the indictment, he said, "Noelle was thinking of your welfare, Claudia. Everyone was."

Nick, while not wanting to butt in, felt he had to find out what had become of Noelle. And what had happened to transform her son Armand into a man whose obsessive fantasy over his mother had developed into an incestuous desire for his half-sister.

But Claudia spoke his thoughts. "What happened to my mother, Ray?" Armand Dantine had lied about his connection to Noelle; perhaps he'd lied about her death, too.

Apparently, however, he hadn't. "Noelle died the year after you were adopted, Claudia. You were here in Chicago with Eleanor and Barton by that time."

282

"I can remember back to my second birthday," she said in a faraway voice. "There were other children. And party hats and favors—" Her eyes began to fill with tears, but she blinked them away. The memory of her second birthday—her first with the Gages—was due partially to actual recall but largely to having seen the party on film; Barton had engaged a photographer for the afternoon to record the children's festivities.

"Your father . . . and I . . . wanted you to be happy with us," whispered Eleanor in a choked voice.

Claudia could withhold the tears no longer. "I was, Mom," she said softly.

Fenwick waited; he didn't want to interrupt the moment he'd hoped would come, the moment where mother and daughter could allow bygones to be bygones. When he saw the smile, however slight, on Claudia's lips, he continued.

Indicating the papers once more, he said, "The rest of these are just the nuts and bolts of how the money in the trust fund has been and will continue"—a quick glance at Eleanor for emphasis—"to be disbursed. When Noelle Dantine died, the trust was given over to her sister, Geneviève, who raised Armand Dantine. His aunt died about ten years ago, but Armand had long since reached majority, so the money had already been transferred into his name."

"What about his son?" asked Claudia suddenly, mindful that if Noelle Dantine wasn't Armand's late wife, she couldn't be Philippe's late mother.

"His son?" repeated Fenwick. "I wasn't aware—"

"Armand Dantine has a child, Ray," interjected Nick. "The woman who lives with him—a woman named Sirena Mars—is apparently the boy's mother."

283

"Nick!" The full implication turned Claudia's face a hot, bright red. Armand Dantine had not only tried to seduce his own half-sister, but he'd made the attempt without a thought for the other woman—his mistress, the mother of his child.

And that gave Claudia the answer to the question that had been nagging at her since she'd learned that Sirena Mars had visited her office while she and Judy were at lunch.

The reason why Sirena had come to Chicago.

She was following Armand!

"My God," said Claudia, sinking again to the back of her chair.

"Claude . . ." said Nick, rising and coming to kneel beside her, "what is it? What's wrong?"

"It's Armand," she replied. "There can't be any other explanation. He's here."

"What on earth for?" demanded Eleanor. "What in heaven's name does he want?"

Claudia was looking into Nick's eyes when she answered Eleanor's question. "Armand wants . . . me."

Claudia was quiet in the car, and Nick didn't press her into talking. But when once they were seated on the sofa in the den at home, he poured brandies and then, clinking his snifter gently against hers, said, "Claude . . . Armand Dantine isn't the only man who wants you. I want you, too. As my wife." He was watching her for a reaction, and hadn't expected to see new tears.

But she was smiling through them. "I'm okay," she said, clasping his hand. Then she laughed softly. "Do you believe it? I'm the one who's trying to reassure the shrink!"

Looking for an answer in her eyes, he said, "The only way to do that is to accept."

Claudia put down her brandy and moved closer to him. For the first time she felt no hesitation, no need to avoid commitment. "Well, Doctor," she whispered, "in that case, my answer is yes."

Chapter 22

They both tried to keep a light tone about the probability of Armand Dantine's presence in Chicago and his reason for being there. When Nick and Claudia checked their mailbox each day, their mutual, visible relief was obvious even to the doorman, who commented, "I've never seen anyone so glad not to receive a letter. Must be the sweepstakes in reverse."

They laughed, but Claudia felt the same apprehension at her office while she went through the day's accumulation of letters addressed to "Dear Claudia." It was similar to waiting for the other shoe to drop.

Four days had passed without any attempted communication from Armand, and the same four days had gone without a reappearance at the *Examiner* by Sirena Mars. Claudia almost wondered if the woman both Bonnie and Josh Samuelson had seen was in fact someone else. A fan, or else a reader who had stopped by with a question and then thought better about taking up Claudia's valuable time.

Still, she adopted the habit of screening all telephone calls at the apartment, and Bonnie, who had previously done so as part of her job as Claudia's secretary, now made a note of any peculiar-sounding caller as well as the caller's name and number. Those who insisted on anonymity were not put through to Claudia.

Nick, although convinced that if Armand Dantine was in the city he wouldn't be foolish enough to come to their apartment, nonetheless alerted the different shifts of building employees—those on the door and all other personnel—that no one other than Eleanor Gage was to be admitted upstairs without an okay from Nick or Claudia. Even neighborhood deliverymen whose faces were known to them were to be screened before gaining entry.

This was only an underscoring of the already existing rules; the staff knew that no patients of Dr. Seward— no so-called emergency cases—were to be admitted upstairs, either, no matter how extreme the circumstances. In this way, the high-rise on the lake became a modern glass-and-steel fortress.

Eleanor had asked Fenwick to obtain some kind of restraining order as an extra precaution, but the lawyer explained that Armand Dantine would first have to show himself and then demonstrate a reason for the legal straitjacket.

Meanwhile, Claudia and Nick had told Eleanor about their engagement. In her customary fashion, especially now that she and Claudia had overcome what she had feared was an unsurmountable obstacle to their closeness, Eleanor now insisted upon a lavish celebration. "Darlings," she announced to Claudia and Nick at dinner, "I'm going to stand firm on this, so you may as well have a hand in the planning. You name the place, and I'll take care of everything."

"Mom," objected Claudia, "why don't the three of us just have dinner together at someplace special?" She laughed at her own words; dinners out with Eleanor were always at someplace special.

"Look," said Eleanor, "I've just about finished all the preparations for the costume ball at the Art Institute. I have some free time coming up, and you know the city is deadly until after Labor Day." Reaching across the table for Claudia's hand, she added, "And to be perfectly honest, darling, it would mean a lot to me— especially now . . ."

"Well, let Nick and me think about it, okay?"

They called a party-truce while Imelda served the lemon mousse and espresso. Eleanor was watching the way in which Claudia attacked the mousse with gusto, and at a certain moment she shook her head and began to laugh.

"What'd I do, Mom?" asked Claudia. "Get lemon on my nose?"

"No, darling. I was just thinking that some things never change. There's an expression that's never failed to cross your face when you're eating that particular dessert. I remember it from your second birthday party—and I just saw it again now."

"Are you telling me I still have no table manners?" Claudia teased.

"Not at all. You were a very ladylike child." To Nick she said, "While the other children got chocolate whipped-cream cake all over themselves and their clothing, Claudia folded her napkin and left the table."

"Where'd she go?" asked Nick.

"Into the kitchen. She'd managed to climb onto a chair and open the freezer compartment of the refrigerator. Of course, we didn't know that until we found her."

"Where was that?" asked Claudia, trying to remember.

"We have a movie of it. You were sitting by yourself, directly under the kitchen table, and having a marvelous time with — what else? — lemon mousse!"

Now they all laughed, including Imelda, who was clearing the empty dessert plates.

"Mom," said Claudia, "I have an idea. Do you know how to run Dad's film projector? I'd be curious to see some of those old movies."

Eleanor shrugged. "If it requires more than the flick of a switch, dear, I'm afraid—"

"I can probably manage it," interrupted Nick. "And I'd love to see Claude on a bearskin rug, Claude in her bubble bath, et cetera." What he really wanted to see — or, more accurately, to observe — was Claudia's reaction to these films, in view of her recent discoveries.

"Well, then," said Eleanor, "let's set things up in the den."

The last scene on the reel was a farewell to the audience, a two-year-old Claudia seated between Barton and Eleanor, all of them waving and mouthing "Bye-bye" to the camera lens.

When Nick flicked on the table lamp, he saw Claudia's hand on Eleanor's wrist. "You know, Mom," she said, "you asked me earlier where we'd like to have our engagement party. Well, if it's all right with Nick,

I'd like to have it here. At home."

Eleanor glanced over at Nick and said, "I'll leave it up to the doctor. Nick, is that all right with you?"

He closed the film can and crossed to the love seat, where the two women were seated. "Ladies," he answered, "it couldn't be more all right."

Sirena was trying to conserve her energy for the right moment, but time was running out. She no longer knew what Armand planned to do in relation to the child, but if he didn't act soon, she'd have no choice other than to confront the Gage woman directly. She'd hoped to avoid that, but Armand never seemed to go anywhere without the boy, and she didn't want Philippe to see her until she was certain of what was to come next; he'd been through enough; he'd already seen and heard far too much for a child of his tender age.

She was staying at an hotel just a short distance from the more expensive Drake, where the boy and Armand were ensconced. Their whereabouts hadn't been difficult to trace; he'd stayed there before on a previous trip to Chicago. Only now she wondered if that visit had involved the Gage woman, too.

Armand had never given Sirena free access to his credit cards or bank accounts; doling out an allowance was his way of maintaining control. However, she had, without his knowledge, opened her own savings account for the sake of the child, and in spite of her haste to follow Philippe and his father to Chicago, she had taken one detour en route to the airport — to make a cash withdrawal for her trip.

With some of this, on her second morning in the

Windy City she had bought "northern" clothes; the silk halter dress in its minty shade of green offset her dark skin; her cascading mane of thick black curls framed her flashing eyes and crimson smile, making her look like a visiting Hawaiian princess. She rather liked the effect until she glanced in the hotel room's full-length mirror and realized that the dress she'd chosen was similar to one she'd seen on Claudia Gage.

They spent an entire afternoon viewing the paintings at the museum. Philippe was enthralled by the collection of French Impressionists, but what he loved most of all were the Thorne Rooms. The miniature replicas on display permitted his imagination to roam, from the simple log cabin of Colonial days to the grand, palatial drawing rooms and entrance foyers of colossal mansions. One room even boasted a minuscule crystal chandelier that looked exactly like the one at home on Royal Street!

Armand had found the museum interesting, but for the most part, it afforded him time. Time alone with the boy, and time to formulate his plan. He had decided on a note instead of the letter, and would hand-deliver it at the right moment.

He preferred the rear part of the Art Institute, the area just outside the art school, where he imagined summer courses must still be in progress. The various smells of pigments and solvents, turpentine and linseed oil, evoked in Armand a nostalgia for his own childhood, in particular those months when Barton Gage had visited the house so often. He'd shown the small boy how to hold the piece of charcoal, then how to

291

mix his colors. He'd even brought Armand the set of oil paints that had set him on his course.

But the man who had given him so much—even a sister!—had taken away more than he had brought.

Now, as Philippe and his father looked together at the model of a 1940s penthouse apartment, Armand's outward appearance belied his inner rage. Yes, he had money. And talent. And he had his son. But Barton Gage had taken away from him what mattered most in all the world: his sister and his mother. They'd all said Noelle's heart was sick. But he knew better. Her heart was stolen; that was why she had died. And only through Claudia could Noelle live once more.

A small, imperceptible smile formed at the corners of his mouth. Yes, he thought. Just as a pen is the writer's medium and paint is the artist's, Claudia will be mine . . .

Eleanor had outdone herself once again. She and Claudia had agreed on a two-color scheme—coral and white—for the engagement party. Imelda and her two cousins had worked for three days with the florist and the caterer to achieve an effect of understated elegance. Nick, peeking at the preparations when Eleanor was out of earshot, commented, "This'll be a hard act to follow, Claude. What is your mother planning for the encore, anyway?"

"Encore?" Claudia repeated, fastening the post of a coral-and-gold earring to her left lobe.

"The wedding."

"Oh, Nick," she said, "Mom gets off on this stuff. And you must admit she's done a gorgeous job. I mean, getting the caterers and the musicians on such short notice—"

"I hope the former isn't through her connections at the hospital, or I'm spending the evening on a diet!"

They both laughed at the thought. Then he said, "Speaking of music, I saw a couple of guys carrying violin cases into the den a few minutes ago. If they're not machine guns, d'you want me to suggest a song or two?"

"Sure," she answered, working at the right earring. "Just make certain it's dreamy and romantic. The way I'm feeling."

"And the way you look tonight." He grinned. "That's it—we'll make it our song. Okay with you?"

Claudia nodded and he left the room.

She was adjusting the strap on her coral silk sandals when the telephone rang. From habit, she didn't wait for Imelda to answer it but reached over to the table beside her mother's bed and lifted the receiver.

"Hello?"

She heard nothing at the other end.

"Is someone there?" she asked.

She could hear breathing. No! she thought. Not tonight! "Look," she said, "we're not accepting obscene calls or heavy breathers this evening, so good-bye—and don't try again!" She slammed down the receiver and thought no more about it.

"Darling, that gown is perfect!" exclaimed Eleanor as Claudia entered the reception hall.

Claudia smiled in thanks; they'd chosen it together. Imelda straightened the white lace apron over her

293

dress just as the doorbell rang, and while she went to answer it, Claudia took another peek at herself in the antique mirror. The folds of pale coral developed into deeper and deeper shades as she turned.

"You're gorgeous," whispered Nick, coming up behind her.

"Thank you, Doctor," she said. "You look pretty handsome yourself."

He did. Nick seldom enjoyed wearing formal clothes, but his off-white silk dinner jacket was casual enough for him and fancy enough for the occasion. He did a Cary Grant imitation in the mirror just as the door opened and the engagement party "officially" began.

Eleanor's apartment, large as it was, did not include a ballroom. However, that didn't inhibit the guests. While the champagne flowed and people dined at small individual tables set up for six apiece, the string quartet played chamber music and old standards. Marble floors, Eleanor had long ago insisted, were not made for disco dancing. And Claudia couldn't argue, then or now. Everyone seemed to be enjoying the party, yet no one had to scream in order to be heard.

"What a fabulous gown!" exclaimed Judy Fargo.

"Thanks. Yours is gorgeous, too," said Claudia. Judy was wearing copper silk, which shimmered whenever she moved.

"Frank looks good, too, wouldn't you agree?" whispered Judy as he waved from across the room. "He's taking the weekend off, in your honor. Or sort of, anyway. He's also looking over a couple of spaces in town, just in case he decides to spend more time up here."

"More time?" repeated Claudia. "Well . . . what d'you think of that?"

Whatever Judy thought had to be put on hold. Nick came up at that moment and whispered to Claudia, "Let's dance."

"Now?"

"Um-hmm. It's the only acceptable way I can hold you in my arms before this shindig's over, so it'll have to do."

"Doctor," murmured Claudia, "when you say it like that . . ."

"When you're *un*dressed like that, there's no other way to say it . . ."

He'd seen the photograph of Claudia on the society page, along with mention of the engagement party. But he hadn't expected it all to be so easy. He'd expected to be told that Eleanor Gage had an unlisted telephone number, yet she didn't. He'd called, but when he'd heard Claudia's voice on the phone, he hadn't known what to say. He wasn't ready yet. Or perhaps she wasn't.

Nor had he dared hope to pass the doorman without being stopped and asked to show his invitation. But entering with a group of other guests had made that simple as well. He'd gotten off the elevator at a higher floor, though not before noting where the Gages' guests alighted.

He'd known there would be music, because the society column had said so. In fact, he'd read everything but the menu of food to be served. He marveled at society's self-inflicted lack of privacy; it made sitting ducks of them all, as though they had extended invitations to anyone wishing them harm.

But Armand didn't intend harm. He didn't even plan to crash the party. He just wanted Claudia to know, to feel, his presence.

Claudia and Nick were dancing—or what would pass for dancing in the eyes of anyone watching. What they were doing was holding each other closely, touching each other discreetly, both of them wanting the party to be over so they could return to their apartment and make love.

The music had included all the standards. The mood was relaxed, and other couples were dancing-holding-touching, too, Judy and Frank among them.

Nick had requested the musicians to play "Just the Way You Look Tonight," but he'd asked that they wait until he and Claudia were dancing; he'd give the violinist a sign. When he did, as they swayed slowly past the impromptu platform, Nick nodded, and received a knowing wink in reply.

When the song they'd been playing came to an end, the violinist cleared his throat and said, "A special request. For Claudia."

She was resting her head against Nick's cheek. The lights had been dimmed, the champagne had flushed her cheeks, and she felt as though she were floating on air. "Oh, Nick," she murmured. "You remembered."

He pressed his hand against the small of her back, and she closed her eyes in anticipation of the song.

The musicians began to play.

Claudia's eyes flashed open, and she felt Nick's body go tense, as tense as her own.

Judy broke away from Frank's arms and reached the musicians on the heels of Claudia and Nick.

"What the hell kind of joke is that!" Judy demanded before anyone else could speak.

The violinist shrugged, bewildered, and handed her the sheet of gray vellum stationery. "The maid gave this to me."

Together, Claudia, Nick, and Judy read the familiar handwriting. *A special request. For Claudia. "Now is the Hour."*

Claudia clutched Nick's arm as Judy said rhetorically, "It isn't over yet, is it . . . ?"

"No," answered Nick slowly. "But it's going to be. Soon. I'll see to that."

Chapter 23

The moment Nick spoke with the violinist, it became clear.

"The maid gave me this note," he said. "All I did was read aloud what was written on the paper."

Imelda confirmed his version of what had happened.

"I opened the door," she explained, "and there was a man standing there. He was very handsome—and elegantly dressed, too. He handed me a note, together with this." Imelda blushed with embarrassment as she withdrew the folded twenty-dollar bill—the tip Armand Dantine had given her—from her pocket.

"He said he couldn't stay," she continued, "and asked me to be absolutely certain to follow his instructions. That's why I went straight to the musicians' platform with his note. So I wouldn't forget."

She looked pleadingly at Eleanor, who said, "That's all right, Imelda. There's no way for you to have known who he was."

"He had such a nice smile and such intense eyes,"

said the maid, "and he told me it was important."

"It *was* important," said Claudia. "To him." But she was feeling better after the initial shock of hearing the song. Someone standing nearby had handed her a glass of champagne, which helped to calm her, even in light of one unsuspecting friend's comment about "not having heard that old song in at least thirty years."

Finally Claudia suggested sneaking off alone together to the den; neither of them wanted to arouse Eleanor's concern unnecessarily, but they couldn't put the matter of Armand Dantine on hold indefinitely; simply ignoring his existence would not make him go away.

"I'm worried about the boy, too," said Claudia. "If Armand has gone off the deep end, what's to become of Philippe? And where is he right now, anyway? Sitting alone in that big house on Royal Street while his father goes sneaking around Chicago followed by his mother?" She still regarded the entire situation as strange—and the fact of Sirena's being Philippe's mother as truly bizarre.

Nick was sitting alongside her on the love seat. "I have a feeling that the child is here, too," he said. "When I went to the house that afternoon to confront Armand, the boy wasn't wearing play clothes. He was dressed up, you know, a shirt and tie, jacket and pants—"

"He always dresses that way," interjected Claudia. "At least each time I've seen him."

"Yes, but somehow he seemed . . . I don't know, but I'm certain the child's in Chicago, too. Poor kid, he's probably sitting alone watching TV in a hotel room downtown, while his father—"

Nick's thoughts were interrupted by the telephone,

and although it was Eleanor's apartment, Claudia made no move answer it. Apparently Imelda didn't, either, so on the fourth ring, Nick rose from the love seat and went to the desk.

"Hello?" he said into the receiver. Then he remembered the way Imelda greeted each caller, and added, "The Gage residence. May I help you?"

No one responded.

"Hello? Anybody home on your end?" asked Nick again.

Silence. But he could hear breathing.

Now Claudia looked up. "Hang up," she said.

"What?"

"Hang up. He won't speak."

"How do you know?" said Nick.

"A call like that came earlier. Just before the party started."

Nick placed the receiver back in its cradle, then said, "Armand?"

"I didn't think so at the time, but now I can't imagine its being anyone else."

Eleanor entered the den just then.

"Everett and Mildred Atkins are leaving, dear," she said to Claudia. "The Fenwicks, too. I told them you'd be out to say good night."

Claudia got up, but as she headed for the door, Nick said, "You don't mind if I explain a few things to your mother, do you, Claude?"

Eleanor glanced from her daughter to Nick. "I was under the impression that Ray explained more than enough in his office not long ago."

"There are a few ... developments," said Nick. "Nothing to be alarmed about, but you should be

300

apprised of them, nonetheless—especially in view of tonight's musical 'interlude' as well as the phone calls—"

"Phone calls?" repeated Eleanor. "So you know?"

"You mean—"

Eleanor interrupted her daughter, who was still standing in the doorway. "Earlier this afternoon. And twice yesterday morning. The first time I answered the call myself. I spoke into the phone and when no one responded, quite naturally I assumed it was a wrong number. But a short while later, after Imelda returned from the florist's, the same thing happened. And this afternoon, she called again."

"*She* . . . ?" exclaimed Nick.

"Why, yes. Oh, of course, you thought the caller was Dantine."

"How do you know it wasn't, Mom—if Imelda took the call?"

"Well," said Eleanor, "I wouldn't be certain, except that the woman asked to speak with me personally. Imelda had to come looking for me in the dining room—I was arranging the centerpiece—and said there was a lady on the line asking for Mrs. Gage." She paused to recall the precise wording. "Yes. Imelda told me—I remember exactly—that the caller had a southern accent, because it sounded as though she'd asked for *Miss* Gage."

"It's possible that she did, Mom," said Claudia, unsure why Sirena Mars would have reason to telephone her anywhere.

While Claudia went to say good night to the

Fenwicks and the Atkinses, Judy and Frank joined Eleanor and Nick in the den. Nick had nothing secret to confide; he'd only wanted to alert Eleanor to any possible aberrant behavior by Armand Dantine—and now, by Sirena Mars as well.

"Eleanor, I'll leave Imelda to you, but if you don't mind, I'd like to speak with your doorman. To find out how Dantine got up here tonight and to make sure it doesn't happen again. Tomorrow I can drop by and hook up your phone to an answering machine—"

"I despise those gadgets, Nick. I've never had one in the apartment before."

"You've never needed one before. But even with Imelda on the premises, she does go out on errands, and she takes a day off—"

"Two. There isn't enough to keep her busy, and she asked for the extra day."

"All the more reason. You're here alone. There's no point in being frightened, yet at the same time—"

"But you see, Nick," Eleanor interrupted, "I have to disagree with you. I don't mean to seem presumptuous by saying this to someone in your field, but if I were to analyze Armand Dantine, I'd say that he might be trying to take revenge upon me. You know, an eye for an eye—"

"What'd you ever do to him, Mrs. Gage?" asked Judy.

"Well, for one, I became Claudia's mother. In Armand's twisted view of things, he may feel that I'm responsible for Claudia's having been taken away from him—and from their real mother. Then when Noelle Dantine died, well, Nick is the one to explain about transference, but it's easy to see that Armand Dantine

302

was . . . in love with his mother, whom he confuses—or identifies—with Claudia. And it's probable that he perceives me as an obstacle. I imagine Nick and I share that honor." Turning to him, she asked, "How am I doing, Doctor?"

He was grinning. "We could use someone like you at the hospital, Eleanor. We're shorthanded, and you're wasting your talents in charity work."

"Look," interjected Frank, who was leaning against the book-lined wall, "I realize this is none of my business, but if you don't mind the suggestion, you could use a little . . . muscle. I can call up a few friends, and—"

"Oh, please," said Eleanor. "Don't let's get carried away over this."

But Nick could see that she was worried. "Let's get back to the Mars woman for a moment," he said. "I doubt that Dantine put her up to making those phone calls to Eleanor. I wonder if he even knows she's here."

"Well, if he isn't involved, what reason did Sirena have for trying to reach Mrs. Gage?" asked Judy. "Or Miss Gage?"

"I haven't a clue," Nick admitted. "We'll just have to wait and see. Meanwhile, Eleanor, about that answering machine—"

"No, Nick. I won't have one. Thank you, though, for the offer. Besides, if this Sirena person should call again, she's far more likely to tell me what she wants than to tell a tape, don't you agree?"

Nick shrugged just as Claudia reentered the den. "Frankly, Eleanor," he said, "there are times when even the doctor doesn't know what's coming next. But I feel certain we're going to find out."

The boy sat curled up on the edge of the bed. The sun was beginning to set, and he had drawn the draperies in the room to feel less lonely as the city grew dark outside. His father had left him some money with which to tip the room-service waiter, but he wasn't hungry yet.

There was a copy of *TV Guide* lying on the table beside the television set. Philippe got up and retrieved the magazine, then flipped through the listings. Most of the movies he had seen before, at home. There were many more channels in this place to choose from, but the offerings were the same.

So he absentmindedly began channel-hopping with the remote-control buttons. He caught the last half of the local news. He didn't pay particular attention to the usual stories of drug busts, mobster convictions; even the weather forecast held little interest with its unvarying predictions of heat.

But the sports report stirred him. "Tonight at Wrigley Field, the second-place Cubs take on the front-running New York Mets in the first of a three-game series. Check your local listings." Suddenly the *TV Guide* that he'd tossed across the bed became compelling reading matter.

Sometime during the top half of the sixth inning, a tablecloth-covered room service cart arrived. The waiter at first observed Philippe with curiosity over his dinner order. But then, as he glanced around the room and realized that the boy had been left alone for the evening, he understood.

"Makes you feel as if you're out there at the field, huh, kid?"

Philippe blinked, then followed the waiter's gaze to the TV set. Only now did the child see what had triggered his craving for two giant hotdogs on buns, slathered with sauerkraut and mustard, plus an extra-large container of popcorn and a bottle of Pepsi.

"You go to many games?" asked the waiter.

"No," said the boy. "I've never been. Maybe someday I'll get the chance."

Onscreen there was a roar from the crowd. It developed into a groan some forty-thousand-strong.

"Holy shit!" exclaimed the waiter, dropping down to the edge of the bed alongside Philippe. "Not a triple, with two men on! Will somebody tell me why in hell they didn't walk him?"

"Walk whom?"

"Strawberry, who else!" Then he looked at the boy. "Hey, what's your name, kid?"

"Philippe," he answered.

"Well, I'm Joe," said the waiter, reaching over to shake his hand. Then, mispronouncing the name, he asked, "Hey, Phillip—what're you doin' here all by yourself tonight? The folks go out on the town without you?"

Philippe didn't know what to answer, but Keith Hernandez hit the ball out of the park at that moment, and Joe grabbed his midsection as if overcome with pain.

"But he just scored a point, didn't he?" asked Philippe, his eyes dazzled by the sight of the ball soaring up and out over the stands.

Joe turned and answered, "A run, not a point. But y'see, he's on the opposin' team. Wait a minute—you from New York?"

Philippe shook his head. "New Orleans."

"Oh, well, that explains it." Joe rose and went to the cart, where he uncovered the food the child had ordered. "Tell you what, Phil. I'm takin' my two boys to the game tomorrow afternoon—it's my day off—and you're welcome to come with us. Ask your folks when they get in tonight. I'll even spring for your ticket if I can have some of your popcorn. By the way, your hot dogs are getting cold."

That reminded Philippe that he hadn't tipped Joe with the money Armand had left under the Seattle space-needle paperweight. But Joe didn't speak like a waiter expecting a tip, and the child didn't want to insult him by offering it now. Behaving like a grown-up was sometimes very confusing. And difficult.

He knew Armand would be furious if he thought that Philippe had forgotten to tip for room service. Just as he knew that his father would never agree to let him go to a baseball game with total strangers. But perhaps if he explained that he'd met a new friend . . .

It was also a way in which he could give Joe the money without making it appear to be a tip.

And if he was lucky, he'd see a live baseball game!

"Joe," he said, going to the paperweight, "I'll ask my father, but even if he says yes, I'm sure he'll insist that I pay for my ticket." He handed over the tip money.

Joe pocketed the bill and said, "Well, okay. My wife, Angelina, is working tomorrow. She's secretary to the manager. So I tell you what. Meet me and the boys downstairs in Angie's office at noon, and we'll go out

306

to Wrigley Field together. Just remember to be on time, though, 'cause we still gotta get you your ticket."

"You're sure they'll have one available?" asked Philippe.

"Hey, Phil," answered Joe with a wink. "Relax. Eat your dinner. You'll be with Joe Buranski. No problem."

Philippe was growing excited. About the game and about being included.

"Shit," said Joe as the bottom half of the sixth inning sent the Cubs down in order. In consolation, Philippe offered him another handful of popcorn.

"Thanks, Phil. See you tomorrow." As he left the room, Philippe heard him mutter under his breath, "Why the hell couldn't they give Goodein the day off . . . ?"

The next morning Eleanor slept late. Imelda and her cousins would be in later that afternoon to straighten up and restore order to the apartment after the party of the night before.

Eleanor hadn't set the alarm clock, so when the noise first penetrated her sleep, she thought it had gone off by mistake. She rolled over in bed, removed her sleep mask, and only then realized it wasn't the clock, which read eleven forty-five; it was the telephone.

She was still too tired to remember Nick's warning. "Let it ring," he'd advised, "unless Imelda or someone else is there to answer it."

"Hello?" she said into the receiver.

"Missuh Gage?" came the southern-accented voice.

"This is *Mrs.* Gage speaking. Eleanor Gage." She wasn't completely awake, but her mind was entirely alert.

"Missuh Gage" came the drawl once more. Eleanor could hear the woman's breathiness, but recognized its cause as nerves, and this calmed her.

"You've called before," she said. "What can I do for you?"

There was a long pause, yet Eleanor sensed again that the woman was seeking courage, not trying to frighten anyone.

Finally, Sirena said into the phone in a very low voice, "Missuh Gage, I need to talk t' you. As one mother to another."

Chapter 24

The restaurant Eleanor had chosen for the meeting was a large-enough but exclusive-looking French establishment that she'd never eaten in before. She didn't plan on eating now, and wanted a sufficiently public atmosphere in case the woman named Sirena Mars might be inclined toward histrionics — or hysterical outbursts; who could predict? Eleanor hardly trusted her own nerves and their possible reaction to this face-to-face encounter.

She'd requested a table toward the back, just far enough away from the kitchen to avoid the clatter of dishes but with constant diversion should the conversation require it.

At first she'd thought about sitting with her back to the restaurant's entrance — she had no desire to be recognized. Finally she opted for the banquette against the wall facing the oak-framed stained-glass door. As insurance, she kept her sunglasses on while focusing her attention on the entrance—it was also the exit. The phrase "just in case" repeatedly played in her mind.

Eleanor was wearing a straw hat, which she removed and placed beside her matching clutch purse on the seat. She was aware that two men in their mid-fifties, well dressed and obviously interested, were staring at her from the bar. The maître d' had done his bit of flirting, too, and while it made Eleanor smile, she was beginning to wonder if Entre Nous had been named for other reasons than its French cuisine.

It was the lunch hour, but Entre Nous wasn't crowded, perhaps because it was Saturday, although the ambience seemed to suggest relaxed luxury and leisure. Eleanor ordered a martini and, after taking several sips, began to unwind. She took off her dark glasses and slid them up over her neatly brushed coiffure. She had no need to hide; after all, she knew nobody here, and if the men at the bar wanted to flirt, she could simply ignore them.

She smoothed the silk of her skirt and took another swallow. The gin warmed her nicely. Perhaps this would all work out. She did question the wisdom of having come to Entre Nous alone, without telling Nick or Claudia of Sirena Mars's call. But what was the point in worrying them? Still, what if Dantine was following the Mars woman? Or what if Sirena was actually in league with him? What if . . . ?

"Would you care to order now, madame," asked the captain, "or do you prefer to await your guest?"

"I'll wait, thank you," said Eleanor. She'd finished her drink, except for the olive. "And I think I'll have another of these."

* * *

Sirena had waited in a doorway until she saw Eleanor Gage enter the restaurant. Then she crossed the street and stopped before the tinted window with its stained-glass casement panels. The maître d' blocked her view momentarily, but when he moved away Sirena could see deep into the dimly lit dining room. She didn't have to guess which of the women was Eleanor.

She observed the expensive surroundings of Entre Nous, then zeroed in on Eleanor. She fits right in, thought Sirena, noting the stylish hairdo, probably dyed that pale blond although it appeared natural; the ruffles at the neck of the white summer silk crepe blouse fell gracefully over the lapels of a man-tailored linen jacket of muted moss green. Diamond-and-gold earrings twinkled, even at this distance; they must be huge, if they reflect out here, mused Sirena. And they'd be real, too. Nothin' phony or second-class about this lady.

It only added to Sirena's discomfort; she felt under-dressed and out of place, and she hadn't even opened the door. Well, she reasoned, best gettin' it over with. You called her, girl; it wasn't the other way 'round. And there's the boy to think of. That's the whole point of this meetin'.

Concern for Philippe gave her the courage she needed, and Sirena entered the restaurant.

The beveled glass set into the handsome oak door reflected her own image back, and Sirena almost changed her mind and bolted. She had been pleased at abandoning her Gypsy look for a simple Indian-cotton summer dress in olive tones. The conservative color and style—a shirtwaist with short sleeves and a modest hem—bespoke respectability, as did the low-heeled

311

pumps. But she hadn't bothered with accessories, and seeing Eleanor Gage through the window had made Sirena realize what was missing. It wasn't that she looked shabby; she looked incomplete.

It was the way she felt without her son.

She tossed her long black curls and, with a swift movement so there'd be no backing out, pulled open the door.

The two businessmen at the bar turned to stare, as did the maître d', who came forward to greet her. Sirena was oblivious to the admiring glances; she had know such attention since the age of thirteen. She was conscious only of the woman seated on the ivory-satin banquette—and of the woman's eyes, which were fastened on Sirena.

Again she fought the impulse to run. This was something she had to do. There was no choice.

"Missuh Gage," she said quietly as the maître d' nodded and led the way.

"Miss Mars," said Eleanor, beckoning Sirena to be seated opposite her. The maître d' pulled out the chair for her and Sirena nodded the way she'd seen women do in similar situations. That had been in the early years, when Armand had occasionally taken her to Antoine's for dinner.

Another time, she thought. Long gone, as if it belonged to a previous life.

She remembered to open her napkin and place it across her lap. When she looked up, she found Eleanor still staring at her and found it unnerving, especially since she knew ladies didn't stare—and Eleanor Gage was definitely a lady.

* * *

"I'm sorry to be late," said Sirena.

"I arrived early," answered Eleanor. "I've already ordered a drink. Perhaps you'd like one."

Automatic pilot, she thought. I'm speaking like a robot, and that's not what this is about. Still, how could she lower her guard in the face of the stunning woman seated opposite her? Eleanor had been prepared for a shrill, brazen, even aggressive hostility, but she could see immediately that Sirena Mars was as tense as she, Eleanor, felt. That, at least, came as a relief.

The waiter set the mint julep down carefully in front of the younger woman. He couldn't keep his gaze from her arresting green eyes, which flashed an unsubtle warning at him to leave the table.

When he did, Eleanor said, "I have only half an hour, Miss Mars, after which I have another appointment."

"Thank you for seein' me in the first place," Sirena answered, stopping before adding "ma'am" to the end of the sentence. She was grateful that Eleanor Gage had agreed to meet with her but was determined not to put herself in a subservient position.

"You've been to Chicago before, I take it?"

Sirena was surprised by the question. She'd expected Eleanor to use her next appointment as an excuse to directly pursue the point of their conversation and then be finished with it—and with Sirena. But maybe this was the way ladies up North handled such matters. Chitchat, small talk first. Or was it simply the way of Eleanor Gage?

She shook her head. "The farthest north I've evah been is Atlanta, which isn't even in the North, if you know what I—"

"I know what you mean," said Eleanor. "I trust you're comfortable?"

"I'm stayin' at a little hotel. It's okay. And I brought a few dollars with me."

Eleanor bristled and tried to hide her reaction. Cautiously she asked, "Then this is, after all, about . . . money?"

Sirena seized the opportunity to plunge right into the heart of the matter. She leaned forward, almost tipping over her drink. "This is about a little boy named Philippe Dantine, Missuh Gage."

"And my daughter Claudia."

"Yes. And about me, and Armand. And you, too. I guess we're all involved. At least now."

"And you think you have a solution, Miss Mars?"

"Call me Sirena. No. I've got no answers to any of this. I just mean to get my boy back. He's here, you know. They both are here."

Eleanor gave a quick nod of her head and took another sip of the martini she'd been nursing. Unsure of how much to say, she needed to stall for time.

But Sirena had seen the nod and knew what it meant.

"He's done somethin' already, hasn't he?"

Eleanor looked up, then away. Sirena covered the older woman's hand with her own. "Hasn't he?" she repeated.

Before she knew it, Eleanor had told Sirena the whole story of the incident at the engagement party the night before. It brought tears to her eyes and she used

314

the damask napkin to dab them away.

"Y'see?" asked Sirena when Eleanor seemed calmer. "I think Armand has gone . . . well, crazy, or somethin'."

"I just don't want Claudia . . . or anyone . . . hurt," Eleanor managed.

"Missuh Gage, I said on the phone that I wanted to talk to you in a mother-to-mother way. My boy . . . Philippe . . . is as important to me as your Claudia is to you."

"Yes, of course he is. I can understand that now."

"And Armand can be dangerous, I believe."

"Nick Seward—Claudia's fiancé—informed me that Dantine threatened him with a gun."

"Well, he's not out to hurt your daughter—he just wants to get her back. Don't be worryin'—"

"Don't worry!" Eleanor exclaimed, then instantly lowered her voice. "The people in my acquaintance, Miss Mars, do not carry guns! They have no need to. An accident could occur, and anyone might be hurt!"

A flash of anger began rising inside Sirena. She had come here for help, not to calm a spoiled, wealthy woman. However, losing her own patience wouldn't get her anywhere. And, she further reasoned, Eleanor Gage has never dealt with a man like Armand Dantine before.

"Look," Sirena said after a time, "we're talkin' about my boy. My son."

"All right," said Eleanor, "how can I be of help? What is it I can do?"

"Armand is . . . oh, what do they call it . . . harassin' you, isn't he? He's harassin' you and your daughter and your daughter's boyfriend. Can't you do somethin'

315

to have him . . . I don't know . . . warned, say, by the police?"

"If you mean a restraining order," said Eleanor, "I've already been informed by my lawyer that nothing can be done legally unless Armand Dantine actually breaks the law. And then it might be too late." She finished her drink, then added, "Besides, we don't even know where he is. Chicago is a very large city, much larger than New Orleans."

Sirena took the last gulp of her drink. The sugar had settled at the bottom and the sudden, unexpected shock of sweetness sent a shiver through her. She realized the futility of her request. She couldn't tell Eleanor Gage that Armand and Philippe were staying at the Drake. The woman—or her daughter, or Dr. Seward—might rethink the situation and take action. God only knew what Armand would do then. In one of his rages, he was capable of anything—anything other than bringing harm to his son.

At least in the past. Would he consider using Philippe as a means of fighting her? Eleanor Gage was right. In Armand's state of mind, he might hurt anyone who stood in his path.

"I'm sorry," Sirena said at last. "I had this idea that . . . well, that with your position in this town . . . and Claudia's bein' famous . . . there'd be some way of getting to him."

It seemed odd to Eleanor that the same thought had occurred to her. Money offered no solution. She'd considered trying to buy Armand off, then realized that he didn't need more money. He had enough for the rest of his life. The irony wasn't lost on Eleanor; Gage money was already Armand's money.

316

"We two are really after the same thing, you know," said Eleanor. "The safety and protection of our children."

Her words touched Sirena. "Oh, Missuh Gage . . . I'm so afraid of losin' my son. I call him my little man, but he's no more than a boy."

"You're his mother. Once we find out where he is . . . well, perhaps my lawyers can do something to help."

"Thank you, but I get this feelin' . . . All Armand wants is to be together with your daughter. It's crazy, I know, but at least . . ." Sirena's eyes were filled with tears and for a moment she was unable to speak. Then she swallowed and said, "Philippe likes Claudia . . . an' I think she's fond o' him, too."

"My dear . . . what are you saying?"

"I'm sayin' that whatever happens, I want to be sure the boy is with someone who'll love him. I'll die if I lose my child, but if he's safe . . . it won't matter."

Eleanor found it impossible to reply. She wondered if Noelle Fournier had once expressed herself similarly.

"Don't speak—or think—that way" was all she could say. "You'll get him back."

Sirena took the napkin from her lap and placed it on the table. "Not if Armand has anythin' to do with it, Missuh Gage."

Armand fastened the last button on his shirt while studying his reflection in the mirror. There could be no rest for him as long as this separation from his beloved continued.

It was simply taking more time than he'd anticipated

317

to formulate a plan. Meanwhile, he would have to satisfy himself with merely watching her, following her, knowing where she went and who she saw.

It was fortunate that the Drake Hotel was a short drive to the apartment building where she lived with Nick Seward. The night had been exhausting, but his wait outside Eleanor Gage's building had brought its reward. The cabbie had grumbled about parking for so many hours, but with the doctor's address and telephone number unlisted in the Chicago directory, the only way to learn the location was to follow them home.

The fantasy he'd composed had occupied his time until the engagement party was over. He envisioned dancing with Claudia all night to their song and celebrating their engagement. Applause greeted them as they left the ballroom hand in hand. Then suddenly, magically, she was in his arms. His formal tuxedo and her flowing gown miraculously disappeared, and they lay naked on the Persian carpeting beneath her portrait, the one he'd painted of her.

For now it was only a dream.

But she knew he was here. Watching her. Wanting her.

The squeak of a mattress spring summoned his attention back to the present. Philippe sat on the bed. He looked so small, so alone. This would all be easier if he weren't here, Armand thought. But there was no way to have left him in New Orleans, no one trustworthy enough to look after the boy in his absence.

Armand was more than wary of strangers, but he feared Philippe himself. The child might tell what little he had overheard or understood, and then what? That wouldn't do. No, it was better to leave him alone, here at the hotel. There was no alternative.

"Are you going out again?" Philippe asked.

"Yes. I must. And I don't know for how long," answered Armand. He sat down on the other bed and slipped his stocking feet into a pair of alligator loafers. "Look, Philippe, I'm aware that this must be very boring for you, but . . ."

"You told me it would be only for a short while. How much longer?"

"I can't say. It has been difficult to arrange a meeting with Miss Gage. She's been . . . unavailable."

Philippe picked up that day's copy of the *Daily Examiner* that was lying at the foot of the bed. "Her column is in the paper every day, so she must go to her office at the newspaper. Why don't you try there?"

"She's very busy, Philippe," Armand answered, snatching the paper from the child's hands. He glanced down at the page bearing the small black-and-white photograph of her beneath the heading, *Dear Claudia*. This morning's entry had intrigued him. He'd always surmised that columns such as hers were written a week or more in advance of publication, but he wondered if today's edition had been an exception.

Dear Reader, The letters I will address today all deal with love that crosses the boundary of obsession. If one or more of you should read this and recognize yourself described in the words of these victims, I beg you to help yourselves and the object of your love. Seek professional counsel. Love which is not given cannot be freely taken.

* * *

She must be speaking to me, Armand reasoned. It was similar to her guarded responses in reply to his own earlier letters. That she was again addressing him only assured him of his importance to her, just as it indicated, in his mind, Claudia's gradual realization of her importance to him.

She knew. It made him smile.

"I must go now," he said. He handed Philippe two ten-dollar bills. "This is for room service and anything else you may want in the way of magazines or reading material. Order whatever you please, and be polite, but beyond that, I don't want you speaking to anyone. Strangers cannot be trusted. Be sure to lock the door after I go out, and again after the waiter has brought your lunch."

Then his thoughts turned to Sirena. She'd know by now that he'd come to Chicago. How stupid of him not to have thought of it before; she'd know where in Chicago because of the last time. Would she try to call? Had she tried already? "If the telephone rings, Philippe, I don't want you to answer it."

"All right," the boy replied obediently. He put the crisp bills under the paperweight and went to the television set.

At the door, his father turned and said, "Perhaps there's another baseball game this afternoon. Why don't you amuse yourself by watching it?"

Philippe looked up and a smile began to form across his face. "I will," he said, and the smile grew even broader when the door was closed and he heard the click of the lock.

In a flash he was seated on the rug and pulling on

320

his shoes. The he glanced up at the alarm clock. Joe Buranski had said to meet him downstairs at noon. He still had half an hour.

He tied his shoelaces, then picked up the newspaper and read the opening paragraph of Claudia's column for the third time. He wished he'd packed a dictionary so he could look up the word *obsession*.

Claudia stepped out of the bathtub and wrapped herself in the soft, voluminous folds of her deep-purple velour robe. The perfume she'd used in the bathwater still clung to her skin, and she felt more rested than she had in weeks.

She and Nick had talked through half the night. She'd voiced her fears, not only of Armand and possibly Sirena, but of her inner conflicts as well. After a time, she'd admitted her warring resentments and sympathies, which fluctuated, often from moment to moment, between Noelle Fournier Dantine and Eleanor Gage.

"Don't look to cast blame on anyone," Nick warned, repeating the word "anyone."

"Meaning?"

"If neither of them is at fault, then someone else must be. Who?"

"My . . . father?"

"And if not Barton? If it has to be someone's fault, Claudia, and you feel guilty about blaming any of them, then who's left?"

"But, Nick, it does have to be someone's fault! Things like this don't just happen! Look at what it's done to Armand—and what he's doing to me! Someone is to blame, Nick! All of them, including—"

She stopped herself and his immediate impression was of a frightened animal, terrified by the sound of a gunshot.

"Who . . . ?" Nick asked softly.

"Me," she answered in a hushed, surprised voice. "If it isn't their fault—any of them—then it's got to be . . . mine . . ."

Tears followed, and he held Claudia and talked gently to her. "It's because you were so loved . . . not *un*loved. Don't you see?"

She finally fell asleep in his arms. If she dreamed, she didn't remember. In the morning, they made love.

"Oh, Nick," she said afterward, smiling. "Thank you . . . for everything."

"We'll forgo my usual fee," he teased, getting up to shower and dress for the office.

Ordinarily they spent Saturdays together, but he'd fallen behind his regular schedule over the past few weeks. This morning was a chance for him to catch up.

"I'll be back by four," he promised.

Claudia barely heard the short, staccato buzzing of the house intercom phone over the roar of the blow dryer. She snapped it off and hurried into the hall. The plush pile of the carpeting felt good under her bare feet.

"Miss Gage?" asked the familiar voice of Byron, the weekend-shift doorman.

"Yes?"

"Well . . ." he hesitated. "I don't mean to worry you . . ."

"What's the matter?" she asked.

"There's a man down here in the lobby," he replied in a low voice. "I had him wait in the vestibule, so he can't hear me. He's—"

Claudia interrupted. "What does he look like?" Her hand inadvertently went to her chest, as though it would help control her quickened heartbeat.

The beat increased in rhythm as Byron described Armand Dantine. "Since he fits the picture of the guy Dr. Seward asked us all to look out for, I thought I—"

"Yes, yes. Thanks, Byron. It does sound like the man. Does he have a child with him? A boy of about eight or so?"

"No, ma'am, he's alone as far as I can tell. But he tried to sneak past me when I had my back turned for a minute. He wouldn't give me his name. I've got my eye on him right now."

"Good. Don't let him come up."

"All right, ma'am, I won't. Still . . ."

"What is it?"

"Well, Miss Gage . . . I can send him away, but if he's made up his mind to go upstairs, he could go through the garage elevator and transfer to a lobby elevator. And it's around the corner, so I wouldn't be able to see him."

God, thought Claudia, he's right! "What did you tell him, Byron?"

"Just that I'd call up. But he's staring at me really hard. I mean, if I say nobody's home, he won't believe me. He sees me talking to someone, so what should I tell him?"

Damn! "The maid—tell him you spoke with the maid and she said I've gone out."

"That's good, Miss Gage," the doorman answered.

"Thanks. I appreciate you conscientiousness, Byron."

"Hey ma'am, it's my job. Who is this guy, anyway?"

"He's . . . you might say he's a fan. Of sorts. It's a long story. Just get rid of him."

"It's done," he said, and hung up.

Claudia stood in the hall and tried to collect her thoughts. She was uncommonly calm now and aware that her thinking was clear, uncluttered by her emotions.

I can't stay here, she realized. Even if he doesn't get upstairs, I won't feel safe sitting alone in this apartment.

She ran to the telephone beside the piano and tried Nick's office number. After four rings, she heard a click on the line and ringing began again. Dammit! That meant the call had bounced back to the main switchboard.

Of course. It's Saturday. Margaret wouldn't be working today.

"Lake Shore General," said the operator's voice.

"Has Dr. Seward signed in yet?" asked Claudia.

"Just a moment, please." Claudia heard pages turning, then the woman's voice again. "No, ma'am, Dr. Seward hasn't checked in at the registry, but I do show him as scheduled to come in today. Would you care to leave a message?"

Should I? Claudia wondered. No, that would only worry him, and I can be there myself in ten minutes. She thanked the operator and hung up.

On a sudden impulse she called Judy, but the answering machine picked up, and Claudia remembered that Frank was staying for the weekend; Judy probably

324

wouldn't check for messages until Monday.

She phoned Eleanor, but her mother didn't answer; she'd mentioned something about a committee meeting for the upcoming costume ball at the museum, and Imelda was always late.

This late?

It reminded her of the time passing. All right, she thought. I'm alone, and I don't want to be. Get out. Now.

Within five minutes she had thrown on a pair of slacks and a shirt. Grabbing her tote, she hurried out of the apartment.

The wait in the hallway for the elevator seemed interminable, but she was afraid to take the stairs. They were at the far end of the hall, and isolated. Even the sign outside read FOR EMERGENCY ONLY.

In a way, this was one. But what if Armand, as Byron had suggested, had somehow managed to enter the building through the garage, in which case the stairwell could prove to be a trap? She considered knocking on her neighbors' doors, but there were only three other apartments on the floor, and all three families, she knew, spent the weekends out of town.

There were two lobby elevators in addition to the service elevator around the side of the building. An attendant was usually on duty there, but what if he'd gone on a break?

The bell signaling the passenger elevator's arrival jangled Claudia's nerves, but the moment the door slid open and she saw that the car was empty, her reflexes went into action. Her finger pressed GARAGE, then she instantly canceled that and pushed LOBBY. Byron could call down to the garage and have her car driven around to the front. It might inconvenience the building employees, but there was no point in taking chances. Not when Armand Dantine was involved.

Chapter 25

Armand knew that Claudia might leave via the garage, just as he knew the doorman was lying to him when he said he was speaking with Miss Gage's maid.

The point was, he reasoned, that now he'd been seen, which in turn meant he could be recognized.

He wanted the doorman to notice his departure, so he stood conspicuously beneath the building-entrance canopy and waited for a taxi to pull up alongside the curb.

"Drive around the block," he instructed the cabbie. "Then circle back and park down the street, but keep the main entrance to the building within view. And make certain we're just out of the doorman's line of vision."

The cabbie's expression, reflected in the rearview mirror, annoyed Armand; nonetheless, he sat back against the seat and fixed his eyes on the entrance doors. Just a glimpse of her, he vowed, and I'll go my way.

As they waited, dark, heavy storm clouds began drifting overhead. Parents wearing swimsuits and carrying towels scurried across the beachfront, their children in tow behind them, everyone intent on finding shelter before the storm began.

"Hey, Mac," said the driver, "it's gonna rain."

"I know," Armand answered. "And the name isn't Mac."

The cabbie shrugged, then turned around and asked tentatively over the front seat, "Well . . . uh, how long are we gonna wait here?"

Armand looked at the face of the driver. He was somewhere in his late twenties. His brown hair was combed into a greasy ducktail left over from the 1950s.

"The meter's running," said Armand. "What does it matter how long we wait?"

"Okay, okay," answered the cabbie. "I was just asking, that's all."

He turned to face front again, while Armand continued to gaze out the window at the building.

Seconds later, he noticed a white Porsche sportscar pulling up to the main entrance. It was driven by a man, who jumped out and held the door open for Claudia, who dashed from under the canopy and climbed in behind the wheel. She gunned the motor, and the tires squealed as the car took off.

"She's in a hurry," the cabbie observed.

Armand remembered his promise to himself. But he couldn't return to the hotel. Not now. Not after seeing her again.

"Follow her," he said.

The cabbie reached for the ignition key. "Just my

luck," he muttered, maneuvering the taxi into the traffic. "A cops and robbers show . . ."

"I'm Dr. Nick Seward," he said to the unfamiliar woman seated behind the front desk. The switchboard buzzed, and while she answered the calls, Nick signed his name in the staff registry.

The receptionist took down a message, then returned her attention to the doctor.

"You had two calls," she said, "but neither woman left her name."

Nick thanked her and headed for the elevators. He passed the ground-floor solarium, where patients in wheelchairs sat with their visitors. Even on a humid late-summer Saturday, there was activity bustling everywhere throughout the hospital. But, he thought, at least most of the administrative staff won't be in today; I can get a few things done without being disturbed. He wondered who had called. Perhaps one of the women was Claudia; he'd try her at home once he got upstairs.

He reached the top floor and noticed an absence of sound; in the hallway leading to his office, thick carpeting contributed to the quiet; downstairs, every step was echoed by shoes clicking on tile.

The morning edition of the *Daily Examiner* was tucked under his left arm. Nick had picked up a copy on his way to the hospital and read Claudia's column in the coffee shop around the corner. Usually he liked reading her advice; she had a good, common-sense approach to human nature and problem solving. But this morning, her column had disturbed him, and he made a mental note to talk with her about it.

He unlocked the door to his office and entered the reception area. It was darker than usual for this time of day. He glanced out the window directly behind Margaret's desk. The view was hardly cheerful under the best of weather conditions. But today it was particularly dreary with the overcast skies that promised more rain. If rain came and didn't let up by the time he was ready to leave, he'd be in for a shower just getting to his car. Why, he wondered, did I park out front today, instead of driving around to the lot. He answered himself with a grin: pure laziness. And not very smart.

Nick was surprised to find the door to his inner office unlocked. He tossed the newspaper onto the leather sofa as his hand went automatically to the light switch on the wall to his right. The door closed behind him.

Sirena Mars stood near his desk and blinked her eyes against the sudden brightness in the room. She looked both frightened and tired.

"They said you'd be in today," she explained hurriedly. "And when I got up here, the cleanin' lady was in, so I ducked inside and hid till she—"

"It's all right," said Nick. "You just . . . well, you startled me."

That explained one of the calls.

"Your telephone rang but I didn't answer it."

He beckoned her to a chair and took his seat behind the desk. Perhaps the second caller was Claudia.

"How long have you been here?" he asked.

"I told you . . . I just . . ."

"No . . . not here in my office. I mean in Chicago."

"Oh." She hesitated, feeling foolish for not having understood immediately. "Since Wednesday, when Armand left."

"You followed him, I take it."

"I had to. He took Philippe." She was sniffling, and her hands had begun to tremble. "I couldn't just stay there and do nothin'!"

"Here," said Nick, offering her his handkerchief. "Blow your nose." He allowed her time to compose herself, then asked, "Now that you're here . . . in Chicago . . . what do you propose to do?"

"That's just it. I don't know. I may as well tell you . . . you'll find out about it anyway. I met with Missuh Gage."

"Eleanor?"

"Yes." She proceeded to tell him the details of her conversation with Eleanor Gage at the restaurant earlier that afternoon. "I thought her family—considerin' how important they are—might be able to help me out, but . . ." Her voice trailed off.

"You probably shouldn't have done that," said Nick. "I imagine it only frightened Mrs. Gage."

"No, she was okay with me. Even wanted to help. But she can't. She said as much, said there's nothin' she could do within the law." Sirena leaned forward. "I've got to get Philippe away from him, Dr. Seward—the child's all I have left!"

Nick reached into the top left drawer of his desk and withdrew a yellow box. He shook five tiny pills into his hand and poured them into a small envelope.

"When you get back to wherever it is you're staying," he said, handing the envelope to Sirena, "take one of these."

"What is it?" she asked suspiciously. But she accepted the envelope.

331

"Just Valium. To calm you down when you're upset and also to help you get to sleep."

"I didn't come here to sleep or to get calmed down with medicine. I've got my own medicine."

"What's that, Sirena? Voodoo?" When she looked up at him, Nick said, "I had a little talk with Uncle Leo."

"That old man always did have a big mouth."

"Perhaps, but what he had to say was . . . interesting."

"I'll just bet it was!" She almost spat the words.

"You're angry with him?"

Sirena gave a single, emphatic nod of her head. "It took me a long time to really use . . . magic. And when I finally did, it got all confused and . . ."

"It didn't work?" Nick asked.

"Not the way I expected. I mean, Uncle Leo should have given me better instructions on how to use this stuff."

"What . . . stuff?"

Reluctantly at first, Sirena told Nick about the buried porcelain rose pin and the lace handkerchief.

He made no mention of how much of the story he already knew. Nick's increasing interest was in the way she told him. Her disappointment was as strong as her belief. She spoke like a child whose prayer to God had gone unanswered. It was too easy to label it as nonsense. His experience as a medical doctor and as a psychiatrist had shown him the power of faith, as well as the consequences suffered by its loss.

Sirena was in tears again by the time she finished. "I swear, Dr. Seward, I've cried so much in the last few days, it's a wonder I've got any tears left." She crumpled Nick's handkerchief in her lap and said, "Armand

332

kidnapped my little man, and—"

"Wait, please, Sirena," he interjected. "Let me explain to you how the police will look at this."

"Okay."

"The three of you are all here. In the same city. But you aren't Mrs. Armand Dantine."

"I'm Philippe's mother!"

"I know, but you're not married to his father. You led everyone to believe you were a salaried servant in Dantine's house. You've never legally claimed the child as yours. Dantine, right now, is entitled to custody of the boy. That's the way the law will see the situation."

"The law!" Sirena was on her feet. "What about the law of Nature! The law that binds a mother and her child!"

"Sirena, please. I'm only trying to tell you how it is, not how it ought to be. There must be a way to—"

"Oh, there's a way, all right, Dr. Seward!" She picked up the envelope of pills and threw them at his chest. "You won't help me, except to give me drugs that'll make me sleep so I won't bother anybody! Well, you can keep your . . . your . . . magic! You can keep your laws!"

She was at the door. Nick tried to detain her, but she shook him off. "I've tried it your way, Dr. Seward. That's not workin', and somethin's gotta be done! I'm gettin' my son away from that man if I have to do it all by myself! And if that happens, I'm gonna be doin' it my way—with my rules! By my laws!"

She slammed the door in Nick's face.

Normally, she would have parked in the section of

the lot reserved for Medical Administration, where Nick usually parked his Jaguar. But the sky had turned a menacing color. The sun was gone, and in its place a fierce wind had come up. Any minute it would start to pour.

The Hospital Administration parking area was just beside one of the rear entrances and a good thirty feet closer than Nick's space around the corner. Directly in front of her, Claudia saw the spot that was unofficially reserved for Raymond Fenwick as a member of the board of directors at Lake Shore General. She wondered why no one ever mistakenly took Ray's spot, since there was no sign bearing his name. Maybe no one dared take it.

Except Claudia. She pulled into the space and checked the rearview mirror again, as she had done countless times since she'd left the apartment.

She saw the same yellow cab. It didn't follow her into the lot, but instead pulled to the curb near the chain-link fence separating the parking lot from the street. She couldn't make out the driver's face, and his passenger might have been invisible for all she could see of him. But she knew, or at least suspected, that this was the cab that had been tailing her; it was too much of a coincidence otherwise.

Claudia alighted and locked the door. She reached the hospital lobby just as the first raindrops began to fall.

Within five minutes, she had passed through the reception area, past the switchboard-information desk, and was upstairs on the top floor, breathless but finally at Nick's office.

The outer door was unlocked. She opened the inner

door and found him seated at his desk. His eyes were closed and he was giving himself a temple massage.

"Headache?" she asked.

He jumped up from the chair, then gave a nervous laugh. He was glad to see Claudia, but she'd scared the hell out of him.

"Sorry about that. Are you okay?"

"I should be asking you that," he answered, coming around the desk to greet her. "You're white as a sheet."

Before she could reply, he'd taken her in his arms and was holding her tightly. Claudia felt better in his embrace. Their lips came together in a long kiss.

"I love you so much," he whispered at last. "Sometimes it's sheer hell being away from you, even for an hour."

His own words reminded him of the immediate situation — and of Armand Dantine's similar but unrealistic feelings about her.

"Nick?" She stepped back and looked deeply into his eyes. "What's happened?"

"You first," he said, leading her to the sofa.

She explained about Armand and the taxi. They were both aware that her hands were shaking as she told the story. While she spoke, Nick got up, opened a wooden cabinet, and returned to the sofa with a bottle and a glass, into which he poured a half inch's worth.

"Drink this," he said.

"Ordinarily, I'd say it was too early in the day . . ."

"But under the circumstances . . . ?" he finished for her. She downed the liquor, and although it made her shiver, she felt better.

"Do you prescribe this to all of your patients, Doctor?" she asked with a grin.

"Valium seemed antisocial," he answered.

Even now, she thought, he knows how to make me smile.

Valium. The word repeated itself in his brain. Sirena's envelope still lay on his desk.

Nick seated himself beside her again. "Listen," he began, "something triggered Dantine's actions today, and I think it may have made him . . . bolder."

"What do you mean?"

"This." He reached behind her to where he'd thrown the copy of the *Daily Examiner.*

"My column . . . ?" she asked.

"Yes. How long ago did you write this?"

"It was"—she stopped to recall the exact day—"when we got back. Before the engagement party was even a definite date. I asked Josh to give it priority over my other columns, in case there was a backlog."

"Claudia . . . didn't you know Dantine would read it?"

"Of course I knew—but I thought he'd be reading it in New Orleans, not Chicago!"

"All right, calm down—I'm not accusing you of anything. It just wasn't the best idea . . . and the timing makes it worse."

"Are you saying that he's doing these things to spite me? Because of what I wrote in the column?"

"No. He likes the attention. It acknowledges that he matters to you in some way. He wants to be important in your life, Claude. This"—he tossed the paper onto the coffee table—"tells him he's on the right track. It encourages . him."

"Christ!" Claudia was holding her head in her hands. "That's exactly what I didn't want! Oh, how stupid of

336

me! I just thought he'd read it—at his house—and see how awful and sick this whole business is!" She lifted her head and rested her hand on Nick's shoulder. "I've received letters from other people in the same situation. I thought the column might help them all."

"And it might. But it hasn't done you any good. And," he added, "there's something else."

"Oh, no. What is it?"

"Sirena Mars was here."

Claudia leaned back on the sofa and listened as Nick told of the woman's visit a short while before. "And I'm afraid I wasn't much help," he admitted in conclusion. "In fact, I may have made things worse. She was very upset, and I think I only aggravated the matter."

"Well," Claudia said quietly after a pause, "I suppose we're even, then."

"I guess we are. I'm surprised the two of you didn't bump into each other. She just left."

"She was probably on her way downstairs as I was coming up." A new thought occurred to her. "Nick! What if Armand saw her leave?"

He paused, then said, "Most likely Sirena will have gone out through the main entrance. If Armand is still where you left him, he won't have been able to see her."

Claudia exhaled a deep sigh of relief. "Good. I . . . I don't want anything to happen to her. She's so alone, Nick. She has no place to go." She pondered this for a moment. "I wonder where she's staying, or if she knows where Armand is."

"She didn't say, unless she told Eleanor. We can call her if you like; it seems that Sirena phoned your mother. And today they had a little meeting."

"When?"

"A couple of hours ago. Unfortunately, there was nothing Eleanor could do to help her."

"Then Sirena's tried getting in touch with all of us, hasn't she?" Claudia said rhetorically, remembering the woman's aborted visit to her office at the newspaper. "Mom hasn't mentioned a word to me about any calls from Sirena."

"Nor to me," he said. "And it's time Eleanor understood that harboring further secrets from us will only do more harm than good."

"You're right, of course," Claudia agreed as Nick picked up the phone.

His conversation with Eleanor Gage was brief, and by the time he'd hung up, Claudia had walked into the reception area of his office. Nick found her staring out the window. The sun, which had disappeared earlier behind darkening clouds, now seemed never to have shone. Torrential rain beat loudly against the glass, which rattled from the wind.

"I told your mother we're on our way."

Claudia said nothing, and Nick followed her gaze to the yellow cab parked on the street opposite the parking lot.

"Do you think he can see us standing here?" she said. Then, not waiting for his answer, she asked, "Nick, what if he follows us to Mom's I don't want Armand to know where she lives."

"Claude," he reminded her gently. "He *already* knows. The party . . . 'Now Is the Hour' . . . ? Don't drive yourself crazy with that kind of speculation. If Dantine wants to find any of us, he will. Accept that as fact. Anyway, he'd be more inclined to follow

338

Sirena."

She looked at him. "You're so good. And none of this is letting you get any work done, is it?"

"No," he replied with a grin. "But this will end. I promise you that. Come on. We should get going."

"How? He'll see us. My car is right . . . there." She gestured out the window to her white Porsche in Ray Fenwick's parking spot.

"Ray will love that. Did you lock it?" asked Nick.

"Yes. Why . . . ?"

"Then leave it there. I'm parked around the front. We'll get soaked—but at least we won't be seen."

"I didn't bring an umbrella," she said as he led her out of the office and locked the door.

"Neither did I. C'mon. Once we get outside, we'll make a run for it."

In the elevator, he said, "Claude, I'm wondering if . . . maybe we ought to go to the police."

She turned toward him but said nothing.

He shook his head. "No, on second thought, what would we say? Dantine hasn't actually threatened anyone except me, and even that wouldn't constitute an act against me."

"That's just it. He hasn't done anything to anyone. He's smart. He knows where all of us are, and none of us knows where he is."

"Damn!" said Nick. "If we could draw him out in the open . . ."

"Meaning?"

"Well . . . he reacted to your column. Something like that—something to force his hand."

"It's a good idea, but I have to admit I'm not wild about the prospect. Got any suggestions?"

"Not a one. But let's keep it in mind. We'll figure out a way."

Claudia hoped he was right. She didn't relish behaving like a fugitive.

Chapter 26

"Can you see okay, Phil?" asked Joe Buranski as they settled into their box seats directly behind home plate.

"Oh, yes!" he exclaimed.

"Hey, Pop," said Mike, the older of the Buranski boys. "Can I have a hot dog?"

"Sure," answered Joe. "Hot dogs for everybody." To Philippe he said with a wink, "I know. We'll get some popcorn and hot roasted peanuts, too, yeah?"

Philippe and Bobby, who had talked nonstop in Joe's car as soon as they discovered their similarity in age and interests, nodded enthusiastically. Mike, who was twelve, was trying to emulate his father, so he maintained a middle ground somewhere between childish glee and preadolescent boredom. He, too, however, had to admit his excitement over their seats.

"Where'd you get these?" he asked. "We always sit in the bleachers."

"Your mom pulled a few strings," said Joe proudly. "It pays to have someone in management." He looked up at the gray clouds. "I just hope those don't get in the way of the game."

Philippe was filled with wonder as he gazed around Wrigley Field. There didn't seem to be any spare seats; in fact, he could see neighboring rooftops spilling over with people. That looked like fun, but it couldn't be more thrilling than sitting here, so close to the players.

"In the game last night," said Philippe to Bobby, "the tall man hit the ball into the crowd, but the man who caught it threw it back!"

"Yeah," said Bobby, "well, that was Darryl Strawberry, and there are some fans who don't like when the other team scores a homer. But just let the ball land in my lap—I'd never throw it back!"

"Wow!" said Philippe. "Neither would I!"

"Too bad your dad couldn't come with us," said Mike, the self-appointed diplomat of the foursome.

"Well . . . he had to go someplace," answered Philippe, thinking that Armand was missing out on a great afternoon.

But thoughts of his father vanished the moment Gregg Jefferies stepped up to the plate. The crowd roared as the lead-off batter, who was only inches taller than Mike, hit a double.

Philippe cheered wildly until Mike grabbed his arm and said, "Hey, Phil, Gregg's with the Mets—you trying to get us thrown outta the park?"

The rain held off until the bottom half of the second inning. But then the first drops appeared.

"Don't be worried, guys," advised Joe, reaching into his canvas tote. "I brought this, just in case." He produced a sheet of bright yellow vinyl. "If it starts to really pour, we can huddle under it." To Philippe he confided, "I was here on the Monday night in '88 when they turned on the lights. They got rained out in the fourth. I was covered by this and didn't feel a thing. I could have stayed, but the guys running the show chickened out and called it off."

"What did you do?" asked a wide-eyed Philippe.

"I went home and came back the next night when they beat your team, Phil."

"My team?"

Joe winked. "The Mets." Smiling, he added, "I'll get you a baseball cap like the boys' if you want, but it'll have a *C* on it. They don't sell Mets caps at Wrigley." Joe laughed at his own joke, but Philippe's face was deadly serious.

"No thank you, Joe. I think I do favor the New York team." He couldn't help wondering, though, which side Dr. Nick Seward would be rooting for if he had come to the game with them.

By the middle of the third inning, the rain was beating down on both teams and their spectators. The apartment dwellers opposite the park had abandoned their free view of the stadium, and Joe had turned his yellow plastic sheet into a poncho for four.

The members of both teams, their uniforms soaked through and more than one covered with outfield mud, continued to play.

"Why don't they go inside where it's dry and wait till it stops raining?" asked Philippe when one ball after another slipped from the fielders' grasps.

343

" 'Cause this looks like it'll keep up all day, Phil,"
explained Mike, "and they want the game to be counted
as official. To be that it's gotta go five innings."

At that moment, there was a smacking sound of
Gary Carter's bat against the ball. It was followed by a
collective cry from the stands as thousands of umbrellas
rose en masse. Joe Buranski and his trio, still shrouded
in their yellow vinyl, watched as the ball was carried up
and gradually back by a gust of wind.

"It's coming here!" shrieked Bobby, jumping up and
down.

"Jesus, you're right!" yelled Joe. "Let's do it!"

He and the boys were getting in each other's way as
they tried frantically to free their arms from under the
plastic sheeting. Philippe, on the end, kept his eyes
fastened to the ball. It was heading straight back down
toward him.

With the rain pelting him and blurring his vision, his
small hands went up into the air—just as the ball
landed with a forceful whomp! Philippe's heart was
pounding as though it might burst. Someone, a stranger to his left, swooped him up and cried, "Bingo! The
kid's got it!"

Philippe was applauded by several spectators nearby
and booed by a dozen others as he clung to the water-
logged ball.

The man put him down and said to Joe, "I'll bet this
is an afternoon he'll never forget!"

Joe grinned philosophically. "I've been coming to
games every year since I was his age, and I never—not
once in my life—got lucky. Not a homer, not even a
foul! Good thing for me I don't play the horses!"

Philippe thought he detected a note of disappointment in Joe's voice.

There followed some thirty thousand notes of disappointment as the announcement came over the loudspeaker system. The game was being postponed due to rain.

"Does that mean what you said before?" Philippe asked Mike. "That it doesn't count?"

Mike nodded. "They'll have to make it up later."

In a smaller voice, Philippe said, "Do I have to give back the ball?"

Mike patted the boy's head. "Are you kidding? Not even if Carter himself comes up into the stands to get it!"

Philippe wondered if that might happen.

His last sight of the ballpark was a blue tarpaulin cover being rolled out over the infield.

"Well, your folks'll be surprised you're back so soon, won't they, Phil?" asked Joe.

Armand! Philippe hadn't considered what might happen if his father arrived back at the hotel and found him gone.

Philippe noticed on Joe's dashboard clock that it was just twenty-five minutes past three when they pulled up in front of the Drake.

"I'll have to drive around to the employee parking lot," said Joe. "But there's no reason why you should get drenched, so I'll let you out here, okay? You can find your room without me, can't you?"

Philippe nodded. "Yes, thank you. And thank you for taking me with you this afternoon. Even though it rained, I had a wonderful time." He shook hands with

Mike, who tousled his damp curls once more, then with Bobby, who returned the handclasp formally, imitating his new friend from New Orleans.

Joe laughed at the scene. Such a little gentleman. "Hey, Phil," he said, reaching over and pulling up the button that unlocked the rear-passenger door. "Y'know what? Me and the boys, we had a great time, too. You're a good kid. You can tell your dad I said so, from one father to another."

Philippe didn't understand why Joe's remark touched him. Nor why he took Gary Carter's foul ball, which he'd clutched tightly all the way back from the stadium, and tossed it into Joe's hands in the front seat.

"Hey . . . what's this, Phil? What're you doing?"

Philippe shrugged, feeling suddenly very sad, as though a door had been opened to him and so soon afterward was about to close. "You said you never caught one before," he answered. "So now you can say you have."

Armand was still sitting in the backseat of the cab opposite the visitors' parking lot at Lake Shore General Hospital. He'd accomplished only two things in his half-hour wait; he'd got the cabbie to extinguish his cigarette, and he'd convinced the already annoyed driver that running the air conditioner while they waited would not ruin the vehicle's battery.

He had to admit, however, that the cabbie was right on one point. It didn't look as though Claudia was planning to come back soon. She'd gone inside the rear entrance—he checked his watch again—thirty-five minutes ago. Who could she be visiting for so long?

"Hey, mister," said the driver, breaking in on Armand's thoughts. "We can park here all day—park or move, it's all the same to me as long as the meter's running. But will you look at the time? I don't know about you, but I haven't had anything to eat since seven o'clock this morning."

"I'm waiting for the woman who went inside, and until she comes out—"

"How d'you know she didn't already? I mean, there's more than one exit to this place, after all."

"She has to come out there," said Armand curtly, indicating the door Claudia had used to enter the hospital. "That's her car. I doubt she'd walk home in this downpour."

"Yeah, well, what if she leaves it here and we don't know about it?"

"Why would she—" Armand's breath caught.

What if she hadn't come to visit a patient—what if she'd come to see . . . a doctor!

"Look," he said excitedly, reaching for his wallet and extracting several twenty-dollar bills. "If that's not enough, I'll double it when I come back out. But wait here—in case she comes out—and whatever you do, don't leave!"

The cabbie glanced down at the twenties. "You got it, mister," he said. "But don't you go disappearing out another entrance, okay? I'm not into games—"

"Just stay here!" Armand's voice was feverish as he threw open the door and, oblivious to the rain now coming down in torrents, hurried across the street.

"A woman," Armand said breathlessly to the woman

347

seated behind the information desk. "She's about my height and coloring, wearing pants and a blouse, and—"

"Excuse me, sir," said the clerk, "perhaps if you could give me her name . . . ?"

"Gage. Claudia Gage. She came in here about half an hour ago—"

"Sir, please," came the soothing voice that agitated him even more. "Is she a patient at Lake Shore General?"

"No! No she's here to see a doctor named . . . Nicholas Seward." Armand realized that he was close to hyperventilating, but could do nothing to stop it.

I must stop it, he reasoned. Otherwise, this woman may refuse to help me.

He tried to lower his breathing and then began again. "I'm sorry. I was supposed to meet Dr. Seward and Miss Gage, but with the rain, my car . . . the traffic . . ."

It was working; he could see by the change in her eyes. He glanced down at his clothes, which were soaked to his skin. "I must be a sight," he said. "But it's important that I find the doctor, and . . ." He let his voice trail off, hoping the clerk would supply the information he sought.

She smiled and reached for a list. "And you are . . . ?"

Armand didn't offer his name.

"Are you a patient of the doctor?" she asked, consulting a row of names on the list.

"Hardly," he answered. "I'm . . . a friend of the family."

"Oh. Well, I'm new, so I don't know everyone on the

staff yet. But Dr. Seward's so friendly, I made a point of remembering him. I suppose the woman he left with must be the Miss Gage you mentioned, because—"

Her words registered and Armand's breathing grew shallow once more. "You say he left? They left? Together?"

"Why, yes. Here it is. He signed out"—she handed him her clipboard, which his mounting fury prevented him from seeing—"not more than ten minutes ago. He's an awfully busy doctor, it seems—"

"Yes, thank you," Armand muttered, turning and running out the way he'd entered, back to the waiting taxi.

The clerk shook her head as she put the clipboard back beside the switchboard. That man is certainly upset about something, she thought. Even more upset than the woman who was here earlier, the stunning dark woman with the Gypsy hair, the one who was also looking for Dr. Seward.

There was a bright flash of lightning, followed by a loud thunderclap.

Maybe it's the weather, mused the clerk, shaking her head once more. It really can affect one's mood.

"Where to now, Mac?" asked the cabbie as Armand climbed into the backseat, shook himself off, and slammed the door.

"I've told you, the name isn't Mac," he said.

"Okay. Sorry. Where to, mister?"

"Give me a moment to think." He pondered the dilemma. If Nick was with Claudia, and she most assuredly knew Armand was following her, the last place they'd go was back to their apartment. And he didn't dare take a chance with Eleanor Gage; Barton Gage's widow must have powerful connections in the city. Harassing Eleanor could be dangerous.

At an impasse, Armand said, "Just take me back to the Drake Hotel."

The cabbie glanced at Armand through his rearview mirror. This guy, whoever he is and whatever he's up to, has got to be rolling in dough, he mused. Didn't anyone where he comes from ever tell him about rental cars? He could be saving a bundle.

Armand hadn't come up with any solutions by the time the taxi had joined the backed-up traffic on Michigan Avenue. He'd have to think up something, and soon. For the boy's sake as well as his own.

"I tell you what," he said as they finally pulled up to the front entrance of the hotel. "I need a driver while I'm here. Interested?"

"You could hire a stretch limo for what the meter's running up, mister," answered the cabbie.

"A limousine is too conspicuous. Do you have a private car of your own—one in addition to this taxi?"

"Yeah. An '88 Pontiac. It rides a lot smoother than this buggy. But, mister, I don't drive a cab for a hobby. It's my livelihood, so if you're looking for a driver—"

"I'll make it worth your while, that I can promise," said Armand, cutting him off.

"Look, buddy, I don't know what you're into, but I'm a clean-living kind of guy. No drugs, no kinky scenes, if you know what I mean. So if you're into anything that could put either one of us away, you'd better find yourself another—"

"I said I'll make it worth your while!" Armand realized he'd almost yelled it. Trying to calm himself, he took out his wallet and said, "Look. See for yourself."

He opened the side compartment of the black alligator billfold and showed the cabbie what amounted to more than five hundred dollars in cash. "There's more where this came from. And you'll be in no danger. I'm simply asking you to be my driver so that I needn't go searching for a taxi every time I require transportation."

The cabbie eyed the bills. "For how long will you . . . require . . . my services?"

"That depends. But not more than a few days. A week at most."

The cabbie considered the proposition, looked at the wallet, then back at his potential client, and said, "You got a name, mister?"

"Dantine," answered Armand. "And you?"

The cabbie took a pad and pencil from the glove compartment and scribbled his name and telephone number on it. "George Tanney. If I'm out, the service will pick up. I check in with them every two hours when I'm out."

"Make it hourly, Mr. Tanney, and I'll be in touch as soon as I need you." Armand withdrew a one-hundred-dollar bill from his wallet and handed it to the driver. "That's your first payment, in advance. To bind the agreement."

George Tanney pocketed the money and said, "Mr. Dantine, you've got yourself a driver." He reached over to an unzipped canvas tennis bag and took out one of the two folding umbrellas inside.

"Take this along, Mr. Dantine," he said, handing it to

Armand. "And try to have a nice day, sir."

Armand was just opening the rear passenger door as he spotted Sirena entering the hotel.

George Tanney had spotted her, too. "Man, will you get a gander at that!" He gave out a low wolf whistle. "What a looker, huh?"

Armand didn't answer. He was already out of the cab and waiting for the lights to change so he could follow Sirena Mars into the Drake Hotel.

She dismissed the lascivious stares of the men standing beside her in the elevator, just as she had ignored the proposition from the middle-aged business executive in the lobby. It struck her as ironic that the better dressed and more prestigious the men, the more obvious their overtures, as though their money and status gave them rights.

Armand Dantine had been no different; she could understand that now. The brooding, mysterious aura that had drawn her to him she recognized now as an aberration, which only added to his arrogance. She could resign herself to never seeing him again.

But there was the child.

The elevator door opened on the ninth floor, and Sirena found herself moments later in front of room 903. Her head grew dizzy at the prospect of facing her son—and his father. She swallowed several times and steadied herself. Still, she felt the heaviness across her chest.

She leaned closer and put her ear to the door. She

heard voices, but realized they were coming from the television set. And then she heard Philippe shout, "Hooray!" And the sounds of clapping. Only one pair of hands.

He was alone.

It would be so easy, she thought. Just knock at the door and say I've come to take him home—and then take him anywhere except there.

But what about the child's welfare? What would Armand do when he came back and found the boy missing? Worse yet, what if Armand was in another part of the suite—perhaps they had several rooms and he simply wasn't in the one with Philippe and the television set?

Beyond that, even if the boy was alone and she did take him with her where his father could never find them . . . how would that affect the child in the years to come? She reflected on Armand's twisted affections; weren't these the results visited on him by his mother and Barton Gage? By one man's desertion and a child's distortion of the facts?

Her throat choking with tears, she touched her fingers to her lips and blew a kiss in the direction of the door. Then she turned down the corridor and headed for the same bank of elevators that had brought her to her son.

Armand had waited impatiently with the other guests. According to the indicators above the doors, all the elevators were currently on the uppermost floors of the hotel.

He overheard a woman say to the man with her,

"Darling, why don't we take the stairs? That way is probably faster."

A terrifying thought flashed through Armand's mind: What if Sirena has taken the stairs, too? What if she's already with him—or gone?

He brushed past the couple and raced to the door marked EXIT. He flung it open and flew up the nine flights, his adrenaline propelling him forward until he reached the door to room 903. His hands were trembling and caused him to drop the key.

Breathless and close to panic, he banged on the door and cried, "Philippe! Philippe, open this door!"

If there's no reply, he thought, if she's taken him, I swear I'll—

The door opened and his son stood before him.

"Philippe!" he cried, pulling the boy to him and almost crushing him.

"Father! Are you all right?" he asked when he'd broken free of Armand's fierce embrace.

"Yes, I'm fine . . . now," he stammered, too winded to notice that the child was shoeless or that he was wearing only an undershirt and a different pair of short pants from those he'd worn that morning.

Nor did he see, when he went to splash water on his face, that his son's wet shoes were drying out on a towel alongside the tub.

He saw only that his son was there, with him, and that the voices he'd heard upon entering were those of the baseball announcers commenting on the recently resumed game.

"So you've been watching television all afternoon?" asked Armand, reentering the room.

"They had to postpone the game until the rain

stopped," said Philippe. "Everyone thought it was canceled, so lots of people went home."

He was aware as he spoke that his lie was one of omission. The first time, with the incident of the lace handkerchief, he had lied for Sirena. This time, he knew, it was for himself.

Chapter 27

On Monday morning at ten o'clock, Claudia walked through the City Room toward her glass-enclosed office at the far corner. The air-conditioning was on high and a welcome relief from the scorching pavements on the street below.

Claudia's coworkers greeted her and she smiled her brightest smile and attempted to concentrate on positive aspects of the day. She was especially happy that the long weekend was over. She felt secure here, surrounded — protected — by her peers.

To further cheer her mood, she'd worn an artist's palette of color. Tangerine silk with kelly-green accents might seem a bit on the dressy side for a typical Monday at the office, but she could justify the ultrachic ensemble; Judy Fargo was coming by and they were "doing lunch" together.

"In another month," she'd said yesterday on the phone, "your book will be old news. So we have to freshen up the image."

Claudia had agreed, although her reason had less to do with staying visible than with spending some time with her friend. She'd alluded to Saturday's events with only "something more has happened. We'll talk. And you can tell me everything about your weekend with Frank."

"Everything . . . ?" Judy had asked with a bawdy laugh.

"Well . . . just whatever's within the bounds of your usual tact and good taste."

"That, dear Claudia, knows no bounds. Anyway, what do you mean about 'something more has happened.' Are you okay?"

"As I said, Judy . . . I'll explain over lunch."

Perhaps that'll help, Claudia thought now. A long talk with a good friend.

She'd had a long talk with her mother, but that wasn't the same. And there had been three of them, Eleanor, Nick, and Claudia, late Saturday afternoon.

Claudia found it interesting that her mother had taken to Sirena Mars. Eleanor had listened carefully to Nick's warning about secrecy—and the gentle reprimand to his future mother-in-law for having met with Sirena and not alerting them until afterward. Claudia had said nothing, but she knew her mother well and was certain that despite Nick's cautionary remarks, Eleanor Gage would continue to do exactly as she saw fit. Claudia felt sorry for Sirena, despite the woman's hostility toward her in New Orleans. Now she realized the reason behind it and wished there was some way to be of help.

Nick and Claudia had passed Sunday as quietly as possible, each of them pretending that it was just too hot to go outside, that staying home and relaxing would be far more enjoyable. They'd rented several films and the neighborhood deli delivered a tray of pastrami, lox and cream cheese, bagels, and dill pickles for a picnic in the den. Incoming calls continued to be screened by the answering machine and, mercifully, none included hang-up calls or heavy breathers.

She was sitting at her desk when Bonnie came in, struggling with two full mugs of coffee and an enormous stack of mail.

"And so the morning ritual begins," said Bonnie.

Claudia was glad to be following a routine; it gave a semblance of order to her tenuously maintained calm.

"Here's the list of the research books I'll need from the library," she said, handing a sheet of paper to Bonnie. The secretary stuck it under her clipboard and ran through Claudia's appointment schedule for the week. Then, as she did every Monday morning, Bonnie placed a smaller pile of letters—what she felt were the most interesting ones from readers—at the center of Claudia's desk.

"You'll see that several of them deal with obsession," said Bonnie, "and—"

"I addressed that subject in the paper two days ago," Claudia said abruptly. "I'm sorry. We'll just assume, or hope, they read Saturday's column."

They went through a dozen or more letters and then Bonnie left Claudia to play back the tape of calls that had come into her office phone over the weekend. The task invariably took up the better part of an hour, and this morning was no exception. Every time one message or plea ended, Claudia waited with growing trepidation for the tape to continue. With each new call, the question: Will the next message be from Armand? Or the one after that?

But the tape held only a series of petitions for help, and Claudia wasn't sure which was worse. She was certain of only one thing: the lunch hour couldn't come soon enough.

At ten-thirty, Josh Samuelson came into her office with a wide grin on his face.

"You look like the famous cat that ate the canary," observed Claudia. "And what are you hiding behind your back?"

"This," he answered, holding up her book.

"Well, my God, you actually sprang for a copy?"

"Don't make me squirm, Claudia."

"Me? It never entered my mind," she countered. "Whatever made you break down and buy it?"

"Barbara. She couldn't believe that it's been out for a month and she still hasn't read it. She bought it, and she wants it autographed . . ."

"Your wife is a fair-minded woman." Claudia laughed. "Here, give it to me."

While she was signing it, Josh asked, "How's it going? Not the book—I know you're on the best-seller list. Which reminds me, the paper's doing photo ads for your column with a book tie-in. But my question refers to your present workload."

She closed Barbara Samuelson's copy of *Dear Claudia* and returned it to Josh. "The work's piled up, the letters don't change, and I'm coping. Isn't that what an advice columnist is supposed to do?" She wasn't about to tell him what was really on her mind—mustn't belabor their business relationship with personal problems, when her business was other people's problems.

For some reason, other people's problems brought Sirena Mars once more to mind. And Philippe. What was he doing while his father was out playing cat-and-mouse? Did the child sit alone in a deserted hotel room? Then Claudia realized that even if Armand spent every moment with his son, the boy was still alone . . .

"Hello," said Josh, snapping his fingers. "Earth-to-Claudia . . . ?"

She blinked her eyes and looked up at him. "Sorry, I . . . was preoccupied, I guess. Ask Barbara to call me when she's finished the book. We can chat."

Josh left, and she began working on the stack of letters Bonnie had put in her priority basket.

Half an hour's reading had tired her eyes, and Claudia was aware of a dull ache at the base of her neck. It required great effort to concentrate without the interfering images of Armand, Sirena, and Philippe crowding in on her.

She glanced through the glass wall at the round clock in the City Room. It was eleven—late enough in the morning to phone Eleanor without awakening her.

"She's on another call, Miss Gage," Imelda informed her, "but I'll put you on hold and she'll pick up as soon as she's available."

"Fine." She's becoming more efficient lately, thought Claudia as she waited. Moments later, Eleanor's voice came on the line.

"Well, darling, good morning!"

"You sound chipper today," Claudia commented.

"Well, I've been up for hours! There's so much to do!"

360

"Do?"

"Dear, I told you, I know I did. We're moving into high gear on the charity ball. The committee, thank goodness, adores the theme. I'd originally thought it should be restricted to only favorite paintings themselves, but then I had this nightmare vision of every woman over size twelve showing up as the Mona Lisa. Worse yet, as Venus on the halfshell. Allowing for the artists as well gives everyone a wider range of costume choices, don't you agree?"

Claudia was only half listening. "Yes . . . yes, of course it does."

"Look, darling," said Eleanor, "I know you have other matters on your mind. And all this fuss over a charitable event probably sounds silly. But it is important, and the money from the ball will go toward completion of the new wing at the hospital—"

"I know, Mom. You don't have to justify it to me. Or to anyone. And if there's any way I can help . . ."

"Well, there is something, I think. In fact I was going to call you about it."

"What is it?"

"You realize this is . . . aside from any plugs you may want to include in your column . . ."

"Mom . . ."

"All right, no harm in hinting, though, is there? I'm going to need as much publicity on this event as is humanly and financially feasible. I want people begging to buy tickets. But you see, all the work is being done on a volunteer basis, and . . ."

"You'd like me to get someone's services for free, wouldn't you?"

"Yes, darling. Judy Fargo. If I can convince her to

take us on—even at a small fee, although she probably wouldn't want that, since it is entirely tax-deductible, and—"

"You're talking about . . . visibility?"

"Exactly! What a marvelous word! Visibility is what we need to make the ball the event of the fall season!"

"Well, I'm having lunch with Judy today. I'll ask her then."

"Claudia, thank you. This really does mean a lot to me, you know."

"I do know."

"Till later, darling." And Eleanor hung up.

Claudia was glad they'd spoken. An entire conversation with her mother, and not once had either of them referred to Armand Dantine. Her eyes felt rested, and the ache in her neck had even disappeared, so she returned to the remaining letters in the priority stack.

She had become so thoroughly engrossed in her notes for a subsequent column that she didn't hear the tapping of fingernails on her glass door. Only when the sounds of the City Room grew louder did Claudia realize someone had opened the door. She looked up to find Judy leaning against the wooden frame.

"Woman at work," she commented, running a hand through her hair. Judy had dressed for a business lunch; the banker's gray silk suit and the beige silk blouse with its stock tie spelled "professional." So did the soft gray ostrich portfolio under her arm. Claudia looked down and saw that Judy's shoes were of matching gray ostrich.

"Nice getup," she said. "I didn't realize it was almost

noon."

"Thanks," answered Judy. "And yes, time does fly. I've reserved a table at Le Cart. My treat, but I booked it in your name."

"Mine?"

"You're the celebrity. For Miss Gage, they'll hold the best table in the place." She checked the gold tank watch on her wrist. "Of course, even for you, they won't hold it forever . . ."

"Just let me run to the ladies' room and fix my face."

"Claudia, my face could use the fixing. Yours just needs a little powder."

"Cute. But humor me. I'll be back in a minute. Here," she said, handing Judy a copy of the early edition, "read something while I'm gone."

Philippe had waited for almost a quarter of an hour before mustering the courage to phone Claudia Gage's office at the *Examiner*. But each time he tried, her line was busy. Finally, unable to wait any longer, he combed his hair, straightened his tie, and slipped out of the room.

It was so easy! Armand hadn't found out about the baseball game on Saturday, even with the wet clothes and shoes. Unless a guest or employee of the hotel saw him now and told his father, no one would know that he was going to see Claudia. In person.

But Philippe was intelligent enough to realize that an eight-year-old child hailing a taxi by himself would be conspicuous. For this reason, he walked two blocks and then asked the doorman at another hotel to hail a taxi for him. "I'm supposed to meet my father," he explained.

"Certainly, young man." The doorman blew his whistle and a moment later a yellow cab stopped to pick him up.

The driver regarded Philippe curiously. "Going somewhere on your own, kid?" he asked.

In his most formal, grown-up voice, Philippe repeated what had worked with the doorman. "I'm meeting my father. Can you please take me to this address?" He held up the piece of newspaper he'd torn from yesterday's edition of the *Examiner*.

"Sure thing, kid—if you've got money."

"How much will it cost?" asked Philippe.

"A few bucks," answered the cabbie, flipping on the meter.

"Yes, I have that." Philippe leaned back against the cool leather in the air-conditioned car and tried to figure out how much of a tip he could give the driver and still have enough to get him back to the hotel with the money Armand had given him for room service.

Philippe hadn't been able to piece together what kind of business his father was involved with; either he was gone for hours at a time, or he didn't leave the room. Such had been the case the day before.

He'd often heard Armand pacing the floor in the middle of the night, sometimes until dawn. This morning was a repeat of Saturday, with an additional warning issued: "Under no circumstances are you to open the door except for room service, and then, only if the waiter is a man. Do not answer to a woman, even if it's just the maid."

"But how will I know who is there if I don't open the door?" Philippe had asked.

"I'll put the DO NOT DISTURB sign out. The maid

shouldn't even knock. But if she—or anyone else—does, you are to say nothing, do you understand? Make no response. Pretend there is no one here."

His father's frenzy had kept Philippe from asking why.

Now he watched as the city's streets flew past. He disliked Chicago as much for its differences from home as for its unfamiliarity. The grandeur of their hotel suite didn't intimidate him; he was accustomed to elegant surroundings. Indeed, the Drake couldn't compare with their house on Royal Street. But in the streets of New Orleans, especially inside the Vieux Carré, he knew his bearings. Here, too, the city rose up into the air, the buildings towering above him not unlike the grand hotels along Canal Street. And yet he preferred the Mississippi to Chicago's Lake Michigan; Royal Street instead of this fashionable avenue named for the lake on which the Windy City stood. Philippe had seldom felt so confused.

The sensation was amplified as the taxi came to a dead stop.

"Are we here already?" Philippe asked the driver.

"Nope. It's the traffic. Must have been an accident up ahead. This could take some time. Hope you're not in a hurry, kid."

"But . . . I am," Philippe answered. He was unsure of what to do. "How much farther is it?"

"Well, it's another ten blocks or so. You could probably hoof it in fifteen minutes. Maybe twenty, considering your size."

No, thought Philippe. It's too far; it'll take too long. "I'll stay here, I guess."

He tried to fill the time by rehearsing what he'd say

when he reached his destination. He patted his jacket pocket. Inside was Claudia's white lace handkerchief. He'd been carrying it constantly for fear that his father might otherwise find it. There was no telling how Armand would react if he knew that Sirena had taken it.

Sirena. Would he ever see her again? Philippe had to will himself not to cry. He was trying to accept the fact that Sirena wasn't coming for him. He'd sensed for some time now that she would not return with them to the house on Royal Street—and that she wasn't waiting there for him now. Yet he knew she had always loved him, still loved him. And that he loved her, too. He would continue to love her, despite whatever was keeping her from coming for him.

There was only one other person Philippe felt he could trust as much as he trusted Sirena. At first it had seemed strange to him that someone he'd so recently met could make him feel so close to her. Perhaps it was because her image had smiled down at him from the parlor wall since his earliest memory. Whatever, some bond between them had been established, and Philippe hoped that she would welcome him.

He wondered if this was disloyal to Sirena. He had no wish to replace her in his affections; no one ever would. But he needed someone, and Claudia Gage was the logical choice.

The gridlocked cars and taxis honked their horns so loudly that Philippe had to cover his ears to shut out the noise. The pandemonium reminded him that he'd better return to the hotel well before his father did; Armand mustn't know he'd gone out. For the first time in his life, Philippe had begun to fear his father. Still, he had to see Claudia, and since she had no way of knowing where he was — or that he was even here — he would have to go to her.

What if she had forgotten him? Suppose she didn't care? Well, he would find out soon enough, the moment they saw each other again. He'd see it in her eyes. Feel it. And should that prove true . . . Philippe wasn't sure what course he would take. The thought of running away had occurred. But it was always followed by a question he couldn't answer: Where would he go?

The taxi lurched forward with a sudden movement that almost threw Philippe to the floor of the backseat. The traffic bottleneck had cleared and cars were picking up speed along Michigan Avenue.

"We'll be there in five minutes, kid," said the cabbie, looking through the rearview mirror.

When they pulled up in front of the massive block-wide structure, Philippe hesitated. He could turn back now and hurry back to the hotel. But he paid the driver with an ample tip and, with a polite "thank you very much, sir," he slammed the door.

Then, before he could change his mind, he dashed into the main lobby of the building that housed the *Daily Examiner.*

Bonnie was applying a third coat of mascara when Claudia entered the ladies' room.

"I saw Judy Fargo on my way in here. She looks great," said the secretary, screwing the cap back onto the mascara wand. "Where does she get her clothes?"

"Well," answered Claudia, withdrawing her own makeup tote from her purse, "Judy does shop a lot."

367

"I never seem to have time," said Bonnie. "I always wind up buying the same styles just because I have to squeeze so much into an hour."

"I'm certain that wasn't a hint," said Claudia. "But just the same, take a good, long lunch today. We're going to, and there isn't a great deal I need you to do this afternoon anyway."

"Thanks, boss—and enjoy!" Bonnie collected her makeup and headed for the door. "See you later, then."

She went out into the hallway and almost collided with a man. He startled her, but then they both broke into polite laughter.

"Pardon me," he apologized in a light southern drawl. "I must have mistaken this for the men's room."

"It's okay," said Bonnie. "The doors aren't clearly marked. It happens all the time." She noted that he was one of the most handsome men she'd ever seen. "You want two doors down," she directed.

"Thank you," he replied.

Bonnie could see a group of people stepping into the elevator. "Excuse me," she said to the man. Then she yelled, "Hold the door!" and tore down the hall.

He looked around. The corridor was empty now. He hoped Claudia would be alone inside. If not, he could pretend once more to have mistaken the door. There was an escape route via the adjacent stairs. Whatever, the risk was worth taking. He had to see her.

And so Armand turned the knob.

Judy Fargo was seated in the chair behind Claudia's desk. She glanced at the stack of letters in the priority basket. Circled numbers in red ink appeared at the upper right-hand corner of each page. Judy was careful not to disturb their order as she skimmed through several of the top sheets.

She stopped reading after the third. Amazing, she thought. A steady diet of this sort of thing would be enough to depress anyone indefinitely. Page after page of broken marriages, young girls molested by their own fathers, people on the edge with nowhere to go. The desperate needs of so many, the cries for help and caring, were more than Judy could take at a single sitting. But it gave her a clearer picture of the true worth of Claudia's book as well as the sincerity with which it had been written. Judy found her friend's ability to handle all these problems—or to advise readers on how to handle them—while maintaining her own objectivity truly admirable.

She returned the last letter to its place and glanced through the glass wall. Then she checked the time. Claudia ought to be back any second now.

Instantly she was on her feet at the sight of a small boy wearing short pants, jacket, and tie. He was standing alone at the far end of the City Room.

The whirl of activity around him made his absolute stillness an immediate focal point, although no one else seemed to take notice of him. His eyes searched the rows of desks. He was obviously looking for a familiar face.

Claudia's face.

Judy went to the door of the office, and when he saw her, his eyes lit up and he broke into a happy smile.

She waved, beckoning him toward the office.

"What on earth are you doing here?" she asked when

he came through the door.

"I've come to see Miss Gage," he said, hoisting himself up on the seat of a chair.

"Are you . . . alone?" she asked. Please be alone! she thought. I can't take seeing your father—and neither can Claudia.

"Yes," said Philippe, "I'm alone. And I haven't too much time. Is she here today?"

Judy nodded. "She should be back in a sec. But tell me, what brings you to the Windy City?"

He told her that Armand was in Chicago on a business matter. "And Saturday I saw my first baseball game ever. Of course my father doesn't know. And I must ask you not to tell him. Please?"

"My word of honor," Judy promised. "How was the game? I missed it."

She listened with amusement to his enthusiastic description. But midway through his story, she glanced again at the clock. Claudia had been gone for quite a while.

"Listen," Judy said after he'd finished his story, "stay here. I'll go and get Claudia."

"Thank you."

"It's good to see you again, Philippe," she said. "We were . . . worried. Claudia will be especially happy to see you.

"She will?" he asked hopefully.

"You bet," Judy assured him as she went out the door.

Judy was right, thought Claudia. I do need a powder touch-up.

She was opening her compact when she saw Bonnie's mascara wand on the edge of the sink. She smiled; how many times had she done the same thing? She reminded herself to bring it along and give it to Bonnie when she and Judy returned from lunch.

Her lipstick tube clinked against the glass shelf beneath the mirror as she set it down. The sound caused a slight echo in the high-ceilinged, tiled room.

Claudia was glad to have a moment to herself before lunch now that Bonnie had left the ladies' room. No muted clattering of computer keys, teletype machines, or printers to disturb the quiet. Lately, peace had been at a premium, and attainable only when she and Nick were alone.

She added a touch of blusher—she needed the color—and a drop of perfume behind each ear. Then a quick brush of her hair. There, she decided, regarding her reflection in the mirror, you're presentable.

Claudia had just dropped her makeup tote in her purse when the door squealed on its hinges behind her. She took Bonnie's mascara and held it up.

"Forget this?" she asked, waiting for her secretary's image to appear from around the corner.

There was no response.

"Hello, Bonnie?" she called softly. Still no reply.

Am I hearing things? she asked herself. The door did open, didn't it? "Is someone . . . ?" she began, then cut herself off. Of course someone was there.

Claudia threw the mascara into her purse and turned to leave.

Armand Dantine stood in front of the door, blocking her exit.

He was dressed entirely in black, a business suit that

371

suggested Edwardian tailoring. The overhead fluorescents accentuated his long nose and firm jawline.

They stood motionless, staring at each other. His eyes traveled the length of her body and came to rest on her face. Claudia could feel her heart beginning to pound wildly. Quickened breathing made it impossible to locate her voice.

But Armand spoke.

"I had to see you," he said.

Still she was unable to reply.

"This can't be a surprise," he told her. "Surely you knew I'd come."

"It's . . . a shock," she managed finally. "But no, Armand. Not a surprise."

"Good."

He took a step toward her, and she stopped him with, "How did you get in here anyway?"

He grinned, brushing a lock of dark hair from his forehead. "I arrived just before you did. I was watching you."

"F-from w-where? I didn't see you."

"I kept the stairwell door open a crack. It affords an excellent view."

"I'm . . . I'm not alone in here," she said quickly, gesturing to the stalls.

"Yes you are. You weren't, but you are now. We're alone." He took another step forward.

"I can scream," she warned him.

He looked genuinely perplexed. "Why would you do that? I'm here to love you, not to hurt you." His heels made a sharp staccato sound on the floor as he advanced, but something, perhaps the fear in her eyes, stopped him. "You . . . can't be afraid of me," he said.

372

"That would ruin everything."

Claudia's words came out in a stammered rush as she fought to control an overwhelming terror. "Armand . . . I'm only afraid of what I might do if you don't leave. This room. This city."

"Gladly. With you at my side."

"Armand . . ."

"Everyone is against us — you can see that, I know. Sirena is trying to come between us, trying to take our child. He's more yours than hers, really."

"Please . . ."

He was less than three feet from her. There was no way around him. Claudia mentally rummaged though her purse, but there was nothing in it that she could use to defend herself, if it came to that.

"I had to leave him alone once more," Armand was saying. "Forgive me. I couldn't bear not being near you."

"Then you must . . . go back to him. Sirena could be with Philippe right now, Armand — she might take him away —"

"If she did, I would find her. But that isn't necessary if you'll simply come home with us."

"Armand," she said, in a last effort to reason with him, "I am home. New Orleans was a long time ago. I have no connection there anymore."

"You do!" he cried. "The house on Royal Street is yours — waiting, as it always has, for you to return! The portrait is only made of paint and canvas. It needs you!"

"I am not the portrait!" she yelled, hoping someone outside would hear her. "Armand . . . I am not Noelle!"

He laughed. "I know that—I'm not insane! But her heart broke when you went away—"

"When I was taken away, Armand—sold!"

"And your leaving killed her—she was taken away from me, too!" He leaned in closer. "Noelle will live again, if only you'll come home and take your rightful place."

"Take *her* place, you mean!" Claudia cried.

He rose to his full height. "Don't presume that anyone could do that. No. Noelle has become you, now. She possesses you."

Claudia felt tears welling in her eyes and throat. "Armand . . . she possesses you. Not me!"

She had backed up against a wall. He didn't seem to hear her—or was beyond listening. His hand moved to caress her cheek, but she averted her face. Don't show him fear, she commanded herself.

"I can teach you what it's like to be worshiped," he whispered feverishly. "I can offer you unknown pleasures—"

She stepped aside, her arms coming up to push him away. He grabbed her wrists and pulled them to his chest.

"I lie awake each night thinking of you," he hissed into her ear. "Thinking of what he's doing to you, while I die!"

She struggled to break free, but his hands were strong. Armand forced her to the wall again and pinned her against the cold tiles. His breath on her neck was quick and hot; his body, hard and moving closer as his words continued. "No one should have you like that! No one should see you . . . touch you . . . like that. Only I, like this. Here. Now."

Claudia's strangled scream was cut off by his hand over her mouth. Her teeth sank into the flesh of his palm. The momentary pain made him release her, and with a free hand Claudia pulled at his hair and cried out once more, while she tried to push him off.

Then the door squealed again, and seconds later a voice yelled, "Get out of here!"

Armand spun on his heels. Judy stood in the doorway. "Get out and leave her alone—or I'll have every cop and reporter in this city on you!"

He stood motionless, looking from Judy to Claudia. "But it's only what should . . ."

He didn't finish the sentence. Instead, he pushed Judy aside and bolted from the room.

Claudia felt herself beginning to slide down the wall as her hands covered her face and sobs burst forth. Judy hugged her, almost rocking her, as she said, "It's all right, hon. I'm here, and everything's okay. He's gone. He's gone."

Chapter 28

Philippe sat in the dark gray and chrome chair at Claudia's desk in her glass-enclosed office and watched with fascination the flurry of activity in the vast room outside. Everyone scurried back and forth. Those who were seated at desks talked into telephone receivers perched on their shoulders, while at the same time they tapped the keys of their word processors as though they were playing music on pianos.

And in a way, the hectic buzz probably was a kind of music, he reasoned. Although with Claudia's office door closed, Philippe could only imagine the exciting things the reporters must be saying into the phone and writing into stories and feature articles for the paper. He wondered if Claudia felt left out, set apart by these glass walls.

No, he decided. She was special, and her office was, too. The rest of the people were the ones who were excluded.

He glanced at her desk piled high with file folders,

opened and unopened letters, copies of *Dear Claudia,* and her personal computer on the adjacent tabletop. He remembered the day he'd purchased her book for Sirena, and speculated on events since. So much had happened, and in so short a time.

Time! He glanced up at the circular clock at the center of the big room. What was taking Judy Fargo so long? She said she'd bring Claudia back right away. If he wasn't at the hotel when his father returned, there was no telling what might happen!

Maybe I should go and look for her, he thought. But he rejected the idea almost immediately; she could be here any second now, and if he went in search of her, they could miss each other altogether.

What would he say to her? He'd read her column two days before, and even if he didn't understand everything she'd written, he realized that it had seemed invisibly addressed to Armand.

He breathed a deep sigh and looked out to the clock once more.

No, he didn't dare wait any longer.

Maybe I can leave her a note, he thought. And then he had an even better idea.

"Are you sure you're okay?" Judy repeated for the fourth or fifth time.

"I'm fine now," answered Claudia. "Thanks to you." She was still breathing shallowly, but her hands had stopped trembling, and she felt her composure gradually returning.

"Nick was right," she mused aloud. "He was so right! And I ought to have seen it. I'll admit it, Judy.

377

Sometimes the advice columnist needs a good, strong dose of her own medicine."

"Hon, there's no way you could have known, so relax. It's like whodunits and crime movies. Everybody says they create criminals. That's a great defense in court, but it doesn't wash. Only a psychotic is going to poison his uncle because he saw it happen on *Murder, She Wrote*. So take it easy. You just didn't realize how far gone the guy is, that's all."

Judy was trying to placate her, but Claudia recognized logic in her publicist's words. For the moment, though, they didn't help much.

"Does Philippe's father know he's here?" she asked.

Judy shook her head. "The kid didn't say, but I tend to doubt it. You don't invite your son along when you're going to try seducing your sister."

That made Claudia laugh, and the physical act served as a nervous release. She had to stop and lean against the wall for support.

"Oh, Judy," she said, "you really are what the doctor ordered. C'mon, let's find"—she paused—"let's go find my nephew . . ."

But her office was empty. Judy and Claudia could see that before they reached the door.

"Where'd he go?" she asked.

Judy shrugged her shoulders. "Want me to check around? I see Josh—"

"No, wait. He left an envelope with my name on it."

"How d'you know it's from him?" asked Judy.

Claudia picked it up and said, "It's not his, it's one of mine."

Sure enough, the envelope had the *Daily Examiner*'s logo in the upper left-hand corner. "Besides," added Claudia, "have a look at the handwriting. How many adults do you know with this kind of penmanship?"

"Dear Claudia" had been carefully, painstakingly written in the center of the envelope in pencil. The letters were formed by someone who had recently learned and was still in the process of perfecting the art of longhand.

"Well," urged Judy, "as the saying goes, don't keep us both in suspense—open it and let's see what it says!"

Claudia tore open the flap and withdrew the contents. "Christ," she said, looking down at her hand.

"You might say that," observed Judy.

Inside the envelope was not a note, but a freshly washed white lace handkerchief. Claudia's handkerchief.

It hadn't been ironed; instead, it was folded neatly, as though Philippe had tried to smooth it free of wrinkles with his hand.

"What do you think?" asked Claudia rhetorically.

Judy's mind went to the scene she'd interrupted ten minutes earlier in the ladies' room—and to what might have happened if she hadn't walked in.

He could have included my porcelain rose, she thought. But she knew that wasn't what Claudia needed to hear, so she didn't answer at all.

Philippe stood at curbside and waved his arm in an attempt to hail a taxi. But this time there was no hotel doorman to assist him, and he had to compete with the taller arms of more than a dozen adults.

One after another, the yellow cars passed him by and

accepted, instead, executives who seemed en route to meetings, or secretaries and receptionists on their way to lunch.

At last he gave up trying and decided he might make better time by walking back to the hotel. If he spotted a taxi on the way, all the better. But with the midday traffic, riding wouldn't be that much faster than walking anyway. Breaking into a half-run, half-skip, Philippe started up North Michigan Avenue.

He paused only to peer over the bridge at the river, then continued on past the Tribune Tower. He saw an empty cab at the next corner, but when the traffic light turned to green, the taxi zoomed away.

A very elegant lady alighted from a taxi in front of Saks Fifth Avenue and Philippe thought he'd give it one more try, but the moment the cabbie's door was closed, the off-duty sign lit up atop the roof of the vehicle.

Philippe quickened his pace, although he took the time to peek at and admire the fancy things on display in the windows of the designer salons. Some of the furnishings in an antiques-store window reminded him of the parlor at home on Royal Street. And the ball gown farther up the avenue in a boutique closely resembled the teal blue worn by Noelle Dantine in the portrait over the mantel.

That still confused him. His head was filled with questions, and the part that saddened him most was the intuitive understanding that never, not now or ever, could he ask his father to explain.

A family passed him. Parents and a little boy about the same age as Philippe. Both father and son were wearing Cubs baseball caps, and they were laughing as they walked along. The mother smiled lovingly at them both, and although he had no way of identifying what he'd never known, Philippe felt a sudden twinge of envy. Not resentment, but it came close to that.

Is that what Armand feels about Claudia? he wondered, remembering his father's expression on the day she'd brought Dr. Seward to brunch. Sirena seemed to have demonstrated a similar reaction on meeting Claudia. Is that what it's like to be grown up? No. There was something strange—he had no idea what—about his father. And, he admitted, about Sirena, too.

He forced himself to erase the latter thought; even its suggestion made him feel disloyal.

The windows had made him almost forget that he was walking a longer distance than he'd ever gone on foot before. By the time he reached the Water Tower, his legs were growing tired. But he recognized some of the buildings, which told him he was almost at the hotel.

Armand hadn't seen George Tanney's car immediately upon reaching the street. He stood at the curb in plain sight and silently swore to himself. He was still in a fury. How stupid to confront her there, but it had been more than he could bear. Logic and reasoning would not bring her to him, so he'd acted. Foolishly, of course. He could see that now. But he had to make her understand. There'd seemed no other way.

He had two choices. Either return to the hotel, pick up the boy, and go back to New Orleans once and for all. Or . . . stay here and make one last attempt to convince her. With intelligence, this time. With patience. And love.

He knew it was his failing if she hadn't yet understood. There had to be some means. If he could maintain control over his . . . mission, he'd find that means.

He refused to call it by the name in *Dear Claudia*'s column. Compulsion. Obsession. Those were extremes inflicted upon other people less devoted, less in love, who thought solely of themselves. He had to make her see that he was thinking of her, too, in his all-consuming passion. Of Claudia, and of the boy.

His ruminations stopped when he caught sight of George Tanney's Pontiac.

"Where to now?" asked his driver.

"Back to the hotel. But drive slowly. I want time to think."

"Mr. Dantine, sir, there's no other way to drive this afternoon. It took me twenty minutes just to circle around the block to pick you up. You're lucky we made a deal. If I was driving my cab and you were paying by the meter, you'd be a pauper in no time flat."

"Do me a favor, Mr. Tanney," said Armand. "Don't talk so much. Just drive on up the avenue."

Philippe could see the familiar outline of the hotel just a few short blocks ahead. He was relieved; the heat was exhausting him. The Indian-summer air was almost as hot and as humid as it was at home.

He heard a car screech behind him, but he paid no attention to the noise. Chicago was a windy, noisy place, and all the cars honked their horns as if they were trying to outdo each other.

382

Then, suddenly, a hand grabbed his wrist.

"Oww! Let go! Leave me al—" Philippe stopped short and looked up into the angry eyes of his father.

"Well, young man, you have some explaining to do," he said, yanking the boy toward George Tanney's waiting car.

"May I come in?" asked Eleanor Gage as she opened the door to Claudia's office.

"Hi, Mom," said Claudia.

"I must say, Mrs. Gage, you're looking terrific as always," offered Judy.

"Same goes for the two of you," answered Eleanor. Then she noticed both women's forced smiles. "What's the matter? Something in the salad at lunch?"

Claudia shook her head. "It's too much to explain right now, Mom. What have you been up to?"

"Oh, just last-minute preparations for the ball." To Judy she said, "I confess, with no false modesty, it's going to start off the season smashingly. I was at the museum all morning, and just wait until you see the decorations!" She glanced at her watch. "Speaking of which, I still have a few things to do there after our appointment, so if we can leave now—"

"Our appointment . . . ?" asked Claudia. "I'm sorry, Mom, my mind's been . . . elsewhere."

Eleanor's eyes were on her daughter's opened Week-at-a-Glance on the desk. "You can't have forgotten, darling. There it is, plain as day."

On the page Claudia had written "Lunch with Judy, 12–1. Costume fitting, 2 P.M."

"This afternoon," she said. "I did forget."

"Well, I can pop into Josh's office and tell him this is important—after all, you're going to model your costume for the society page, so he'll have to concede—"

"Oh, it's not that. I'm caught up on work, aside from all these letters." Claudia's eyes fell on Philippe's envelope. Maybe an hour with her mother at the costumer's would do her good. She'd moped all through lunch with Judy.

"Mom, I'm all yours."

"Grand. Do you need to powder your nose before we leave?" asked Eleanor.

She didn't understand the look that passed between her daughter and Judy as Claudia answered, "No, Mom. The ladies' room is off-limits, thank you."

In Eleanor's car on the way to the fitting, however, Claudia explained everything that had occurred earlier that day. She omitted only the physical details concerning Armand's confrontation.

Eleanor listened, and as they pulled into the parking lot behind the costume warehouse, she said, "I don't want you to worry about this. I think we may be ready for Ray Fenwick to take legal action."

"Mom," said Claudia, "on what grounds?"

"Darling, he attacked you—or would have, if it hadn't been for Judy. That also means we have a witness. Please. Leave it to me."

"But what can Ray possibly do?"

"I don't know yet, but I'm sure he'll think of something. In the meantime, don't go anywhere alone. You have what people call a network around you. Make use

384

of it. Nick, Judy, and me."

"Mom, forgive me if for a while I misunderstood your . . . motivations."

Eleanor squeezed her hand. "There's nothing to forgive. Now come and let's see what famous paintings we're going to bring to life at the ball. I've already chosen mine."

"What?"

"Change the What to Who. There's a stunning portrait by Joshua Reynolds. It's not in the Institute's collection — in fact I can't recall whether it's at the Metropolitan or at the Frick in New York. But I've always vainly sensed a slight resemblance . . . ." Eleanor's eyes sparkled, but Claudia knew that only part of her mother's enthusiasm was genuine; the other part was her attempt to dispel Claudia's concern. And her own.

The fitting went quickly once Claudia had decided upon which portrait she would "become" for the ball. Her knowledge of paintings and their artists stemmed from Barton as well as from history courses she'd taken in college. At first she'd thought to come dressed as a famous woman painter. She'd envisioned herself in a huge hat with feathers, a sumptuous gown of satin and lace, and something in the way of a palette or sketchpad that would identify her as the beauteous Angelica Kauffmann of London's eighteenth-century Royal Academy. Or perhaps as the less stunning but brilliantly talented Adelaide Labille-Guiard, after her self-portrait at the Met in New York. But the costumes were all too billowy-skirted, too fussy with frills. Claudia wanted

385

something simpler.

Eleanor unwittingly gave her the idea. "Darling," she suggested, "think of your deepest, secret fantasy and the way you see yourself in it. Perhaps that will help you decide."

It more than helped.

When Claudia came out of the fitting room to model the ensemble, the dressmaker and her assistant both applauded.

Eleanor looked up and beamed. "Sargent couldn't have done better, darling. It's perfect!"

"Good!" exclaimed Claudia. "That means you've guessed."

"Well, after all, I know the portrait. But I must say, even your pose matches hers. It's an inspired choice."

The gown itself, of lush black satin, was starkly simple. The skintight bodice, suspended from thin, jeweled straps, plunged to a provocatively sharp *V;* the skirt both captured and reflected the light.

Claudia's long dark hair was swept into a French twist, helped by a handful of bobby pins borrowed from the seamstress. She stood absolutely still, her face turned to the left in a perfect profile as she mimicked John Singer Sargent's famous beauty on canvas. The effect was strong. Dramatic. Almost defiant.

It suited Claudia's frame of mind.

She modeled the gown for Bonnie and Judy when she returned to the *Examiner.* The three women had appropriated the fashion editor's office; Trish was out for the day, and hers was the only office on the floor that didn't have glass walls.

"I don't feel like playing Madame X in a fishbowl," Claudia joked.

"That's exactly what you'll be doing at the Art Institute," said Judy. "Décolletage like that is not for the modestly inclined, Miss Gage . . ."

Josh Samuelson wandered into the office at that moment and echoed Judy's remark. Knowing Claudia's aversion to wolf whistles, he stood in the doorway and shook his head.

"Is that disapproval, Josh, or the opposite?" she asked.

"Oh, definitely the opposite. I don't think we should shoot you for the society page. Or fashion. We could boost the paper's circulation by several million if we put you on page one!" He paused for effect, then added, "Of course, we'd have to run a warning from the surgeon general — you know, cigarette-pack stuff . . . This photograph could be hazardous to the health of anyone with heart or circulatory problems . . ."

"Thanks and then some," Claudia said with a grin.

"You asked me, I told you. Now I'd better get some air, so if you ladies will excuse me . . . ?"

"I'd better change out of this and get back to work. I have a zillion letters to answer."

Bonnie said, "Oh, I almost forgot. Dr. Seward phoned while you and your mom were at the costumer's. Said for you to call him."

"I'll do that now," replied Claudia. Then almost cautiously she asked, "Were there . . . any other calls? Or messages?"

Bonnie thought for a moment. "Nothing pressing. The usual fan stuff. And your editor. The book's still holding the top spot on the best-seller list."

387

"Well, that's good news! And I can use some good news."

"I'm sure it's due to the promotion tour," said Bonnie. "You never can tell how much the personal touch can do, don't you agree?"

Claudia and Judy looked at each other before Claudia said, "No, you never can tell . . ."

Nick was still at his office when Claudia returned his call. "Bonnie said you phoned."

"Right. She told me you and Eleanor went off for an afternoon of fun."

"Well, not exactly," answered Claudia. "Costume fittings for the ball. You'll have to come as John Singer Sargent."

"I will? Why?"

"You'll see tonight. I'll model the gown for you before Josh sticks it on page one."

"Page one . . . ?"

"A joke. But someone on the committee—Mom, most likely—thought it would be great publicity for the big event if a well-known author is photographed in one of the costumes for the society page."

"Mmm," said Nick, "they couldn't have chosen a better model. And that's a terrific idea—"

"What's so terrific about it? We're talking two hours under hot lights when I could be sleeping late instead."

"Sorry," said Nick. "I was referring to what you said earlier. About Sargent. You know how I hate wearing costumes."

"Almost as much as you hate formal wear?" she teased.

"Well, almost is the key word. But now I'll be able to get by in the lesser of two evils. White tie and tails."

"What kind of costume is that?" asked Claudia. "The theme is painters and their subjects, remember?"

"Portrait of the artist as a middle-young man," said Nick. "Sargent always wore tails. And since you're obviously coming as Madame X, I—"

"You guessed! Damn! Nick, when I get my hands on you tonight, I swear—"

"Promises, promises," he said. "I didn't mean to spoil your surprise. It's just that I don't know any of his other paintings by name. Anyway, you sound in good spirits, so I take it there's been no word from . . . southern quarters?"

She wasn't about to tell him over the phone. "I'll be home early this evening. I'll do something special for dinner."

He thought he detected evasion in her too-light tone of voice, but he didn't pursue it. "Okay, see you around six."

Over chilled wine and stir-fried scampi, Claudia told him about the visits from both the younger and older Dantines. She finished by saying, "Mom's going to talk with Ray Fenwick about getting some kind of restraining order. Not that it'll do any good."

Nick nodded; Armand Dantine's psychological profile would place him, at least in his own mind, above the law.

"I'd like to find out where he is," said Nick. "I know there's no way to convince him that he needs help, but there's got to be a way to get through to him."

"To what end?" asked Claudia, pouring them more wine.

"To his getting the hell out of our lives once and for all," he answered, draining his glass. "I know I'm not speaking the way a shrink ought to speak, but there are moments when I'm furious enough to strangle the son of a bitch! Maybe it's a good thing we don't know where to find him!"

Claudia rose and began clearing the table. She needed to change the subject. "Espresso? I've already set up the pot."

Nick shook his head and reached for the wine bottle, which was almost empty. "No, I'd prefer more of this." He glanced at the label. "There should be another bottle in the refrigerator."

"I'll open it."

"I have a better idea," said Nick. "I'll get the wine. You model your Sargent concoction."

"Now?"

"What better way to end dinner than with a fashion show?" he asked.

They both laughed as other alternatives crossed their minds. "First things first," he said.

It was the Madame X costume that sparked Nick's inspiration. Claudia pulled her hair up as she had done at the costumer's, then added black peau de soie sandals. She entered the den and did a three-quarter model's turn to Nick's head-to-toe appraisal.

"I bet the *Examiner* sells out when you model that."

"Josh said as much. I take it to mean you like it?"

Nick's mouth curved into a mischievous grin as he

390

nodded and came closer to her.

Claudia's arms went around his neck as Nick's fingers began tracing the folds of satin that outlined the plunging *V* and her breasts. He slipped a hand inside the fabric and with his other hand eased the slender straps from her shoulders.

She helped him, but their kisses interfered with her effort to step out of the gown.

"Nick . . ." she whispered.

"Mmm-hmm?"

"This is a rental — we've got to be practical, or we'll tear it."

He was trying to free her from the tight bodice. "I am being practical, Claude. That's why we're taking it off."

"Nick . . ." she protested feebly.

"You said that already. C'mon, let's get you out of this."

Moments later they were both lying naked on the carpeting.

"Hey, Madame X," he teased, "I had a really rough day . . ."

"So?"

"So, it's your turn . . ." He pulled her gently until she was astride him, straddling him just below his chest. Then he eased himself into her, and she abandoned all thoughts of Madame X, costume balls, and Armand Dantine.

Afterward, still on the floor and still in each other's arms, Claudia sighed contentedly and glanced over at the heap of black satin they'd tossed onto the chair a short while ago.

"Now that would make quite a picture," she observed.

Nick turned and laughed. He and Claudia, along with the shiny black fabric reflecting in the mirror opposite them, presented an image of wanton disarray.

"I mean, speaking of sellout copies of the *Examiner* . . ."

"Claude!" Nick exclaimed, sitting up. "That's it!"

"What's . . . what?"

"The way to Armand Dantine!"

"I don't understand. You mean it's something I said?"

"Yes! We'll find Dantine by using your picture — the one that's going to be on the society page. There's bound to be information about the ball — the details about date and time, all that. He's a painter; he'll jump at the bait."

"But Nick, who says he'll read the society page?"

"He reads your column, doesn't he?"

"But the society page is nowhere near the advice page. It's in the fashion section." Claudia considered her own words. "Unless . . ."

"Unless?"

"Maybe we can get Josh to run the picture on the cover of the Sunday magazine — we can make use of the celebrity status the book has pulled in."

She saw the look of concern on Nick's face and said, "Of course, there's no guarantee he'll show up. And even if he does, with so many people in costumes and masks, he might not recognize us — or vice versa."

"Masks?" he asked absently.

"Well, it is a masked ball, at least until midnight.

That was Mom's idea, so judging of the costumes can be impartial. Which brings up another point. The entire event is by invitation only, and tickets will be scrupulously checked. Crashing Mom's party was easy, with Imelda at the door; at the Art Institute, it's something else."

Nick had been thinking, and the dangerous ramifications loomed stronger and stronger in his mind. "Look," he said, "let's forget my suggestion, okay?"

"Why? It's a great idea!"

"It's too risky. The guy is obviously coming unhinged." He laughed at his choice of words. "In my professional opinion—"

She interrupted. "Unhinged. The language is perfectly clear. But that's just it—if he weren't, he'd have left by now. He's obsessed—or possessed—so when he sees my picture in the paper—"

"Claude, when he sees your picture in the paper, Dantine and everyone else in Chicago who reads the *Examiner* will know what costume you'll be wearing, mask or no mask. That makes you a sitting duck."

"Or a decoy, darling," she said. "And I've sat back passively far too long, while Armand plays his little games as if we're his . . . toys!"

For the first time in days, Claudia's fighting spirit was returning. "Nick," she said, "if my posing as Madame X will bring him out into the open, I prefer that to having to sneak out back exits and use your car, while my heart moves into my throat every time I step into an elevator or go to the ladies' room!"

She had given Nick the same details of her encounter with Armand as those she'd given Eleanor, but she knew that Nick could easily fill in the blanks.

Which apparently he had. "Claude," he said, "I don't want you getting hurt. The man is mentally disturbed, and the more desperate he becomes, the more he's likely to try anything."

"Nick, he's also strong and healthy, and it may give him some kind of perverse pleasure to stalk me like this. He could enjoy it so much that he'd move up North and continue this indefinitely. And I want it to end!"

"There's got to be another way."

"Fine. Let me know if you think of it. But in the meantime, I'm due at a photo session tomorrow morning at ten. Dressed as Madame X."

Chapter 29

Sirena Mars stared at the full-length photograph on the cover of the *Daily Examiner* Sunday magazine section. Claudia Gage was modeling a daring black evening gown. In the lower right-hand corner of the cover was a color inset depicting the painting of another woman, posed and dressed in an identical gown. In white letters across the bottom were printed the words: "Life Imitates Art: Society Paints the Town." Sirena turned to the article and read:

Next Saturday night the lights of the Art Institute of Chicago will be burning brightly long after closing time.

The glittering evening is a fund-raiser for both the museum and Lake Shore General Hospital, but with a definite twist.

"We wanted a theme that would reflect the purpose of the event, in terms of encouraging creativity, life, and beauty," said Mrs. Eleanor Gage, who organized the charity ball. The answer? Some four hundred invited guests, costumed as artists or as the subjects of paintings. Admission will set attendees back a pricy five hundred dollars per person, and tickets are almost sold out.

The *Daily Examiner*'s own Claudia Gage, pictured on our cover and costumed as John Singer Sargent's infamous "Madame X," said, "My mother has worked endlessly to make this an extraordinary evening. Costumes will compete before a panel of judges, and the grand prize, a trip for two on the Orient Express, will be awarded to the most authentic. A musical cue will announce the midnight unmasking."

A musical cue? the *Examiner* asked.

"Yes," replied Miss Gage. "The orchestra will play 'Now is the Hour,' a song with a very special meaning." She went on to explain, "It's a favorite of someone I personally wished to invite to the ball, someone I've been unable to locate."

One of her readers? we asked our popular advice columnist and author of the best-selling *Dear Claudia*.

"Yes," she said. "And if he dresses as Gainsborough, he'll be admitted without an invitation."

We asked about possible gatecrashers. "Few portraits exist of Gainsborough himself; his paintings, such as 'The Blue Boy,' are far better known. But anyone costumed as Gainsborough will be asked a specific question; the inability to answer will identify an imposter."

The rest of the article described the museum's history, its extensive renovations in recent years, and information about current exhibitions.

Sirena leafed through the colorful photographs of canvases on display. The modern ones were unfamiliar to her and painted by artists whose names she couldn't pronounce. But she recognized Monet's lilies, a Rodin statue, and several more from the earlier, better days with Armand, when together they had toured New Orleans museums. With few exceptions, he had regarded the works as insignificant, the talents, inferior.

I should have taken warnin' when he locked his studio to me, she reflected. Then none o' this would be happenin'. He's sick with blindness in his soul, but so am I, or I'd have seen it before.

Before, she thought. Before Noelle—and Claudia Gage—became his obsession. And before Philippe.

Nine years. So long ago. She looked up from the paper and glanced at her image in the mirror over the dresser.

The years with Armand Dantine had begun to show. Untying the belt of her cotton wrapper, she let it fall to the floor and studied the full reflection of her naked body. It, too, had changed. She was thinner than her curves suggested. Her stomach was flat, and a slim waist led upward to high, firm breasts. Men still wanted her, she knew. Any man except Armand.

Sirena felt a pang of the anguish she carried with her constantly. Her contempt held no bearing on her aching need of him. People were burdened by all kinds of afflictions. And she was forced to admit that Armand Dantine was hers.

The thought returned her mind to the costume ball she'd been reading about. And to the invitation Claudia Gage had openly addressed to him with her interview in the paper.

Why, she didn't know. But he'd be there. She was as certain of that as she was that he would read the article.

Would he bring Philippe? And would that place her child in danger?

Sirena let out a cry that was half sob, half whimper, then fell upon the bed. Her own longing for Armand was loathsome to her; to still want him after he had taken — stolen — the only meaning left to her life was nothing short of madness.

"Philippe," she whispered over and over through her tears. Just to see him, hold him, once more. Was it too much to ask? All the years of submission to Armand's will, even to denying herself the joy of calling Philippe "Son" and hearing him call her "Mother." Was there nothing she could do?

She sat up suddenly.

It wasn't yet a fully formed idea, more like a flash of some remote possibility. She grabbed the magazine section and hurried to the article once more in search of an address.

Forty-five minutes later, Sirena walked up the steps to the Michigan Avenue entrance of the Art Institute of Chicago. She wasn't unaware that men's eyes lingered on the sway of her hips and the way the late-summer breezes caught her full skirt and sent it flying up around her thighs. Or that the wind played with her hair, which fell long and free over her shoulderless dress.

She paid the suggested donation, then waited, unsure of which direction to take within the cavernous lobby.

She couldn't ask at the information desk; she didn't

know what she was looking for. People, families, or groups of tourists, for the most part, were milling about, checking their maps and catalogs.

Sirena randomly followed a blue-jeaned and T-shirted couple nearby; they seemed to know their way.

Without realizing she was behind them, they led her through several rooms, or galleries, filled with wonders from the East, and another with the treasures of antiquity. Then farther, down a long hall filled with armor and evil-looking swords and weapons.

"Want to stop for coffee?" Sirena heard the young man, bearded and in his twenties, ask the girl.

"Later," she answered. "Otherwise, I'll be late."

They went through a door at the right, and Sirena stepped back. She'd heard voices coming from within, but she had stopped for another reason: the odors that reached her nostrils were the strong odors of turpentine and linseed oil. Her stomach did a turn, not because the odors were unpleasant, but because of their instant association. They were the same as the smells in Armand's studio.

The door opened, and now a clean-shaven boy in his late teens came out. He wore overalls that were spattered with red and ocher paint. When he saw Sirena, he said, "Excuse me, ma'am, but you look as if you're lost."

"Y-yes . . . I guess I am," she answered.

"Well, that's easy enough since the renovations, unless you're here on a regular basis." He gave her a once-over, then he smiled. "You must be one of the new models," he said. "I can show you where you can change. It's next to the class—"

"No . . . I'm not a model," she answered quickly. Then she understood. This had to be the art school

399

the newspaper article had mentioned.

If she was neither a model nor one of the students, what was she doing here?

"I . . . got turned around," she said shyly. "I was lookin' for the ladies' room, and—"

"Oh, you went right instead of left," said the boy, eager to help. "You want to cross over there"—he indicated the direction with a nod of his head—"and it's next to the Rubloff Auditorium. Once you're on the Monroe Street side of the building, you can't miss it."

"The auditorium," repeated Sirena. "I thank you very much."

"That's okay," said the boy with a grin. "I'm just sorry you're not one of the models. Most of them—in my classes, anyway—should all be on starvation diets." His pale face turned crimson, and it made Sirena laugh. He's so sweet, she thought. And so innocent.

She was aware that the boy was still standing there, still watching her as she moved away. No matter. Something unknown was urging her forward, and something equally as obscure within her was responding. Maybe it was magic, or maybe there was no such thing as magic. That didn't matter, either.

She followed the boy's directions until she came to the entrance to the ladies' room. And the Rubloff Auditorium. A line of women stood waiting just outside the ladies'-room door. She'd used it as an excuse; no need to wait on line. Without thinking, she opened the unlocked door to the auditorium and stepped into the darkened theater.

The rows and rows of empty seats reminded her of the time Armand had taken her to the opera in New Orleans. He'd reserved a box and insisted they arrive early, while the theater was still dark.

"There's something special about a theater before it fills with people," he'd said. "As though the spirits inhabit the premises. Then the philistines invade and drive the spirits out."

Sirena had found his remark more than odd. "Don't you need people in the seats before you can have the show onstage?" she'd asked.

His look of contempt had silenced her. But why, she thought, am I reflectin' on that now? Maybe I'm losin' my own mind the way he seems t' be losin' his . . .

Nonetheless, visions of ghosts danced through Sirena's head as she stood engulfed by the stillness. It wasn't a stillness brought on by fear—nor like the silence of unexpressed rage.

Armand's rage.

That summoned her back once more to the reason she'd come here. She reviewed her movements since entering the museum. From what the student had told her, she was on the Monroe Street side of the museum. Michigan Avenue, where she'd come in, must be at least a full block to the west—where the costume-ball guests presumably would enter. But according to the newspaper, the ball was to be held in the South Building. Sirena made a mental note to pick up a map on her way out; that way there'd be no mistake.

She came out of the auditorium and again noticed the women waiting their turn outside the ladies' room. The line had grown shorter.

That prompted the idea. Sirena understood at last not only what she needed to do, but how it could be done. There remained only one final hurdle.

The answer came inadvertently as she headed back

through one of the corridors in which watercolors and drawings hung on display. A guard smiled and said, "All you'd need is a flower tucked behind your ear."

"Excuse me?" she said.

"The Gauguin. You've seen it?"

"The what . . . ?" asked Sirena.

"The Gauguin. It's on loan."

When she still seemed not to understand, the guard instructed her. "The hall over there, then make the turn, through to the next gallery, and you can't miss it. You'll be surprised, I guarantee. Maybe even flattered. You should be."

Sirena recognized the artist's name from one of Armand's books, although she couldn't remember what any of his paintings looked like.

However, the moment she stepped into the gallery, she knew. Rows of paintings lined the wall, but the Tahitian girl was the surprise the guard had promised. And she was flattered.

Only two other visitors were in the same gallery, and they stared as openly as Sirena did as she looked at the face of the brown-skinned beauty on canvas. Curly black hair like her own fell loosely over naked shoulders; the fuller figure was wrapped in a colorfully flowered sarong that clung to her form and hid none of her sensuous curves, curves that Sirena, too, possessed.

And now, with more than curious interest, she began to study the costume in the painting. Bright red and orange. White flowers. Simple. Nothing more than a large piece of cloth tucked into itself over the right breast. And a hyacinth in her hair.

She became excited as the solution became more apparent.

This is no accident, she decided. This is the way it's

meant to be.

Maybe the magic is workin' after all . . .

Claudia had been sitting in an Indian-style position without saying a word; she was waiting for Nick's reaction to the newspaper article. What was taking so long — was he reading it twice?

Finally he dropped the magazine section to the floor and turned to her.

"Well?" Claudia asked eagerly. "Do you think he'll show up?"

"Yes, I do," he answered, rising from the chair and coming to sit beside her on the sofa. "That's what has me worried, Claude."

"Don't. I can take care of myself."

"Look," he said quietly as he ran his fingers through the hair at the nape of her neck, "the guy is potentially dangerous . . ."

"You'll be there," she countered. "And you understand him psychologically . . . better than any of us."

"Now don't put up a brave front for me," Nick replied. "You can't be without some fear about the outcome."

"I . . . I am afraid — that someone else could get hurt. I don't think he'd try to harm me. But you . . . or Mom. . . ." She breathed, then exhaled, slowly. "I keep thinking about . . . the gun he pulled on you."

"I'm not the one he's after, Claude."

"Nick, he's jealous — and you're his rival . . . at least the way he sees it. I'm even worried about Sirena Mars. He said he could find her, and he probably can." Claudia tied the ribbon closure of her gray silk peignoir and got up, then walked to the terrace windows. "Do you think Sirena might try to find Philippe and take him away?"

"It wouldn't be a wise move, but I couldn't blame her if she did," answered Nick.

"Neither could I. Nick . . . is he desperate enough to hurt the child?"

Nick shook his head. "I doubt it. Dantine wants to reunite the boy with his . . . mother."

"But Sirena is Philippe's mother—"

"Not the way Dantine sees it. Nor the child, Claude. He's been told since his birth that the woman in the portrait is his mother. And *that*'s who Armand Dantine wants her to be."

"But . . . I'm Noelle's daughter."

Nick joined her at the window. "Forget that, Claude. Forget that she's your mother—and Armand's. What he really wants is Noelle, not you. Your resemblance to her has pushed him to the limits of his sanity, where he can no longer make the distinction."

Claudia leaned her head back against his chest. "You know, under other . . . more normal . . . circumstances, I'd find it flattering. It's all so confusing, and he's so warped, Nick. I wish we could help—and have him out of our lives, too."

"Well . . . if the piece in the newspaper works, we can personally confront him. It just may be enough to snap him out of it. Or . . ."

"Or what?"

Nick shook his head and didn't reply, although he wondered if their attempt to bring him out in the open might be too much. Armand Dantine could not only snap—he could easily go over the edge.

Aloud he asked, "Incidentally, what's the so-called password—the question that'll make sure he's the right

Gainsborough, if he does show up?"

"He'll be asked his son's name," she said, rubbing her temples to ease the tension there.

"Headache?" he asked, taking over the massaging for her.

"Mm-hmm. But it's only six more days. I'll manage."

Nick kissed her hair, then turned her around to face him. "Six more nights, too," he said, taking her hand and leading her to the bedroom. "We'll have to do something to help you relax . . ."

Chapter 30

"Mom, don't you really think a limousine is overdoing it?" asked Claudia as the sleek black car headed south along the Outer Drive.

Nick nudged her gently and said, "I'm not a male chauvinist, Claude, but you have a wise mother. So even if I didn't mind your parading downtown dressed—rather undressed—like that, Eleanor wouldn't allow it. Right?"

Eleanor Gage laughed nervously. "Right, Nick. But even if Claudia were costumed in tatters, considering what we've all been through recently, I'd go as far as locking her in her room rather than have her wandering around town alone." To Claudia she said, "Darling, I agree that a car this size is a bit on the pretentious side. However, the window glass is dark, and the driver"—she lowered her voice—"is more than just a chauffeur engaged for the evening."

"Mom," said Claudia, "you're not telling me you hired a bodyguard, are you?"

"From the tone of that question, darling, I'm not telling you anything. Besides, we're almost there."

Claudia nodded and gazed through the window at the towers lined up alongside one another.

Nick rested a hand on her knee and she involuntarily shuddered. "Mmm," he said. "Nice to know the effect I have on you." In a softer voice he asked, "You okay?"

She nodded. "Nervous as all getout. But yes, I'm okay. I'm just wondering if all this is going to work. And what we can hope to expect if it does."

"Darlings," said Eleanor, "I hope you'll both relax enough to enjoy the ball. The committee and I have gone to quite a bit of trouble to make this an unforgettable evening."

Yes, thought Claudia. And what about Armand Dantine . . . ?

Eleanor had refused to model her costume for Nick or Claudia in advance. "It's part of the fun, keeping it all secret," she'd insisted. Now as the three mounted the steps guarded on either side by the Art Institute's familiar bronze lions, Eleanor wrapped her voluminous, floor-length black satin cloak around her and held her matching, rhinestone-studded mask up to her face.

"Excuse me," said the man at one of the doors, "may I have your name?"

Eleanor smiled indulgently and handed him her engraved invitation. As soon as he checked her in, she hurried off. "I must finish dressing," she said. "See you downstairs."

Claudia nodded and whispered to Nick, "I can hardly wait to see who she's come as. I couldn't even get it out of Imelda."

As their invitations were checked against the guest list, Claudia glanced ahead. "Well, I see two women who could each pass for Marie Antoinette. I hope my idea is more original."

"I don't care whether it is or not," said Nick. "I think you should always wear black satin cut down to there." He indicated "there" with his eyes, and Claudia wondered if the maître d' nodded approvingly at that precise moment because of the way she looked, or in response to Nick's remark.

It turned out to be neither; he'd found their names on the list. "Miss Gage, Dr. Seward, go right in."

"Where will we find Eleanor?" asked Nick as they passed Fullerton Hall on their left and the libraries to their right. Flowers and festooned ribbons fashioned into still more blossoms had been hung or draped everywhere the eye could see. Ushers were posted at entrances to the Oriental and Classical Arts galleries. They were obviously intended to direct guests to the stairs or elevators that would take them to the South Building, where the actual festivities were being held. The effect, however, was anachronistic, given the setting.

"Miniature Mozarts just don't fit in with the armor," Nick commented as they entered Gunsaulus Hall. Then, noticing that a number of the ushers were young girls, he added, "Androgenous little Mozarts, aren't they?"

Claudia laughed. Nick wasn't far off the mark. The ushers were costumed as eighteenth-century pages, complete with white wigs, satin vests, and velvet jackets covered in a tapestry of beads and rich embroidery.

At the end of Gunsaulus Hall, Claudia and Nick took the elevator to the lower level, then continued through the American Arts galleries and on to the South Building. Sheathed in pale limestone and with its restrained door frames and windows, it was the perfect setting for a gala costume ball.

"They could hold the Super Bowl in here," commented Nick.

"There seem to be that many people already," agreed Claudia. "How will we ever find Mom in this crowd?"

Everywhere around them were "paintings" that had, as Eleanor had predicted, come to life. Several "Rembrandts" strolled by; one couple, dressed as Grant Wood's "American Gothic," walked stiffly as though they had just stepped off the model's stand after decades of posing for the artist.

And then, from the center of a glittering crowd, came the sounds of Eleanor's familiar laugh. Nick said, "We may need another invitation to get near her!"

"It's Mom's evening," said Claudia. "But I've got to see what she's wearing." Claudia and Nick edged their way through yards of hoop-skirted elegance, and past a woman dressed as Whistler's mother. At last they discovered what Eleanor Gage had been keeping secret all week.

"She must have been hiding a trunk under her cloak," Claudia observed.

Eleanor had wrapped yards of white silk into a turban around her head. A long gown of black satin fell in graceful folds to the floor and into a train behind her. In one hand she held a mask, a dagger in the other.

"Mom . . . ?" said Claudia, finally moving in next to her.

Eleanor held the mask up to her face and asked, with a hint of mischievousness in her voice, "Well, darling, what do you think?"

"Think? It's stunning, of course. But . . . who are you supposed to be?"

Eleanor smiled imperiously and answered, "Mrs. Siddons, darling. 'The Tragic Muse.'"

When neither Claudia nor Nick responded immediately in recognition, Eleanor explained, "The title of the painting is 'The Tragic Muse.' It's by Joshua Reynolds. I finally remembered that I'd seen the portrait in London, not in New York. She was a great beauty, but I can state immodestly that it's the title that first gave me the idea. And," she added dramatically, "the props." She lifted the mask to her face once more, but Claudia's eyes were on the dagger. It was real.

"Mom . . .?" said Claudia.

"Never fear, darling. Medea killed her children. I, instead, am ready to kill anyone who tries to harm mine."

On their way to the bar, Claudia observed wryly, 'The Tragic Muse. Perfect.'

Champagne glasses in hand, they took a visual tour of the costumes on display. Clearly, great imagination had been at work.

A "still-life" twosome strolled by; the man wore red tights, and the upper half of his torso had somehow been enveloped in papier mâché to resemble an apple; his female companion wore green tights and a neck-to-knees cluster of grapes. Together they had managed to attach themselves to an oversize Blue Willow-patterned plate.

Claudia herself was aware of stares as the vast space filled with more and more guests. Acquaintances and friends stopped to admire her striking costume — which, because of its attendant publicity, identified her at once, despite her glittering mask.

Nick was masked, too, and he was amused that people were addressing him as Mr. Sargent. His formal attire got him off the costume-hook, and its unspectacular aspect afforded him freedom of observation as each newly arrived guest joined the swelling crowds. He was intent on keeping a protective eye on "Madame X," although he knew Armand Dantine, if he swallowed the bait, would try to put distance between them both.

Women's voices as they entered the ladies' room told Sirena that the ball had begun. She waited until she saw hems and borders of half a dozen jeweled gowns filling the space between the cubicle door and the tiled floor. Then she straightened the creases of her red-orange-and-white-flowered cotton sarong, fixed the silk hyacinth behind one ear, and joined the rest of the women at the mirror over the sinks.

The other women were staring, and at first Sirena feared that it was because they knew. But then she glanced up at her reflection and realized the stares were from envy—and because she really did look like the painting she'd seen. As though the Gauguin had come to life.

Strange, she thought, running fingers through her long black curls. A painting come to life.

The same as Claudia Gage.

Sirena opened the ladies' room door and went out into the crowd.

As Claudia sipped her champagne, she looked about and marveled at the ingenuity of the creative mind.

She saw a tall, thin man with a craggy face. His short-cropped hair was red—obviously sprayed that color for the night. He wore a simple brown corduroy jacket and nondescript, paint-smeared pants. But his "signature"

411

was the conspicuous—and clearly fake—bandage covering one ear. In his hand he carried an enormous sunflower and an artist's palette, and the mask covering his face was an impressionist's canvas of thick, primary-colored impasto.

"Van Gogh would be flattered," quipped Claudia. "The only thing missing is a pitcher of iris."

Nick laughed. "Oh . . . there's Ray Fenwick, looking older than Methuselah! Let's say hello."

"How do you know it's Ray?" asked Claudia. "I can't tell for sure with those rubber wrinkles covering his face."

"Trust the doctor, it's Ray. But who's he supposed to be, I wonder?"

She answered just as the Gages' lawyer joined them. He wore a flowing robe of an off-white color, and a wig of long, stringy hair. A velvet artist's hat capped his head, and his mask made him appear to be well over ninety. "It *is* the original Renaissance man, isn't it?" Claudia asked.

Fenwick bowed ceremoniously. "I'm glad someone guessed," he said, kissing her on the cheek. "Of course, when Gloria is at my side, that makes it easier. She's dressed as the 'Mona Lisa.' "

Claudia remembered Eleanor's remark about matrons above size twelve, and laughed. Gloria Fenwick could just about squeeze into a fourteen.

"Well, Signor Da Vinci," said Claudia, "you're up against some pretty stiff competition, artistically. I've seen Van Gogh and a few Rembrandts stalking the premises tonight."

Just then Nick looked up and commented, "There's something to be said for modern art." He was referring to the couple passing them: the man a perfect double for

412

Andy Warhol, and on his arm, a masked champagne blond wearing a skintight white halter dress whose skirts flared the way Marilyn Monroe's had in *The Seven Year Itch*. Her mouth was set in a Monroe pout.

"Well," said Fenwick. "I was under the impression the costume parade wouldn't begin till eleven, but I see it's going on all around us." His eyes were following the derrière on the Monroe lookalike. "You'll both have to excuse me. I want to browse around the . . . uh . . . modern-art collection. See you later, all right?"

"When the band strikes up 'Now Is the Hour,' " said Nick.

His words made Claudia's stomach churn.

The orchestra was playing and guests were dancing, but she was sitting this one out. Claudia and Nick had waltzed and tangoed, but she was still unable to relax, feeling a constant need to glance about in search of another artist—the one they hadn't seen. Claudia found the ever-present uncertainty of whether he would show up—and what might happen if he did—an enervating experience. Waiting games were more difficult, she reasoned, than knowing the answers and dealing with them. This, together with the fishbowl-like attention her Madame X costume had attracted, made Claudia feel that she was center stage, even when, as now, she was seated on a marble bench and waiting for Nick to return with refills of champagne.

She was gazing at the glamorous array of costumes and the excitement that her mother's efforts had garnered. Eleanor had done herself, the museum, and the hospital proud.

She noticed someone approaching in a beeline for her.

413

Claudia's antennae would have gone on alert, but she could tell, from the shapely legs extending beneath the wildest array of ostrich feathers she had ever seen, that this splendid "bird" was a female.

The bird's feathers were bursting with brilliant colors — cerise, orange, yellow, and purple — even her head was covered with them. A half-mask hid the upper portion of the bird's face, as high spike heels — on jeweled pumps of purple and pink — propelled her forward. When she reached Claudia, she stood before her and bowed deeply.

Claudia shook her head in wonder and heard her voice ask, incredulously, "Judy . . . ?"

"Shit!" came the reply, followed by uproarious laughter. "How in God's name did you figure that out?" She arranged her purple-feathered tail to one side and seated herself on the bench beside her friend.

"Deduction," answered Claudia, smiling. "That costume has to be a Chagall painting. And knowing your perverse nature, I thought, Judy's the only person I know who would come dressed as a painting by her least favorite artist."

"You're a smartass, Gage. Speaking of my other least favorite artist, has *he* dared to show his face yet?"

Claudia's apprehensive feeling was returning. "No. He may not."

"He'll be here. He's too sick to just forget about you and go home alone to his mausoleum in the French Quarter."

Judy saw that her remark wasn't being taken as lightly as she'd intended it. But Nick was coming toward them with two champagne glasses.

"Judy!" he said, handing her one of the glasses.

You, too!" she exclaimed, crestfallen. "Now look, I know I didn't tell you my feelings about Chagall!"

414

"Chagall?" he said, shaking his head. "Oh . . . sure, one of his birds. No, I recognized those gorgeous legs."

Claudia kicked him playfully and said, "Sit down. We'll split my drink."

The three made small talk, but each was aware that the evening was progressing and so far there had been no sign of Armand Dantine.

"Well," Nick reminded Claudia, "if he got the message you sent him through the paper—and he'd have to be dead not to have understood it—he'll show up at the appointed hour, and not a minute before."

"What if whoever's on the door slips up?" asked Judy. "I mean, even if the so-called message to Armand is clearly an invitation, how do we guarantee he'll get in here without a ticket?"

Nick took a sip of Claudia's champagne and replied, "The maître d' at each post has been alerted to admit any man fitting Dantine's description and giving Claudia's 'password.' If he turns up, he'll be admitted."

"And hopefully committed," quipped Judy. But immediately she noticed Nick and Claudia's identical reactions, and she added, "Listen, you two, I'll shut my beak. In fact, I'll go powder it. Where's the nearest john?"

On her way to the ladies' room, Judy passed a woman who was what Frank referred to as a real knockout. A Gauguin painting in the flesh! No wonder the artist had chosen Tahiti over Paris!

She found herself staring openly, along with other masqueraders, at the woman in the striking yet simple costume. It was clear, even with a dimestore half-mask covering her eyes, that the dark woman in the flowered cotton sarong and thong sandals was a stunner.

Judy entered the ladies' room and observed her own costume's reflection in the mirror: Chagall's bird was glamorous, elaborate, expensive, and while spectacular in its way, the Tahitian woman hadn't needed any of that.

Well, she reasoned, drawing her powder compact from within a feathered pocket, I've seen only one woman in recent memory who could get by without makeup or artifice of any kind and still make us all look like drudges by comparison.

The thought made her dizzy.

Is it possible? she wondered.

Is Sirena Mars here, too?

And if she is, should Claudia know . . . ?

Nick and Claudia had alternated dancing with wandering through their favorite galleries, and nibbling hors d'oeuvres and canapés from the lavish assortment her mother's food and drink committee had arranged.

They'd seen very little of Eleanor for much of the evening so far. "She's been as secretive about the way they're going to judge costumes," said Claudia, "as she was about her muse."

"I hope whatever she's doing will be less obscure," said Nick. "For us plebians, that is."

"Well, Mom said it'll be more fun than just having one costume after another parade past a reviewing stand."

"How long do we have to wait?" asked Nick.

"Till eleven. Mom feels it'll take about an hour. She's hoping the prizes can be awarded in time for the unmasking at midnight." Claudia felt another twinge, but now she knew why.

She'd expected Armand Dantine to appear before the costume parade began. Someone with his ego would have no wish to be upstaged, she reasoned. Once the judging started, everyone else would be relegated to the background.

Unless he's waiting for that so he can create a diversion. This particular thought unnerved her; she hadn't considered it before.

But if Armand Dantine had entered the museum, none of the principals—Claudia, Nick, Judy, Eleanor, and Ray Fenwick—had detected his arrival. Nor, it seemed, had museum security, whose personnel had been instructed to alert several plainclothesmen who owed Fenwick a favor. In addition, the array of jewels adorning many of Chicago's most prominent socialites had brought out extra security in full measure. Claudia had seen several men wandering about looking like refugees from Modigliani canvases, but when she asked Fenwick if they were detectives or simply unimaginative in their costume choices, the lawyer said he wasn't sure.

Finally the orchestra played a fanfare. Claudia pulled back the sleeve of Nick's frock coat and checked his watch. "Well, it's time for Mom's surprise," she said with more enthusiasm than she felt. The waiting and wondering were beginning to wear her down.

Nick's arm went around her waist. "Don't be disappointed, Madame X," he said. "You can't compete for the costume prize, because it would smack of nepotism. So try to relax and enjoy the show." But he knew as well as Claudia that the tension he felt at the base of her spine had nothing to do with costumes or prizes.

They moved closer to the long wall upon which a

temporary stage had been constructed. A red velvet drapery hung across and over whatever Eleanor had hidden beneath.

"It looks like a painting's going to be unveiled before the judging begins," Claudia whispered as a drum roll summoned the vast gallery to silence.

Eleanor Gage climbed the portable staircase of six steps at the far left of the stage and made her way to the center just alongside the red velvet drapery. A microphone and podium had been set up, and nearby were five chairs facing whatever lay beneath the covering.

Eleanor approached the mike and cleared her throat. Then she began. "Ladies and gentlemen, friends and patrons of the Art Institute of Chicago and Lake Shore General Hospital." She offered a small welcoming speech and then said, "We won't keep you in suspense any longer. You've probably been wondering if I'm going to unveil the museum's latest acquisition—but we can't afford another Van Gogh at today's prices."

The gallery was sprinkled with polite laughter.

"Well, I'm going to unveil—unmask!—as many paintings as there are guests present tonight." Eleanor took a corner of the red velvet drapery and with a single, swift movement flung it aside to reveal a carved-gilt antique frame measuring more than five feet across and six feet in height.

"But it's empty!" exclaimed Claudia. "What is Mom think—"

"Shh!" whispered Nick as Eleanor continued speaking into the microphone.

"The judging of costumes is about to begin," she said. "Each guest—or group of guests—is requested to mount the stage"—she indicated the end opposite the one occupied by the judges' chairs—"and then, if the costume or

418

costumes represent an actual painting, the subject will step into the frame. If, however, the entrant is dressed as the artist, he or she will stand beside the frame. Naturally, in the event that a group covers both, the artist will take his or her place next to the 'portrait.'

"You will note a number written at the bottom of your ticket. These denote only the order in which costumes are to be judged. The names and numbers, by the way, are unknown to our panel of distinguished judges, who are impartial members of the board of directors of the Art Institute.

"To ensure fairness we request that each entrant give only the name of the artist and/or subject he or she has chosen to impersonate. In case of duplication, these costumes will be listed in their order of appearance, for example, Mona Lisa one, Mona Lisa two, and so on."

Nick nudged Claudia. "I've seen three already, and Gloria Fenwick isn't going to be thrilled. The two chubbier ones look more like the real thing."

Claudia smiled just as Eleanor was concluding.

"Finalists will be asked to wait at the end of the stage so that prizes can be awarded promptly at midnight, when we find out 'who's who.' " As a closing quip, she added, "That is, the who's who—among the 'who's who.' "

Her remark was greeted with vociferous applause, after which Eleanor stepped away from the microphone and led the five judges, each of them costumed and masked as well, to their chairs opposite the gilded frame.

Another fanfare, and the costume parade began.

Claudia felt as though her mind, not just her brain,

were divided in two. Half of her watched the costume contest onstage with enjoyment as her mother's inspiration entertained everyone present; the other half kept the various exits in her peripheral vision in case Armand made his own "appearance."

She knew Nick was nervous, too, although they pretended, for each other's sake, to be concentrating solely on the parade.

The penultimate entry was an historic canvas depicting two beautiful Frenchwomen, possibly mother and daughter. Both wore sumptuous satin gowns of iridescent pink and cream, covered with beads and pearls. Their powdered white wigs were entwined with jewels. But what intrigued Nick was the Nubian slave, complete with a palm for fanning the two ladies.

Nick leaned over and whispered into Claudia's ear, "I've never heard of the artist or the painting, but I think they swiped the idea from the ballroom scene in *To Catch a Thief.*"

Despite her increasing nervousness as the hour approached twelve, Claudia couldn't help laughing at his remark.

Nick's joke had momentarily taken her attention away from the stage. The applause made Claudia's eyes return to the frame opposite the judges.

She hadn't heard the announcement. But she had no need to, even with the mask.

"Nick!" She almost gasped. "It's . . . Sirena Mars!"

At that moment, Gauguin's Tahitian beauty was asked to wait with the rest of the finalists. Claudia watched as Sirena joined the dozen or more people at the far end of the stage.

Claudia also watched as Eleanor rose and strode to the microphone. At first she thought her mother was going to ask for Sirena's invitation. Certainly Eleanor must be wondering the same thing she was: How did Sirena get past the security people at the door?

And if she had, what about Armand? Had he avoided detection, too?

Her question was answered moments later.

Eleanor cleared her throat and said, "Well, ladies and gentleman, you've had the opportunity to view our 'guest paintings' and their 'artists.' I see that midnight is almost upon us, so without further adieu, let's ask the judges to perform their task. If it were up to me, I'd award prizes to you all, but—"

"Just a moment, Eleanor," called one of her committee members standing near the stairs that had been used by each entrant in approaching the contestants' frame. "Ellie, there's one last entry!"

Everyone turned. Claudia and Nick were too far back to see at first.

But then he stepped forward. His hair was dark and curled, and he was dressed in satins and lace, with an artist's smock tossed casually over one shoulder.

He stepped behind the gilded frame to help the small, curly-black-haired child, who was dressed in an eighteenth-century blue satin suit, into the center spot.

Then he bowed to the judges and announced, "Gainsborough. And 'The Blue Boy.' "

Chapter 31

Nick winced from the force with which Claudia grasped his hand.

Around them, the glittering guests were gathered below the stage, where the last two entrants, Gainsborough and 'The Blue Boy,' had joined the line of finalists.

"My God," Claudia whispered. "What if he wins?"

"What if he does?" Nick returned. "I doubt that he expected this to happen."

"When will you try to talk with him?"

"As soon as it's time to unmask. I'll be able to deal with him more easily if we're face-to-face."

But while they whispered to each other, Claudia could see Armand's eyes sparkling through his black half-mask. He never once looked away from her.

Claudia glanced at Philippe, who stood at his father's side but was turned to his left and staring at Gauguin's Tahitian woman. She was closest to the podium and every now and then looked furtively back toward Philippe. My God, thought Claudia, what's she planning to do?

Eleanor Gage had laid her Tragic Muse's dagger on the

podium while she searched the crowd for her daughter. When she located Claudia at last, Eleanor's brows formed an unspoken question, and Claudia nodded as if to say, "Go on with the presentation . . . there's nothing else you can do."

One of the judges, a man dressed as Napoleon, rose from his chair and handed Eleanor a slip of paper.

"We . . . we . . ." Eleanor began, but her voice faltered. She cleared her throat and tried to control her trembling hand, which now held the name of the judges' choice.

"We have our winner," she said finally. "Georges de la Tour's 'Adoration of the Magi.' "

Eleanor started the applause as the three costumed kings came forward to accept the certificate.

"You'll have to employ wisdom," she quipped weakly. "The Orient Express grand prize is a pair of tickets for two." She was still shaky as she handed over the envelope to "Balthazar."

His offer of a brief thank you was followed by similar phrases of gratitude from his cohort-kings.

"Damn!" Nick cursed under his breath. "Get on with it, will you?"

Then Eleanor took her place at the microphone once again. "I see that we're right on schedule," she announced. "It's midnight . . ."

The sound of a harp filled the air. Then came the violins. Soon, all the musicians had joined in and the ballroom was enveloped by the lush arrangement of "Now Is the Hour."

Nick and Claudia remained standing where they were, their eyes on the stage, and hundreds of dancing couples around them.

"Everyone . . . unmask!" Eleanor called to the crowd, her voice cutting through the string section that carried the melody line of the waltz.

A shout went up and laughter rang out in counterpoint to the quickening tempo as guests removed their masks and feigned surprise at so many sudden "recognitions." Cries of "I knew it was you!" could be heard throughout.

Eleanor had lowered the mask from her face, and was turned toward Armand. Still staring at Claudia, he ripped his mask away and threw it to the floor. He made no other move; his face wore no expression, no clue as to what he might be thinking. The intensity of his stare made it impossible for Claudia to look away, despite her desire to do so.

He stepped off the small stage and started toward her. The sea of waltzing guests parted and opened a pathway to him.

"Nick . . ." was all Claudia's voice could utter.

"I'm here," he assured her.

Armand was standing directly before her. He extended his hand. "Will you?" he asked. "One last dance . . . ?"

"Dantine . . ." Nick began, but Claudia silenced him with the tip of a finger on his lips. She could see rising anger on Nick's face, determination on Armand's. There mustn't be a fight between them. Not here. Not now.

"I will . . ." she said. "If you'll be reasonable, Armand. We want to help . . ."

"Dance with me, then."

Reluctantly she offered him her hand and allowed him to lead her out onto the floor.

Claudia glanced back over her shoulder. Nick stood watching her, but other couples were crowding in around him, and soon he was no longer visible.

Armand had let go of her hand. She felt his fingers at the back of her head as he worked the knot of her ribbon. Slowly he peeled the mask from her face and it fell to the ground to be immediately crushed beneath the shoes of dancers surrounding them on all sides.

"There," he said, smiling for the first time. "Now nothing remains between us."

He spun her in circles, and the three-quarter tempo of the waltz seemed to quicken, growing louder and louder in her ears. The room, too, was spinning, the couples turning and whirling in a frenzied kaleidoscope, with Claudia and Armand at its center.

"Our song," he said, laughing.

She was becoming increasingly dizzy as his grip tightened around her waist. The sound of the music crowded out every image, every thought.

Claudia broke into a cold sweat as suddenly she understood. She was waltzing, wide-awake, through her own dream.

Her nightmare, come true.

She gasped, unable to catch her breath. Armand held her fast. She pushed away from him and struggled to stay on her feet, while the room seemed to tilt on its side.

Then the spinning stopped.

Claudia was standing still, her vision blurred, diffusing the sparkling lights from everywhere around her. She heard her mother's voice cry out.

On the small stage, the Tahitian woman had lunged forward, kneeling and taking 'The Blue Boy' in her arms.

"Little man," Eleanor heard her whisper to the child. "Oh, my little man!"

"Sirena!" Philippe's hands were locked behind her neck as he wept happily over the blaring music.

Instantly, Armand was pushing through the crowd and dragging Claudia helplessly behind him. They had almost reached the stage, and couples nearby complained as Armand shoved them from his path.

Sirena looked out onto the dance floor and watched as Armand and Claudia drew closer.

"No!" Sirena cried out.

The orchestra stopped playing, and now the only sound in the vast ballroom was the muttering of general confusion by the guests.

Everyone had turned to face the stage.

Sirena looked left, then right. She saw Eleanor's dagger lying beside her mask on the podium. She grabbed it and met Armand's stare in challenge.

He'd left Philippe alone for so little time—only the time required for one last dance! How stupid! he thought, cursing her, cursing himself.

He watched as Sirena's fingers entwined with Philippe's, as together they bolted toward the exit door behind the stage.

"Stop!" Armand yelled. His hand went inside his satin coat and fumbled through the tight brocade vest until he found the small pistol. His arm extended fully before him, he aimed at the blur of orange, red, and white.

Guests screamed, and fled to the farthest corners. Claudia's hand reached out and pulled his arm down before he could fire the shot.

"No!" she cried. "You can't!"

Armand shrugged her off, but refused to let go of his hold on her wrist. Claudia almost tripped on the folds of her long gown as he yanked her along behind, across the stage after Sirena.

He careened into the podium; it tipped over and crashed to the floor. The live microphone wailed with an earsplitting shriek. Claudia looked up and saw Eleanor, now flat against the wall and not four feet from them. Her mother seemed frozen, incapable of movement or speech.

Claudia turned to glance back, and in that instant she

426

saw Nick. He was rushing through the startled mob. Behind him followed a group of costumed men.

Armand tugged her arm so hard that Claudia feared it might come loose from its socket. The pain ceased as the man dressed as Van Gogh managed to get ahead of them. However, before he could connect with a punch, Armand swung his arm—the arm holding the gun— against the man's throat. "Van Gogh" dropped to the floor. Then Armand pulled Claudia past the man writhing in pain and together they headed for the exit through which Sirena and Philippe had made their escape.

"Nick!" cried Claudia. And the door slammed hard behind them.

Inside the ballroom, a near riot was breaking loose. Nick pushed his way through the crowd and tried to get to the stage. Somehow, Ray Fenwick had elbowed his way to Nick's side.

"Let me by, goddammit!" Nick yelled to anyone blocking his path. Why the hell did I let this happen? he thought, cursing himself for not having known how far Armand Dantine would go. Or Sirena. "Ray!" he called as a spike heel dug into his toe. "Where does that door lead?"

"Across to one of the study rooms, I think!" Fenwick shouted back. "But they could have gone anywhere! This place is a maze!"

It took nearly two minutes to reach the stage. Then they ran to the exit and out into the hallway, leaving pandemonium in their wake.

Nick looked up and down the corridor. Empty. The doors before them had to be the study rooms Ray had mentioned. He tried the knob of one. It was locked. Then he noticed the white silk hyacinth Sirena had worn

427

in her hair.

The security guards were barking orders to each other. "Shut up!" Nick yelled. "Maybe we'll be able to hear them!"

One by one, the men fell silent. Then, from far off, they heard an echo of running footsteps, followed by Claudia's voice. She was calling Nick's name.

"Come on!" he shouted, and they headed for the garden restaurant at the end of the hall.

"Wait!" Sirena cried out in a panting whisper. "I've got to catch my breath!" She leaned against the locked doors, her chest heaving as though it might burst.

Philippe gazed up at her. It wasn't advisable to stop like this, but he trusted her completely, and he could see that she needed a moment's rest.

"Sirena!" he whispered. "We have to hide!"

She ran a hand through his hair. "You do, anyway," she said. The blue satin of his costume was soiled and torn at the knee.

Sirena's eyes searched their surroundings.

There's got to be someplace up here to keep Armand from findin' him! If he shoots at me and Philippe gets in the way, I'll kill myself! If that happens, I'll get Armand, first!

That was her silent vow.

She clutched Eleanor's dagger tightly. It was wet and clammy in her hand, but she was afraid to lessen her grip in case she might drop the knife. No matter what, she reasoned, the boy must not be harmed.

But before it came to that, maybe she could get them both out of the building. There just might be a chance because Armand didn't know the museum's twists and turns any better than she did.

428

She'd thought to get away through the garden café but instead they'd wound up in the administrative area, where rows of locked office doors barred their escape.

A hallway filled with architectural displays had led them to another lobby at the bottom of a stairway at the rear of the building. Up ahead she saw an exit, but again the doors were bolted shut.

The lobby was dark, the only illumination coming from the dim lights at the far end of the corridor.

What'll I do? she thought, fighting down her rising panic. She had to maintain some kind of control; Philippe mustn't know the degree of her desperation.

"Sirena . . . ?" she heard him say.

"What is it, little man?"

His voice was barely more than a squeak as he said, "I have something to tell you."

"All right, honey, but you'd better make it fast."

"I . . . I gave Claudia her handkerchief. You said she should have it back, and . . ."

"Oh, Philippe!" she answered quickly. "You're . . . you're such a good boy."

That white lace! she thought. It had brought far more trouble than it had been worth!

For an instant she remembered back to New Orleans and Uncle Leo. His magic! What good has it done if it's all endin' like this!

And in that moment she realized that there was no magic, never had been. It was all a big joke, and she'd fallen for it. A great lie, and he'd led her to believe it. Now, it just might be the death of her.

But not of Philippe!

She heard the scuffling of shoes echoing in the stairwell and knew that Armand was gaining on them.

"What are we going to do?" Philippe asked.

Directly in front of them Sirena saw the answer. It had

429

been there all the time, but she hadn't seen it: an information kiosk. A perfect place.

She grabbed his arm and together they ran to the back of the enclosed booth. "You're goin' to hide in here while I try to find us a way to the street." She pushed him inside. "Get down on the floor and . . . and don't come out till I . . . or till someone . . . not him . . . comes for you! Understan'?"

She knelt and held his shoulders. "If Armand finds you . . . you run, hear? You get away from him and stay away for all you're worth—and then you find the Gage woman or her doctor friend!"

Philippe nodded, but he could no longer hold back his tears. He began to sob, and his soft cries nearly broke Sirena's heart. She held him tightly to her breast. "Little man," she said, choking. "Oh, my little man." She could taste his tears mingling with her own as she added silently, *My son.*

She broke the embrace at the sound of Claudia's voice.

"Philippe," murmured Sirena, looking deeply into the bewildered eyes of her child. "I love you more than anyone or anything in this world. No matter what, always remember that!"

She rose to her feet. There had to be a way out! A door, a window, some way!

"But where are you going?" whispered Philippe.

"Hush now! Get down!"

And she was gone.

"A little farther," he said, "and we'll have found him."

"Armand!" cried Claudia, covering her eyes with one hand. "I can't! I . . . just can't!"

They were in a long corridor, but exactly where, she couldn't be sure. It was too dark to gain her bearings.

430

Claudia knew only relief for their having stopped running. She'd managed to kick free of her high-heeled shoes, but not before she'd tripped several times. She rubbed her tired calves. The cool floor felt good under her stocking feet.

"They're just ahead!" Armand hissed. He still held the gun ready. "Get up! You must get up!"

"What if I can't go on, Armand? Will you shoot me?"

He sank to the floor and caressed her cheek. "How can you think of such things? What must I do to convince you that this . . . all this . . . is for . . . us?"

Claudia tried to pull away. She hoped the darkness would hide her revulsion. "Armand . . . leave Sirena and Philippe alone! Help me back! I can't go on . . . I think I've sprained my ankle," she lied.

"Are you in pain?" he asked. "I would never wish to cause you pain."

"I'll be fine . . . if you'll just . . ."

"Take you home," he answered for her, nodding. "Yes . . . I'm going to take you home."

They heard a noise. Claudia wasn't sure what it was, but Armand turned on his haunches, and when he moved, Claudia could see past him. Up ahead there was an expanse of lobby. The rear lobby! she realized. We're at the other end of the building—nobody will ever think to look here!

He turned back now and said, "I'll come for you . . . with Philippe. Soon. Until then . . ."

He leaned over to kiss her tenderly. She didn't dare refuse him.

"Armand!" she pleaded, calling out after him. "Please don't—"

He didn't wait to hear the rest. His silhouette became smaller against the light, and the sound of his footsteps grew faint as he hurried away down the hall.

Sirena was running across the length of the lobby when she heard Claudia call Armand's name.

God! she reasoned. He's close! She stopped and looked in every direction. Staircases to her left led only to the closed restaurant or to more displays. The elevator might be out of service—or he might be on it. There was no choice but to go straight ahead, to lead him as far away as possible from where she'd left Philippe.

There was another corridor to her right. Then she remembered; there was a place! She forced her weary body ahead and ran so fast, so blindly, that she inadvertently banged smack into the facing wall. She ached from the blow, but there it was: the door to the auditorium!

Oh, please! she prayed. Please, let it be open!

But, like the magic, her prayer went unanswered and the door remained shut.

She was locked out and had nowhere to turn.

Armand had spotted her just before he reached the end of the hall.

He listened, certain he'd heard a whimpering sound. A child's whimpering.

From there, across the lobby. The information booth, of course!

He'd come back for the boy later. For now, he had to deal with Sirena.

Armand had heard the impact, although he couldn't see exactly where the noise had come from. He decided to check the darkened area around the corner near the elevator.

His grip tightened on the pistol.

The hall was dimly lit. Sirena was about to dart farther down the corridor to her right.

She found nothing there. No exit. The narrow passage-way ended at the ladies' room. If she stayed here, she was trapped. With no time left to think, she ran.

Armand appeared at the mouth of the corridor. Just a shadow, an outline of black. At its center, the pistol, its short barrel dully reflecting in the dim light.

She skidded to a halt, her heaving gasps for breath the only sound until he spoke.

"He's mine. You took him." Armand's voice was devoid of all emotion, all feeling.

He was three feet from her when he fired.

The bullet hit her just below the rib cage. Sirena screamed and doubled over.

The pain was unbearable. She could feel her strength waning. Her eyes, blurring now, allowed her only the time to see Armand turn his back and start toward the lobby.

To the information booth, she knew.

Sirena stumbled forward, still clutching the dagger in her hands. She raised her arms over her head.

Armand heard the scuffling of her sandals on the floor and wheeled around.

Their final confrontation spanned the years in a single moment.

Then Armand fired again.

Sirena doubled forward, but before she fell, she plunged the blade into his chest.

Claudia lifted her gown to maneuver the last of the steps down into the lobby.

On her left was a gallery, and just ahead, the wall,

where Armand's silhouette had turned and disappeared.

The rustle of her underskirts seemed amplified in the stillness of the deserted space.

She had reached the spot where the wall ended and was just about to turn the corner when she heard a sound — an explosion — that reverberated through the museum.

Then came the scream. Sirena!

Claudia fought her fear — fear for the child! Where was he?

She shuddered and stood motionless, waiting. Listening.

From behind, there were distant shouts. Men. Nick! He was calling her name!

A second explosion, which she now recognized as a shot, echoed, repeating itself over and over until it faded away, only to be replaced by a terrible silence.

Then the heavy, sickening thud of something — or someone — hitting the floor.

Her breath choking her high in her throat, she crept around the corner from where the shots had come.

"Ohhhh! Nooooo . . . !" Her cry was more of a wail as she stepped into the light of the corridor.

They were lying on the floor, together.

The voices . . . Nick's among them . . . were very close now.

"I'm here . . . !" Claudia cried through a strangled sob, still gaping, immobilized, horrified by the scene.

Slowly she moved forward. Her toe touched something. The gun.

She knelt and looked at them: Armand, on his back, his right hand resting in the tangled mass of curly black hair; Sirena, lying across his body, one arm stretched to grasp his shoulder, the other with its hand pressed against his chest in a fatal embrace.

The shining handle of Eleanor Gage's dagger protruded from Armand's breast, as though the weapon were part of the painter's costume. The blade was encircled by blood.

His face was in repose, the ever-errant lock of hair over his brow.

His eyelids fluttered and opened.

Claudia drew a sharp breath. The irises of his eyes seemed a more intense blue than she had ever seen them, as he stared up at her in sudden recognition.

He smiled, and his lips moved to form a single word.

"Noelle . . ." he whispered, and died.

Nick was the first to reach her.

Claudia fell, sobbing, into his arms.

The other men arrived, and minutes, perhaps seconds, later, Nick led Claudia slowly away and down the hall.

From across the lobby, she thought she spotted a flash of blue satin in the light.

"Philippe . . . ?" called Claudia.

The small figure emerged from the information kiosk. His arms were outstretched, his face contorted into a voiceless plea.

He collapsed in Claudia's arms and together they wept. She reached up and took Nick's hand, the tears streaming down her cheeks.

"It's over," she whispered softly, rocking the child gently. "It's all over, little man."

Epilogue

Claudia glanced around the room to make sure she'd packed everything she'd need for the weekend. The intercom buzzed, and she called, "Mom, would you be a sweetheart and answer that?"

Eleanor Gage lifted the receiver on the wall in the foyer.

"Mrs. Seward?" said the doorman.

"This is her mother," Eleanor replied.

"Right. Well, ma'am, Dr. Seward asked me to tell Mrs. Seward that he's waiting with the car."

"Thank you; Mrs. Seward and Miss Fargo will be downstairs directly." She hung up and returned to the bedroom.

"Nick and Philippe are ready," she said.

"Then I guess we are, too," answered Claudia. Turning to Eleanor, she said, "Oh, Mom, I wish you'd reconsider and come with us. It's only for a weekend, just for the opening."

Her mother responded with a bittersweet smile. "Darling, please understand. I think it's wonderful that you're opening the house to the public. Also that Armand

Dantine's paintings will at last be seen by the world." Eleanor shook her head sadly. "But even with his leaving the house to you, I still feel as though it belongs to someone else. In a way, because of Barton. I've considered the matter at length, dear, and it's better that I stay here, where your father "—she almost choked with tears at the word—"and I shared so many good years. As much as New Orleans and the house are part of your past, they're better gone from mine."

Claudia went to her mother and hugged her gently. "I do understand, Mom. And you're quite a lady."

"That's what people tell me," she joked, trying to shrug off a sudden melancholy.

"Well, then," said Judy, who had been sitting on the edge of Nick and Claudia's king-size bed, "are we ready?"

Claudia nodded and started to close the lid of her suitcase. But something stopped her. "That reminds me, speaking of the past . . ."

She went into the living room and picked up the small wooden music box from the coffee table, where it had spent the preceding eight months since Armand's death in September.

"It's beautiful," said Judy, standing in the doorway.

"Yes, it is." Claudia wound the tiny key under the box, then lifted its lid. The lilting waltz began to play.

Holding the music box, Claudia walked to the terrace windows and gazed out across the glasslike surface of the lake.

"You know, Judy," she said as the melody continued, "I don't have the nightmare anymore. I still have the dream occasionally, but now it ends happily." The simple tune began winding down, and Claudia closed the lid of the box.

"What about Philippe?" asked Judy. "Do you really

think it's . . . healthy . . . for him to see the house again? To ever set foot in it?"

"Nick has been working with him for months, and he wouldn't have suggested it if he didn't feel that Philippe is ready. In a way, this will enable him to say good-bye. There's got to be part of him that still hasn't accepted the finality of it."

"Look, hon, that even took you a while. The kid's just turned nine, and—"

"Yes, and when we asked him what he wanted for his birthday, he's the one who requested coming with us. 'I'd like to attend the opening of my father's museum.' They were his exact words. So he's gotten past the denial phase—also the anger." She watched as a lightning-class sailboat sliced a path through the water.

"That part took the longest, the anger. Not over Armand, but because of Sirena."

"Does he know . . . I mean, that she was his mother?"

Claudia nodded. "Somehow I have the feeling he's always known. Or sensed it on some level. He wouldn't talk about it in the beginning—he refused to cry for almost the first month he was with us."

"You haven't mentioned most of this till now," said Judy.

"Look," answered Claudia, "with you traveling all over the country and calling long-distance from God-knows-where, what was I supposed to do—start relating every last detail? The important thing is that he's made tremendous progress. Nick's wonderful with him—"

"You both are. A little love goes a long, long way."

"Thanks. You know, Nick's been right all along. He's felt from the start that Philippe's psychological adjustment is due more to his being treated like a normal nine-year-old kid than to all the therapy in the world. Children are amazingly resilient, and Philippe is no exception. Stick him in a Mets uniform—not Cubs, mind you; he seems to have this 'thing' about the Mets—and he's in paradise. I mean a regular baseball fanatic. Nick got him into Little League, and he's not half bad. Even has the scabby knees to prove it."

"Speaking of which," said Judy, "two members of the 'team' are waiting for us in the car."

Claudia went back into the bedroom and placed the music box carefully inside the side compartment before closing the lid of her suitcase.

Judy noticed, but said nothing. Instead, she squeezed her friend's arm and said, "I'm really glad it's turned out like this, hon. For all of you."

Eleanor was on the terrace, and she turned as Claudia knocked on the glass.

Coming back inside, she said, "Well, then, you're ready . . . ?"

Claudia went to kiss her mother on the cheek. Picking up the single suitcase, she said, "All set. See you on Monday, Mom. In the meantime, remember how much I love you."

Eleanor's eyes misted. "There was only one moment, dearest, when I ever doubted it. But I never stopped loving you."

Philippe wore his Mets cap in the car and throughout the plane trip. He removed it only when he and Nick and Claudia were ensconced in their sumptuous suite at the Royal Orleans. Judy was staying at Frank's apartment until his new condominium was ready in Chicago, where he'd decided to open a Cajun restaurant.

On the day of the press opening, the group lunched together, after which, en route to Royal Street, Philippe led them on a tour of the French Quarter. Apparently he knew nothing of Sirena's parentage; they strolled like tourists past Uncle Leo's voodoo shop, and the child never once displayed any sign of recognition.

Claudia and Nick had discussed at length the reactions Philippe might experience upon reentering the house in which he'd lived his first eight years.

As they came up the stone walk to number 1130, Claudia wondered if the child could possibly be as nervous as she was. She glanced at Nick, whose hand rested on the child's shoulder as Philippe reached up and rang the bell.

There was a few moments' wait, then the door was pulled open by an efficient-looking young woman from the historical society. Both Nick and Claudia looked down at their adopted son, who removed his cap upon entering the foyer. Claudia was reminded of Sirena's phrase when she'd called him her little man.

At Claudia's request the house had remained unchanged, except for the walls, which were now adorned with the paintings Nick and Claudia had found in Armand's studio.

They'd framed and hung the numerous canvases in what would be known as the Dantine Museum. Noelle's portrait still hung in its place of honor above the parlor mantel.

Directly opposite on the facing wall, where before had hung an antique mirror, was a stunning portrait of another lady of the house: Sirena Mars. She was dressed as a Gypsy peasant, and the fire in her eyes burned as vividly on canvas as it had in life.

Initially Claudia had wondered, when they'd found the painting buried beneath stacks of others, if Sirena had ever seen it. Or whether she, like Claudia, had posed only in the artist's imagination. The two portraits were indeed a study in contrasts; the first, a creation of distorted love; the second, one of unbridled lust. Now, as she stood at the center of the room, Claudia surveyed her surroundings with an objective eye, and smiled. She was pleased at her decision to open the house yet keep it as it had been.

She walked to the mantel and reached into the bottom of her tote bag. Withdrawing the music box, she placed it under Noelle's portrait.

"It looks right, there," said Judy, standing beside Claudia.

"It belongs there," she answered, gazing up at her mother on canvas.

No. She amended the thought. Her mother was Eleanor, who had been wise enough to stay at home. The phrase "everything in its place" somehow seemed appropriate for the first time.

She and Judy toured the house. The furnishings throughout—and the interior work of the rooms themselves—dated back to pre-Civil War days. The history, as well as the splendor of the architecture, was sufficient to attract visitors for more than the sole purpose of viewing Armand Dantine's paintings. These, however, complemented the rooms in which they were hung so that the atmosphere created was one of elegance, without the imposition of overbearing formality.

With Nick and Philippe out in the courtyard, Claudia and Judy went to the kitchen and shared a glass each of wine.

"Got to feed the press more than the story," Judy commented to the air. "The vultures swoop down, eat and drink all the freebies, and still say what they please. But at least with full bellies, they're likely to be more expansive—in our favor, as well as in their midriffs."

Claudia smiled. "I hope you're right." She reached over to a silver-plated tray that one of the caterers was in the process of filling. Stealing a canapé of spiced shrimp on a toast point, she observed Nick and Philippe through the kitchen window. "I wonder what he's thinking," she said. "And I know it's senseless to worry about it." She turned to Judy. "But I can't help it."

"Congenital, hon. You're a mother now. It has nothing to do with giving birth. We're talking responsibility, not biology."

"Funny, isn't it," mused Claudia. "My relationship with Philippe has taught me so much about mine and Eleanor's when I was a child."

"Mm-hmm," answered Judy, swallowing the last of her cracker. "I'll just bet. Eleanor must have had her hands full."

The doorbell rang. "Well," said Judy, wetting her lips with her tongue, "ready or not, the vultures have landed. Shall we go and greet the press . . . ?"

Judy's comments were right on one count; the guests devoured every morsel of food and every drop of wine. Philippe bowed politely whenever he was introduced to someone, but for the most part he stayed in the background, preferring to sit in the courtyard beside the Spanish moss. At one point, Claudia thought she'd seen him talking to someone or something. Nick had noticed, too. They agreed it was wiser to say nothing, rather than make the boy self-conscious.

Claudia allowed herself to be interviewed, but maintained a careful distance whenever questions arose about the enigmatic painter and former master of the house. Claudia had anticipated these questions and was therefore prepared beforehand; Armand Dantine had too long been the center of rumor and gossip to have them suddenly disappear.

She admitted that he and she were siblings, separated in childhood and reunited only shortly before his death. The charming but firm tone of her voice set up the invisible boundary. Not quite a barrier, but a line clearly defined and reminding guests that they and she were gracious, discreet, genteel members of a common estate: the press. And, unseen as the boundary was, no one tried to cross it.

When the food and drink—and therefore the guests—were gone, Claudia flopped down into a chair and said to Judy and Nick, "God, I'm glad that performance is over. Poor Philippe, he must be bored to tears."

Judy said, "Maybe we ought to let him know the coast is clear. I saw him sitting in the courtyard."

"He's spent most of the afternoon there," said Claudia. "I'll go out and get him."

She left, but returned moments later without Philippe. "He must have come inside while we were in his father's studio. I'll check upstairs."

They met on the landing; Philippe was on his way down.

"Everyone's left," said Claudia. "We thought we'd be going soon, too."

"To dinner?" asked Philippe. "I'm hungry, but I didn't want to take too many of the canapés."

Claudia ruffled his black curls. "What would you like to eat tonight?"

Philippe thought for a moment, then shook his head. "Is there someplace we could get hot dogs? Or maybe a Big Mac?"

"Well, if there is, we'll find it." She took his hand and they descended the stairs.

The members of the historical society staff had finished the day's work and said good night. The caterers were outside packing their truck. Claudia and Philippe

443

joined Nick and Judy, and together the foursome headed toward the front door.

"I'll be right there," said Philippe, turning back down the hall.

"Is everything all right?" asked Claudia.

"Yes. But I almost forgot something."

"We'll wait for you at the gate, Philippe, okay?" said Nick.

"Okay. I'll just be a minute."

Claudia looked questioningly at Nick, who said quietly, "He needs to be alone. C'mon."

"I'll be with you in a sec," said Claudia. "I've forgotten something, too."

She waited until Nick and Judy had gone out the front door, then she headed toward the courtyard.

Philippe had tiptoed into the parlor. Holding his baseball cap under one arm, he approached the mantel and reached up for the music box. As Claudia had done earlier, he wound the little brass key and lifted the lid. "Now Is the Hour" began its tinkling waltz, and for a moment he watched the studded metal roll as it turned and the innocent tune poured forth.

He gazed upward at the portrait; it seemed as though the music were playing for them alone.

No. For him alone.

Philippe listened, then gently closed the lid of the box and returned it to its place on the mantel. "Good-bye, Noelle," he whispered.

Now he turned toward the opposite wall, to the portrait of Sirena. The boy saw none of the sensuality that his father had painted there. He saw only love.

He patted his pants pocket. Inside was the piece of Spanish moss he'd taken from the courtyard, just so he'd

444

remember.

His eyes filled with tears, but he swallowed hard and blinked them away.

She'd called him Little Man. Mustn't cry like a baby. Not anymore.

A sweet, sad smile formed on his lips as he looked up at her face and said, "Good-bye, Mother."

Then he donned his baseball cap and left the parlor.

Claudia had returned from Armand's studio with the canvas under her arm. It was still covered with the paint-spattered sheet she'd used to wrap it with before hiding it from display.

She stayed in the shadows of the hallway until Philippe was gone from the house. Then, without hesitation, she tiptoed into the parlor, locked the doors, and crossed directly to the fireplace.

Beside the music box on the mantel was a silver matchbook holder. Several exhibition catalogues lay on a nearby table. Claudia picked up all but one and placed them on the grating. Then she took a match, struck it, and lit the edge of the catalogue she still held in her hand. The glossy cover caught fire. Quickly she tossed it atop the rest.

She waited until the red-hot flames had almost consumed the catologues. Then she added the single canvas excluded from the Dantine Collection — the nude that Armand had painted of her.

She watched, transfixed, as the wooden stretcher cracked. Red-orange darts of fire danced on the portrait and leapt into the air, followed by a brief burst of blue-green sparks. The canvas imploded upon itself, Claudia's image crumbled, and Armand Dantine's masterpiece was gone.

The embers smoldered and died, leaving only ashes in their wake. The spring evening was warm, yet a penetrating coldness shrouded the room.

It was time for Claudia to depart this house; nothing remained to hold her here.

She unlocked the parlor doors and, without turning for so much as a farewell glance, she went out to the front gate, where Nick and Philippe and Judy were waiting.